THE SILENT DEAD

CLAIRE McGOWAN

headline

First published in Great Britain 2015 by
HEADLINE PUBLISHING GROUP

1

Cataloguing in Publication Data is available from the British Library

ISBN 978 1 4722 0440 0

Typeset in Sabon by Avon DataSet Ltd, Bidford-on-Avon, Warwickshire

Printed and bound in Great Britain by Clays Ltd, St Ives plc

Headline's policy is to use papers that are natural, renewable and recyclable
products and made from wood grown in well-managed forests and other
controlled sources. The logging and manufacturing processes are expected to
conform to the environmental regulations of the country of origin.

HEADLINE PUBLISHING GROUP
An Hachette UK Company
Carmelite House
50 Victoria Embankment
London EC4Y 0DZ

www.headline.co.uk
www.hachette.co.uk

To Sarah and Angela

Acknowledgements

This book would be substantially different (or possibly flung into the sea by now) without the insightful, comprehensive, and generous feedback I received from my agent Diana Beaumont and my editor at Headline Vicki Mellor. Thank you both so much for all your time and energy. Thanks also to everyone else at Headline, especially Caitlin Raynor and Jo Liddiard.

Thank you to my parents and sister, brothers, and brother-in-law, who put up with me doing a final edit at home, staring at the laptop and muttering to myself, and forgetting to use coasters on the Good Table.

Thanks to Debs and Bob for hosting me at Retreats 4 You in Devon, where I was able to nail down a first draft thanks to all the peace and quiet and wine delivered to my desk.

Thanks to the two lovely bookshop-owning Davids – David Torrans at No Alibis Belfast for all his support, and David Headley at Goldsboro Books London, scene of many a party.

Thank you to Kate Pearson for the loan of her lovely Edinburgh flat.

Thanks to Jamie Drew for some fantastic headshots (and lunch).

Thanks to City University, especially Jonathan Myerson,

for offering me gainful employment, and everyone who's hosted me for a talk or teaching session, especially Arvon Lumb Bank, Guardian Masterclasses, the Belfast Book Festival/John Hewitt Society, and the Derry Verbal Arts Festival. Thanks also to Brian McGilloway and William Ryan for generously including me in events.

Thank you to Dr Laurance Donnelly, forensic geologist and police search adviser, for geology help (any mistakes all my fault of course!)

Thanks as ever to the crime fiction world and all the lovely people in it. Jake Kerridge and Stav Sherez for gruesome lunchtime chat. Katherine Armstrong, Anya Lipska, and Jamie-Lee Nardone for drinks. Theakston's Old Peculier festival in Harrogate and Crimefest for top-notch book festivals. Imogen Robertson and Ned for dinners and wine. Tom Harper for Scooby Doo inspiration and whiskey. Kevin Wignall for all the fine dining. Thanks to Stuart Neville and Adrian McKinty for including my story 'Rosie Grant's Finger' in the anthology *Belfast Noir*.

To my non-criminal friends, for all your support during what has been something of a turbulent writing period – I couldn't have done it without you. Thanks to Gareth Rubin for help with the title and to everyone who read early drafts, offered me house room, and generally helped me along, especially Alex, Sarah, Angela, Kerry, Kelly, Beth, Hannah, Isabelle, Jillian, Sara, Freya, and Jo.

Thanks to everyone who has taken the time to read or review my previous books – it really does mean the world to the writer plodding away on their own. If you have any thoughts on this one, you can contact me at www.ink-stains.co.uk or on Twitter at @inkstainsclaire (or find me on Facebook).

Prologue

I'm dead.

I don't mind. I want to be dead. Nothing could be worse than staying alive, not like this. But all the same I'm running away.

I can feel the blood between my toes, my feet slipping on the roots and branches. They've taken my clothes from me. You're dead, they say. No one will miss you. You're evil. The world is better off without you.

And I know they're right, but I'm running anyway.

I know they will catch me – I'm lost, no idea where I'm going, and after what they've done I can hardly stand, but I'm running. In the dark the forest is full of eyes, and branches claw my face like scratching hands. Overhead, the moon is as white as a face with the flesh stripped back.

My own warm blood is splashing on my skin. My heart is bursting in my chest. You have no heart, they told me. You are dead inside. You are scum. Yes, yes, it's all true, but, but, but. I can hear them nearby in the trees. The high voice of the wee girl. Saying my name. I know they'll find me, panting and stumbling, but I can't stop. I am so afraid. I've never been afraid like this.

The noise stops. The moon lights up the path ahead, empty, and I run, and as I run I'm thinking one thing: *my baby. Oh my baby.*

Chapter One

Ballyterrin, Northern Ireland, April 2011

'We are gathered here today to join this man and this woman in holy matrimony.'

Paula's lilies were wilting already. She shifted on her swollen feet. The bulk of her belly meant the only way she could comfortably stand was with one hip jutted out, leaning on it, and she didn't think such an insolent pose would cut it before the altar. She'd already seen the priest's eye travelling over her stomach and then pointedly not looking at it. Catholics – they were good at pretending things that did exist didn't. And vice versa.

She stared straight ahead, her legs buckling under the cool satin of her dress, glad that its length hid her puffy ankles and enormous underwear. *What am I doing here?* The church smelled of incense, and cold stone, and the slightly rotting sweetness of the flowers.

Across from her, Aidan was also staring rigidly ahead. He was tricked out in a new grey suit, clasping his hands in front of his groin in that position men adopted during moments of gravitas or penalty kick-offs. She wondered if, like her, he was having to stop himself mouthing the too-familiar words of the Mass. *Lord have mercy (Lord have mercy) Christ have mercy (Christ have mercy) Lord have mercy (Lord have mercy)*. The phrases found a treacherous echo in her bones. She heard Aidan cough, once, in the still, heavy air of the church. On that warm spring day, it was full of the ghosts of candles, and dust, and long unopened hymn books. *What are we doing here?* She wanted to catch his eye, but was afraid to.

'Do you have the rings?' Aidan stepped forward and deposited them on the Bible, two hoops of gold, one large, one tiny. Then he moved back into position, eyes downcast.

'Repeat after me,' said the priest. The bride and groom arranged themselves in suitable positions. 'Patrick Joseph Maguire, will you take Patricia Ann O'Hara to be your lawful wedded wife, for richer for poorer, for better for worse, in sickness and in health, to have and to hold from this day forth, forsaking all others, as long as you both shall live?'

Paula's father – PJ – spoke in a rusty voice. 'I will.' His bad leg was stiff but he stood up straight in a new black suit bought for the occasion. Paula suspected he was hating it all, but he'd have done anything for the woman standing next to him in an ivory suit from Debenhams, several nests' worth of dyed feathers attached to her head.

Aidan's mother, Pat O'Hara, said her vows quick and earnest: 'I will.'

They would. They were both so sure. How could you be sure? Paula stole a glance at Aidan – what was he now, her stepbrother? – and saw his dark eyes were wreathed in shadows, his hair tinged with grey over the ears. She'd never noticed that before. He saw her watching, and both of them looked away, her belly as big and unavoidable as the lies between them. *Oh Aidan, I'm sorry. I'm so sorry.*

Then it was done, and Pat and PJ were wed, and they trooped down the aisle like a bride and groom in their twenties. Aidan grasped Paula's arm without meeting her eyes, escorting her out, because that was what you did. His hand was cool on her hot, fat skin. Everything about her was squeezed. The ridiculous lilac bridesmaid dress, strained over newly discovered breasts, was like a cocoon she might burst from at any moment. Aidan could barely look at her. She didn't blame him.

They were out now, and posing for photos taken by one of Pat's friends, who couldn't work the camera, and Pat was all smiles and tears, kissing Paula with her five layers of lipstick. She'd had her colours done for the wedding, plunging into manicures and spa days and shopping trips like a first-time bride. Paula had tried to play along, because she loved Pat, but it was hard to be excited about a wedding when its very occurrence hinged on the fact that your mother, missing for seventeen years, had been declared legally dead. And maybe she was dead – dead as Pat's husband, who'd been shot by the IRA in 1986. But maybe, just maybe, she wasn't.

Maybe. When you got married you did not say 'maybe'. You said 'I will', you put your feet on the good, solid stone of certainty. 'Maybe' was like shifting sand. She wished so much there was something, anything she could be sure of. Whether her mother was alive or dead, for a start.

It was warm outside, and the sunlight played around the old church, which was painted in crumbly lemon-yellow.

Paula had made her First Communion here, and they'd also chosen it for her mother's memorial service back in the nineties – no funeral, of course; nothing to bury. Now Pat's friends had gathered to throw confetti, twittering women in their Sunday best suits, lilacs and yellows and blues covering crêpey arms, hats pressed out of boxes and set atop tight-curled hair. Many greeted Paula – *hello, pet* – some kissing her cheek, though she barely recognised them. She knew they'd be looking at her vast pregnant belly and bare left hand, and speculating about her and Aidan and what might be going on there. He'd been her boyfriend when she was eighteen and he was nineteen – was he the father of the wean? Honestly, she'd have told them if she knew.

Suddenly it was too much, all of them there, and the kiss of the sun on gravestones, and the sight of a small plaque in the vestibule bearing the name *Margaret Maguire. In loving memory.*

'Maguire?' It was Aidan, speaking his first words to her all day. In months, in fact, since she'd told him about the baby. She realised she was sagging gently down to the steps, like a deflating balloon. 'You all right?'

'It's just the heat – the sun . . .' It wasn't especially warm – it never was in Ireland, of course – but her body seemed to produce its own waves of heat now.

'Sit down.' Aidan led her inside to the incense-scented dark. She slipped off her tight lilac shoes and the stone floor was cool under her feet.

'Thanks. I'm OK.'

Aidan sat beside her in a pew, leaning forward so his tie flopped between his knees. 'Weird day.'

'It is that.'

He looked at her, and the old ache came back. 'Are you feeling well? I mean in general.'

She shrugged. 'I'm like a beached whale. Still, won't be long now.'

Aidan said, 'We need to talk. I know that. I've been meaning to see you.'

'I've been here.'

'I just couldn't . . . you know, after you told me it was either me or him. Christ, it was such a shock. It was like you'd done it on purpose almost. To punish me.'

'Yeah, you're right. I got pregnant and I'm the size of a cow just so I could make you feel bad. You're totally right.'

He made a noise of annoyance. 'I know, OK? It was just a lot to take in. And him – you see him every day, like, you must be close.'

She tried to explain. 'He's my boss. He – well, it's complicated too. It's not as if we're—' With spectacular bad timing, that was when her phone went, trilling in the depths of the (also lilac) clutch bag Pat had forced on her. 'Oh, sorry. I better get this.' It echoed in the silent church. She pressed the green button. 'Hello?'

'Paula?'

Her heart sank at his voice. She could see Aidan had recognised the name which flashed up; he was once again scowling intently ahead.

'What's up?'

'I know you have the wedding today, and I wouldn't bother you if I could help it, but—'

'Something's happened?'

'There's a body. I thought you'd be annoyed if I didn't tell you.'

'Is it one of them?'

'We think so, but—'

'Where?'

'Creggan Forest. But listen, Paula, don't—'

'I'll be there in twenty minutes.'

'No, Paula, that's not what I—'

She ended the call. The menu of Poached Salmon, Roast Beef with Julienne Vegetables, and Summer Fruits Pavlova would have to wait, and after the day she'd had she was almost weepingly grateful for the certainty of human flesh, a crime scene to analyse, a case to solve.

Aidan spoke bitterly, still not looking at her. 'You're going then.'

'I have to. It's one of the Mayday Five, we think.'

She offered it as a small sop – Aidan, editor of the local paper, knew the significance of the case more than anyone. But he didn't budge. 'If you think that's more important than today.'

'I don't. I'll be an hour, tops – anyway, they'll be snapping photos for ages yet.' He wouldn't move to let her out, so she clambered awkwardly over him. '*Aidan.*'

'Oh, it's OK. Go to him. Don't mind me.'

She bit down the enraged retort that he'd ignored her for the best part of four months. 'Where's your car?' she demanded.

'You're not really going to feck off during a wedding?' But he sighed and slapped the keys into her hand, on a football key ring Paula knew had to have been a present from Pat. Unless someone was getting done on corruption charges, Aidan had zero interest in sport.

'See you later. Look, I'm sorry – try to understand?'

'You've made your choice,' he muttered. She pretended not to hear. Then she ran down the aisle in her bare feet,

8

shoes in one hand, bag and wilted flowers in the other, her lilac dress rustling around the folds of her unwieldy body.

Soon she was heading out of town, on her way to a small village in the shadow of the Mourne Mountains. Stone houses, Lego-green fields, the sea opaque with light. As she drove she felt her shoulders, crunched up all the way through the ceremony, gradually relax.

Her father was married. To Aidan's mother. Even when he'd told her about it months back – told her he planned to have her mother finally declared dead so he could marry Pat – it somehow hadn't sunk in until now, seeing them before the altar. Everyone else was moving on, and after seventeen years you couldn't blame them. So why could Paula not give up? Why did she have her mother's case file in her desk at home, full of questions and blind alleys and no answers at all, after all this time?

The car park near the forest was full of police cars and vans. Paula was beginning to realise her bridesmaid's dress was not the most practical of garments for a crime scene. No matter. She wasn't going to miss this.

She parked and staggered up to the police cordon on the path leading into the forest. DC Gerard Monaghan, an ambitious Catholic recruit in his twenties, was on his mobile nearby, and burst out laughing when he saw her. 'Jesus, Maguire. Are you lost on your way to a formal?'

She was panting already, slick with sweat under the man-made fibres. 'You found something.'

'A walker phoned in a body in the trees. Some local uniform was first on scene.'

'And how did we get in on it, if he's dead?' They were walking, so she tried to tuck up the hem of her dress.

'Well, Corry and Brooking are on bestest terms right now.'

'Hmm.' Paula wasn't sure how she felt about this rapprochement between DCI Helen Corry, head of Serious Crime at the regular PSNI in the area, and DI Guy Brooking, their boss at the missing persons unit, seconded in from London. At first the two had thoroughly trampled on each other's toes, but lately Corry had been nice as pie about sharing jurisdiction. Paula wasn't sure why.

But none of that mattered right now. 'Is it definitely one of the Five? Which one?'

'I doubt they can tell.' He was leading her to the cordon and nodding to the uniformed officer at the tape. 'Here's Cinderella, late for the ball.' She glared at him and he laughed. 'She's with us, pal. Dr Maguire, forensic psychologist.'

The officer eyed her sweaty face and bulging belly, but let them pass.

'Why can't they tell?' Paula asked, as they trotted up the forest path. Dappled sunlight fell on them, and a warm pine scent filled the air. She knew that Gerard, six foot four in his socks, was shortening his stride for her, but even so she felt dizzy with the effort. Around them was the silence of the forest, small clicks of insects and leaves rustling.

'You'll see,' said Gerard. 'It's a grim one. You don't have to be here, you know.'

'I do. I can't get a sense of it otherwise.'

'All right.' Gerard gave an on-your-head-be-it eye roll and directed her down a small side path. She lifted her skirt to step over roots, her flimsy shoes already in flitters. This was stupid. This was, in a competitive field, one of the more stupid things she'd ever done.

Trees parted to reveal a small gap in the woods, and a cluster of CSIs and detectives surrounding something she couldn't quite see. Corry and Brooking had their heads together, looking at a piece of paper.

'Look who turned up,' said Gerard cheerfully.

Helen Corry was the type of woman who, whatever they had on, you looked at it and realised – *that's exactly what I should have worn.* Her short-sleeved white shirt and grey trousers were cool and fresh. She wore gloves, and a stern expression. 'So I see. Being seven months' pregnant can't detain you from crime scenes, Dr Maguire?'

'Or being at your father's wedding?' added Guy.

Paula sighed. They were awful united, much worse than any of their disagreements. It was like being looked after by an extra set of cool, young parents. 'Who is it?'

Corry peeled off her gloves. 'We think it's Mickey Doyle. Hard to tell from the face, but we'll know soon enough.'

'So they didn't leave the country then, the five of them? Do we think they were kidnapped?'

'Should you really be here, Paula?' Ignoring her question, Guy moved towards her. He too looked cool in a blue shirt and red tie, his fair hair brushed back from a stiffly controlled face. 'I mean, the baby—'

'The baby's fine.' She pushed forward, irritated. 'Let me see him.'

Then she did.

Hanging victims all had a look in common. Eyes popping, tongue protruding, face red and livid. That would be why they couldn't identify him yet. Also common was the loosening of the bowels, which Paula could now smell on the fresh pine breeze. She'd seen it lots of times, so it was strange and very bad timing that this particular victim should cause her to black out suddenly, the forest floor swimming up to meet her.

'I told you.' Guy had caught her before she fell. 'Look, you're not up to this. Sit down.' He marched her to a tree stump. 'I'll get you some water.'

Paula acquiesced, breathing and blinking hard. His expression, she realised, was exactly the same one Aidan had adopted towards her, stoical and distant, with just a touch of resentment. Perfectly timed to remind her that, while the pregnancy had granted her a temporary reprieve, as soon as this baby was out, all three of them were going to have to find out which of the two men was the father.

Kira

When she woke up, she was covered in blood again. In that second when you're still mostly asleep, when you're sure everything you've dreamed is true – like when you look in a mirror and can't recognise your own face – she could only see the blood all over her arms and feel it warm on her skin, going into her mouth even, metallic and hot.

Rose's blood.

She put on the little light beside her bed. She'd tried to sleep with it on after what happened, but Mammy said she was too big for it, and always came in to turn it off. Mammy and her slept at different times now, as if they couldn't both be awake at once. She imagined that even now, as she staggered up, heart hammering, Mammy's eyes would be closing in front of the TV. She'd find her there when she got up for school, the bottle of vodka slumped so low it would be spilling on the carpet.

In the light she could see herself in the mirror. No blood.

She'd just been crying in her sleep again, big, spurty tears that drenched her pyjamas. And her arms, it wasn't blood on them, of course, it was the scars. She was glad about the scars, even though people made comments behind her back – *oh, poor wean, she was the one, you know the sister, blah blah.* She was glad of the scars because it showed she survived.

On her dresser was the photo of Rose and her. Rose was hugging her tight in it, the two of them on a sea wall down on the coast. After that they'd had salty chips and ice creams with flakes in, two each, because Rose said sure why not?

Today was the day. Today it was finally going to happen. She knew she wouldn't sleep again, so instead she sat cross-legged on the carpet in the dark and wondered when it would start.

Chapter Two

'Come on, everyone, shake a leg!' It was Monday morning and the small team that made up the Missing Persons Response Unit was filing reluctantly into the conference room, cups of coffee in hand, suppressing yawns. It had been a long weekend – it had been a long week, in fact, ever since the disappearances.

Guy waited until they were settled. His deputy, Detective Sergeant Bob Hamilton, ex of the RUC, still of the Orange Order, was blowing his nose loudly on a cotton hankie, the others reluctantly shuffling papers and slumping in seats. Guy frowned. 'Where's Avril?' He looked at Fiacra Quinn, a young Detective Garda from over the border who was their liaison with the South.

'How would I know? Got her nose in some wedding magazine again, no doubt.'

'Would you fetch her? We need to start.'

'Monaghan can go,' said Fiacra grouchily.

Gerard, sleeves rolled up and tie askew, gave a sort of grunt. 'Nothing to do with me.'

'Sorry, sorry!' Finally in came Avril Wright, flustered and dropping papers, revealing the magazine she was carrying in among her briefing notes. A woman in lace and silk smiled out, radiant, and Avril hid it, blushing. The young and pretty intelligence analyst, who did her very best to overcome the disadvantage of being Bob's niece, was getting married in the summer and had gone from being efficiency itself to an airhead with her nose never out of bridal magazines. Between her and Pat, Paula never wanted to hear the words 'three-tier red velvet cake' ever again. She herself was the sixth team member, though the bump of the baby was so huge it could probably count as a seventh for health and safety purposes. As Avril sat down, both Gerard and Fiacra shifted slightly in their seats, Fiacra to watch her, Gerard to pointedly ignore. Several months before, Paula had caught Gerard and Avril in some kind of strange, intense moment in the corridor. She'd never got to the bottom of it, and didn't want to.

It was no accident that this joint team was situated in Ballyterrin, biggest border town in the North, a crossroads of smuggling, terrorist activity and general shiftiness. No-man's-land, they called it. The team was supposed to coordinate missing persons' cases north and south of the border, make sure the right people were looking for the lost, see that no one fell down between the imaginary lines of the border. But sometimes, as with the case in front of them, it was difficult to understand why anyone would want to look for those who were gone.

Guy gripped the back of his chair and launched into it. 'Mickey Doyle.'

A small sigh went round the room. Relief, maybe, or something else.

'Definitely?' Gerard.

'He had his driving licence in his pocket.'

'Did he hang himself?' asked Fiacra, who hadn't been at the scene.

'He died by hanging in Creggan Forest Park, yes. But

whether it was suicide or he was forced we don't know yet. The car park has CCTV, which shows a white van driving up into the forest around two a.m. last night. It left again half an hour later, and Doyle certainly wasn't driving it. No number plate visible, but it's a start. There's also this.' Guy switched on the projector, illuminating something on screen. 'The autopsy hasn't been done yet, but the FMO found this in Doyle's mouth.'

On screen was a scrap of lined paper, and written on it in big, shaky capitals were the words: COLLATERAL DAMAGE. 'Does anyone recognise that wording?' asked Guy.

'It was in their statement,' said Avril, with her forensic recall of documents. 'Ireland First. They made a statement after the bomb saying it wasn't them, but even if it was, some loss was always inevitable in a war, something like that. Collateral damage, they said.'

Bob Hamilton was shaking his head. 'Terrible thing. Terrible, terrible thing.' Paula knew he'd been working on the day it happened, back in 2006. So had Helen Corry, for that matter. Everything about this case was too close to home.

But the idea of Bob working on it, or any case, made doubts worm in her mind again. She tried to focus.

Guy was nodding. 'So this seems to rule out suicide, and also the idea that the Five skipped the country together.'

'It was kidnap then,' said Paula. 'I thought it must be. I knew Catherine Ni Chonnaill wouldn't have left her children like that.'

Finally, Guy looked at her, in that sideways manner he'd developed, as if holding up his fingers to block out her bump. 'I agree. But who took them? With the memorial service coming up too, I don't like the timing.'

Gerard leaned back in his seat. 'I guess Jarlath Kenny'd want them out of the way. Talk is he's going to run for Westminster.'

Paula saw Bob's face contract at the mention of the name. The fact that Kenny, Ballyterrin's Republican mayor, was a former member of the IRA did not sit well with her either, even though you weren't supposed to mention these things in this post-conflict, all-friends-here Ireland.

'What about other dissident Republicans, sir?' asked Fiacra.

Guy said, 'You know what they're like. One mad man and a dog, some of them. No one's claimed responsibility.'

They all considered it for a while. After the ceasefires and Good Friday Agreement of 1998, when Paula had been taking her A-levels, the Republican movement in Northern Ireland had fractured into several smaller groups, intent on keeping up the fight which the IRA had stopped. The peace of those past years had wobbled several times – defused bombs, shootings of police officers, the odd riot or two – but had held, so far held, thank God, and they did every day, whichever God you believed in or even none. It was over. They weren't going back.

But for the people whose pictures Guy now showed on screen, the past was still alive, and pumping hot as fresh blood.

Guy switched the projector off, weariness sounding in his voice. 'Corry's team are treating Doyle's death as murder. Our priority is to find the other four, and fast. It seems likely they've been taken together. So the question we now have to ask is, if Republicans aren't behind this, who else would want them dead?'

And the answer, Paula thought, and the particular problem with this case, was who *wouldn't*?

Paula managed to escape to her desk after the briefing without being alone with Guy – her main objective at work these days – and for what felt like the thousandth time since the Mayday Five had gone missing a week before, she read the case notes.

Nearly eight months since she'd come home to Ballyterrin, determined to consult on just one case then leave, but ending up pregnant, trapped, tied down by silken threads of family, friends, obligations. Love. It was hard to believe that for years she'd managed an almost nun-like life in a Docklands flat in London, working on missing persons with a big inner-city unit. That was where she'd been when the Mayday bomb exploded in a small village outside Ballyterrin – on 1st May 2006 – and she'd sat disbelieving before the TV all day as the death toll went up. Some man had been there with her, some transient bank holiday boyfriend – Adam? Alan? – and he'd been bewildered at her shock and horror. 'Did you know someone there?'

She'd been unable to speak, explain how it was. That you grew up holding your breath while shaky ceasefires lasted a year, eighteen months, then exploded into shootings and bombs, that you hardly dared hope 1998 could be the end, but it was, after the stinging final horror of the Omagh bomb, biggest death toll ever in the Troubles, and still it held, five years, six years, eight years, and you'd let your breath out and it was going to be OK, almost.

Then it wasn't. Another bomb in a small town, a vague warning, going off too soon. Sixteen dead. Babies blown up in the street, teenagers, old people. Paula had never met any of them but she knew their faces, she felt it like a slap from someone you had come to trust, and she went to bed that night crying angry tears, the blundering boyfriend sent home. *We thought it was over. You told us it was over.* And determined: *I'm never going home to that. Never.*

And here she was.

The facts of the case. Mickey Doyle, now deceased, had gone missing a week before, on 1st April. On that same day they had received word of a further four missing people – Callum Brady, Ronan Lynch, Martin Flaherty, and one woman, Catherine Ni Chonnaill. Ni Chonnaill had texted her mother to pick up her children, as she'd be late home from work. Except she'd never turned up. Lynch had similarly not arrived at his job. Brady's flat had been in disarray, furniture knocked over as if he'd left in a hurry, a half-eaten breakfast of microwave burger sitting on his fold-up kitchen table.

All five were part of a small Republican splinter group calling itself Ireland First, dedicated to continuing the armed struggle and disrupting the peace process. They were best known as the defendants in the Mayday bomb case, the trial which had collapsed the year before without a conviction, although everyone in the area considered them guilty as sin.

She looked at their faces again. There was Doyle, now dead, a father and husband, a small, rat-raced man with a cigarette hanging from his mouth in the surveillance photo they had of him. He'd been a binman. Lynch was handsome in a seedy way, tall and fair, and worked in a warehouse. Brady was overweight, unemployed, a pale wreck of a man captured outside a betting shop. Martin Flaherty was the leader – tall, greying, fiftysomething. An ordinary-looking man in glasses and a good wool coat.

Then there was the woman. Even in the blurred police shots she was beautiful, her fair hair pooling down her back as she strapped a child into a car. The child's face was not visible, but Paula touched the photograph reflexively. Whatever she'd done, Catherine Ni Chonnaill's loss would be felt.

Who would want them dead? Guy had asked. God, who would want them alive? They'd most likely made, armed and planted a massive bomb on a busy high street, then driven away. Their target was an Orange Order parade due later that day, but the bomb had gone off early, when the streets were crowded with families. They'd blown up sixteen innocent people, maimed many more. They were going about their lives unpunished. A memorial to the bomb victims was to be unveiled on the fifth anniversary in a few weeks' time, and that was supposed to be the end of it. But the Five were gone, and now one was dead, and there were still no leads.

She looked down at the faces of the Five again. Ordinary people. That was the worst bit.

'Hello.' When she finally left the office that day, Guy was at her car, wiping spring pollen off the windscreen. 'I was just—'

'Thanks.' She got her key out but didn't move towards the car.

'So I'll see you tomorrow?'

'I suppose. Do you really think it's a good idea?'

'They have the most obvious motive, so yes, we'll need

to get their alibis. Hopefully we can at least rule them out.'

They had arranged that Paula and Guy would visit the Chair of the Mayday Victims Support Group, to update him on the investigation and explain that they'd have to interview the families of the dead. Paula was already dreading it. She fiddled with the key. 'How's Tess?' She tried to ask the question innocently, like a concerned colleague, but there was no way to innocently ask a man about his wife when you'd slept with him.

A guarded look came over Guy's face. 'She's all right.'

'Doing OK now she's home?'

'Yes, Katie and I are looking after her.'

'That's good.' A family, that's what they were. However much it hurt, she made herself press into the point of it. Guy had a teenage daughter, and a wife who'd suffered something of a breakdown before Christmas. After the murder of their young son in London, the Brookings had come to Ballyterrin to try a new life, and Tess had done her best to get pregnant again, with no success. They'd split up for a while, which Paula constantly reminded herself of when the guilt got too much, but now Tess was back. That meant Paula had no idea where she and Guy stood.

Guy was still hovering there. The evenings were growing lighter, the pearly twilights of an Irish summer not far away. 'How are you feeling?'

Was he asking as a boss or as a prospective father? When she'd finally told him it was either him or Aidan, Guy had wanted her to sign a statement that would go to the Chief Constable. He'd been ready to resign, take the flak for sleeping with a junior colleague, but Paula had refused. Helen Corry, who knew the full story, was also keeping quiet. As long as people did their jobs she didn't really care whose bed they went home to. Since then Paula and Guy had lumbered on in daily working contact, trying to ignore the situation as it visibly swelled between them. She shrugged. 'Fine. Well, I'm enormous, but otherwise OK.'

'How was the wedding in the end?'

'All right. I made it back for the meal.'

'O'Hara was there, I suppose.'

'Of course. His mother being the bride and all.'

'Sure.' He stood awkwardly. 'How is he?'

'Aidan? You're asking the wrong person. We haven't been chatting much.' *Like you and me*, she wanted to say. The hardest thing about the pregnancy – aside from not fitting into any of her clothes and being sick ten times a day – was how it had damaged her relationship with Guy. Once it had been so perfect, a calibrated professional curiosity, so in tune that they could conduct interviews without even having to say a word to each other. Aidan, sure, things had never been right between them, not since he'd dumped her when she was eighteen. But being Paula, she'd slept with Guy, unable to leave it at a productive attraction. And Guy had backed off – since he was still married, after a fashion – and she'd slept with Aidan on a stupid sad impulse, and now she was carrying around the fruit of these mistakes like a balloon up her jumper. Even for a lapsed Catholic, it seemed an overly harsh punishment.

Extract from *The Blood Price: The Mayday
Bombing and its Aftermath*, by Maeve Cooley
(Tairise Press, 2011)

*When you look at them, the faces of the Mayday Five
seem to radiate evil. Is it because you know what
they've done, or can something human in you sense
that here are ruthless killers, delighted to murder in
the name of long-dead politics? But the worst of it is
they are human too. Catherine Ni Chonnaill is the
daughter of former IRA Commander Danny Connell,
and after he was shot by the UVF in 2004 she
was pictured on TV weeping angry tears for him,
collapsing behind his coffin while heavily pregnant
with her first child. Four of the Five – Doyle, Lynch,
Flaherty, and Ni Chonnaill – have been married and
have children. Ni Chonnaill's are still at primary
school, a boy and a girl she had with Lynch before
they split, and there's also a young baby by an
unknown father.*

*Yet these five people conspired one bright summer
day to blow up sixteen men, women, children, and
babies, with a bomb so massive it destroyed a whole
street, tore the heads right off some victims, and
produced so much blood it fell down on the High
Street like a red rain for a full ten minutes after the
blast.*

*What can we say in the face of such horror? What
the Five have said amounts to – we were not involved,
and even if we were involved, we didn't intend to kill
civilians, and anyway, some must always die in the
war for freedom. We know the story. As I will show*

in this book, the guilt of the Five is indisputable, yet a series of legal and policing errors mean they have not been brought to justice. For the families of the sixteen people who died that sunny spring day, and the dozens maimed, blinded and paralysed in the blast, the end of the road has been reached.

If you ever ask yourself the price of peace, then this is it – to go out in your home town and see the man who murdered your child filling his car with petrol, whistling a Republican tune, free and alive and getting off scot-free. Ask yourself – is that a price you'd be willing to live with?

Chapter Three

Paula returned to an empty house that night. The idea was that now Pat and PJ were married, he would move into her bigger and nicer house across town, where the bathroom could more easily be adapted to his bad leg. Injured in an accident years before, he'd been badly wounded again just before Christmas, when a killer had broken in looking for Paula. Since then the locks had been replaced by shiny new bolts, but still she didn't feel safe until she'd checked all the doors and windows every night.

Having completed the rounds, she stood in the kitchen. Under her loose maternity top, her hand found the scar on her abdomen, where an insane woman had tried to cut her baby out. But the baby was still in there, safe for now. A girl. Paula hadn't wanted to know, but the woman's sister, who claimed to be psychic, had told her, and now she knew it was hard not to picture the child. Would she have red hair? Paula sighed. Seeing Guy every day, his features were too easy to picture, the fair hair swept back, the rigid bones of his face. She remembered what the psychic, Magdalena Croft, had told her, seeing her with Guy: *oh, he's the one, is he?* It wasn't true. The woman didn't have visions, it wasn't possible. She was a fraudster, a liar, and she deserved the prison sentence she was now serving. *But was she right?* And then there was Aidan, of course, dark, angry, whose face she saw every time she shut her eyes.

Paula touched her stomach and spoke aloud in the silence. 'It's OK. We don't need either of them. We'll have each other.'

It was strange she should feel lonely here. She'd loved living alone in London, shutting the door and keeping out friends, lovers, would-be boyfriends. Waking to the river's shifting colours, running along it at night with her breath in her ears and the pounding of her own feet the only sounds. Sitting in her window seat watching the lights of boats go past, perfectly happy in her own company, working on missing persons for a big station in Rotherhithe. Work had mattered, and nothing else.

Then she'd come home, and got stuck here. And this house was haunted. There in the kitchen, that was where her mother had stood the last day, rinsing off breakfast dishes. Paula, then just thirteen, had eaten her porridge without looking up, school uniform on and eyes bleary. When the police asked about it later, when she'd been home for hours and no one had come and she had to give in to her rising panic, she'd not even been able to remember what her mother was wearing.

Her mind turned, restless, to the doubts that lurked at the back of it. Several months ago Guy had handed her the file of her mother's case. A jailed IRA member had suggested he knew something of the case, and might even talk if he could get early release. And then there was Magdalena, whispering more of her poison: *your mother's still alive. She's alive, and over water.*

Bob Hamilton had been the lead officer on her mother's case, back in 1993. Paula remembered him coming to the door, her father's former partner, there to arrest him for the possible murder of his wife. Of course PJ had been released, but his job had never been easy again, and he'd been let go for good in 1998 after the Good Friday Agreement. Bob Hamilton had been the one to deliver the news. Forced to work with him, Paula had asked him to reopen the case, but he wouldn't talk to her about it. She'd spoken to everyone who might know something, anything – her mother's old boss, Pat, Bob himself. She'd learned nothing concrete, but still the doubts would not go away. Had they done everything they could? Was the psychic right, had she really seen something? *What if?* The what if, it could drive you mad if you let it.

Restless, Paula checked her phone – nothing. Nothing from Aidan, nothing from Guy. Nothing from Saoirse, her best friend – or she had been before Paula left town anyway, who knew now – who'd been strange with her since the pregnancy. There was no one else. Her London life, her friends there, her colleagues, it had all been washed away in the move across the water.

She shivered and tugged her dressing gown round her bump. 'You OK in there? This is where we're meant to live when you come out. What do you think?' She looked round at the brown seventies cupboards and patterned lino of the kitchen. 'I know, not the best, is it? We're getting it fixed up. Hardwood floors and that.' Her dad was going to pay. The idea was Paula and the baby could live here 'for as long as you want, pet', and then it could be sold. Which was until when? Could she go back to London as originally planned, with a tiny, helpless baby, pick up her life of dark bars and late nights and always the escape of her empty flat? Could she stay here and live in her parents' sad terraced house, a single mother in her thirties?

She wandered into the living room, itching with doubt and boredom. She picked up the local paper, but that only reminded her of Aidan, its editor, and anyway it featured a large profile of the Republican mayor Jarlath Kenny and the success he'd made of attracting investment to the town – something of a puff piece for Aidan, but no doubt he'd printed it for reasons of his own. Jarlath Kenny didn't even try to hide his IRA past, as if everything that happened before 1998 had been wiped out by the Good Friday Agreement and no questions asked. Now he was launching a Westminster bid – the local seat was going to be vacant when the current moderate MP retired in September and he was widely seen as a shoo-in. It was strange that Kenny, once as much of a terrorist as the Mayday Five, was running the town, while the Five had disappeared. It was entirely plausible that the local Republican movement had dealt with them, bent as they were on derailing all the progress made since 1998 and stirring up awkward memories of the not-so-long-ago time when many politicians had themselves been no stranger to the detonator or the Armalite. And then there was the Mayday Victims Group, vocal, angry. Denied any justice since the trial had collapsed the year before.

But Paula didn't want to think about that. Hopefully they would all have alibis. Hopefully the visit to the Chair would be just a formality.

She was actually glad when the phone rang and it was PJ checking up on her.

'Make sure you don't let that water heater overboil. It does be awful temperamental.'

'It's fine, Dad. Are you all right? How's your leg?'

'Ah, not too bad. Have you put the heating on? You don't want to catch a chill with the baby.'

'Of course.'

'Don't go out now and leave your straighteners on or anything like that. I put a new battery in the smoke alarm, but you never know. Oh, and the bins go out on a Tuesday.'

'Dad! I'm not a kid!'

'I know, I know. Listen, would you ever call in on Mrs Flynn next door if you've time?'

'I'm so busy, Dad, I—'

'Just for a minute, see she's OK. Now I'm not over the fence she's got no one. Her weans all went to England and sure they never make it back to see her.'

Had Paula chosen, she could have read books between the gaps in her father's words. 'OK. I'll call in when I get a minute.' Though the Lord only knew when that might be.

'And you're OK up there on your own, you're not getting into bad thoughts or anything?'

Paula thought again of all the years she'd lived alone in London, barely seeing her father for months on end, just stilted phone calls straining across the water. But this house was haunted – for him, too. 'I'm fine.' She could almost have said it, said, *Dad, I know you think she's dead, but I'm just not sure, and I have to keep on looking, whatever it means. Whoever it hurts.* 'Honestly, I'm just going to go to bed. We're so busy at work.'

'Oh yes, with the fella in the woods. Can't say I have too much sympathy for him. Well, goodnight, pet. You're sure you're OK?'

After assuring her father she was fine, she was thirty and

had lived alone for many years, and hadn't fallen down the stairs or electrocuted herself on the toaster, Paula took herself to bed to read a book published a month before, to much controversy, about the Mayday bomb. In it the author, a Dublin journalist, had publicly named the five people believed to be behind the blast, who due to various legal and jurisdictional blunders had never been convicted. Having followed the story with interest, Paula knew that Ireland First were in the process of suing the author and publishers, a small independent press – until the Five had vanished. And now Mickey Doyle had turned up in the forest with a rope around his neck.

Lying on her bed in the dark house, she tried not to see his mottled face. The book's journalist author, Maeve Cooley, was a rising star in the South, loved for her cynical style as much as for her blonde beauty. She was also a good friend of Aidan's, often helping him on stories, and by extension a sort-of friend of Paula. Except that the last time Paula had seen Maeve, Aidan had been in her bedroom in Dublin, wearing just a T-shirt and boxers. They were old friends. Could have been nothing. But she wouldn't ask, same as he wouldn't ask her if he was the father of her child, and this was the game they were playing, had been playing for twelve years, until they were so good it was hard to say if either had won or both had lost.

The cover was adorned with a picture of Maeve, soulful, lovely, clever. Damn her, she was funny too. You couldn't not like her and Paula had done her best. She began to read.

CLAIRE MCGOWAN

Extract from *The Blood Price: The Mayday
Bombing and its Aftermath*, by Maeve Cooley
(Tairise Press, 2011)

*No one got up that morning with any premonitions.
Those who say they did are wrong, and worse, they
do an injustice to the dead. For who would have
gone into Crossanure that day if any pall or shadow
hung over the bright sun, who would have strapped
babies into buggies, taken elderly parents for a day
out?*

*On a farm outside town, John Lenehan was up
tending to his cows. He'd later send his son Danny
into town, to buy animal feed and change some
money for Danny's upcoming holiday to Majorca –
his first ever with friends. He'd got his passport the
day before. All over town people got ready. They
were there buying a Communion dress, getting a car
serviced, picking up new glasses, changing library
books. Hundreds of people were in Crossanure that
day. A funfair had set up in the park, spilling out
popcorn smells and disco music. The Orange parade
was due at two p.m., the first of marching season. It
was Monday 1st May 2006, a bank holiday. By the
end of the day sixteen people would be dead and
hundreds wounded, the still-beating heart of the
small town ripped right out. In this book I will try to
make some of their voices heard, through speaking
to those injured and those left behind to grieve.*

*This is what happened. But no, that isn't the right
wording. It didn't just happen. This is what someone
did. And in this book I will go on to name them, in*

31

the hope that they may one day face the truth of the
murders they committed.

Paula put the book down. It was all coming back to her: the death, the screaming, the shock. Blood misting the camera lens. In all the horrific litany of the Troubles, this bomb was somehow the closest to home, the nastiest last sting in the tail. And here she was trying to find the likely perpetrators, help them, save them. She didn't want to think too much about that.

Chapter Four

Paula could hardly believe the change in John Lenehan – he'd suffered a stroke after the Mayday trial collapsed, she knew, but it was still shocking to see him, his hair turned entirely white, his back stooped. Despite being permanently confined to home, he wore a shirt and tie under his jumper. 'Would you like me to get that, Mr Lenehan?' He was struggling from the kitchen on a walking stick, but the look he flashed her as he put down the tray of tea was pure steel. 'I'd be dead and buried before I'd let a woman in your condition serve me, miss. You sit down.'

'Thank you.'

With much difficulty he arranged his own tea, the cup and saucer rattling, as he lowered himself into an old upright chair. Everything was near at hand, the crossword, the glasses on a string, the bottles of pills. The walls were lined in holy pictures and framed family shots of a handsome boy and a pretty woman in her fifties. Mary Lenehan had been thirty-five when she wed, nearly forty when Danny came. Several months after her son was blown to pieces on Crossanure High Street, her husband had found her body hanging on the landing of the house they now sat in. John Lenehan was seventy-three. Before Danny died, he'd been an active man in his late sixties, still farming, a Eucharistic minister and devout Catholic who got on well with his

Protestant neighbours in the rural belt outside Ballyterrin. Now he was . . . like this.

'What was it you were wanting me for?' He had perhaps noticed Paula's eyes wandering to the pictures. His words had a slight slur – you could hear him forcing them out.

'You may have seen that a body was found at the weekend.'

'Michael Doyle.'

'Yes. Mickey. We're sure it's him.'

John nodded grimly. 'He hanged himself, I heard.'

'Well . . .' Paula hesitated. Guy was still outside on his phone, chatting to his best bud Corry, no doubt. 'He was hanged, yes. But we aren't sure if he did it himself.'

The ageing man sat up very straight in his chair. He leaned forward and set the shaking cup upon the coffee table – old, scarred, just like him. The manoeuvre took a full fifteen seconds. 'What is it you're telling me, miss?'

'We think someone killed him. There were certain . . . signs that it wasn't suicide.' They'd agreed not to release information about the note in the mouth, as a way of weeding out confessions. 'So I'm afraid we're going to have to speak to the families. We need to eliminate them from the investigation.'

John was silent for a moment. She realised he was looking past her head, at the picture of his wife and son. He didn't say anything for a while.

Paula spoke. 'Mary . . . she couldn't go on after it?'

He looked at her. His blue eyes were leached of colour, his eyebrows white caterpillars. Paula let him look at her for a long time. She didn't need to say anything. Eventually he shifted. 'You came to tell me it was murder, miss? If indeed it's possible to murder a man like that. Do you need to have a soul to be murdered, or is it more like putting down a rabid dog?'

'Is it?'

'I'm a Christian, miss. Nothing that happened changed that. If we can't forgive we have to endure. Now what did you want with me? The man's dead, seems not much can change that.' He paused. 'That was their argument too, as I recall. The Ireland First lot. Too late to bring people back, so what was the point in a trial?'

'The other four are still missing, and we think it's now looking orchestrated – a mass kidnap, with the intent to harm.'

'They said they had no intent,' he said, still looking over her shoulder. 'You remember that? Plant a bomb on a busy shopping street, but not meaning any hurt. There was a lot of talk about *intent* back then. What makes a crime. What makes a sin.'

'Mr Lenehan . . . I understand not everyone is part of your support group—'

'No. There were a few disagreements along the way. Human nature, sadly. Some wanted to fight in the courts, some preferred to get on with some kind of life.'

'And you?'

'It's not much living when you're like this.' He indicated the walking stick, the house settled about him like an old coat. 'As I said, I'm still a Christian.'

It wasn't really an answer, Paula thought. 'We wanted to let you know as Chair that we'll have to speak to the families and survivors. We'll be as tactful as we can, but we do have to speak to everyone involved and try to get alibis. If you could relay that message, it would be very helpful to us. Thank you.' She went to get up, then realised she couldn't. She was entirely sunk into the soft cushions. 'Er . . .'

'Here.' Shifting to his feet, the old man helped her up. His hand was very cold. Paula righted herself. 'Thank you. I'm a liability at the moment.'

'When are you due?' His voice was gruff.

'In two months, God willing.' Yes, she'd said God willing. Some atheist she was.

'May God bless you.' He said it like he had a direct line to the man himself.

The door opened and Guy came in, tucking his phone away. 'Mr Lenehan, so sorry to keep you. I'm DI Guy Brooking.'

Paula and John Lenehan exchanged a look. 'I've spoken to the doctor here,' he said. 'Get her to tell you what I said. Look after yourself, miss.' He stumped off to the kitchen with their cups rattling a shaky fandango in his hands.

She indicated to Guy they should go out, shutting the door quietly behind him. 'What was your call about?'

'The autopsy's been done on Doyle. Traces of a sedative in his system. They're trying to isolate the compound now, as it could be a good lead. But one thing's sure – it definitely wasn't suicide.'

He opened the car door for her, unthinkingly courteous. 'What do we do next, then?' She got in, with difficulty.

'We interviewed the families of the bombers when they went missing, but we better go back now we've found Doyle, see if they know anything else. Perhaps you'd go with Gerard – I'd like your insights.' Guy started the car.

'You can't come with me?'

'I have to go to Belfast tomorrow. Big meeting.'

She waited for him to tell her what the meeting was

about, but he didn't. 'OK . . . who should I go to?'

'We've spoken to Doyle's wife already, and Lynch and Brady didn't have close families. You should speak to Catherine Ni Chonnaill's mother. She's looking after the children.'

'What about Flaherty?' Martin Flaherty. Paula thought back to his picture. In it he was carrying a thin plastic bag from the corner shop which clearly contained a copy of the *Irish News* and a packet of ham slices. He owned a car dealership in town and had done well out of it. Yet this harmless-looking man had orchestrated the deaths of dozens of soldiers over the years, booby-trapped cars, bombed a pub in Manchester killing four students, and likely been the driving force behind the carnage of 1st May 2006. 'Flaherty's widowed,' said Guy. 'Lives alone. He has one daughter, Roisin, who's in Dublin.'

'Are we seeing her?'

'No, they haven't spoken in years, apparently.'

'Doesn't really matter. If people are in trouble they nearly always go to family first, however long estranged.'

'Would you like to visit her, then?'

The question was surprising. 'Well, sure, but am I not needed here?'

'We can call you in if we need you.'

Paula understood – sending her to Dublin was an entirely pointless errand, a safe way to get rid of her and her embarrassing cargo. Out of the front line. She stared out the car window, annoyed. 'OK. After that we interview the families of the victims?'

'Unless we find some answers before then. Really we should have questioned the mayor by now, but apparently that would "inflame" local sensibilities.' Guy sighed, changing gear as they slowed down in the traffic nearing town. 'It's a very odd case.'

That was true. For a start, it wasn't often you had more sympathy for whoever the killer was than the victim.

Kira

Kira told everyone she couldn't remember the bomb. It was easier, and it made them feel better. She could see them relax, and sometimes they'd say things like, *ah, it's for the best. Poor pet, she's blocked it out*. But what it was really like was having something under your bedclothes, twisting and turning around, like when the cat's in there so you can't see it but the shape's there and you know it's about to come out. For a long time it was like that. Then she woke up one night too scared to scream. Her tongue in her mouth was dead and the breath crushed out of her lungs. What she'd remembered had no eyes but the smell was there – burned, and something yellow she knew was blood. And the sound – the little noises you knew were people trying to scream, but everyone had the wind knocked out of them and your ears had gone and the silence was the most frightening thing. You'd been blown over, so your back was raw against the ground. Bits were falling down on you like burning rain. Plaster. Brick. People.

You tried to breathe. No one knew for ages it was a bomb. You just knew the world blew up. You were born the year peace came. You never knew about bombs.

For a long time you could see nothing and that was a blessing, but it was there waiting. One day you saw Rose after the bomb. Her face was gone. There was her hair, her lovely blonde hair all dirty, and then a space of just blood, and then her body. You saw something on the ground and it was Rose's leg, twitching, blood pumping. It had blown off her. Her leg wasn't attached any more.

Rose was still not dead then and making a noise through the place where her face usually was. You went to her, though you were eight and it was horrible and you couldn't believe any of this.

Your arms were all red. Her blood. Rose's blood blown all over you and in your eyes and mouth and nose. You could hardly see anything, eyes swimming in a line of blood, like when your goggles filled up at the pool.

Rose was making a noise. Kind of like *Mmmmmok . . . kay?* You couldn't talk. You held her hand, which couldn't stop twitching, and told her it was OK somehow, even though she had no face or leg any more. There was blood all over the pavement, running down it like rain.

'Mm . . . OK?'

She was asking if you were OK. She was dying and she wanted to know were you OK.

'It's OK,' you croaked. 'It's all fine.' Your last words to her were a lie. You knew that she was dead before she did.

Chapter Five

'You OK with the belt?' Gerard and Paula were driving to one of the dodgier parts of town in a police-issue Skoda. He'd reluctantly agreed to leave behind his beloved Jeep – it was too recognisable as a PSNI vehicle, and in the area they were visiting, that was enough to get you two slashed tyres, and if you were very unlucky, a car bomb underneath.

'I'll manage.' She arranged it awkwardly round the bump.

'Not long now then.'

'No.' She ran her hands over it, stretched tight. 'It's very heavy – it'll be a relief in some ways.' But not in all, because then she'd be forced to take time off work. She winced as a foot caught her kidney. Gerard saw it and his eyebrows went up in alarm. 'Relax, I'm not going to break my waters all over the car.'

'Say if you are. I wouldn't have a baldy what to do.'

Paula also wasn't keen on having her child by the side of the road with only Gerard Monaghan's big lug for assistance. 'I've a while yet. Just take me there.'

Gerard was eating a packet of Tayto Cheese and Onion crisps, the smell filling the car, turning her stomach. 'I am,' he said through a handful. 'It's not the best area, you know. I'm surprised—'

'What?'

'Nothing. It's just, in your condition . . .'

'I'm not dying.'

'Hm.' He kept stealing glances at the bump, his fingers crumbed with crisps. 'I'd not want my wife working right up to the day of the birth.'

'Oh right. I must have missed something, then. Do you actually have a wife?'

'No, but— . . .'

'She's unlikely to be working, then, is she? Since, you know, she doesn't actually exist.' Gerard sulked, rattling the last bits out of his crisp bag. It was pure revenge that made Paula say the next thing. 'I see Avril's set a date for the wedding.' She watched him for a reaction, but none came. Nothing had happened since that odd moment at Christmas – Avril was getting married, Gerard flirted with every female in sight, and Fiacra, who'd taken Avril's engagement hard, had morphed from a cheerful young country boy to a moody, ambitious thorn in all their sides. Although he had other reasons to have changed, admittedly. 'I wonder if we'll be invited,' she said.

'Dunno. You'll hardly be able to go anyway, with the wean.'

'Hmm.' She relented – she was hardly the person to poke her nose into other people's affairs. Although officially no one knew Guy might be the father of Paula's baby, she was sure everyone had noticed the spark when they'd first met, and if they could count at all, it wasn't a huge leap to make. She shut up, and they drove the rest of the way in silence. Soon they were passing walls covered in murals – Hunger Strikers, Peelers Out, Bloody Sunday memorials. Centuries of bitterness slapped up there in lurid colours. They parked in a rundown estate where the kerbs were painted green, white and gold. Immediately a crowd of kids gathered. 'Here, mister, that's a nice car.'

'Thanks.' Gerard locked it. 'Who's gonna keep an eye on it for me?'

'Me, me!'

He picked out the tallest lad, freckled in a Celtic jersey. 'I'll give you two quid if it's all in one piece when I get back. Come on, Maguire.'

'I see none of them were prospering, anyway,' said Gerard. 'Bit of a dump, this.'

Catherine Ni Chonnaill lived with her three children in a sad, pebble-dashed end of terrace. The overgrown grass in the front yard was mined with bin bags and broken toys, and when they rang the bell the paint on the door was flaking.

It was opened a short while after by a sixtyish woman, shouting at a pit bull terrier to be quiet as it worried around her heels, pressing its wet nose into Paula's leg.

'What do yis want?' The eyes travelled to Paula's bump.

'We're with the MPRU,' said Gerard. 'The Missing Persons Response Unit. Could we come in, please, ma'am?'

The 'ma'am' usually did the trick. She stood aside to let them into the dingy living room. It smelled of fags and the brown carpet was marked by cigarette burns. Two children, a boy and a girl, sat watching cartoons on a big TV. They didn't look up as Paula and Gerard came in. There was nowhere else to sit – the kids were on the crumby sofa, and propped on the brown velvet armchair was a baby, sniffling, his face encrusted with baked beans. The woman, who was presumably his grandmother, wiped his face with a tea towel and asked again what it was they were wanting.

'We need a word with you about your daughter,' said Gerard. 'It'd be better if the wee ones didn't hear, though, if you see.'

'Tara, Owen, go outside.'

'Wa-ah!' The boy, who had two pierced ears and a Man United shirt, grumbled.

The grandma swatted him with her towel. 'Get out of my sight, you wee skitter.'

It was windy outside, and a light drizzle pattered down, but the children went, both in bare arms. Seven and five, Paula knew they were. 'Well?' said the grandmother. 'I'm feeding the wee one so I can hardly put him out.'

'What's his name?' asked Paula.

'Peadar.' The third child, the one who wasn't Ronan Lynch's. He stopped grizzling when a plastic spoon with more beans was shoved in his mouth, but Paula couldn't tear her eyes from him, the food mess, the snot round his pudgy nose, and the smell of dirty nappy wafting from his little blue jeans.

'Mrs Ni Chonnaill,' she said. 'I'm a forensic psychologist, so my role in the unit is to produce reports on the missing to see if there's anything that might have made them go.'

'It's Mrs Connell. I don't hold with that Irish rubbish. And you'd be better served looking after your husband, love, 'stead of parading about with all and sundry looking at your belly.'

Paula blinked. 'Er – well – never mind me. I need to ask you about Catherine. Obviously we're very worried about her, since Mickey Doyle's death. Where do you think she is?'

It was a question so obvious it rarely got asked, but Paula found it could be surprisingly useful. Know the person and you'd often know where they were. 'Who knows with Catherine? She's most likely annoyed the Ra again and gone off.'

'You're saying she sometimes left the country to escape the IRA?'

'Aye, two or three times. Around the Belfast Agreement. They don't like all that Ireland First business, the Ra.'

'Your husband died in 2004, I believe?' Gerard was making notes again.

'Not soon enough, ould bastard that he was.'

The child put up his dirty hands for the spoon. Paula averted her eyes. 'And these other times, did Catherine tell you she was going?'

'Oh aye. She'd ring from phone boxes and that. I told her to stay away, make a life in England, but her da wanted her back.'

'But she hasn't phoned this time?'

'Not a word since the text. She said she was late at work and would I lift them from school. What did your last maid die of, I texted back, and could she not have rung me at least? But she never answered.'

'I see. And she hadn't been to work that day, it turned out?'

'So they said. Never turned up.' Catherine had last been seen getting into her car after dropping Peadar at daycare. Somewhere between there and her office on the outskirts of Ballyterrin, she'd vanished.

'Mrs Connell,' Paula hesitated. 'Is it fair to say you're not overly worried about your daughter? You don't think she's been abducted, you think she's safe somewhere?'

'Missus, I've been expecting her dead since she was ten years old, but she scrapes through. She'll be grand, you'll see. I'm more worried about being landed with these weans.'

'The oldest two, they're Ronan Lynch's children? He has also been reported missing, as you know. Could they have left together?'

'In his dreams. She wouldn't piss on him if he was on fire these days, useless galoot that he is.'

'I'm sorry, but are you able to tell us who the father of – Peadar – is?' Paula lowered her voice, as if the child could understand. He looked on with watery blue eyes, uncomprehending.

'You'd have to ask Catherine.' The grandmother was suddenly tetchy. 'I've no more idea than you do. Is that all now? I'm a busy woman.'

'All right. Thank you.'

Behind her, the baby had seen something on the muted TV and was pointing at it. His granny poked the spoon at his mouth. 'Quiet now, what's wrong with you?'

He was crying now, pushing the food away, reaching out for the screen, his sobs turning to wails. Paula followed his gaze. On the TV behind them, the news, and on it the pretty, sulky face of Peadar's mother. Catherine Ni Chonnaill was forty years old and looked thirty, a beautiful, fair-haired woman with a strong, ruthless gaze.

'Shut your face, Peadar,' said his granny, poking the spoon at him once more.

'He wants his mother,' said Paula quietly. And who had taken her away from him?

Extract from *The Blood Price: The Mayday
Bombing and its Aftermath*, by Maeve Cooley
(Tairise Press, 2011)
Interview with John Lenehan

*I sent my son into town that morning. He wouldn't
have gone otherwise, you see. He was like all young
lads – he'd lie in his bed till teatime if you let him.
He'd this holiday booked in Majorca and I said he
shouldn't be going unless he could earn the money.
You do hear all sorts of stories. Drinking and carrying
on. So I says get up and change some currency if
you're going. Take it out of your post office account.
His mammy'd paid for the holiday, but she was soft
on him. I didn't want him spoiled, you see. He was
our only child – his mammy was near forty when she
had him.*

*Anyway. I make him get up and go to town and I
tell him to get his mammy some shopping while he's
there. She'd usually let him keep the change but I said
I'll check the receipt. He was nineteen, you see, miss.
I thought he should be working. So we had words,
and he went off, all sulky like. Mary went after him
and she gave him a big hug at the gate. So she had
that at least. I'd been fighting with him. I have to live
with it.*

*I was working on the farm that day, painting
a fence. Mary came down about one. I could see her
running out of the house. She'd no shoes on, just
running in the mud. Her hair all falling down. I
knew something was wrong but I just went on
painting. Until she got there, you see. Until she told*

me and it was all going to be different.

There's been a bomb in town, *she says, and her face was all wild.* They're saying on the news. Come quick, come quick.

So she runs to the house and I just put the lid back on the paint. Don't know why I did that. And I walk. Slow like. She's the TV on and there's High Street and it's all smoke. It's like a film. Neither of us says anything. Then I goes, He'll have been heading home by now.

He might have gone to the shops.

Sure he's no cash of his own.

She didn't look at me, and I knew she'd given him the money. Did you phone his mobile? *I hate those things, terrible waste of money they are, but I was right glad he had one that day.*

He's not answering. *Mary's voice was all funny.*

They'll have no reception. It'll knock down the wires or something. *Mary turns to look at me. I was well past forty when I wed her, and she was the most beautiful girl I ever saw. Danny was like her, he'd her dark hair and her eyes. I'll never forget her blue eyes.* Will you go, John, *she said.*

So I get in my van. I wish to God I never saw what I saw that day. A lot of the families, they stayed at home, or they didn't hear about it till later. I went, you see. I couldn't get in the whole way, the army was there, but there was blood running down the street. It was sort of raining blood onto your face. The petrol station was on fire and the bank had fallen down, they said. I just keep thinking he'll be finished by now, he'll be finished. I kept shouting, Danny,

Danny*! And they're saying,* You can't be here, sir, go to the hospital if you've lost someone, he might be there. *There was all sirens and you could hear people screaming – you've seen the video, aye? It was like that, but it was worse. Alarms going off everywhere. You could smell it. The oil, and the blood, you know.* Sir, *they said,* you have to go, *and they're in their masks and suits, and I look up and there's the tree and in it somebody's arm. A woman's. The watch still on it.*

Anyway, I went to the hospital, but I couldn't get in for traffic so I just got out and left the van there in the road and walked in.

Yes, I found him there. He was – well, he was still alive at that point. But I told his mother he wasn't. I told her he was at peace. Sometimes you have to lie to people if you care for them.

Chapter Six

Although Paula hadn't known Maeve Cooley for long, she'd already started to think of her as a friend and colleague. But both Maeve and she had been distinctly cool for the past few months – Facebook messages long unanswered, no kisses at the end of text messages. For Paula's part, which she knew was irrational – he hadn't been her boyfriend since she was eighteen – it had been finding Aidan half-naked in Maeve's bedroom that day in Dublin. For Maeve's part, Paula guessed Aidan had passed on the news she'd given him one grey January day in Ballyterrin General Hospital, windows lashed by melting snow, herself recovering from a knife attack and barely able to walk. 'So you know I'm . . . eh—'

'Pregnant. Yeah,' he'd mumbled, staring at the floor. She was telling him now because she'd almost died and that ought to give her a small amount of leeway, surely?

'How much . . . I mean, when . . . ?'

'Three, four months or so.' She watched him adding up, his head sinking lower.

'Oh,' he'd said.

Paula decided just to say it, ripping off the bandage. 'I slept with Guy.'

Aidan's head had jerked up. She went on hastily. 'Before

us, I mean. It was – we'd found Cathy Carr's body, and I – it just happened.'

Aidan took this in, his face slowly hardening. 'It's not mine, is that what you're saying?'

'I'm saying I have no idea. Honest to God, I don't. It could be . . . either.'

'Can you not count? You've got a doctorate, for fuck's sake.'

'It takes two, you know? I don't remember you saying let's stop and find a condom.'

'I was pissed!'

'Well, I was – oh, I don't know. It just happened. And you lambasting me about safer sex really isn't going to help. And someone just tried to kill me and take the baby, so I'd really like to not get in a row, OK?'

Aidan had stared at the floor some more, rubbing his dark head with one hand. Nicotine stained, bitten-nailed, story notes smudged in ink on the back. His hands made her sad. 'Have you told Brooking?'

'No. I'm telling you first.'

If she'd hoped that would placate him, there was no sign of it. 'If you want money, tell me. Or whatever you decide.'

She earned more than him, but didn't say this. 'You don't have to – I decided to have it . . .' (Her – it was a girl, but she felt squeamish saying this to him. For him, it was still just a massive problem.) 'I thought about it a lot, you know, but in the end I couldn't— . . .'

'You were going to have an abortion.'

She'd shut her eyes. 'Aidan, if you go all pro-life on me, I swear to God I will kick your head in. As soon as I'm able, I mean. You don't get to be arsey with me and moralistic.

This might be my body it's happening to but I didn't do it on my own.'

He looked angry, muttered, 'Wish you hadn't slept with him too. He's fucking married and all. I never thought you'd be the type, Maguire.'

Her hands clutched in the pillows. 'I really will kick your arse when I'm better. I didn't cheat on anyone, did I? Anyway, I thought she'd left him. She was in London. And – you dumped me, remember?'

'Ah, here we go. It was years ago! Anything else you want to bring up? Did I do something in the Famine too, or at the Battle of the Boyne?' He blinked a few times. 'I'll leave you be. Tell me what you want me to do.' He paused at the door. 'You're not even sorry, Maguire. I know you didn't mean it, but – me, and him, for fuck's sake. The Brit cop. You're so taken up defending yourself you never even think to say sorry.'

And the news had clearly filtered through to Maeve. She'd of course taken the side of Aidan, her friend since university – more than a friend, maybe. It was something Paula tended to dwell on late at night, as the baby kicked at her insides. That's if she wasn't thinking about Guy playing Happy Families with his wife and daughter.

She'd emailed Maeve to say she'd be in Dublin but there was no answer, so she drove down alone, parking her car in a side street in Donnybrook and waddling out in the warm spring sunshine. Was it OK to park there? She couldn't make sense of the sign, it was all hours and numbers and her brain couldn't take it in. The place was a red-brick Georgian town house, with a shiny navy door and bay trees in pots outside. Paula climbed the ten steps with difficulty and leaned on the bell. Nothing happened for a while, then it was opened by a grey-haired women holding a duster.

'Yes?'

'Mrs De Rossa?' Surely not, she looked too old.

'Are you press?'

'No. I'm – here.' She handed over her police ID. 'I'd just like a quick word.'

'She's not seeing anyone.' Presumably this was the cleaner or something. Roisin Flaherty, married to the head of a big Southern bank, had come a long way from the farm she'd grown up on. The door shut as Paula thought of what to say and she found this rather rude – she was pregnant, for God's sake.

She leaned heavily on the bell, and the cleaner opened the door again. 'I'm sorry, miss, you—'

'Could I please have a glass of water? I'm so sorry. You see, I'm pregnant, and it's awfully warm today, can I just – I'm a little faint.'

'Let her in, Nancy, for God's sake.' A voice had come from further back in the house, from the hallway smelling of polish and lilies. In the gloom Paula could see a woman not much older than she was, with set blonde hair, in a cashmere jumper and dark slacks. Silver bracelets up one arm. Expensive. 'Do come in and sit down. Nancy, would you get her some water – or tea, if you prefer?'

'Tea would be lovely,' Paula murmured, as she was led into a sitting room that was painfully formal and clean. Like a hotel, almost, with a deep grey sofa and a mirrored coffee table, navy silk paper on the walls. 'I'm sorry. The heat gets to you, doesn't it?' She knew Roisin had children.

'Oh yes. I remember it well.' She stood, twisting her hands. 'Is this about what I think?'

'I'm afraid it's about your father, yes. I'm Dr Paula Maguire from the Missing Persons Response Unit in Ballyterrin.'

The woman flinched, as if from a physical blow. She had a chunky silver necklace about her neck, which she fingered nervously. 'I don't think I can help.'

The door opened and the cleaner appeared with tea on a tray, white china cups and a pot, a plate of shortbread which slender Roisin De Rossa would not eat. The woman gave Paula a fierce stare and went out, shutting the door loudly.

Paula settled into the sofa. May as well use her situation to extract the maximum cooperation from witnesses; it was good for precious little else. 'I'm sure this is a very anxious time for you.'

'I don't—'

'I mean, he's still your father, isn't he?'

Roisin took a deep breath, closing her eyes for a second. She checked the door to see if it was securely shut, then picked up a remote, which she aimed at a black stereo on the bookshelf. It looked more like a pebble in the river than electronic equipment, which showed it had been very dear indeed. 'How do you work this thing – oh. There.' Loud pop music came pouring out, One Direction or something, setting Paula's teeth on edge. 'Sorry. Kids. There we are.'

Soothing classical, the soar of heavenly voices. Paula understood this was to mask their conversation.

Roisin sat down, twitching at her trousers until she was ready. 'I'm sorry you came all this way – Dr Maguire, was it?'

'Yes. I'm a forensic psychologist but I work with the police team. I'm working on your father's case.'

Again the flinch. 'Please, I don't – I can't help you. You see, I don't know him any more.'

'You're estranged?'

'Of course we are.' Her lips tightened. 'When I was wee, of course, I didn't understand, and at university I was in that crowd, you know – we thought we were doing right . . .' She trailed off. 'I never knew what he was at. That he was actually involved in it.'

'The IRA?' Paula didn't lower her voice, and Roisin turned pale.

'Please – my kids. They have no idea. They've never met him. They don't know my maiden name. We never go north.'

Why would you, Paula thought, if you could sit in splendour in Dublin 4, with organic vegetables and clothes from Brown Thomas? 'Mrs De Rossa. I understand you want to distance yourself from your family.'

'My childhood,' she corrected. 'I made my own family here, with Dermot and the weans.'

'OK. But we can't find anyone who knows a thing about your father. He left the IRA, I gather, after the Good Friday Agreement?'

'Yes, he was very angry. We – we still spoke, back then. He felt I'd betrayed him, you see. When I left mostly I gave up following politics. I thought there was enough fighting and blood spilled. My weans – I didn't want them part of all that. I wanted them safe.'

'And when did you find out about his role in the bomb, his alleged role, I mean?'

Roisin lowered her gaze, biting her lip. 'I had no idea. Really, I don't – I mean, he was political, and he talked the talk, but to do that . . .' Paula realised she was angry. 'I was pregnant at the time. With my second. And that wee baby who was killed . . . Oh God.' She gave a shuddering sigh. 'I'm not asking anyone to be sorry for me, not when all those poor people died, but it was awful, just awful.'

'I can imagine. So who told you about it?'

'It was on the news. We were having our dinner and Dermot said turn that up, and I was carrying a bowl of couscous and didn't I drop it down on the flagstones and it broke everywhere. Sixteen dead – and then his picture came up. They said maybe it was linked to his group.'

'Did you believe it?'

'Not at first. I rang him. I was in hysterics. Daddy, I said, they're saying it's you. Did you do it? He was quiet. He didn't say no. Then he said, you should get off the line, Roisin. That was it. So – I knew. We flew to France the next day for a month. Dermot has a sister there. It was—' She got a hold of herself. 'So I didn't talk to him after that. And the trial and all . . . I didn't go. I stopped watching the news and we don't take the papers. Dermot takes them in the office, but I told him he's to tell me nothing. Unless Daddy actually dies.' She looked at Paula suddenly. 'Is that—'

'We don't know that he's dead. But we've found the body of one of the accused Five, and the others are still missing. We couldn't find anyone who really knew your father. Is there any other family?'

'Mammy's dead. Thank God. She never believed he'd hurt a fly.'

It was especially sad to be glad your own mother was dead, and this made Paula feel a certain kinship to the woman. She'd often thought it would be better to know for sure that her own mother was dead, if it was peaceful, if it would have been quick. She shifted again; she needed to pee. 'Did you know any of the others? Catherine Ni Chonnaill – she's not much older than you.'

Roisin's lips tightened further. 'Mammy used to say that woman would shoot her own baby for a united Ireland. She's evil. Pure evil.'

And probably also dead, Paula thought. 'So you can't think of anyone your father might have talked to, spent time with?'

'I wouldn't know. But he cut a lot of ties after the bomb. Even the Republican hardliners, the Thirty-two County Sovereignty Movement and the Continuity lot, they felt it was botched. The warnings weren't right, it went off too early. There was no need for civilians to die, and it cost them a lot of support in the States. That sort of thing.'

How did she know this, if she hadn't spoken to him since 2006? 'Roisin. He got in touch, didn't he?'

'No, I . . .'

'Please. When was it?'

She sagged. Her voice came from somewhere near her feet. 'A week ago. The day that he – went.'

Right before they'd disappeared. Paula leaned forward. 'What did he say?'

'Oh, I don't – I didn't know it was him, of course, or I wouldn't have answered . . . I told him never to call and he didn't have the number, I thought – but it was him. Thank God the kids were at school.'

'What did he say?' Paula asked again.

'He said – he was sorry. I said I'd put the phone down. He said, I mean I'm sorry for you, Roisin. It was your life too. And I'm sorry for all of it. And I said – I said it was too late for sorry.'

56

'And?'

'And he said he knew, but he had to say it anyway. And then he said, goodbye, Roisin, pet. God bless. And he hung up.' She was weeping now. 'And then a few days later I heard he was gone.'

'You think he knew something was going to happen?'

'I was waiting to hear he'd killed himself,' Roisin sobbed. 'I thought that's why he called. I'm sorry.' Her tears were leaving streaks in her make-up. 'It's just he was my father, and I used to love him, and I've lost him too, but I'm not allowed to say. I'm not allowed to grieve, because he was a monster, but—'

'He was your dad.' Paula reached for the woman's cold hand. 'It's OK, Roisin. You've done your best. Look . . . you've a lovely house, lovely family – you did your best. None of us can do any more than that.'

Roisin looked up, her face pale as bone. 'He doesn't realise,' she said. 'He doesn't realise how many people's lives he ruined. And I don't just mean the ones he killed.'

Kira

Kira was eating her tea when it came on the news. She always ate it on her own now, ever since Rose died. Then, she used to come home from school and do her homework while Rose would sit with her college assignments (she was studying childcare) and they'd work away, sharing biscuits off a plate and with a pot of tea on the coaster. Jammie Dodgers were their favourites but sometimes Rose would get a new kind in the shop and they'd try them. Then Mammy would come home and they'd all eat tea with the news on.

Not now.

Mammy never ate dinner any more. She put Kira's tea in front of her and stood in the kitchen, wiping everything, staring at nothing. Tonight, like sometimes happened, she hadn't made any tea at all. It got to six and the oven was still cold and empty and Mammy was in front of the TV, her plastic bottle that she said was water beside her. So Kira put a frozen pizza into the oven and ate it at the table on her own, though it hadn't cooked right and the doughy bits got stuck in her mouth.

Times like this, she could imagine Rose there. She had a little chat with her in her head. Rose would be washing the dishes, putting them shiny-wet in the rack.

How was the Maths test?

OK. I got a hundred percent.

Good girl yourself. And did that Marian Cole give you any bother?

I told her to eff off like you said.

Just right. If she starts again you tell her she's as big a hoor as her sister.

Rose always knew the right thing to say.

Kira could get so into these inside-head conversations she'd forget where she was. So she jumped when Mammy made the noise, as if she was choking. She had knocked over the bottle onto the carpet so Kira went in to wipe it. Mammy was on her knees in front of the TV. On it the newsreader, the nice lady with the blonde bob, she was saying about someone being found dead in woodland. Then some pictures came up on the screen. A man, all scary looking. Then three other men and a woman. Five of them. *The* Five.

She knew what was coming then but it was too late.

58

Mammy was running from the room, knocking over the bottle again so it ran into the pink carpet, and slamming the bathroom door. You could hear her crying, *Rose Rose oh my Rose my angel.* Kira stood there and watched the picture come up, the street with the petrol station and the security tape, the collapsed buildings, and she knew that street. She'd lain there, paralysed, while Rose died in front of her with her face blown away.

Kira turned off the TV. She got a cloth and sponged the carpet. She threw away the crusts of the pizza and washed the plate, the way Rose would have, and dried it up and put it in the cupboard. Clean and tidy as you go, Rose would say. Then they'd have tea and eat Club bars and watch *Friends* on Rose's box set. Kira leaned against the sink the way Rose used to, the sleeves of her school uniform rolled up, her hands wet and wrinkly.

It had started. It was time.

'Thank you,' she whispered out loud. 'Thank you.'

Rose smiled.

Chapter Seven

'Are you almost back?'

Paula adjusted the hands-free kit; Guy's call had caught her driving back to Ballyterrin. It was hard enough as it was to reach the wheel over the bulk of her body. 'I'm on my way. Why?'

'There's been a tip-off about a white van acting suspiciously on the A1 near the border.'

She was instantly alert, hands tightening on the steering wheel. 'So . . . maybe dumping another body?'

'Could be. Trouble is, it's a very large area, and we aren't sure where the van was going exactly. Corry wants us all at the station. Can you make it?'

'Of course!' She'd been so afraid she'd be left out of this investigation. 'Are we going out to the bogland?' She'd need strong shoes if so, boots even. She had her wellies in the boot just in case.

'We may, if it turns out there is a body. There's a team out there already.'

'Are you at the station?'

Guy seemed to hesitate. 'I'm still in Belfast. I'll try to make it, but I'd like you to be there.'

'That was a long meeting.'

'Yes.' Once again, he didn't tell her what it was about.

'OK. Listen, I'll tell you about it properly later, but it

seems like Flaherty's disappearance wasn't a surprise to him. He called his daughter the day he went missing – they hadn't spoken in years before that. So maybe he did skip the country after all.'

'Hmm. He'd also just changed his will, according to his lawyer. Two weeks before the disappearances. Leaving everything to the daughter – save for a sizeable donation to the Mayday Victims Fund.'

Paula almost veered out of her lane in surprise. 'Really?'

'That's top secret, by the way – it would cause all hell to break loose if it leaked to the press. He's always denied any involvement with the bombing, despite the overwhelming evidence. So let's keep it to ourselves.' Paula knew he was thinking of her connection to Aidan. He went on. 'It's an odd thing about Flaherty. Unlike the others, his house was clean and locked up, and his milk delivery was cancelled.'

'Maybe he got out before they came for him.'

'But he didn't show up on passenger lists on any planes out of the country and there's no sign of him on the mainland. It seems he's just vanished into thin air.'

Paula realised the turn-off for Ballyterrin was nearing. She had to start paying attention or she'd miss it. 'I better go. I'll see you at the station?' She waited for him to say she couldn't go to the scene, wasn't fit. He didn't.

'OK. See you there.'

Half an hour later, in her stylish attire of wellies, cardigan and maternity jeans, she lumbered into the main station, passing a knot of reporters outside the main door, shivering in the spring breeze. She couldn't help but look, and hated herself for it – but Aidan wasn't among them. She sensed he was still annoyed at her for leaving the wedding. She went in, slapping her pass down on the automatic door. Corry had reluctantly let her have one, largely because Paula was still flirting with the job offer she'd been made several months before. Corry wanted her to join her team permanently – so far Paula had managed to put off giving an answer, her pregnancy offering a convenient get-out, but she'd have to decide sometime.

The team had gathered in the large conference room – Paula didn't recognise everyone, they must have brought in other officers from outside Ballyterrin. The room buzzed with chatter, and as usual men outnumbered women, so Paula, her belly huge, drew every eye. She looked for Guy and didn't see him, but at the last minute he rushed in, still holding his coat, and stood against the wall, as every seat in the room was taken.

Corry rapped the table for quiet. 'OK, everyone. No confirmation yet, but I'm betting we have another body by the end of the day, and we need to be ready. Who, we don't know yet. The bog is a large area. I'd like this done as quickly and tidily as possible, so I've decided to get some help. Fortunately – or unfortunately – we have some experience round here of searching bogland for bodies. I want to bring in a search team to find the other four – hopefully alive, but they'll also be looking for disturbed ground that might indicate graves.'

There were some murmurs round the table. Bob Hamilton cleared his throat. 'Ma'am – does this mean we're bringing in outside experts?'

'Four more bodies.' Corry was staring at the combined teams as if it was their fault. 'That's what we could be looking at, if we don't find the rest of the bombers, and fast. Four more dead bodies surfacing God knows where.

I'll use whatever resources I can. So yes, I'm talking about bringing in a private firm.'

'The others could be anywhere,' said Gerard gloomily. 'Where are we supposed to start looking?'

'And Doyle's body wasn't hidden,' said Guy. 'It was quite clearly meant to be found, and fast.'

Corry ignored him. 'Nonetheless, we need to start being proactive. I'm not waiting for more corpses to land on our doorsteps. I've already got reporters camped outside. And isn't this your remit, to find the rest while they might be still alive?'

Gerard raised his eyebrows at Paula across the table. The *glasnost* between Corry and Guy hadn't lasted long. 'Getting her excuses in early,' said Gerard under his voice.

'What do you mean?'

'You'll see. This fella they've got running the search team, they say he has all the women eating out of his hand. Good-looking bastard, by all accounts. You'd want to watch yourself, Maguire.'

Paula glared at him. 'I'm sure I'll be able to control myself.'

'This time,' said Gerard, with a pointed look at her belly, and raised his hand to ask Corry a question before Paula could bite back. 'What leads do we have, ma'am?'

Corry said, 'There's this white van, like the one in the forest car park when we found Doyle. We couldn't get a plate this time either, though. As for suspects, I believe you're looking into an IRA connection, DC Monaghan?'

'I thought they were the most likely culprits, ma'am – a mass kidnap like this takes a lot of organisation. I've got some feelers out, but the most I could find out was that Jarlath Kenny wasn't pleased about the Mayday bombing

– didn't go down well with his funders in the States, too close to nine-eleven.'

Guy was nodding. 'I agree with DC Monaghan – I feel we should question the mayor as soon as possible.'

Corry frowned. 'Oh yes. Jarlath Kenny. He's an interesting one.' That was putting it mildly – on the one hand, illustrious local mayor, running for MP in the summer. On the other – former Republican terrorist who'd served time in the Maze prison for handling arms. 'We need to speak to him directly at some point, yes, though we have to tread lightly. I think that should be an MPRU task. You're perceived as more impartial.' In other words, they could do the grunt work and stay out of her way. Paula saw Guy's mouth tighten as Corry went on. 'As for the families of the bomb victims– well, no one likes it, but I think someone should go to the relatives' group. They're the ones with the strongest motive, if we rule out Republican in-fighting.' Her eyes went round the room. Paula tried not to catch her gaze – *not me not me*. 'Dr Maguire.' She looked up to Corry's sweet smile. 'I think you'd be best. A police officer, it's more threatening. You're . . . cosier. Tell them you've come to update them on the situation, and see what you can suss out. We'll probably have to interview them all separately if we do find a body today.'

'Cosier.' Paula glared at her. Corry's eyes took in Paula's cardigan, the falling-down plait of red hair. All she needed was some knitting to be every police officer's nightmare of a civilian expert. She could hear Gerard chuckling, and even Guy was frowning, as if trying not to laugh. 'Whatever you say, ma'am. I'd certainly not want people to feel threatened, after what they've been through.'

She didn't care. At least it got her close to the action,

and if anyone underestimated her because of her bump and dishevelled clothes, well, they'd soon realise their mistake.

There was a knock on the door. Corry's head snapped round. 'Yes?'

It was a young constable, her hair in a net. 'Ma'am – phone for you.'

Corry put out her hand for the mobile and took the call in front of everyone. 'Yes. I see. And where is that exactly? Is there access? Right.' She stowed it in her pocket like a gun in a holster. 'We've got the body. Shallow grave – barely hidden, in fact, as you said, DI Brooking.'

Guy nodded, slightly mollified. Paula found her voice. 'Is it . . . a man?'

Corry looked at her for a moment. 'Yes. Callum Brady, by the looks of it. ID on the body again.' The team was already stirring, getting ready to go, and Corry picked up her jacket. 'I'm going there now. DI Brooking, gather what team you need. The body's on the hillside just off the A1. The land is marshy so they're setting up duckboards. I'll need a press statement assembled too – a second body, this is going to get a lot of attention. We have to be careful how we play it.'

'He's been murdered?' Guy was shrugging on his jacket. 'Yes.'

'We can be sure this time?'

'We can be sure.' She was moving to the door. 'I said they'd found a body, but what they haven't found is his head.'

A brisk wind was blowing, tossing the white cotton of the bog flowers, whistling forlornly through the trees as Paula struggled out of her car. There was the usual large group of people milling about, some in white protective suits. Among the crowd, a familiar face. She lumbered to where a short, dark-haired woman was getting into a silver Mondeo. 'Well,' she said, in greeting.

'Well, he's dead. If that's what you wanted to know.'

'I gathered that. Him not having a head and all.'

Dr Saoirse McLoughlin was the FMO on call, a doctor in the local A & E, and for many years Paula's best friend. After years of absence they were rebuilding some kind of friendship, but it wasn't easy.

Saoirse eyed Paula as she put her bag away. 'You're massive.'

'Yep. I'm the thing the planets orbit round. Haven't seen you for ages . . . how's Dave?'

'He's all right.'

Paula wanted to ask, but couldn't think how, when Saoirse was going to start her course of IVF. Her friend's face already looked puffy from the drugs she'd been injecting every day. 'You're feeling OK?'

'I'm fine. I'm not the one who looks like a beached whale.'

Paula smiled weakly, though she wasn't sure it was a joke. 'I better report in. Meet up soon?'

'Yes, maybe.' No invitation to call round. 'Aidan's seeing Dave on Thursday. I'll see if he's free sometime too.'

Yes, because a social occasion with her ex-boyfriend, possible father of her unborn child, was exactly what would pass for fun in Paula's world right now. 'See you.' She trudged over to the cluster of officers and vehicles.

'Paula, meet Lorcan Finney.' Corry was standing by the police van with a big hunk of a man, hidden under goggles and a white suit. This must be who Gerard had been talking about, the leader of the private search team.

She held out her hand, aware that with her pregnant belly and chunky-knit jumper she was a walking stereotype. 'Mr Finney—'

'Doctor,' he interrupted. 'I'm a forensic geologist.'

She lowered her hand. 'Well, I'm Dr Maguire. Psychology.'

Rocks, she was thinking, just as he was probably thinking *mad theories* about her.

Corry said, 'Dr Finney here is an expert at locating burial sites. He helped us find Brady's body so quickly.'

'Don't the cadaver dogs do that?'

The man took off his hood and goggles to reveal a wide, weather-beaten face and flattened sandy hair. His eyes were a startling shade; almost violet in the afternoon light. 'Aye, the dogs do a good job. They just bring me in for the plod work.'

'I actually don't remember sending for you, Dr Maguire,' said Corry pointedly. 'In fact, are you not meant to be on lighter duties? I thought I asked you to visit the relatives' group.'

'DI Brooking sent for me,' she lied. 'There's a meeting this evening which I'm going to. I'm just trying to understand the ritual of all this. That's two now, one hanged, one decapitated, you said? Is there a note with this one?'

'We haven't found the head yet, so if it's in the mouth we can't be sure.'

'Is there anything useful?' She was going to have to justify her presence there, in a soggy field, her bump heavier than a small suitcase.

Finney finally seemed to relent. 'This one wasn't killed here.'

'How can you tell?' Paula raised her eyebrows. A change in MO.

'No blood in the soil,' said Finney. 'His head was removed somewhere else. So if you can work out where—'

It could be the lead they needed. 'And can we?'

'Well, that's where I come in. I analysed the provenance of soil from the previous crime scene, including some we got off Doyle's shoes. It showed a type of mineral which is quite rare in this area, and certainly doesn't belong in a forest or a field of boggy soil.' He slammed a boot on the ground below them, rich and oozy. 'I need to check with a few local experts, but the good news is this will narrow the kill site down to a few locations nearby. We also found some footprints this time, which were difficult to recover in the previous woodland setting. I think there's clay mixed in with them.' He indicated what looked like a toolkit by his large feet. 'When we find a suspect, samples will show us if they walked in the same clay.'

Corry was looking like a cat who'd found a very interesting mouse to play with. 'Good, isn't he? All that from soil.'

Paula tried to regain control. 'The footprints – do we have a gait analyst on the force, or a forensic podiatrist? We used to have one when I was in London. Often they can tell you lots, like if it's a man or a woman who left the imprints, or how old they were, all kinds of things.'

'London,' repeated Lorcan Finney, fixing her with his odd eyes. 'I hear they have all manner of things over there. Have you heard that, DCI Corry?'

Corry laughed. Paula scowled – so much for solidarity. Corry said, 'I'll put in a request to the forensic service. The site will be combed down, and there's a huge amount of debris about, so it'll take a few days. But if we can find this other site like you said, Dr Finney, there's a chance we can recover Flaherty, Lynch, and Ni Chonnaill alive.'

Finding and saving vicious murderers. No one wanted to say it, but cases like this sometimes made you question what your job was actually for. And who.

''Scuse us, boss.' A uniformed officer approached, clearing a space. Paula lumbered back, as past them came two white-suited techs carrying a stretcher. It wasn't possible to get the ambulance any closer on the muddy ground.

'Oh, they've found it,' said Corry, sounding pleased. The stretcher came closer. On it sat the head of Callum Brady, the hair brown with soil, the eyes clogged with it, the teeth bared in the final agony of death. The neck ended in shredded flesh and veins.

Paula, automatically and secretively, made a small sign of the cross as the cargo passed them by. She looked up to see Lorcan Finney watching her with an odd expression on his face. He gave her a small nod. *Catholic*, she found herself thinking, though his name alone could tell her that, and then immediately felt ashamed.

Kira

She couldn't remember a time when she didn't know where the man lived. Of course there must have been one. He'd not touched their lives until *that* day, when Kira was already eight. But she knew it as if she always had – he lived in that big white house her bus passed on the way from school to Crossanure, out on its own. Of course there were other men too, but everyone knew he was THE man. The important one. The ringleader, it sometimes said on the news, and it made Kira think about a man with an evil smile and a top hat and whip, tigers dancing round him.

This was back in March. After everything had been decided. After the trial didn't work for those complicated reasons she couldn't get straight in her head. It was easy in the end. Sometimes it was as easy as just getting up and doing it. Luckily Charlene wasn't speaking to her anyway, so she didn't have to explain too much. She'd got off at an earlier bus stop, with the girls from the Tooley estate. Charlene's head snapped round, her frizzy curls bouncing. 'Where're you going?'

Kira stuck her nose in the air. Charlene had sat down the back of the bus with Lucy and Sam today. So obviously it would be one of those days when they ignored Kira, laughed those loud laughs and said words she knew were about her. 'I'm visiting my friend,' she said coldly, gathering her bags.

'You don't have any friends,' sneered Lucy. Kira gave her the look Rose had taught her – one that said, *you are like a scummy little beetle under my shoe*. Amazingly, Lucy shut up. Kira's face was burning as she climbed down off the bus, but maybe no one noticed. She stayed fiddling with her bag and PE kit until the Tooley estate girls had walked off. They'd given her some weird looks and weren't above having a go or making fun of her shoes. Soon the road was quiet. She got out the map she'd drawn herself, using the computer in school, and set off down the country lane.

It was a nice day. Sun fair splitting the stones, Rose would say, which apparently was something Daddy also used to say way back. Little birds played in and out of the hedge and there was a nice coconutty smell off the gorse. She took off her blazer and rolled up her shirtsleeves as she walked along. She wished she had a drink. Rose used to give her a Capri Sun for the journey home, but Mammy never remembered. It seemed to take a long time to get to the man's house, but eventually she did. She stared at his gates, which were closed and locked with a big padlock. It was very quiet. She could hear birds, and far away someone cutting their grass. It smelled like the countryside, a bit ripe and rotten, but in a good way. Kira decided to climb over the fence. It was high and jaggedy and she tore a hole in her school skirt, but she made it. Then she picked up her school bag and sneaked round the house.

It was a really ordinary house. Quite big, but just with plain white walls. No flowers in the garden. There were three cars in the drive, white, black and silver. They looked like expensive cars. Jamesie would know what they were. She wondered would she ever see him again. She crept around the house, peering in the windows. A lot of the rooms seemed empty, with no carpets even or beds. One was a sitting room – sofas with plastic still on them and a massive TV. And the back of the house was a little patio with chairs on it, all dusty since it hadn't rained in so long. He didn't use any of this. You could see that. The back of the house was all windows, so you could see right into the nice white kitchen. Kira turned the handle – it opened.

She wasn't even scared. She realised she was supposed to go in all along. And Rose was with her, so she'd be safe. Inside felt quiet and a bit cold, like no one lived there. On the counter there was a plate with a crust on it and a paper – the *Irish News*. They never got that, it was the Catholic paper. It was open at the crossword, half filled in. Kira looked to see could she answer any but knew not to write on it. She wanted to open the cupboards, see what he had for his breakfast, this man. The Bad Man. Her feet made a squeaking noise on the white tiles; she'd left a bit of soil from walking on the grass in the middle of the road. On the fridge was a magnet of Ireland which was holding up a leaflet about bin collections. They had the same one in their house, only it hadn't been pinned up; it was in a big pile of papers Mammy never went through. Kira knew because she'd started looking in it for important things. Bills. Hospital appointments. The letters from the counsellor woman.

She ran her hands over the counter. It was marble and it felt cold. She was just wondering what she was meant to do when she felt the air sort of move and her hair all stood up and her stomach went 'blurp'.

'Who might you be?' said the man, standing in the doorway to the hall.

Chapter Eight

Paula entered the small church hall, with the same smell they all had, lino and dust. Old Christmas decorations sagged from the walls with posters for singing classes, am dram, dog obedience. But this was nothing so benign. This was a meeting of the Mayday Victims Support Group. Everyone in the dim room, lit by cobwebbed fluorescent bulbs, they'd lost someone that day, or they'd been hurt themselves. That was the thing about a bomb. It didn't just tear through buildings, reducing them to rubble and ash, and it didn't just tear through people, so bloody parts ended up yards from their owners, so the teeth of one victim might be found embedded in the leg of another. It tore through lives, leaving everything a mess, a heap of ruins, a raging fire.

She inched along the wall awkwardly, very aware that her body was ripe with life. It seemed almost an obscenity, when so many people had lost their children on that day. It seemed wrong to be so whole. She'd have liked some way to tell them she wasn't whole at all, she had her own wounds. You just couldn't see them.

A young woman was putting plates on a table, on which sat bottles of squash and packets of Jaffa Cakes. She had salon-shiny hair, and nice suede boots. Then she turned slightly and Paula saw she had only one eye. It was a pretty

73

turquoise blue, and on the other side was a patch. She recognised her. This was Lily Sloane, who'd been practically blinded by glass shards when she was eighteen. It made Paula's chest ache to see the girl, how she'd grown her fringe over the damaged side of her face, but she put on a smile. 'Hello, sorry to interrupt you all. I'm with the MPRU – they said I should come on down today?'

The girl put down the plate and flicked at her fringe. 'Oh right. I'll get Dominic. I'm Lily.'

I know, Paula almost said. 'Nice to meet you.' She knew who Dominic was too. An angry, energetic man in his late thirties, he was the father of Amber Martin, the toddler who'd been killed that day. Paula thought she'd also heard that the Martins' marriage had not survived losing their only child. There was no sign of John Lenehan. Dominic Martin was up on stage behind the shabby green curtains, talking to a man who looked like the caretaker. Lily approached him, walking with the easy grace of a twenty-three-year-old. Briefly, he looked at Paula, then carried on talking to the man.

'Sit down,' Lily called back. 'We'll add you to the agenda.' Paula obeyed, sitting heavily on a plastic chair. She let out an involuntary sigh as she eased into it – standing was getting harder every day. More people had arrived, and it was difficult not to match them up with what she knew of the victims. There were people of all ages – men, women, older, younger, even a teenage girl who slipped in near the end and sat behind Paula with her feet up, where she could see her from the corner of her eye.

'I don't know you,' the girl said suddenly, over the hubbub of getting ready. Dominic and a woman of about sixty were seated at a trestle table in front, with one chair empty. The others sat in rows of chairs, a steady murmur of talk going up. Paula felt all eyes were on her.

'No,' said Paula, startled. 'I'm with the police. You know . . . I'm here about the missing people.' Would the girl know about such things, or was she too young?

'Oh yeah,' she said, sounding largely uninterested. 'We don't talk about them much. Not here. This is a space to keep them out, John says.'

'Well – I'll be respectful, I promise.'

Dominic had stood up. 'I hope everyone is keeping well? I think we'll start.'

'What's your name?' Paula quickly asked the girl, on impulse.

Nothing for a few moments, then, very quietly – 'Kira.'

She hadn't time to say her own, but anyway Dominic was looking at her. 'Welcome, everyone. You'll notice we have a visitor today.' He managed to make 'visitor' sound like 'sinister interloper'. 'Dr Paula Maguire is here from the missing persons unit in Ballyterrin. We've been asked to talk to them. She'll update us on a few things.'

She waved. 'I'd get up, but I'm not sure I can.' A few people smiled, as she'd hoped they would, but Dominic and the woman to his left remained stony-faced.

Dominic went on. 'First bit of business is that John has sadly decided to step down as Chair due to ill health. I'm sure you'll all join me in thanking him for his years of service. Before the next AGM I'll act as Chair, with Ann carrying on as secretary.' Another murmur went up, which Dominic seemed to ignore. Ann was presumably the grim-faced woman – who was she? A mother, a daughter, a wife? Ann coughed and read out the minutes in a dry local accent. Paula tried not to tune out. She'd never been any good on committees – indeed, as a doctoral student, had been kicked off the organising team for their graduation ball after she'd stood up and shouted 'I don't give a fuck about rocket!' during a two-hour debate about menu choices.

It was a succession of minutiae: discussions over the memorial, a reminder to pay subs for tea and biscuits, lengthy updates about the failed court case. Only one thing stood out. In the same voice she'd used for the rest, Ann said, 'A vote was taken on options for proceeding in the light of the failed court case. There were three against, five for, and the rest abstentions. Minutes by Ann Ward,' she finished, and Paula could place her. Out with her family that day, she'd lost her husband Patrick, and the six-week-old grandson he'd been wheeling in a pram, also Patrick.

'Any matters arising?' asked Dominic.

No one spoke for a moment. Then a man cleared his throat. 'I think there's a few issues to go over, Dominic. What with everything that's happened . . . you know.' Paula was sure he was looking at her. She tried to keep her eyes on the floor.

'There's plenty of time on the agenda for any issues arising,' said Dominic easily. 'Now. Let's start with remembering.' He shut his eyes and everyone did the same. 'Amber Martin,' he said tonelessly. 'My daughter.'

Then Ann cleared her throat. 'Patrick Ward, my husband. Patrick Ward Junior. My grandson.' Her voice didn't change from that in which she'd read out the minutes.

The litany moved around the room, as if they did this every meeting, a well-practised round. Two middle-aged men seemed to have come together. One said, 'Rita Smith, my wife.' The other, 'Colette Cole, my wife.' Paula remembered them – the two women had been friends, although from different sides of the divide, and were out collecting money for Guide Dogs when they were killed.

'Siofra Connolly,' said a woman in her early thirties. 'My little sister.'

'My sister too,' said the man with her, a bit younger, dressed in paint-stained clothes, as if he'd come from a building site. Siofra was one of the teenagers killed, along with her French exchange partner. Lily had been a friend of theirs – the girls were hit when the windows of the bank exploded.

'Tom Kennedy,' said a woman in her forties. There was something in her voice, a defiance. 'My husband.' Something went round the room at that, barely perceptible, the shadow of a murmur.

'Penny Garston,' said a middle-aged woman who'd brought knitting. 'My mother.' That was the oldest lady who'd died, the devout Catholic with thirty grandchildren. Her funeral had been so big they'd had to put up a marquee.

'Daniel Jones,' muttered an old, old man at the front, hunched over his walking stick. 'Grandfather – I mean, he's my grandson.'

Daniel, who'd been ten when he died, wearing the strip of his favourite team, Arsenal. Paula found it was all coming back to her, the horrific roll call of the dead.

The teenage girl at the back was last. She stood up, which no one else had done, and cleared her throat, raising her chin. 'I'm here for Rose Woods. She was . . . mine.'

There was a short pause. Dominic read, 'We also remember Danny Lenehan, Monique Leclerc, Sergeant Andrew Patterson, Lisa McShane –' again, the odd murmur went round – 'Idris Adebayin, and Constable Raymond Sheeran.'

Those who'd been born overseas, out of this crucible, but brought to the town that day by steps of malign fate. The Sheerans she knew didn't get involved. And Lisa McShane – Paula wondered why no one had come for her.

He left a pause. 'Now. I think we'll pass over to Dr Maguire to explain why she's here.' His eyes settled on her, cold, and she realised he'd done that litany for her benefit. *Remember what we've been through.*

She felt she'd better stand up, so she lumbered to her feet, one hand on her back. Funny how the body knew these things, knew how to stand like a pregnant woman. 'I know it's difficult and we're very keen that the families are treated with respect . . . eh.' She faltered. 'Why I'm here is that the members of the so-called Mayday Five have gone missing. I'm sure you've all seen this.'

There was no response, and she had a sudden moment of panic – what could she say to these people, who'd lost so much? Would they be able to see she'd lost someone too? She soldiered on. 'One of the Five, Mickey Doyle, has now been found dead. And this hasn't been announced, but we believe we found the body of another of them this morning. The injuries are quite severe.' She waited, but there was no reaction. 'Um . . . we think the other three may be captive somewhere, and so – we'd like to ask people to come to us, if they know anything, anything at all, about where they might be. We're attempting to be respectful, but we do also have to look at who would have wanted the Five gone. I'm afraid we may need to interview some of you, establish alibis and so on.' Silence. She took a breath. 'So – you can speak to me, in confidence, if you need to. I'm not a police officer, I'm a psychologist, and we have oaths of confidentiality. That's all.' More silence. She sat down more heavily than she'd intended, making a slapping noise on the chair.

'Let me just check – was it Dr Maguire?' said Ann Ward, writing.

'Yes, um, not medical, obviously.'

'I see. Are you asking us to help find these people? You think we know where they are?'

'I'm asking you to help us unravel what happened. It's still possible the other members of the group have skipped the country, trying to evade justice. We just want to know where they've gone. We have to . . . check with everyone. Just in case.'

'Justice.' Dominic repeated the word. 'It's a weighted word in here, Doctor. What justice has there ever been for us? My Amber had barely learned to walk when they blew her to bits. She wasn't even two years old. What justice did she get?'

Paula swallowed. 'Yes. We do understand that.'

'You understand it.'

Bad word to choose. 'We're . . . mindful of the situation. But we do also have to try to find people, if they've been reported missing. We still have a job to do.'

There was more silence. Dominic Martin continued to watch her. His eyes were green, and held so much pain and rage Paula had to look away. 'We'd be very grateful for any insights you could give us,' she said. 'Thank you for your time.' There was a silence. She realised she should go. Dominic began talking about costs for the memorial, which would be unveiled in a few weeks' time, on the fifth anniversary of the bomb.

Behind her, the teenage girl leaned forward so her voice sounded low by Paula's ear. 'Meet me outside, miss.' And she slipped out of the room on quiet feet. After a moment,

Paula bumbled to the door, bumping chairs with her belly and trailing cardigans and bags, then on shutting the door behind her she waddled away as quickly as she could in case they started talking about her. It had been a bad idea to go there. Of course these people weren't going to help, even if they did know anything.

'Missus?'

She turned to see the teenage girl standing on one leg. 'Oh hello. Kira, isn't it?'

'Kira Woods.'

'Of course. I'm sorry about your sister.'

The girl swished her ponytail at that, like an irritated horse. Paula should have known better. Why be sorry when you had nothing to do with it? Kira was dressed in the uniform of the local Protestant school, navy blue with a short skirt and white knee socks. Her blazer was studded with pin badges and she had fluorescent green marker on her hands. 'I'm sorry if I upset people,' Paula said. 'I just had to ask. It's my job.'

'Do you want to see the graveyard?'

Paula was bone-tired and embarrassed enough for one day, but the girl had left the meeting for a reason, and so she said, 'Sure. Thank you.' And the two walked round to the graveyard behind the church hall. Kira moved with a kind of lilting skip, and Paula wondered how old she was, then decided just to ask. Thirteen, was the answer.

'So we you were eight when . . .'

'Yeah.' She swung the gate into the graveyard, riding on it for a few moments like a kid. 'There's a memorial there, look. There's a couple, you see, in the different churches. We wanted to put up a proper one – they're always on about it, money and planning and I dunno. They're going to open it in town on the anniversary. Not open. What's the word?'

'Unveil?'

'Yeah. They're going to unveil it. They've been making it for ages.'

'Do you go to every meeting?' They were crunching along a raked gravel path.

'Yeah. Rose would want me to. She says it's really important not to let people down once you've joined something. Like Girl Guides and that.'

The use of the present tense was jarring, for a sister who'd been dead for five years. 'I see. Is it the same people every time?'

'Nuh-uh. At first people came from foreign. That French girl – her parents were here one time. They cried a lot. And there was a black lady came from London – I think he was her brother, the man who died in the petrol station. Idris. She had this really cool turban thing.' Kira was hopping along the sides of the graves, as if on a gymnastics beam. 'That soldier too, he had a da who came from Liverpool, but then I think he died.'

'Oh. And everyone local, does someone come for them?'

'They're supposed to. No one comes for Lisa, and the Sheerans, they don't like to mix cos of their religion.'

'Lisa McShane?'

'Yeah. People say she was like, having an affair. You know Tom Kennedy? He was Methodist. She was Catholic and they worked together, and they were both in his car that day, you see, parked behind the garage. I think they like got trapped in the fire. They weren't meant to be there. People only found out when they got their bodies out.'

'Oh. I see.'

'Her family sort of like disowned her, I think. She has three wee kids and everyone says her husband won't talk about her any more. Supposed to be after she died he found all these texts on her phone from him – Tom.'

'I see.' Paula was walking very slowly, the baby pressing on her. It was a beautiful evening, the light soft and warm, the kind she remembered from her childhood, staying out late, playing in the street. 'And you, Kira – you were there too that day? Were you hurt?'

In response she shoved up the sleeves of her blazer, revealing arms pockmarked with scars, and long, livid burns, silvered. 'And here, see?' She lifted her lank fair hair to reveal more burns all round her neck. 'We got caught near the garage,' she explained. 'They fixed me up a bit. Lucky I wasn't as pretty as Lily. She even got spotted by a model scout one time, in Belfast. But that was before. This is it.'

They paused before a granite stone, just as Paula was sinking under the weight of stories, of loss. It was a simple grey stone, marked with a list of names, and above them a dove etched in white. Kira traced it with a bitten finger. 'Some people don't like him cos it's a sign of peace, and they don't think we should be peaceful. But we lost the case, so, what can we do?' She shrugged.

'There were arguments in the group?' Paula asked. 'You know, about how to deal with it?'

'Oh yeah. The McShanes won't join at all, like I was saying, and the Sheerans, they're sort of Free Presbyterian.' She said it matter of factly. 'They think Catholics did the bomb so they hate John being Chair.'

'John Lenehan.'

'Yeah. He leads us. He's a Catholic, you know.'

'Yes, I know, but – where was he tonight? He's stepped down, has he? Did you know that was going to happen?'

Kira shrugged again. 'Dunno. He's like really old.'

They stood looking for a while, trying to absorb the names and the life behind each. *We will not forget*, said the inscription. Paula got the feeling that could be construed as a threat. She hoked about in her shoulder bag.

'Listen, would you like to give me your number, Kira? I'll text you mine, and then you can call me any time you need to, OK? If you have any questions or that about the investigation.' It bit deep. The girl was the same age Paula had been when her mother went, similarly lost, grief-stricken.

Kira took the proffered pen and scrawled a number on Paula's notebook. 'That's it.'

'I'm sorry this is so hard. We do understand, OK? We just have to do this.'

Kira stared at her feet in their sensible shoes. 'They're bad people.'

'They were acquitted, though. That means we can't treat them like criminals.'

'But they did it! Everyone knows they did it!'

She didn't know what to say to that. 'I'm sorry. This is just the way it has to be.'

Finally Kira lifted her eyes – the same blazing blue Paula recognised from the photos of her sister, but burning with rage, with the injustice of it all, and Paula heard the words as clearly as if she'd said them: *No, it isn't.*

'You can get in touch if you need something,' she said again, weakly. 'If there's anything I can do.' Except, of course, there wasn't.

Paula thanked Kira for showing her round, and the girl

shrugged it off, refusing a lift and heading off down the street, trailing her hand over the railing of the park, her large school bag weighing her down. She was an odd one, a strange mixture of childish impatience and adult understanding. Paula looked back to the hall, where the meeting was still in progress. She could hear raised voices within, as if some intense debate were in progress, but she knew she couldn't go back there. She cringed as she thought of the reception they'd given her. But what could they do? The Mayday Five were people too, and had to be looked for, no matter what they'd done.

She thought about it some more, wondered what it was that had bothered her about the meeting. And it was this – no one had seemed remotely surprised, even though she was there telling them about kidnap and torture and murder. Not even a flicker. She tried to suppress the worry. She couldn't face bringing even more pain into these people's lives. She'd seen the look in Dominic Martin's eyes. That man had identified the body of his daughter on three separate stretchers, she'd been so badly injured. His wife had gone. Everything had gone. But all the same she couldn't link them, this motley crew of grandmas and kids with their squash in plastic cups, with the simultaneous kidnap of five hardened terrorists. How would they ever have pulled it off? No. She couldn't see it. She refused to.

Feeling her stomach stretched tight and aching, Paula went back to the car and headed home to the cold, empty terrace, taking her ghosts with her.

CLAIRE MCGOWAN

Extract from *The Blood Price: The Mayday
Bombing and its Aftermath*, by Maeve Cooley
(Tairise Press, 2011)

*I initially contacted Niall McShane as part of my
research for this book. I was hoping to get as many
perspectives as possible on that day, though I didn't
expect many families would want to talk. In the end
most did, apart from those who are overseas or who
didn't comment publicly at all. It was a way of
bearing witness for some, and ensuring their loved
one was not forgotten. Mr McShane said no to begin
with, which was to be expected given the rumours
surrounding his wife's death (Lisa McShane died in
the car of her colleague, Tom Kennedy, which was
parked behind the garage when it exploded). But
some time later he contacted me requesting an
interview – what follows is the transcript.*

I met Lisa, my wife, in 1999. The first thing I
noticed about her was her eyes – she'd the strangest
colour eyes. I never saw anything like them before or
since. She was pregnant soon after and we got married.
We used to joke I only had to look at her and she'd be
expecting. Lisa'd no family, she was adopted as a
wean, so she wanted loads of her own. We had three
in five years. When she died they were six, four, and
one. Money wasn't good, and we were fighting a bit,
and she was fed up doing all the housework and
minding the kids. So she got a wee job in an office
doing the filing and that. They sold building supplies.
They liked her, I think – she was good at chatting to
the ould fellas and that. She seemed happy.

I did wonder the odd time if there was someone else. She'd get a call at home and she'd look a bit funny, but she'd just say it was work. And she'd hide her phone all the time when I walked in. Then once she'd to go to a conference overnight and we had a fight. I didn't see what conference was so important she had to leave me with the weans. She only did admin, for God's sake. But it's hard to say if I knew or I just remembered it all after. Anyway, that day she was so jumpy, picking fights, shouting at the kids. She said we needed groceries and I said I'd go later, I'd to call into work anyway. She was raging, saying she'd go, I never let her set foot out the door. I didn't think that was right and we had words. The last time I saw her she was getting into the car and sending a text. I was standing in the window with Sinead – our youngest – trying to get her to stop crying. I remember thinking that when Lisa came back I'd try to talk to her. I'd put the washing on and that might cheer her up.

I'm sure you know all about that day. I waited for ages – I didn't put the TV on, I was too busy round the house– then my ma rang to say there'd been a bomb and was I OK? I said I hadn't gone into town, but Lisa had, and no she wasn't back. I waited with the kids. I thought maybe there'd be roadblocks or something holding her up. The kids knew something – they were in wicked form. Then the mammy came round and I went to the hospital. We didn't say anything. I think we knew.

At the hospital it was chaos, every corridor full and people going about shouting names and crying.

There was blood all over the floor, and people had stepped in it. You could see all these footprints down the middle, and you could see even the doctors and nurses were scared. You could see it in their eyes. I didn't shout for Lisa. I just kept asking people and they'd look at lists and then they sent me to a wee tent out back. There were all folding chairs and people sitting about looking like the world had ended. I waited. It was the worst moment of my life until then, but even so I didn't want it to end, because then I'd have to know for sure. In the end it was dark and everyone was still there. They came out and said, Mrs Kennedy? That was your woman, the wife, you know. Anna, I think you call her. And she got up. Then they sort of looked at me too. It was a wee girl with a clipboard. Are you Mr McShane? *she says.* We need you too, please.

And we're looking at each other, me and the Kennedy woman, never seen each other in our lives before, and then we both go behind the curtain. I let her go first, thinking I was being polite. I always remember that. I thought it was good manners. Then we saw them.

They told us a clatter of things that day. Lisa had been in the Kennedy fella's car, and did they know each other? They'd found her phone blown clear and some of the messages suggested they'd gone to meet up and . . . you know. When we saw the bodies, they were still holding hands. They'd sort of burned together and couldn't be separated. Your woman, the wife, she turned round and looked at me like it was my fault. Did you know? *she said. Like I should have.*

Well, that was just the end for me. I'd my kids to think of and all that talk about their ma carrying on with some man. The oldest is near twelve now. She hears things. At school, you know. I had to protect them. The Kennedy woman, she goes to meetings, but I just stay away. At least Lisa had no family round here – she'd been adopted, she was put in a children's home when she was wee.

The worst thing was reading those messages. Sounded like he was trying to finish it with her and she was begging. Tom, Tom, I love you, please will you meet me, you owe me that much. *When I think of that, and about their hands, I can't help wondering, was she crying before she died? Was she hurting so bad she'd maybe have been glad when it came?*

Chapter Nine

'So it's definitely Brady.'

'Surprised they can tell,' muttered Gerard. 'His mother would hardly know him like that.'

On the office's projector screen, the pictures of Brady's severed head, soil-stained, were indeed hard to match to the bloated, unhealthy pictures they had of him in life.

'They found a licence on the body again,' said Guy. 'There's no attempt to conceal identity. He was hardly buried at all, just put under some scattered soil. His head was found on the other side of the bog, propped on a stone.' Guy illustrated this with a map of the bogland, red dots marking the body and the head.

'Was there a note in the mouth again?' asked Paula.

'We don't have the full autopsy results yet, but yes, there was a note.'

'And?'

He frowned slightly at her impatient tone. 'And it's the same, ruled exercise paper, what looks like the same writing. This time it says "unforeseen escalation".'

'Unforeseen escalation,' she repeated. 'Is it—?'

'It's another phrase from Ireland First's statement,' Avril confirmed. 'From the time of the bombing. They said there'd been an "unforeseen escalation", what with the bank collapsing and the petrol station going on fire – even though they still didn't say it was them planted the bomb.'

Guy leafed through some papers. 'Forensics did manage to analyse the note in Doyle's mouth – no DNA there, but we can source the paper to a standard exercise book sold in several outlets in town. Nothing unusual, unfortunately.'

'And the writing?' asked Bob.

'That's interesting. It went to a graphologist, who believes the note was maybe written by a child, or a young person.'

They all stared at him. 'There's no way a child could manhandle a fella like Martin Flaherty,' Gerard scoffed. 'The man's six foot four in his stocking soles.'

'Right. It could also possibly be a young woman. So what this suggests is—'

'More than one person,' murmured Avril, who was taking notes.

'Exactly.'

Fiacra groaned. 'Ah, *no*.' Everyone hated cases with more than one perpetrator – messy, and hard to pin it on one or the other.

Guy said, 'I know, but let's face it, there was never any way one person could have lifted all five of the bombers on the same day. We have the white van as well – we've been able to pull some CCTV from near Brady's flat and one was seen driving by there on the first of April. We think it's the same one as was seen at Creggan Forest and out near the bog, as there's no plates. So – it must be more than one person, yes. A group, probably, who could plan the kidnap of five strong adults, without being seen or caught. If it was five. There's also the fact that Flaherty seems to have known he was going to disappear – the will changing, and the fact he contacted his daughter. But the other four appear to have been forcibly taken, certainly, and not everyone could do that.'

Gerard jumped in. 'That's why I favoured Kenny's lot for it. Word is him and Flaherty go way back, joined the Ra together in the seventies. That journalist who wrote the book – she said Kenny and Flaherty were thick as thieves back then.' Maeve's book, he must mean. Paula wondered if there was any connection there, the book coming out, then the Five going missing. Gerard went on. 'I'd like to chat some more to a few of my boys, see what they've heard. I mean, he'd have had help. He wouldn't get his hands dirty himself. I hear talk too that Kenny's hold is slipping with the local Ra.'

'The local IRA he isn't officially part of now,' said Guy drily. 'Why?'

'People think he's gone soft. Sucking up to the cops and about to go over to Westminster and take his seat, they reckon. Will I talk to my boys then?'

Avril tutted audibly but said nothing. His informers, was what Gerard meant. He was a big fan of the 'ear on the street' approach. It was a source of great sorrow to Gerard that he'd joined the force in the days of the PSNI and PACE. He'd have been much happier skulking about in stakeout cars, slamming his fist against interview-room tables, smoking in the office while wearing a trench coat.

Guy said, 'That's acceptable, as long as you keep it at strictly a voluntary, informal chat. We can't authorise any covert human sources at this time. Is that clear, DC Monaghan?'

'Some cash would help,' said Gerard nonchalantly. 'These boys don't talk for free.'

Bob made a noise of disgust and Guy said, 'Not now, I'm afraid. Just talk to them.'

Paula thought again of their faces – the two remaining men, the woman. So many people with reasons to want rid of them. The children who'd be left without a mother. 'What's being done to find them, the other three?'

Guy shuffled his papers again. 'As I said, we don't have the full results yet, but Brady appears to have been killed in the past twenty-four hours – so there's a site somewhere else we need to find, where he's been held – it seems likely the others are there too. He also has over a hundred small injuries to his body. Look at this.' He passed them some sheets of paper and read it for them. 'Glass poked into him, small burns on every patch of skin, what looked like injuries from bricks or stones dropped onto him. His left eye had a large piece of glass sticking out of it, so it was oozing vitreous fluid.'

'He was tortured, then?' asked Bob, with distaste. He was clearly finding it hard to work on this case. Paula could only imagine what it had been like to be on duty in the aftermath of the Mayday bomb.

'Yes. The injuries were all done pre-mortem, though he was likely dead by the time they cut through his oesophagus. Like Doyle, he seems to have been drugged. Too soon to say here, but the compound used on Doyle was a kind of animal tranquilliser. So anyone with access to a farm could probably get it.'

They all fell silent. Avril was staring down at the laptop, pale, though her fingers never stopped moving.

'We've also had the analysis back from the geologist,' said Guy, after a moment. 'I must say, he's worked very fast.'

'Is that what that rocks fella was doing there?' said Gerard. 'Taking wee samples of dirt – it's a weird job.'

'He gave out to me for stepping on a bit of ground,' complained Bob in injured tones. 'It wasn't even cordoned!'

'I know. He did seem to have rather a sense of entitlement.' From Guy that was damning. 'However, DCI Corry's rather keen on him.'

Gerard rolled his eyes. 'She is indeed.'

'Anyway,' Guy pressed on, ignoring this. 'It's interesting reading, the report, if you could turn your attention to it, please.'

The report certainly didn't look interesting – a dry table of words and chemical compounds, and on the page after, a map with geological terms on it.

'What is it?' Fiacra was squinting. 'Looks like my old chemistry homework.'

'It's the different rock compounds found on the victims' shoes, and areas in this locality where these are found. It might lead us to the kill site.'

'They weren't *victims*,' said Avril quietly, eyes on her laptop. 'They were killers.'

'We don't know that,' said Guy severely. 'They were acquitted in court, and even if they had been convicted they're entitled to the same justice as anyone else. That is in fact the meaning of "inalienable rights".' There was silence around the table. 'Is everyone clear on that? I don't want any further discussion of this matter. We're going to do the same for the Mayday Five as we would for anyone else. That's the reason we have laws – it's not up to us to decide on who gets justice, with all our own history and pain. OK?'

No one said anything. He went on. 'Now, the most

significant compound is highlighted there. On page five . . .'
They all turned over, the sound like a brief flap of wings in
the small room. 'Dr Finney has highlighted where this
mineral can be found near Ballyterrin. One site is the scree
above the Drumantee mountains, and the other is the sea
caves down by the coast. He feels the latter is more likely,
as it's very remote and it would be quite possible to hold
someone there without detection. Apparently the IRA used
to use the caves for smuggling arms.'

The word IRA always sounded different in the mouths
of English people. Round here they were the Provos or the
Ra, familiar names to cover up the fear and pain they'd
caused. Reducing them to a joke, like so many painful
things in Ireland.

'So are we searching the caves?' Gerard pushed aside the
paper, which he obviously couldn't be bothered reading.

'Yes. We're going out as soon as we assemble a TSG.
Paula, I'd like you to examine the scene too, see if there's
any cultural or ritual significance to the site. Even if they're
not there, we might find some leads to the other three.'

'How will she get down there?' said Fiacra bluntly. 'I've
been. You have to climb down a path, and look at the size
of her.'

'She's not an invalid,' said Avril, still typing.

'She's not deaf either,' said Paula, glaring at Fiacra.

Guy held up his hands for quiet. 'If the caves are safe,
we'll approach via the beach. It should be doable.' He
turned to her again. 'What did you find out from the
relatives' group?'

'I'm not sure. They were reluctant to discuss it in front
of me, but John Lenehan has stepped down as Chair – too
sick, they said. And there was some kind of vote at their

last meeting – about options for proceeding, they called it.'

'John is over seventy,' said Guy. 'And it's true, he didn't seem in the best of health.'

'And that group is all he has. His son was blown up, his wife hanged herself, and his farm's gone to the wall. So why would he suddenly leave?'

Avril spoke up. 'Dominic Martin did make death threats after the trial collapsed – I found the video footage of it, what he said in the courthouse when they let the Mayday Five go.'

'You can hardly blame him,' said Fiacra, a little nastily. Avril bit her lip, dropped her head.

'It doesn't make everything allowable,' Paula said. 'Grief . . . it's not an absolution.'

'I think you're right, Paula,' said Guy. 'We'll have to interview the families. But it will be very difficult, both for them and for us.'

'But you're sure it's justified?' said Gerard. 'You don't reckon an IRA feud is much more likely than the families knowing anything about it? I mean, they're just kids and old folks, most of the relatives – they could hardly kidnap five terrorists, could they? That fella Martin Flaherty, rumour has it he'd kill you as soon as look at you.'

Paula sighed. 'Believe me, I'd like nothing more than to pin this on Kenny and his ilk. It would give me the greatest pleasure to see him thrown into jail, Armani suit and all. But – everything I've said still stands. There was something going on in that meeting. Hopefully it's not what I think, and we can clear them. But we need to speak to them.'

Guy was nodding reluctantly. 'It'll need very sensitive handling.'

'Yes.' She could hardly imagine how she'd go about it.

'Who would we start with?' And there it was, the easy assumption, the knowledge that they worked in a perfect team, which meant she couldn't walk away from him.

She almost smiled at him. 'We should start with Dominic Martin. He's the ringleader of whatever's going on, I'm sure of it.'

'All right. Let's pay him a visit then. But after the caves, if we don't find anything, I think we should talk to Mr Kenny first. If local Republicans do have anything to do with this, he's the man who'll know.'

'He's agreed to meet us?'

'Let's just say he wasn't given much of a choice. It's ridiculous. If this was England he'd have been the first person we questioned.'

Paula looked at Bob, who was staring at his papers, wondering what he thought of all this – the terrorists he'd spent his life hunting now running the town. He caught her eye for a moment, then averted his gaze. She knew he didn't approve of pregnant women working – barely approved of women working at all, she suspected. But she could imagine how hard he was finding this, having been there that day, having walked down the street after the bomb went off and seen it running with blood. Paula was also thinking of Catherine Ni Chonnaill's children. Left behind – forever, if they didn't find her and fast. Like Paula, spending the rest of their lives asking questions into a silence that never answered back.

Kira

'Who are you?' he said. 'What are you doing here?' The funny thing was he didn't even seem annoyed. He wasn't surprised, she didn't think. He was so tired, like the most tired man she had ever seen.

'I'm Kira.' Her voice sounded funny in the big marble silence. Echoing. 'Kira Woods.'

'And who might Kira Woods be?'

'Rose Woods . . .' Her mouth filled up with spit and she swallowed it down. 'She died in the bomb. The Mayday one.'

'Your sister?'

She nodded. It was easiest.

He looked at her for a long time. His hair was going white and his eyes were wrinkling. 'And what brought you to my door, Kira?'

'I want . . .' She didn't know, she realised. She didn't know what she wanted. 'I want you to do something.'

He moved as if he was cross. 'There's nothing to be done. Your sister's dead, you said. There's nothing in the world can bring her back.'

'I know that! It just isn't right. She was – the best person. Now she's dead.'

'These things happen. My da died when I was round your age. Brit soldiers, they shot him down in the street. Minding his own business, he was, on his way to mind his wee shop. Those fellas stayed in the army, not a bother on them. But you didn't see me asking them to do nothing. What can you do when someone's dead? Nothing.'

Kira rolled up the sleeves of her school shirt. There was biro on the cuff. 'Rose's blood,' she said. 'It went on my face. In my mouth. And look.' She showed him the scars – on her arms, silvery pink now, like drops of dirt except she could never wash them off.

He looked. He did this, she told herself. He did this and

97

he killed Rose. Her heart was pounding so hard it made her shake. He rolled up the sleeves of his T-shirt. His arm was all tattooed, but at the top there was a big gouge out of the skin as if someone had bit him. 'Hand grenade,' he said. 'UVF. You'd be Protestant, Kira Woods, with a name like yours?'

Her heart beat even faster, but she wouldn't deny it, like St Peter in the garden. 'Yes.'

He just nodded. 'Have you a mammy, Kira?'

'Yes. She's – not too good now. Since Rose.'

'Then that's a shame, but you should go on home to her anyway. A nice girl like you shouldn't be breaking into people's houses.'

'I didn't break in! The door isn't even shut.'

'And the gate?'

She said nothing. He nodded again. 'Kira, go home and look after your mammy. Do your qualifications. Get off this bloody island. That's my advice. Go on now.'

She moved to the door. He held it open. She was rooting in her bag, her hands shaking. Her fingers closed on it, all clammy over Rose's face. She took the picture out and held it up to him. In the picture Rose was being a bridesmaid for their cousin Shelly, who'd been in bad form all day because everyone said Rose looked like a model and people said Shelly looked lovely but only to her face and you could tell they didn't really mean it. In it Rose had on a pink floaty dress and flowers in her hair, all blonde and pretty. She was smiling in a way that made you know she was laughing at the state of the dress and the long, boring ceremony where the minister had a lisp.

'Look at her,' said Kira, holding it up. 'I want you to at least look at her picture.'

The man almost pushed her. 'I mean it now, girl. Go on home. Don't make me phone someone.'

She thought he meant the police, but later she thought he probably didn't mean that.

Mr Collins was Kira's favourite teacher at school. He thought she was 'very bright', he'd once told Mammy, and he lent her books and didn't make her talk out loud in class or feel sorry for her. Or not too much. One day he had looked at her a bit funny and said: 'Kira, I think you're very brave. I just wanted to tell you.'

She'd have liked to say that was silly. It wasn't brave to have something bad happen to you – you didn't get any say in it. One book he gave her was about religions of the world, and how they thought about death. It was very interesting. There was one bit that said in India, if someone did you wrong – stole from you, say, or killed someone in your family – you went and sat outside their house for days and days until they gave you some kind of restitution. It was called *dharna*. In other countries, if someone killed you they could pay your family a thing called blood money. She asked Mr Collins what restitution meant and he perked up like a dog and started explaining it was when someone had taken something off you, or done something wrong to you, and they had to make amends for it. Restitution. She liked that word, rolling it over and over in her mouth, and the next day she read it again. And again.

Chapter Ten

'Is it safe?'

'It's empty. The TSG have searched it. You can go in.'

As Paula moved from the warm, windy beach, April sun sparkling on the waves, into the cool drip of the caves, she felt a chill descend and couldn't hide her shudder. Her feet slipped on seaweed and she heard the bladders pop under her feet. She'd given up any concession to fashion and was wearing walking boots and old tracksuit bottoms with the elastic all gone.

'How far back do they go?' She vaguely remembered learning about the sea caves in Geography at school.

'We're not sure.' She could feel Guy's hand almost brush her arm – as if he desperately wanted to take it, and in truth she wanted him to, but neither of them would move the extra inch. That seemed to sum up their relationship at the moment. 'Dr Finney says it's not all been explored and it may go back for miles. So don't wander off.'

After high tide the only way into the caves would be by boat, or risking a very cold swim. The entrance was a shallow plane of rock, treacherously slippy, and as they moved in it opened up into a gloomy natural hall. Paula felt her heart quicken as the daylight receded and the only light was from the wavy halogen lamps the team had affixed. Corry was there shouting at everyone, zipped up like Lara

Croft in black trousers and a jacket. 'Careful of the walls! If there's damage the council'll have my hide.' She rolled her eyes at Paula's approach. 'Is it too much to ask that you might just look at photographs, Dr Maguire?'

'I need to see it with my own eyes. Let me take a look?'

'If you must. Up here.'

Paula climbed another PSNI walkway into a slightly higher part of the cave. Below her it opened out into a sort of room. A room people had been living in. Clutching the stone walls, she peered down at Corry. 'What is it?'

'We don't know. Go up and take a look.'

Up there the floor was sandy and dry, and she felt safer walking. The space was about four metres high and twenty across, vanishing at the back into a darkness full of drips and echoes. Five chairs had been put in a semi-circle. Ordinary chairs with wooden legs and arms, like you might get in a school. From the arms of each sagged heavy ropes, nylon ones like you could buy in B&Q, looping all the way down the legs and on to the next chair, so they were tied together. The other furniture in the room was a table, of similar dull office stock, and three chairs behind that.

There was a bucket underneath the table which gave out a very bad smell, and on top of the table was a ruled exercise book, the shreds of a few torn-out pages clinging to it. Several officers were walking about in white suits, taking pictures and dusting the items of furniture.

'Don't touch anything,' said Corry, scrambling up behind Paula.

Paula ignored her; of course she wasn't going to touch anything. 'They were kept here? All five?'

'We think so. It'll be easy to check for DNA. The bucket is full of faeces and vomit, and look.' She pointed to the arms of the nearest chair, which was crusted with a dried rusting substance – blood. Now Paula looked, she could see the sandy floor beneath each chair was also covered in dark stains.

She turned back to Corry. 'Any prints?'

'Loads. The whole place is full of them. Local kids come down here sometimes to drink and get up to no good – explains the stink of booze and piss.'

'And the other three bombers?'

Corry shrugged. 'You can see for yourself. Five chairs. Two bodies. There's no sign of the others.'

'The exercise book – is it the same one?'

'We'll be able to reconstruct from indentations, we hope, but yes, it looks like the same one used for the notes. There's been several pages of dense writing on top of it.'

Paula turned and scanned the space, the expanse of dark rock overhead, full of moving shadows, and in the middle the dusty, nondescript chairs and table, their odd vines of rope and what she assumed was blood underneath. Her hands crept under her waterproof jacket to find the mound of the baby – warm, alive. In the dark, she could make out something stuck to the walls. 'What's that?'

'Take a look,' said Corry.

Paula stepped forward uncertainly, peering at the damp walls. It was pictures, fixed onto the walls with masking tape. The edges of the photos curling up. Faces and faces and faces. She counted – yes, sixteen. 'All of them.'

'Yes. Every victim of the bomb. A picture of each one.'

'What do you think happened here?' she asked Corry, after a moment taking it all in.

'I was hoping you'd tell me. That is your job after all.' Corry sighed. 'I just don't feel right bollocking you when you're the size of a house. Can you not just have it and come back?'

'I'm trying. I think – this is just a first impression.'

'Go on.'

'It reminds me of a courtroom. You know, the trial.' She pointed. 'A small person's been tied to that middle chair – see the ropes are looser. In court, during the trial, they sat with Ni Chonnaill in the middle.' She counted it off, squinting as she tried to remember the illustration in Maeve's book. 'From left – Flaherty, Brady, Ni Chonnaill, Lynch, Doyle.'

'A courtroom.' Corry was nodding. 'I can see that. Passing judgement. Giving them the proper trial the government failed to provide.'

'Yes. So this is our kill site, we think?'

'One of them, anyway. There's a large amount of blood in that corner there, consistent with Brady's head being removed here.'

'I'd agree.' A white-clad figure was tramping across the floor to them, putting down its hood to reveal sandy hair and a handsome face. 'Dr Maguire.'

'Dr Finney.' Their greetings were about as warm as the chill from the walls of the cave. She wasn't sure what he was doing here – surely finding the site should have been the limit of his involvement.

He went on. 'This is one of the few locations of the mineral we found on Brady and Doyle, so coupled with the odd set-up and obvious signs of restraint, this is the kill site.' He pointed to the mouth of the cave. 'There's a large number of impressions there. It's highly likely we can still find deposits on the shoes of the killer, or killers, and match it to those from the original crime scenes.'

'It must be more than one killer,' said Paula uneasily. There were three chairs behind the table. 'Surely one person couldn't have got them all here, set all this up.'

Finney nodded. 'I'd agree with that too.' *I wasn't asking you*, she thought tetchily.

There was movement at the opening to the cave. A young constable in uniform approached, stepping gingerly on the wet rocks, calling out to Corry. 'Ma'am, they've found something in the woods. It was caught in the trees. Also, there's some journalists at the cordon. Word must have got out.'

Paula tried not to show that she'd immediately thought of Aidan. He was world-class at working out the lie of the land in Ballyterrin.

'Send them off,' snapped Corry. 'No one can see this. We have to keep it quiet as long as we can.'

'Yes, ma'am,' said the constable nervously, licking his cracked lips.

'Show me what they found.' Corry made a gesture with her hand. A CSI in a blue suit and mask appeared, handing something to her in a clear bag. She peered at it in the dim light at the cave's entrance, then reached impatiently into the pocket of her jacket and flicked on a small torch. Paula saw what it was, and her heart dipped with a quick dart of nausea and fear. 'Hair,' said Corry, looking at it. 'Blonde hair.'

'Is it hers?' Paula swallowed, her mouth suddenly dry. 'Is it Ni Chonnaill's?'

'Looks like it. So she was held here, along with the others. Only question is,' said Corry, glancing around, 'who was sitting in judgement on them?'

* * *

'Paula! Look at you!'

'I know, I'm huge.'

'Not at all, you're glowing. Come here.' Saoirse's husband Dave was always so nice. He clasped Paula in a bear hug so tight a small gasp escaped her.

'That's good, I'll be in labour in no time with more of that.'

'Sorry, sorry. What can I get you? No drink, I suppose.'

'Sadly, no. I'll just take a juice or something. Is – eh, is Aidan coming?'

Dave always seemed oblivious of the issues between Paula and Aidan, though he couldn't possibly be. 'He'll be down later,' he said. 'Working late, it's deadline day.'

Of course. She used to know things like that, in the brief hiatus when they were friends, or something, again.

Saoirse came into the living room, wiping her hands on an apron. She looked flushed and happy. Paula noticed because on seeing her, her friend's face instantly fell. She tried to hide it. 'Paula! Glad you could come. Might be the last time for a while, eh?'

'It might indeed.' She sank into the squashy grey sofa Dave indicated. 'I can't imagine another two months of this. I'm seriously about to pop.'

Saoirse's expression didn't change much, but Paula was reminded of a long-ago conversation, before she knew she was pregnant, and Saoirse was discussing her fertility issues: '*What I can't stand is women complaining about their kids, or being pregnant. They don't know how bloody lucky they are.*'

'Anyway – how are you both?' she said.

'Well, I start stims next week. Then we wait for the egg harvesting.'

Paula couldn't help but twitch. 'Oh yes?'

'All being well we could be pregnant by May,' said Dave. Paula looked at Saoirse, knowing it wasn't like her to be this positive. Luckily the bell went. Paula braced herself – was it, was it – yes. She heard Aidan's voice. Her heart turned upside down.

'I'll go,' said Dave, setting down his bottle of Peroni.

Saoirse was watching, her eyebrows raised. 'I did say he'd be here.'

'No, I know. I wanted to see him. It's OK.'

Saoirse rose to kiss Aidan as he came in. He said to her, 'Well, missus. You're looking grand. When are you gonna ditch this fella here and run off with me?'

Saoirse laughed. 'He could break you in two, pet.'

'I know. Why do you think I'm pals with him?' He spotted Paula and the laugh was gone from his face. 'Hiya.'

'Hi.'

'You OK?'

'Yep. Just . . . getting by.' She waved her glass of juice feebly and resolved to go home after the main course.

When they were sitting down to the meal of Heston Blumenthal roast chicken, made by Dave, Saoirse brought up the case. 'So you're still looking for the Mayday lot? It's been all over the news. Two of them are dead now?'

Paula set down a chicken bone. 'Yeah. We're still looking for the rest.'

'I was working that day.' Saoirse was also not drinking, which made for a sober, quiet gathering. Aidan had three beers and stopped, as if making the point that his drinking was under control. When things were bad it was whisky he went for, or more specifically, cheap supermarket bourbon, chasing oblivion at the bottom of a bottle.

'In the hospital?' They'd fallen out of touch back then, Paula and Saoirse. She'd never known her friend was in the thick of the bomb, while she watched it on TV in the safety of her London flat.

'Yeah.'

'It must have been awful.'

Saoirse toyed with her food. 'We got word something had happened, and then they started coming in. I've never seen anything like it – we just weren't equipped. Hundreds and hundreds. People were driving up and dropping out of the back of cars, just sliding out, there was so much blood. It was on my shoes, all the way up my legs even. And I just knew there were people I could – but there wasn't time. There wasn't time to get to everyone. I saw this wee girl – she'd been brought in on a stretcher, but she wasn't – God, she wasn't even whole, they should have seen she was dead but I suppose in the confusion – I always remember her. Only a baby, really.'

They'd all fallen silent.

Saoirse gave a short, humourless laugh. 'Sorry. I forget not everyone spends their days up to the eyeballs in blood and guts.'

Dave cleared his throat. 'It was a terrible thing.'

Saoirse said, 'I've been thinking a lot since then about why things happen. I mean, why did those people die and others didn't? They were good people.'

'There's no reason to it,' said Aidan, fiddling with the label on his last beer. 'Things just happen.'

'I mean, look at me. I tried to do everything right. Got married, worked hard – I help people all day long. And I have no baby while other people my age are on their third.'

'It's not fair,' Aidan said again. 'But life isn't fair. All of us at this table know that. I was there that day too. I was stringing for one of the nationals back then and they sent me. Bonus to the first person to get a picture, they said. I got behind the cordons and I saw . . . I saw some of it. People laid out, like. They wrote numbers on their heads, some of them, to try to keep track. With a marker, like.' He tore the label off his bottle. 'Course, some of them didn't actually have heads.'

Dave caught Paula's eye over the table, and she saw his expression at the turn this conversation had taken. 'Well,' she said firmly. 'It was very sad. But I'm sure you both helped people a lot that day.'

'I don't know about that,' Saoirse said quietly. 'There were so many people I couldn't get to.'

'I wasn't even trying to help,' said Aidan. 'Just to get shots of them dying.'

'Well now,' said Dave vaguely. 'We all do the best we can, and we can't do more.'

Paula stared down at her empty plate as silence fell again. 'I should make a move,' Aidan said, as if reading her mind.

'Me too,' she said, with relief.

Saoirse snapped out of the reverie she'd fallen into. 'You'll be over the limit, Aidan, you should leave your car here.' He opened his mouth to protest. 'Paula will leave you back.'

She glared at Saoirse, who stared pointedly back, and realised she did need to talk to Aidan alone after all.

Neither spoke during the short drive to his flat in town, but she was aware of every breath he took, every shift of his legs and creak of his leather jacket. He filled the car with a scent of tobacco and mint and something else that she could have picked out in a crowd as being the smell of him. 'This is me.'

She pulled up, wondering what the flat was like inside. If he had his vinyl, his guitars, his books, cups of half-drunk coffee everywhere. How could someone mean so much to you when you'd never even been to their home?

He took his seat belt off, hesitated. 'It was good to see you tonight.'

'Was it?'

'I said so, didn't I?'

'Aidan. I'm sorry. You said I wasn't even sorry, back in January. Well I am. I didn't plan any of this.'

'I know. But it's happening, isn't it?'

'Yes. But maybe after . . .' He waited, and she realised she didn't know how to finish that sentence. She rubbed her eyes. 'This case is a real killer, you know.'

'Have you any leads?' He held up his hands. 'No no, just making chat, not digging for a story.'

'Gerard thinks it's the local Provos. Getting rid of the embarrassing country cousins so they can put on suits and go to Westminster. We keep hearing that Kenny and Flaherty used to be friends, but he denies it.'

Aidan rubbed his chin. 'Aye, Maeve put that in her book. The publishers didn't want her to, but she insisted.'

Paula found that, at the mention of the journalist's name, she was clenching her fists, imagining him once again in Maeve's bedroom, half-naked. 'What's happening with that?' She tried to keep her voice neutral.

'Ireland First were trying to sue her, last I heard. I guess not any more, now.'

'That must have been tough for her.'

'Not at all. She did it on purpose.'

'On purpose?'

'Aye. If there was a libel trial it would all be heard in court again, wouldn't it? It was one way to get something for the families, she thought.'

Which was a bloody selfless thing to do. 'Oh.'

'Anyway, do I sense you don't think Kenny actually did the kidnaps?'

'There's a lot that doesn't fit. And . . .' She couldn't tell him about the notes in the mouths, the photos on the cave wall. 'There are signs that link it to Mayday.'

'Revenge?'

'I think so. Some kind of . . . restitution, maybe. I went to the relatives' group and there was definitely something up with them.'

Aidan rubbed his chin, and it almost killed her how much she missed this, asking him for advice. 'You'd want to be careful. The families went through so much they're near canonised round here. You wouldn't want to accuse them of being mixed up in it.'

'I'm not. I just . . .'

'You just have doubts.'

She smiled weakly. 'When do I not?'

'OK.' A silence welled between them, full of unsaid things. She gripped the steering wheel. She didn't even know what she'd say if she could speak. After a moment, Aidan opened the door. 'I'll see you around then. Is Saoirse OK, do you think?'

'You'd know as well as me.'

He thought a bit. 'She'll have to be, I suppose. There's no remedy for it.'

'No, but I don't think it helps seeing me like this.'

'It's not your fault.'

'Thought you said it was.' She smiled at him weakly to show she was joking and he half-smiled, half-grimaced back.

'Well, let's not go there, as they say. Night, Maguire.'

His old name for her. It was something, anyway.

Extract from *The Blood Price: The Mayday Bombing and its Aftermath*, by Maeve Cooley (Tairise Press, 2011)
Interview with DCI Helen Corry, Ballyterrin PSNI

I was thirty-seven when the bomb went off. I don't know why I feel that's relevant, except that my life was cut in two by it. I can't describe it any other way.

I'd been doing OK before that. My husband wasn't failing me. Not yet. We had money. The recession hadn't hit. My kids were seven and nine. Still sweet, energetic wee things who didn't hate me for working all hours. I had an au pair. I'd been made a DS already, despite missing a year for each child.

I was leading the team on 1st May 2006. Crossanure is a small town outside Ballyterrin. I'm sure you know that, but perhaps your readers won't. More of a village really. There was an Orange parade later on that day, so we were monitoring it from the control room, with officers on the street. I remember it was sunny, and I was in a bad mood at missing the bank holiday. My husband was annoyed and kept phoning to ask things like where were the barbecue tongs and did we have any suncream.

Sorry. You don't need to know that.

The call came in at 11.03 a.m. I remember because I could see the red lights on the clock blinking on the control desk. It was a constable out on the beat, Raymond Sheeran. Eh . . . He came on the line then said nothing.

Constable? *I said. I was pressing down the button on my phone, irritated.*

I think something happened.

You'll need to clarify, Constable. We're a bit busy for 'something'.

There's a car, *he says. This lad was in his early twenties, no more. No bombs for a good twenty years, remember.* There's a car in the middle of the High Street. It's kind of parked weirdly.

Weirdly how?

Eh . . . sort of abandoned like. In the road. *I could hear the hesitation in his voice. He didn't want to say it. We didn't want to think it.* Have any threats been called in?

No, of course— *but then I saw a flicker of something in the dispatcher's eye.* Hold on, Constable. *I glared at the dispatcher. She was sitting right beside me.* What? Tell me.

That's right. Susan Markey was her name. Yes she was . . . let go after the incident. But I'm afraid that's a confidential matter.

It came in earlier, ma'am, *she said hesitantly.* I wasn't sure it was anything but . . . it's in those papers.

You put it on my desk? Jesus, Susan. You always put any threats right into my hands.

It sounded liked kids. *She was trembling.* There wasn't a code word. They didn't say a car, anyway, they didn't say anything really. They weren't making any sense and half of it was in Irish. They said something about the High Street, about continuing the struggle . . .

Give me it. *I read the whole transcript of the call, gulping it with my eyes. She was right – it was mostly gibberish, but all the same my blood was running cold. I shouted,* Order an evacuation. Everyone out of that end of the street. *I diverted all my officers and ordered Constable Sheeran to lead the operation.*

Ten minutes later the bomb went off. Not in that car but in a bin outside the Methodist church. On the route of the Orange Order parade, but several hours early, and exactly where I'd been sending all those people. The car was just an unfortunate coincidence. Constable Sheeran died. I heard him screaming through his phone. He'd been assisting an elderly woman, who hadn't a scratch on her. It happens that way in a bomb. It moves through like the hand of God, knocking down the young, leaving the old, taking the well, missing the sick. There is no order. Afterwards it was concluded that grouping everyone at that end of the street most likely led to the very high loss of life. We'd walked them to their deaths.

My supervisor shot himself a month after the inquest. That's right. In the mouth, with his service rifle. Me, I got divorced. But I don't blame myself. The only people to blame are those who made the bomb, who placed the bomb, who phoned in a vague and misleading warning. No one else should have been punished for it.

   I think we'll have to leave it there, if you'll excuse me. Thank you.

Chapter Eleven

'Nice place.'

'As long you're not a Protestant, a Catholic they don't agree with, or English.'

'We're screwed then.'

The pub was exactly the kind of one Paula would normally have crossed the street to avoid. It was called the Starry Plough, and was infamous as the scene of the shooting of Derek 'Funster' McCourt, one of the town's most notorious drug dealers. He'd been gunned down there in 1997 in a small misunderstanding over a missing consignment of ecstasy tablets. Paula was sitting opposite it in Guy's BMW, and her mind was currently failing to take in the idea of Guy Brooking, all English vowels and handmade suits, going inside the pub's wired-up windows and faded paintwork. 'You really think this will be all right?'

'They've agreed to see us.'

'But – don't they know you were with the Met?'

'They agreed to speak to me, and they know I'm neither Catholic nor Protestant. I'm told a priest will mediate.'

'You know what they used to do to the English over here?'

'Paula. It was all years ago. I understand perfectly if you feel apprehensive – I did say you should perhaps stay—'

'*I'll* be fine! I'm Catholic.'

'A Catholic working for the police.'

'Hmph. OK. Let's both go then.'

'I suppose you won't listen if I suggest it's not the best place for you.'

'Nope.'

'And if I mention the baby, you'll get cross?'

'I'm very well aware of the baby, sir. It's hard not to be when it's sitting on my bladder.'

He almost smiled. 'All right. Let's take it nice and easy.'

She walked across the road with her belly held awk-wardly in front of her, like a ship's prow. He hovered at her elbow, not quite taking it. The place smelled like all Irish pubs, as if every stick of wood in the place had been marinated in Guinness for forty years. It was so dark it took a while for Paula's eyes to adjust. There was one man behind the bar wiping glasses, a radio softly giving out Irish. There were two other men at a corner table, one in a dog collar. The other, she knew, was Jarlath Kenny, IRA commander of the area in the nineties – allegedly, of course – and now mayor of the town, possibly soon to be MP. He was dressed in a polo shirt and tracksuit bottoms rather than the Armani suits he was known for, and drinking water from a pint glass.

Guy approached, all suit and smile. 'Father McCracken, is it? I'm DI Brooking. Pleased to put a face to a name.'

The priest hesitated, then shook his hand. 'This is Mr Kenny.'

Paula held her breath for a second, but the ex-Army officer and ex-terrorist shook hands without incident.

Guy turned to her. 'This is my colleague, Dr Maguire. She's helping us build up a profile of the missing people.'

As was so often the case, the men's eyes floated over her,

taking in her relative youth, her bump, her messy civilian clothes, and passed on. Jarlath Kenny gave her a hard stare for a moment. '*Dia duit.*' The Irish greeting was basically saying – are you Catholic?

'*Dia is Mhuire duit,*' she mumbled, hating herself. Yes, Catholic Maguire. After that they ignored her. Really, Paula didn't mind being so dismissed. It allowed her to see things without being noticed. She and Guy sat on stools, which were too small for her bulk, so she held herself awkwardly. The walls were lined with Republican memorabilia.

'Well, Inspector,' said Jarlath Kenny, with control. 'What can I help you with?'

'It's about this Mayday case, Mr Kenny. You may have seen that the five Mayday suspects – or sorry, the five who were rumoured to be involved – have gone missing, and two have now turned up dead.'

'I have.' He took a sip of water. The glass was smeary with fingerprints.

'Mr Kenny, I understand you're a very knowledgeable man. What we'd like to know is, have you heard anything that might suggest there's a reprisal element to these disappearances?'

'Do you mean do I know who took them?'

'We can't even be sure if they were taken. But several of their families have commented that the Five were wary of local Army Command.' She had to hand it to him, Guy used their faux-military language with what could pass for respect. 'Given Ireland First's attempts to derail the peace process, it would hardly be surprising if there was some . . . intervention.'

Kenny took another sip, choosing his words as carefully

as Guy. 'The Mayday bombing was condemned by everyone who's committed to peace,' he said. 'Flaherty and his cohorts were neither supported nor aided by any groups I know of. It may be they were advised to leave the area, for the sake of local sensibilities . . . the memorial being unveiled soon and the fifth anniversary coming up. But whether any pressure was applied to hasten their departure – no. I know nothing about that.'

'Hmm.' Guy thought. 'Am I right to say that if it happened, you'd be the man in the know?'

He watched Guy closely. 'I would hope so, Inspector.'

The priest spoke, in a dry, nervous voice. 'Mr Kenny is very well connected in the area, where he's worked tirelessly to bring the Republican movement to the way of peace. And although the bomb was condemned as an atrocity, of course, any retribution against the perpetrators was strongly discouraged.'

Meaning: they'd been asked to ease back on the kneecapping or punishment beatings.

'Is there anything we could try?' asked Guy. 'We're in something of a bind here. I believe you knew Mr Flaherty when you were both younger?'

Kenny shifted. 'I wonder where you'd have heard a thing like that, Inspector.'

'You would have moved in the same . . . circles?'

'I may have met him once or twice, but not to my knowledge.' Everyone was choosing their words so delicately it was making Paula hold her breath. Under her smock and cardigan, she stroked the firm rising bump of her pregnancy. This was flesh and certainty, a fresh start, untainted by the past, of the fear she would be born into. Paula just hoped the baby wouldn't sense where she was.

'So you don't know anything about it,' Guy was saying.

'I've told you all I know, Inspector. We have no contact with rogue elements intent on destabilising the peace process.'

'And your own Westminster bid? Any truth in that?'

'I'm in talks with the party about my selection, yes. I've been open about that.'

'But you don't know Mr Flaherty, and you have no idea where he might be?'

'As I've said, no. Several times.'

'So why is it then a journalist recently alleged that you and Mr Flaherty were very close friends?'

'How would I know what you've heard, Inspector? I don't care to repeat myself again.'

Something had shifted – Paula realised the barman had switched off his radio, and was listening intently.

Kira

The next time she went to the house, Kira didn't climb over the gate. He'd been right about breaking in – it wouldn't be good to get arrested herself. She got off the bus as before and then just sat on the wall, dangling her legs. March was warm and dry that year, lucky for her. Eventually he came home. It was seven o'clock and his headlights picked her out in the gloom. He must have seen her sitting there hunched, her school bag beside her and regulation school coat on. The gates opened automatically and he went into the light and safeness of his house. After a few minutes Kira got off the wall and started trudging back to the main road. Mammy didn't ask where she'd been. She never asked any more. Probably she didn't know what time it was.

The next day, she did it again. And the next. Then it was the weekend, so she couldn't get there, as there weren't any buses. On the Monday she went again. Same walk up, same chilly wait in the darkening road, same car getting home and ignoring her. On the Tuesday things changed. He drove his car in as usual, but then he came back. He walked over the lawn towards her. He was wearing a black wool coat. 'What is it you want, girl? Why are you here, bothering me?'

'*Dharna*,' she said, and her voice sounded funny, because she'd sat there all the other days without saying a word.

'Eh?'

'I'm sitting so you can see me. Then you have to make me restitution.'

He looked at her for a long time. She realised she was shivering, had been for ages, just hadn't noticed it.

'You better come in,' said the man. 'You're freezing, so you are.'

This time the house seemed brighter, more lived in. 'Stay there.'

Kira waited in the kitchen. There was a plastic bag on the side with a Pot Noodle in it – beef kind. Her stomach groaned – she knew there'd be no dinner for her later, Mammy nearly always forgot to make it these days. Sometimes she made herself a Pot Noodle too, that she bought from the corner shop. She looked all round the place, drinking in the details of where he lived.

The man came back. He'd put on a jumper and taken off his jacket. He leaned on the counter. She realised she was very hungry, and very tired. 'You've been sitting at my door all week,' he said. 'What is it you want me to do? I know your sister died. But what can I do about it?'

'Restitution,' Kira whispered. It was the only word she could say.

'It doesn't work like that.'

'Why not?'

Silence. On the fridge she saw a letter pinned up. She recognised the logo of Ballyterrin General Hospital. It was where she'd had all her surgery after it happened, five in a row trying to fix her arms and face after the fire had burned her. It was where they'd taken Rose, where she'd died. She saw the words swim into view, words she could read but didn't understand: *metatastes . . . stage four.*

She looked back at him. Understood it all, suddenly, in a strange way. As if Rose were breathing the truth into her ear. 'You're sick.' She saw the grey tinge to his skin, the dark circles round his eyes.

He kept on looking at her. 'I'll be punished soon enough, lass. It's all going to be over for me. You know what that letter means?'

'Sort of.' She did, somehow, in her bones.

'Well then. Maybe you'd go along now. I'm not long for this world.'

Kira didn't budge. 'Are you afraid? Do you think maybe you'll die and God will judge you? Do you worry you'll see them, all the people you hurt? The little babies? Rose?'

His knuckles whitened as he pressed down on the worktop. 'Why have you come here, child? It's over. There's nothing more to be done.'

Kira said, 'There's always something. You're wrong. You can always do something.'

Chapter Twelve

Dominic Martin's house told a sad story. It was the kind of large bungalow people bought round Ballyterrin when they started a family, but the windows upstairs were uncurtained, the place unkempt. A bachelor sports car stood in the drive, low-slung with a canvas top. In the back garden there was a swingset, the grass grown up around it.

Guy saw her look. 'How old was his daughter?'

'Two, or a few days off it.'

'And the wife—'

'She left, apparently. I heard she has a baby with someone else now.'

Guy pushed his shoulders straight. 'It's very sad – it's tragic. God knows I can identify. But we have to do our jobs.'

'I know.' She tried to cover her bump, again feeling how much pain she must be causing to people who'd lost their own children.

'What did you think of what Kenny said?' he asked.

'Slippery customer. He'd say anything to cover his own back. He must have known Flaherty, surely. He didn't like you asking about it.'

'Until we have proof, though, we have to play nice with him. Let's go in.'

Dominic answered the door in a tracksuit and T-shirt,

unshaven and bathed in sweat. His T-shirt clung to him. He just looked at them.

'I'm sorry to call so early,' Guy began.

'I'm just back from a run,' he interrupted. 'Can you wait till I get a wee shower?'

'Of course.'

'In there.' He lightly slapped the door of the living room and jogged up the stairs, making the roof shake. Paula was glad to sit down – even walking a few steps seemed too much effort now. The room was the same mismatch: a stained family sofa, but free weights on the floor and a jar of body-building protein on the table. On the mantelpiece was a corkboard tacked over with pictures of a small girl. She'd lost her front teeth in one, and smiled at the photographer with pink gums from someone's arms. Paula recognised Amber's mother from the files. She'd stayed at home that day, wanting a bit of peace, while Dominic took Amber into Crossanure to watch the parade. She'd never seen her daughter again.

Soon Dominic was back, in a different T-shirt and jeans. He smelled of some fresh lemon shower gel and his brown hair was dark with water. 'Would you take coffee or something?'

'No thank you.' Paula indicated her bump. 'Not supposed to.'

He nodded. His eyes seemed to trace the contours of her, but unlike most people, he didn't make the obvious comment about her not having long to go. 'What can I help you with?' His tone was the same as at the meeting – polite and totally blank, while his eyes said something else that Paula didn't want to decipher.

'It's about the Mayday case,' said Guy. 'I'm afraid we

will need to interview some of the families.'

'Is there any evidence pointing to a specific person?'

Paula said, 'It's the MO, you see. Certain . . . signs have been left that seem to clearly link the deaths to the bombing.'

'We'd go to John Lenehan,' added Guy. 'But apparently he's stepped down as Chair.'

'Well, John isn't as young as he used to be.'

'Was that the only reason?' In response to her question, he just stared back. He had green eyes, very clear and piercing. He was, she realised, a very attractive man.

'I'm happy to give a statement,' he said formally. 'I run my own business, as you probably know.'

'Green energy, isn't it?'

'Solar panels, wind turbines, consultancy. So I don't have an alibi as such for the day they all went, if that's what you're after. I'm nearly always out on the road. Now I don't have childcare to do.'

The room fell silent. Somewhere in the house, Paula thought she could hear music.

'OK,' said Dominic, as if they'd asked him something else. 'I'll speak to the group and explain you might be calling round. Some of us just can't stand to talk about it at all, you should know. Not all the families even joined the group.'

'Mr Martin,' said Guy. 'We've come to you first partly because you're Acting Chair, but also because we're aware of the comments you made to reporters after the trial concluded. You recall what you said then?'

'I believe I said they should be strung up,' he said calmly. 'Something like that, anyway.'

'As you know, Mickey Doyle literally was.' Guy was hesitant. 'He was hanged.'

'In a better justice system he'd have been hanged by the state. Culled like a dog. But they failed us.'

'Are you saying someone else finished the job then? Did what the state couldn't?'

A pause. 'I'm not saying anything. Just that it wasn't undeserved.' Another silence. Dominic broke it again. 'I'll assist you in whatever way I can, Inspector. Give me a day to talk to the group and I'll send you a list of all the families. Some are very sensitive about certain issues – the compensation, for one. They didn't understand why one life was valued more than others. It created . . . divisions. Let me just ring Ann and ask her to dig out the records for you. She has all the minutes, going back five years.'

He left the room, and Paula and Guy looked at each other. She opened her eyes wide to express helplessness. There was nothing they could say to this man. His loss made him invincible. There were light footsteps on the stairs, different from Dominic's heavier tread, and a figure appeared in the doorway, wearing just a man's T-shirt over long, lovely legs. Lily Sloane.

'Hello,' she said, rubbing her face. 'I heard voices. Dr Maguire, isn't it?' She advanced on Guy. 'I'm Lily. I was in the bomb too.' She lifted her sweep of long hair to show her face. She wasn't wearing a patch today, and so the hole in her face could clearly be seen, a red puckered mess.

'I'm very sorry,' said Guy, not flinching away from the sight. 'We'd like to speak to you about the incident too, if we can. We're speaking to everyone in the group.'

'We don't call it an incident.' Her fingers, never still, raked through her caramel hair. 'We call it the day, usually. Cos like we all know what day we mean.'

'Of course. Lily, do you get on well with everyone in the group?'

'S'pose. What do you mean?'

'Is there any disagreement?'

Lily sighed. 'Oh, you know what they're like. It's so boring sometimes. That trial. Years they were on about it. Blah blah blah judicial review.'

'There was some issue about compensation, I gather?'

'Mmm-hmm. I got money.' She pointed to her eye again. 'You see, they do it on like how much earning you might have lost. And I was going to be a model and actress, so Dad got them to give me more. I had a good lawyer.' She said this like a child, mouthing words. 'But some people didn't get anything.'

'Did it cause problems?' asked Guy.

'Dominic sorted it.' Her face went gooey. 'He always knows the right thing to do. He explained it was the law and it wasn't meant to pay us back, nothing could, it was only meant to make life a bit easier. And he got us to agree that any money in the Victims Fund could be for families who didn't get much. Fairer like. Most people were OK with that.'

'You and Dominic—' Paula began.

Lily looked wary. 'Yeah?'

'You're together?'

She shrugged. 'Whatever that means.'

'He's your boyfriend, is he?'

'I don't call him that. He's special. We're . . . close.'

'Are you in a sexual relationship?' asked Guy awkwardly.

'Ew. Why does that even matter?'

Paula glared at him. 'I'm sorry, Lily. I'm sure you think it's none of our business. It's just that, legally, if you were, we might not be able to use what you tell us about him.'

'Why would I tell you things?' She genuinely seemed puzzled. Paula turned to Guy again.

He said, 'Ms Sloane, as you know, we're investigating the disappearances of the so-called Mayday Five.'

'Yes.' Her voice was cold.

'Dominic previously said they should be strung up. After the court case failed. And we've not been able to get an alibi for him.'

'You want me to be his alibi?'

'No, that's not . . . we want to know if you think he meant what he said.'

'Duh,' she exhaled. 'They blew up his little girl. He loved her. *Loved* her. His stupid wife blamed him cos he was with her. It ruined his life. It's only cos he's so amazing he keeps going at all.'

Paula sensed a certain relish in Lily for the role of victim, supporting her broken-down man, nurturing the darkness in his soul. Was she exactly the same? She was very aware that Guy's own loss of a child was what kept her stuck there, even though he was married, and Aidan's brooding grief over his father's death was likewise what made her chronically unable to get past him.

'So do you know his whereabouts that day?' Guy was saying.

'No. I can't remember, like.'

'Ms Sloane, you really need to tell us the truth.'

'I'm not NOT telling you the truth.'

They'd annoyed her. She turned her head away, revealing once again the raw, ruined side of her lovely face. She was very young, Paula reminded herself. No one could imagine what it had been like for Lily, so beautiful, to lose all that at just eighteen. 'We didn't mean to upset you,' she said gently.

'Well, you have.' Lily's voice was angry, with a telltale shake that made Paula want to give her a hug. There was silence, and Lily's snuffling tears. Paula looked at Guy. He was glum. They'd made Lily Sloane cry, on top of everything she'd been through in her young life. She gave a trembling sigh and wiped her face with her hands, her T-shirt lifting slightly to reveal the edge of lacy pants. 'Tell Dom I went upstairs.' Her voice was thick.

Paula watched her slim long legs depart. 'That's a development,' muttered Guy. 'He must be twice her age.'

'Not quite.' Paula was thinking about Lily, and realising this: there was one way to get to someone who'd lost everything, and that was to give them something else that could be taken away.

'Let's go,' she said. 'I'm sure he'll get back to us.' The house had taken on an uncomfortable air, naked and embarrassing. As they went out to the car she noticed Guy staring round the side of the house. 'What do you see?'

'The Lotus he drives . . . not very practical for a job putting up solar panels, is it? He'd need something else too, wouldn't he?'

'I suppose. Why?'

Guy nodded to what he was looking at, and she saw – parked around the side of the house, not hidden in any way, was a dusty white van.

Extract from *The Blood Price: The Mayday*
Bombing and its Aftermath, by Maeve Cooley
(Tairise Press, 2011)

Martin Flaherty was set on the path to murder almost
as soon as he was born. Raised in a staunch
Republican family in South Armagh, his father was
killed by an Army patrol in 1971, right at the begin-
ning of the Troubles. The soldiers responsible were
not only not prosecuted, they remained on active
duty. Young Martin quickly had to take on respon-
sibility for the family. He joined the Armagh Brigade
of the IRA in 1972, alongside many current
Republican luminaries, including Jarlath Kenny,
now mayor of Ballyterrin – although Kenny has
officially denied any knowledge of Flaherty or of IRA
membership. Flaherty called Kenny a 'turncoat
bastard' after the 1998 Good Friday Agreement.

In 1999 Flaherty set up a splinter Republican
group, calling itself Ireland First. They were on anti-
terror radar from the beginning, but dismissed as a
small operation, no more than ten people. However,
sometime between 1999 and 2006, the group
managed to get hold of large quantities of plastic
explosive. During March and April 2006, unbe-
knownst to intelligence, they were building a huge
bomb at Flaherty's home near the border. On 1st
May 2006 they drove this bomb into Ballyterrin and
concealed it in a bin that was on the route of a
planned Orange parade later that day. They put it
there and walked away, planning to detonate the
bomb by mobile phone at the moment the parade

passed by. The aim was to kill members of the Orange Order, disrupting the peace process and taking down a Unionist politician who was leading the parade that day. However, the bomb went off ten minutes after they walked away – a vague warning had been phoned in, without any recognised code words. A car had also been parked haphazardly further down the High Street, and police efforts were focused on trying to move this. No one realised the danger was in the bin, near to where people were being evacuated. The bomb exploded at 11.17 a.m. on 1st May 2006. Ten people were killed instantly, hundreds injured. Six more died later in hospital.

The PSNI immediately suspected dissident Republicans, and the leaders of Ireland First were arrested within days of the blast. Despite Flaherty owning the mobile phone that was linked to the detonator, and there being clear traces of the agricultural products used to make the bomb in Lynch's car, and the presence of Doyle's van in the town that day, and DNA linking Ni Chonnaill to detonators found in other devices, Brady's own semi-confession, and many other obvious clues, a series of procedural blunders and plausible deniability meant that when the Five were eventually brought to trial in 2010, it collapsed. It is now not possible to bring another criminal case against them. They have, in the words of Dominic Martin, walked down the street covered in blood and gotten away with it.

Chapter Thirteen

'What did Corry say?'

They were back in the car. Guy hung up the phone and shook his head. 'She says it's too circumstantial – lots of people have white vans round here, and we never got a reg from either crime scene.'

'Can we search it?'

'Think how it would look. She's not keen. I think we need to carry on with these interviews and see what else comes up.'

She sighed. 'All right. What about the caves, did we find anything more? There was lots of DNA found, right, not just from the Five?'

She didn't want to say what she was thinking, but he knew. 'Corry won't authorise DNA testing right now either. Not until we have a clear suspect in mind with other evidence to back it up. Same with handwriting samples.'

'So what can we do?' She was shaking her head in frustration.

'Just keep looking. The other three must be somewhere, after all. The search team's been out in the mountains – they must have been moved somewhere else after the caves. Let's see if we can get any information today.'

'All right.' She turned a page in the file on her lap. Paula kept track of the interviews via a series of photos. On each page a dead person, and their immediate family or significant others. A map of loss, the dead and the roots still holding them in place. A map of devastation. Now they were at the Woods' house – this was the family of the odd, helpful teenager, Kira. The father had died years before.

Like every house they came to, it seemed to be marked by an invisible sign of grief. The lawn wasn't cut, and the paintwork on the door was peeling. It took a long time for it to be answered, by a shuffling middle-aged woman in a tracksuit. She had chipped red polish on her nails and they could smell alcohol on her breath. It was eleven in the morning. 'Mrs Woods?'

'Yes. Who is it?' She was blinking as if she'd been asleep, squinting in the daylight.

Guy spoke. 'We're from the MPRU – the missing persons unit. I wonder if we might ask you a few questions?'

She moved to let them in. All the curtains were drawn, and the house had a foetid air, as if the bins hadn't been taken out. 'What's it about?' In the living room she sat down on the sofa, yawning.

'About the Mayday case, Mrs Woods. May we sit?'

'Oh. All right.'

There was a noise of light feet and Kira appeared in shorts and a T-shirt with a puppy on it. Her hair wasn't brushed and she had a wary expression.

'Hello, Kira,' said Paula, sinking into a saggy armchair. 'Are you off for your Easter holidays?'

She stood poised, as if ready to bolt. 'Er – yeah. Why're you here?'

'We're talking to all the families separately. This is my

colleague, DI Brooking.' She was slightly younger than Guy's daughter, Katie.

He smiled warmly. 'Pleased to meet you, Kira.'

Kira crossed the room to the sofa where her mother was. She was doing something furtive with her feet, which puzzled Paula, until she realised the girl was trying to hide her mother's bottle of vodka from them. She averted her eyes. 'Kira was very helpful to me at the group meeting, Mrs Woods.'

'I don't go there,' she said listlessly. 'It brings it all back, you know. It's upsetting.'

'Is that Rose?' Guy indicated the large studio portrait over the TV. A pretty girl with a smile that suggested she'd tell you all her secrets and keep yours. She'd had that naturally fair hair which is so rare.

'My little girl,' said Mrs Woods, with a small sob.

'I'm your little girl too,' said Kira, too loudly. Her mother ignored her.

Guy pressed on. 'Mrs Woods, we're just doing routine enquiries to see if anyone in the group has knowledge about the disappearances of the so-called Mayday Five. I know this must be very hard, so if you could just tell us what you know, we can be on our way.'

'What would I know? I don't know anything. First I heard was on the news. They showed the pictures again – the petrol station burning. I can't bear it. Every time I just think, that's where my Rose died. That's her dying, that smoke rising up.'

Kira rolled her eyes. 'Mammy doesn't know anything. She doesn't go out. Do you want to see where we were on the day they went missing, is that right?'

'Yes.' Paula was impressed; the girl was quick.

'An alibi.'

'That's right,' said Guy. 'We need to just collect them, then we can leave people in peace.'

'Mammy was here,' Kira shrugged. 'She won't have an alibi but she sometimes rings people during the day so you can check that.'

'What people?' Guy was writing.

'Psychics and that. The government, to complain about stuff. The doctor.' Kira's mother was staring into space.

'Thank you. Can I ask about your father, Kira?'

She started. 'What?'

'Your dad, Rose's dad, he passed away?'

'Yeah, he's dead. I was like three. I can't remember. I was at school that day they went. If you need an alibi for me too.'

Guy was almost smiling. 'Thank you. That's very helpful. Dr Maguire was right.'

Kira didn't look pleased at the compliment. 'Will you go to everyone? Lily too?'

'Yes, we'll see Ms Sloane.'

'Even the McShanes? The Sheerans? Not everyone comes to the group, you know. Sometimes people get too upset.'

Mrs Woods seemed to rouse herself. 'Are you trying to get the people who hurt my Rose?'

'We're trying to find them, yes,' said Guy gently. It was technically true, after all, if not in the way she meant. She was crying again.

'My poor Rose! She never hurt a fly. She made mistakes, but sure don't we all do that! Please can you find them? Please.' Her body had gone slack, knees gaping, mouth open and wet with tears.

Kira shifted over and patted her mother's shaking shoulders.' It's OK, Mammy. They're doing the best they can.' She looked up, and her eyes were the oldest and wisest Paula had ever seen. 'You should go.'

They rose, Paula with some difficulty. 'I'm sorry.'

As they went to the car, she tried to identify the hard nugget that had lodged itself in her gullet. Shame. She felt ashamed. These people had the heart torn right out of them, ripped and gutted while still beating, and here she was smearing more blood on their door.

'You OK?' Guy was putting his seat belt on. 'I must say, this is one of the most difficult cases I've ever worked on. I can't keep track of moral north.'

He was being kind, giving her a chance to say she was also struggling, her system flooded with hormones, balanced herself on the edge of life and death. Instead she heard herself say, 'I think we're going to have to look at Martin's van. It's too much of a link to ignore. Can we try to persuade Corry?'

'OK. I'll try.'

Requisitioning the van of a grieving father. That would go down well. They drove back to the station, sunlight glinting off car windows and the dark river at the heart of town almost navy today. Paula found she couldn't shake the image of Rose Woods, and the smile that said all she'd expected out of life was to love and be loved back.

Kira

The road to Rose's place was along a street of houses. Ugly little ones, with bins in the small front gardens and those stones stuck into the walls. Rose had told her this was called *pebbledash*. It wasn't where she'd have liked to go to chat to Rose. Ideally they'd have gone to the café Rose liked after school and had milkshakes out of the blender, or driven out to the beach and paddled their feet in the cold waves, or even just sat at home in the warm kitchen. But this would have to do as Rose could only be in this place from now on.

Rose loved flowers. Daffodils best. They look like hope, she'd say, cramming them into every glass in the house until Mum shouted to get those mucky flowers out of there. It was a kind of magic, how you'd put in tight buds and even if you stood there watching them you'd never catch the moment they opened, but they did. Magic. One of the houses on the street had some in its garden, all yellow and happy and with a smell that reached down the street. No one was looking. She put down her school bag and hopped over the low stony wall. The stalks of the flowers were thick and juicy, and she grunted as she snapped them, getting soil and sap on her hands. Was it like the flower's blood? Did it hurt them?

Don't be silly, pet.

OK, Rose.

She took them in one hand and walked to the end of the street, where she swung open the rusty gates of the graveyard. Rose was at the end of the row, next to an old lady who had high black walls round her, handy for sitting on, and those sort of green stones over her. Rose just had grass. At first, it got very long – Mammy never came, and Kira didn't know how to cut grass. Then an old man saw her with some scissors, crying over it, and he did it from then on.

'Hiya,' she said out loud. 'I got these. Do you like them?'

There was nowhere to put the flowers. She needed a jar or something. She made a little hole and stuck them in the ground, then took out the two Capri-Suns she'd brought from home. One she popped and one she left for Rose. She always brought one. It was always gone when she came back.

She drained the juice; it was a long walk from home. 'They found one of the men,' she said, hesitantly. But maybe Rose knew already. 'It was on the news and Mammy sat in the bathroom crying all night. I couldn't get in to pee. They said he hanged himself but it wasn't that. You know.' She'd told Rose before. 'So what do I do?'

No answer, only the breeze through the graveyard, and far away, a family raking over the stones on someone's grave. Someone they loved. That's what you did when you loved a dead person. You put up shiny black stones and jewel pebbles and threw away any rotting flowers. Rose's stone was grey, and unlike some it didn't have a picture of her. It just said *Rose Sarah Woods. 1983–2006. Beloved daughter and sister.*

She crouched down and pressed her head to the stone, until it hurt a bit. It was very cold. 'I miss you, Rose,' she whispered.

There was no answer. Sometimes, if she listened very hard, she could almost hear Rose in her head.

'Will I do it? One of them's gone. The rest will go too. And they want me to . . . will I? For you?'

No answer. In a tree at the corner of the graveyard, a bird began to sing, high and piercing.

Chapter Fourteen

Extreme grief had a look about it. It was like being very tired or very hungover. Your movements slowed down, your eyes heavy and blinking, as if the world had gone into slow motion. It was a look common to the families of the Mayday dead.

On arriving at Ann Ward's house, Paula was surprised to find the place full of people. Then she remembered – it was Easter Monday, which had almost entirely passed her by. The door was opened by a middle-aged man holding a toddler on his shoulders, chocolate smeared round its face. 'You must be the police. I'm Sean Ward, come in.'

Paula was trying to place everyone as they were led through to a kitchen/living room full of adults and children, who all stared at her bump. Sean was the other son – the one who wasn't the father of the baby who'd been killed. Both the child and his grandfather had been called Patrick Ward.

Ann was there, a child of about three sleeping half in her arms, half on the sofa. The child was sucking her thumb while the house around her rang with shouts and screams and the low-level hubbub of chatter. Open Easter eggs were much in evidence. A crowd of young women were in the kitchen doing things with cling film-wrapped dishes.

'Would you take something to eat?' said one to Paula and Guy as they were led in.

'No thank you.'

'Clear over there,' said Ann to a boy of ten or so who was engrossed in an iPad game. 'Turn that ould thing off and let the lady sit down. Go out and play.'

He went, grumbling, and Paula sat down on the sofa beside the other, sleeping child, who stirred, fidgeting. Guy perched on a stool. Ann wore the same boot-faced expression as always. 'So you've questions to ask, do you.'

'Yes, but is this a bad time? We don't want to interrupt the party.'

Ann seemed surprised. 'There's no party. This is Patrick's family, and it's only right they're here to see what you have to say.'

'All right.' Guy looked about him – people were carrying on their conversations, and a seemingly endless conveyor belt of children ran in and out from the garden where a trampoline was drawing shrieks and howls. 'Should I just—'

'Mary!' Ann shouted. A pale, very young-looking woman detached from the gaggle in the kitchen and came over, leaning on the arm of the sofa. 'This is my daughter-in-law,' Ann said. 'She's the mother of wee Patrick.'

'I'm very sorry,' said Guy. The woman didn't react.

'Wee Patrick's daddy is in the garden,' Ann went on. 'He won't talk to you. Patrick Senior and myself, we'd two boys and three girls. All these –' she indicated the house and the hordes of people in it – 'these are our family. Every single person here lost a father or grandfather that day, and a nephew or a cousin or a child.' Mary Ward dropped her head but said nothing.

'We understand that,' Guy began.

She fixed him with a glare. 'Do you? Then I have to wonder why you'd come round here trying to help the people who took our hearts and smashed them.'

'We have to ask all the families,' said Guy. 'We just want to rule people out, then we can leave you alone.'

'And it's alibis you're wanting, is it?' She made the word sound ridiculous. 'Well, I do mornings at Victim Support in town and I'd have been in the office that day. You can check with them. Same with all my family. We've all jobs, all hard-working people. I'm sure you can follow that up easily enough.'

'Thanks,' said Guy, making notes. Paula was sure it was just to give him something to do. 'And I understand you've been secretary of the group since it began?'

'I used to be a school secretary,' she said, 'so I know what's what. I do the minutes and make sure we follow the law, and keep track of the bank accounts and compensation and all that. Some people weren't too good at filling in the forms, you see.'

The child on Ann's lap stirred again, sitting up and rubbing her eyes. 'Who's these people, Granny?'

'Never you mind. Go to your mammy.' She passed the little girl over to Mary with surprising strength, and Mary walked the child off to the garden, still without a word.

Ann saw Paula watching. 'That one was born two years after we lost wee Pat. He was their first, God love them. He'd have been five now.' It was too easy to imagine another child running around. 'It was me made Mary leave him that day,' Ann went on. 'We were in town getting a wedding dress for my daughter Eileen, that's her there in the pink top, and Mary came with us for the outing. She was bridesmaid. I said leave the wean with his granddad, he'll only cry in the shop. So big Pat took him for a stroll in the pram. Up to the High Street.' She paused. 'They were right beside the bin when it exploded. We never even found a trace of wee Pat. Only one wee bootee – it was blue, it had cars on it. So we knew it was his.' She pushed her glasses up her nose. 'Well. I'll do what I can to help, I'm sure. What is it you'll be wanting?'

Guy couldn't seem to speak for a moment. 'Minutes of all the meetings, please. Anything you have. Activities of the compensation scheme, and ideally alibis we can check for all your family.'

Ann gave him a steely gaze. 'Do you have family, Inspector?'

'Yes.'

She nodded. Her eyes passed over Paula's bump without comment. Paula drew her hands tightly around it, protective. 'Well,' said Ann. 'I hope you'll remember what some people lost that day. Not all the families are doing that well. Remember that.'

She got up, and so did they, taking their cue to go. Another child ran in, this one a girl with ginger hair. 'Granny, Granny, Bobby fell off the swing!'

'And is he all right?'

'Aye, he's laughing.'

'Well, that's OK then.' She began walking, hands on the child's back, batting her outside. She reached into a desk by the door and took out a pile of exercise books – A4, red covers, lined inside. She handed them to Guy, who made a show of putting them in his briefcase. 'I haven't had a chance to type them all up, but I've neat handwriting so you should be grand. Is that all you're needing for now?'

Paula glanced at them very quickly – not the same hand as the notes in the mouths; Ann's writing was spiky and neat. But the notebooks looked identical to the one found in the caves. She felt she had to say something more. 'How long were you married, Ann? You and Patrick Senior?'

Ann stood in the doorway, screened in sunlight, her family moving around her like the parts of a clock. 'We're still married,' she said. 'They couldn't take that away from us, at least. Anyway, I'd best be getting on now. Goodbye, Inspector, Miss Maguire.'

And she went out into the sun, shouting was Bobby OK and didn't she say that trampoline would only end in tears?

At the end of the week they'd heard countless statements of unendurable loss, recounted in matter-of-fact tones by the flesh and blood relatives of the dead. Mothers who'd seen their babies blown up. Parents bereft of children. Husbands and wives living on without the other half of themselves. Every time Paula closed her eyes she saw them: the stoic widowers of Rita and Colette; the extended family of Penny Garston, the oldest victim, who'd been killed while out buying a Christening card for her newest grandchild; Arthur Jones, grandfather of ten-year-old Daniel, who couldn't stop the tears trickling down his face at the mention of the dead child. It was overwhelming. Anna Kennedy, shakily defiant, explaining what a good man her husband Tom had been, all three of them sitting there thinking about how he'd been found burned alive, still holding the hand of Lisa McShane in the car park behind the petrol station.

At the home of Siofra Connolly's family, her mother and father and grown-up brother and sister described how every year they were visited from Tours by the family of Siofra's French penfriend Monique, who'd died alongside her on the day of the bombing. Monique had been spending a fortnight with them and as it was her last day, Siofra's brother Liam had taken the girls into town to see some of the traditional Irish culture in the form of the Orange parade. The girls had died side by side in the newsagent's, blown right through the window and into the street. Monique had still been holding the can of Fanta she was about to pay for.

'They should have been strung up,' her brother Liam muttered, pounding one fist into another. A builder, he was the young man in the paint-stained clothes Paula had seen at the meeting. He'd echoed Dominic Martin's words; was that a coincidence?

'Were you hurt yourself, Liam?'

He stared at her. He was no more than twenty-five, she was sure, but his blue-grey eyes looked ancient. There was a small fleck of red paint in his stubble. 'I'd gone down the street to buy some cans. Told the girls I'd meet them after – 'cept I never did. Our Siofra died and I was just one street away. Only had cuts and bruises myself, and she was . . . well, they said she went quick. I just hope that's true.'

'I'll always blame myself,' said Siofra's mother, in the matter-of-fact tone all the families seemed to use for their loss. 'If that wee French girl hadn't come here she'd be safe and well in France. She'd be twenty-one now, same as Siofra. Maybe they'd have stayed friends. Anyway, her family doesn't blame us, they said. Lovely people, they are. Come over every year to lay a wreath at the site.'

Before they left, Siofra's sister Aine displayed her two-year-old son and said how much she wished Siofra had met him. 'She'd have been a great auntie, she loved kids.'

The message was clear: we're good people, we're the victims here. You need to leave us alone with our grief.

Paula and Guy went to his car, both stiff and weary. He scrolled through his BlackBerry as they walked, made a noise of annoyance. 'Christ.'

'What is it?'

'Dominic Martin – he's reported his van stolen. Just when I'd persuaded Corry to search it.'

'For God's sake. He couldn't have known, could he?'

'I don't see how. And we've found out nothing useful this week. A total waste of time.' Guy dropped the phone into his pocket, frustrated. 'I'll drop you home,' he said, exhaustion sounding in his voice. 'Take the rest of the day off, will you? Get some rest. It's been a tough week.'

She buckled herself in. 'It has that. What are you going to do?'

'Oh, another meeting.'

'With the Chief Constable?'

'In Belfast, yes.'

She watched him closely. He didn't look at her, staring out at the road. She opened her mouth to ask him what was going on, then shut it again. Maybe sometimes it was better not to know.

Paula was in her thirties, and weeks off giving birth, but standing in Mrs Flynn's porch made her feel seven again, sent round by her mother with an apple tart or flapjack or something to take to 'the ould busybody', as Margaret had called her. She'd finally given in to guilt and called on her neighbour, at the end of the long, fruitless week talking to the relatives. Her mind turned over and over with a screensaver of faces: victims, the helpless dead, the grieving left behind. They were no closer to finding Catherine Ni Chonnaill or the others, and all she'd done was cause more grief to people who'd already suffered the worst. At least she could visit her neighbour, do a small act of kindness. She knew it wouldn't make her feel any better, though.

It took a long time for the door to be answered. She could see Mrs Flynn through the glass of the door, fumbling with the chain. 'Ye-es?' The large eyes blinked behind glasses.

'How are you, Mrs Flynn? Dad asked me to drop in on you. Eh . . . it's Paula.' She was never sure if people would remember her or not, she'd been so young when she left.

'Wee Paula?'

'That's me.' She was a good foot taller than the shrunken old woman, but no matter.

The chain had come off now, so she interpreted this as an invitation to go in and followed Mrs Flynn into the front room. The house was laid out just like theirs, except this one was stifling from the gas fire and smelled like a chemist. She insisted on making a cup of tea, which took ages, leaving Paula in the living room staring round at the family pictures, the Mass cards, the cheap glass figurines. Was this how her father would have been, had she not come back to Ballyterrin? Sitting alone, with only pictures of a child across the water, the ticking clock, waiting for someone who was never coming home?

'Here you go.'

'Thanks, lovely.' The milk was on the turn, bits floating in the tea. Paula made a mental note to buy her some groceries and drop them off. 'How's Mark and Kelly?'

'Oh, they're well.' She reeled off a list of their

achievements – Mark was an accountant; Kelly had married a lawyer and they had three children, all doing well at some London private school. Paula remembered now she had never much liked Mrs Flynn, a fussy woman who'd never stopped blowing even then about her Mark and her Kelly. She remembered one time, kissing Aidan in his car outside on the street, only to see Mrs Flynn's pale face peering out of the upstairs window. The memory gave her a lurch.

'So you're back then?'

Paula tuned in to the wavery narrative. 'Oh yes, I've been back a while now.'

'And you're married? Your daddy never said.' She nodded to the bump.

'Eh – yes.' It was easier than explaining.

'English fella, is he?'

'That's right.' Luckily Mrs Flynn still preferred to talk rather than listen, and didn't ask what the imaginary husband was called. Joe, she'd decided, or Jim. A straightforward kind of guy. Probably wore jumpers.

'And they never found your mammy after all that time.'

Paula froze. People did this sometimes, casually mentioning it, as if determined to show it didn't faze them. Otherwise they didn't mention it at all. She wasn't sure which she disliked more. 'Um – no, they never did.'

'The peelers never came back to see me either. I thought they would.'

She frowned. 'You mean – you didn't give a statement?'

'Of course I did, pet, sure I saw the whole thing, the men knocking on the door. They're just wee boys playing soldiers, I wasn't afraid.'

The tick of the clock seemed very loud, the spaces between it just the same as always, even though time had

CLAIRE MCGOWAN

somehow slowed. 'Mrs Flynn – I'm sorry, but we were always told none of the neighbours saw anything. Your statement wasn't in the file.'

'Well I don't know, I told them what I saw. Two men at the door, looking for her, that same day she went.'

'Do you know – did she let them in?'

'I couldn't say, pet. I went to ring the police, and when I come back they'd gone, so I thought she was at work like normal.'

'You don't remember what time this was? I know it's years ago.'

'Oh aye, it was lunchtime. I'd the news on. I turned it down to see could I hear anything.'

'You're saying you rang the police to tell them men were at my mother's door? On the day she disappeared?'

'That's right. I thought they might be burglars.'

'And no one came to see you, follow it up?'

'Of course they did, I gave a full statement. I'm not afraid to help the police, even the ould RUC back then. They weren't all bad.'

'You don't remember who interviewed you?' asked Paula, even though she was sure, deep in her bones, that she already knew the answer to this.

'That Orangeman.' Mrs Flynn lowered her voice. 'You could see he'd never been in a Catholic home in his life, kept staring at my Sacred Heart pictures. Something Hamilton, that was him.'

Bob Hamilton. Bob Hamilton had interviewed their neighbour about her mother's disappearance. So why wasn't the transcript in the copy of the file in Paula's desk next door? 'Can you tell me, Mrs Flynn, do you know anything else?'

'That was all. And you never found her, after all this time?'

'Well, no.' Duh.

'I always thought she'd come back. I thought she'd gone off to get away from them men that was looking her.'

'Why do you think that?'

'Hmm?'

'Why did you think that, Mrs Flynn?'

Her eyes had wandered to the road again, where a van was passing with a rattle and suck of air. 'Isn't it awful, the speed they go flying down there? The council should put in those bumps. You'll want to watch that when your wee one comes. Is it a boy or a girl?'

'Girl.' She didn't often tell people this, superstitious, but Mrs Flynn maybe hadn't long for the world. 'But, listen, Mrs Flynn. Did you see her leave? Mrs Flynn?—'

'A girl, that's lovely. Will you bring her in to see me, pet, when she's here?'

As if the baby were on a long journey to them, perhaps by ocean liner. 'I will, of course.' She tried one last time. 'Mrs Flynn, is there anything more you could tell me, please – about the men, or my mother? Did you ever see . . . ?' But Paula realised she was afraid to ask the question forming in her mind. 'Never mind. Thank you for the tea.' As she took her leave, she wondered why her mother had disliked Mrs Flynn so. *Interfering, nosy old busybody,* she'd once called her . . . why? What exactly had she been nosy about?

A familiar burst of anger went up in her, like a spurt of lava. Why had her mother left them with so many questions, never to be answered? Couldn't she have sensed somehow she'd not be back, and left a list of answers, everything from where she kept the key to the meter box to why she'd been off work the day before she vanished?

Paula went into her own house, standing again in the kitchen where her mother had last been. Every surface was scrubbed and clean, but the smell was ingrained – damp, and hope left to slowly fester. She had to find out where that transcript had gone.

A memory rose up like a ghost, making her chest compress – the psychic she'd encountered before Christmas, Magdalena Croft. *Your mother is alive. She's alive, and across water.*

She remembered what her father had told her, when they'd last talked about it months ago – they'd arrested him because there was only Paula's word her mother had been there in the morning. PJ had an alibi for the day of the disappearance, had been out on a case, but there was only a thirteen-year-old girl, stunned with grief, to say her mother had been there to make her breakfast. Yet this report from Mrs Flynn, it could have been proof her mother was in during the day – proof that someone had come and taken her.

Paula hadn't known any of this. She'd closed the door that morning and never seen her mother again. That was how it often was. You didn't get the chance to say goodbye. And you'd think, knowing what Paula did, this would make her hang on fast to the people she loved, whisper words that could be the last, every time, but it didn't. Sitting in the cold, dark kitchen, she found herself thinking of Aidan. It always returned, like a bad case of the flu, when she was at her lowest ebb.

Paula couldn't settle that night. She couldn't eat the dispiriting healthy mess of vegetables and noodles she'd cooked for herself, couldn't concentrate on TV or Maeve's book or even the case files. The house was so large by herself. In London sometimes she'd go out if she got like this, pull on trainers and run through the silent residential streets of Docklands, past sleeping tower blocks and lights drowned in the river. Here someone was bound to notice if she went out at three a.m. and phone up her dad, wondering had she lost the run of herself altogether? She couldn't go out anyway with her massive bump. She sighed, tapping her fingers in a light rhythm on her belly. She'd not be alone much longer.

She was in the woods.

It could have been the same ones where they'd found Mickey Doyle's body, his skin turned purple. These woods also smelled like death, but old and wormy.

She was looking for something. She was tripping over roots, her breathing hard in her ears, her heart punching in the drum of her ears. She was very, very afraid. Somewhere in the woods a baby was crying, heart-rending. She had to get to that sound but it seemed to be all around her as she stumbled. The cries went on and on and on, dragging at her, pulling her flesh from her bones. Then she was on her knees in the dirt, smelling soil and something rotting, and she was digging her fingers into it and snapping her nails. Overhead a bone-white moon came out from the clouds, and then she saw it reflected in the ground – the gleam of a skull, and around it a shawl of red hair.

Paula was awake now, and it wasn't real, it was a dream. Her mother was not in the ground, alone in the woods. No one knew where she was. Her baby wasn't lost and crying, she was still inside, she was safe, under the tight drum of skin.

She sat up, panting. It was early, the sky outside cut with icy blue. Now she could hear the phone ringing downstairs – she'd stopped sleeping with her mobile since the baby – and waited drowsily for her dad to pick it up, then remembered he was gone. She hauled herself down the stairs one at a time, gripping the banister. 'Hello?' The hall was cold and the microwave clock read 4.48 a.m. Work? No, PJ. 'Dad, are you OK?'

'Aye. Were you sleeping?'

'Not really.'

'Look at your wee phone there, pet. Something's happened. Work didn't ring you?'

'No. How do you know?'

'Sure I can't sleep in this place, and Pat has that News Twenty-Four yoke.'

She could picture him downstairs in the dark, his bad leg on a cushion, cup of tea beside him. It swam through her head – *Dad, did you know Mrs Flynn made a police statement? Did you know Bob Hamilton had it all this time?* She couldn't ask him. 'OK. I need to hang up, though.'

She opened her browser and waited for the slow 3G connection to kick in. Northern Ireland news was reporting a body found in the hills outside of town. One of the Five? No pictures yet. She dialled the number for the MPRU, expecting the answerphone, but instead it was picked up by Gerard. 'What's going on?' she said, startled.

'Maguire? You need to get off the line, I'm waiting on the boss ringing through.' Behind him Paula could hear phones and voices, as if it was four p.m. not four a.m.

'Why did no one ring me?'

'Boss said not to.'

'He *what*?'

'Look, I'm not getting involved, OK? I have to go.'

'Wait, Gerard – is it one of them? It's not a woman, is it, it's not Catherine?'

He'd hung up. Fuming, Paula slammed down the stupid smartphone. They'd found one of the Five and no one had even told her. Well, she would see about that. She couldn't face getting out of her cosy maternity pyjamas in the frigid room, so she pulled on a hoody and Ugg boots. They'd pass for tracksuit bottoms at this hour. She wound her long red hair into a plait, noting in the mirror her dark eye-bags and pallid skin. Wasn't it meant to be after the birth that you couldn't sleep?

She thought of how Saoirse would scold her for getting out of bed in the middle of the night. Saoirse with her birth plans and morbidity studies. Paula would have just liked to crawl away on her own in the dark and deliver, like a cat under the stairs. She grabbed her car keys and headed out.

Extract from *The Blood Price: The Mayday Bombing and its Aftermath*, by Maeve Cooley (Tairise Press, 2011)

Dominic Martin was the most difficult of the families and survivors to interview. Some, like the Presbyterian family of Constable Sheeran, would not speak to me at all – they have retreated into their faith to deal with what happened. This is not what I mean by difficulty. When I rang Martin first, he asked who I was. He said was I at the trial. Yes, I said, I'd been covering it for my paper, the Daily Tribune. *One of the vultures, he said, repeating what he'd said that day, when he'd made the comment about feasting on their pain. I've had this reaction before, of course, all journalists have, now that door-stepping and cheque-book journalism are so rife.* Mr Martin, *I said.* I want to write this book to give a voice to the victims.

My daughter didn't have much of a voice, *he said.* She wasn't even two yet.

Three days short, *I said; he went silent and I wondered if I'd gone too far.*

What's the point of a book, *he said.* More slow-motion tears, sad music? What does any of it do? Nobody needs to remember Amber except her mother and I. Well, I think of her every minute of every day, and her mother does too, I imagine, though she hasn't spoken to me in some time.

I'm going to name the bombers, *I said.* All five.

You'll be sued, *he said. Impatient.*

I hope so. That way we could maybe get a libel trial going.

We, *I'd said, by mistake, and I wondered if he'd be angry, me jumping in on their grief.*

Come round, *he said, instead.* I'd give you the address but you most likely already know it. *He put the phone down.*

I have decided not to transcribe my conversation with Dominic Martin. It's rare for a journalist to be reminded that we are nothing in this – we're just a conduit to twist words, and arrange them convincingly, and ultimately to sell papers.

When I spoke to Martin I realised he'd been twisting me. And it was no more than I deserved. It's unusual for a group of victims to have such an articulate and active spokesperson. The media have tended to gravitate to John Lenehan, the group's Chair, a grave and measured man, suffering etched into his face. He's a good victim – praying and accepting and urging peace. Dominic Martin is not accepting anything. He is angry, furious, protesting at the obscenity of a world where his child could die beneath him on a sunny May day. I was struck by one thing he said during our talk – I can't even call it an interview. What's the point of all these words? It can't be understood in words. When is someone going to do something?

I couldn't answer this and I still can't. We failed Amber Martin and the other silent dead – we failed to do anything, to save them or punish their killers. This book, such as it is, is my own paltry attempt at doing something.

Chapter Fifteen

Outside dawn was creasing the sky, breaking pale blue in the east. She could see her breath. There was little traffic and the drive through town was peaceful until she reached the unit, where she found the whole team, dressed hastily and running about between phones and computers. Even Avril was wearing jeans, an unheard-of event. 'Paula,' she said, covering her phone headset with one hand. 'I thought you weren't coming in?'

'Well, no one told me,' she said shrewishly. 'Was that DI Brooking's decision?'

'Maybe he thought you'd need to rest.'

Paula humphed. 'Where is he?'

'In his office, but . . .'

She stomped off, but found her feet were taking her past Guy's closed office door and into the small cubby beside it – Bob Hamilton's office. Little more than a cupboard. She opened the flimsy door without knocking. He was at his computer, staring at the screen. He'd never mastered the new databases they used to log missing persons.

'Miss Maguire?'

It was too much suddenly. The number of times she'd asked him to call her Paula, or even her proper title of Doctor, but he insisted . . . the way he averted his eyes from her belly, as if she revolted him . . . 'I need to talk to you.'

'I thought you weren't coming—'

'Not about this.' She shut the door behind her, so it reverberated through the chipboard walls. 'About my mother.'

'Miss—'

'Yes, yes, I know you don't want to talk about it, I know the case was closed – but tell me this, Bob. Tell me what you did with Mrs Flynn's statement.'

He looked uncomprehending and that just made her angrier. To forget something like that, a key piece of the puzzle that had consumed her all her life . . .

'Our next-door neighbour. Nosy lady. She said you interviewed her, back in ninety-three. She said she saw men at our house on the day Mum went – why's it not in the file, Bob?'

He looked slowly down at his hands, the fingers red and chubby, on the keys of the old computer. She waited. He said nothing. The silence grew and thickened. Paula opened her mouth and was horrified to feel tears swell in her throat. 'I . . . please tell me. You must know something. Why isn't it there? What did she tell you?'

Bob looked away from her as he spoke, his voice dry as papers in a filing cabinet. 'I don't know what you're talking about, miss. And I don't think you're supposed to have a copy of the file, are you? It was a long time ago.'

He wasn't going to tell her. But she could sense it, feel it between them that he knew something all the same. She could almost grasp the contours. Her voice shook. 'I don't know why you're doing this. Did you have something against my dad? You arrested him – but maybe Mrs Flynn could have proved it wasn't him? I mean, you only arrested him because we couldn't prove Mum was there in the morning, wasn't that right?'

He said nothing. Paula took a deep breath. 'Right. You aren't going to help me. But I'm not giving up. So . . . just thinking about what I said. Try to do something right, for once in your life.'

She stormed out, bumping into Fiacra in the corridor, who was also visibly gloomy. 'Are you not meant to be off?' he said.

'Did everyone get this memo except me?' she exploded. 'I'm still working, aren't I, I'm not an invalid!'

'Jesus, OK, don't shoot the messenger. We thought with the wean—'

'It's none of your business, Garda Quinn!'

He pushed past her, muttering that she'd made it his business.

Paula blinked. 'What was that?'

He turned. 'How is it not our business, OK? You ride the boss and prance about here with your belly out and we're supposed to ignore it? My sister lost her baby. She nearly died and she was only going shopping, and there's you running about with not a thought for your own safety!'

Paula's mouth fell open at this unexpected savaging from the sweetest member of the team, and to her horror she felt the tears gather in her nose. 'I . . . I just couldn't sit at home with all this going on.'

'Well you have to. You're having a baby. Even I know you can't carry on the way you do.'

'Here, wait there, son.' Gerard, a mere year older than Fiacra, had come out of the main office to shove his oar in. 'Leave her be.'

'You can stay out of it. Seems myself and ould Bob there are the only ones who stick to the rules round here. There's a reason you're not supposed to sleep with your colleagues, you know.'

'Hey!' Gerard shouted. There was a crash behind them in the main office; Avril had knocked over her keyboard. 'What are you trying to say, son?'

'Don't call me son, you fecking eejit, you're no older than I am. You know rightly what I'm trying to say.'

Avril was moving, a blur of anxiety. 'Gerard, stop, I—' She was in the corridor, wringing her hands. 'Look, just leave it, OK?'

'Quite the team, aren't we?' Fiacra looked between them nastily. 'Very cosy indeed.'

Bob came to his door, bewildered, refusing to look at Paula still. 'What's the racket out here?'

'Nothing,' said Fiacra sulkily. 'I'm just sick of people not doing their jobs and I'm sick of pretending no one knows why she's knocked up. We're not bleeding stupid, you know.' He turned back into the main office, giving the wall a frustrated kick as he went. Paula turned away; she couldn't bear it if Bob and Gerard saw her crying. At that point Guy opened his door. 'What's going—' He saw her face. 'Back to work, everyone. Would you supervise, DS Hamilton? Thanks.'

He indicated she should go into his office. As soon as the door shut she put her hands to her face, the tears flowing thick and fast. 'Did you hear that?'

'Enough. Are you OK?'

'No – I don't know. It's just. I can't bear it, you know. You don't even tell me you've found a body! You're at all these meetings you won't tell me about . . . I mean, what's next, will I be fired?' Then she'd be alone in the house, with just the baby and the ghosts for company.

'Sit down.' He motioned her into the chair, and she sat, wiping away tears and gulping as fast as they came.

'Look. Paula. I'm in a difficult situation here. I can't tell you what the meetings are about, not yet, but it's nothing to do with you. And I know you want to keep working, and we do need you, but look at you. It's difficult to have you at crime scenes – there's the insurance for one thing. And for another, people aren't stupid, they know you and I are – close. And now you're pregnant.'

'I haven't told anyone! No one knows it might be – you know.'

'They can guess.' He ran a hand over his eyes, and she saw the wedding ring he still wore, and her stomach heaved. It was too much. At least while there'd been work she could shut out the fact that she'd felt things for him, and then his wife had come back, but without work—

'I found something out,' she said, still blinking back tears, the grey squares of carpet dissolving into a blur. 'My mother. Sergeant Hamilton was the investigating officer on her case – you know that.'

'Well yes, but—'

'There's a statement missing from the file. Our neighbour, she saw some men come to the door the day my mother went missing. You'd think, wouldn't you, that something like that would be in the file?'

'How do you know?'

'She told me. And yes, she's not as young as she was, but she'd hardly make up something like that after seventeen years. Sergeant Hamilton took her statement. And it's not there now.'

'Are you suggesting he suppressed evidence?'

'No.' She thought about it. 'Yes. I don't know. I think he must have. I want you to look into it for me.'

'Paula. Are you saying you want to make a formal complaint? As a relative, not as a member of staff?'

Before this, everything had been done under the table, allowing Paula glances at files, whispers in corridors. But fuck it, they were freezing her out, and she didn't have much time left. Panic seemed to grip her. 'I am a relative, aren't I? We always talk about keeping the families informed. Well, that's me. And I believe the officer in charge deliberately hid information.'

'Why would he do that?' Guy was keeping his voice measured.

'I've no idea. Had it in for my dad, maybe. There's some bad blood between them, I never knew what. Maybe he lost the statement, then covered it up. But I want to know where it is and what happened to it.'

'Paula . . . are you sure about this? It was a long time ago, and Sergeant Hamilton is a valued member of the team . . .'

'Would you say that to one of the families, ask if they could be bothered digging it all up, finding out where their loved one disappeared to?'

'All right. I'll look into your complaint.' He made a note. 'I'm afraid in light of that, I will have to ask you not to work on your mother's case any more. And certainly not to visit any witnesses.'

She stared very hard at the carpet. Time was running out . . . the baby would be there soon . . .

'Paula. I'm sorry. But you know it has to be this way. You're . . . things aren't the same now. They never will be again, when the baby comes.'

She nodded dully, tears pattering onto her stupid hoody. 'So what can I do?'

'I think you need to scale back. Work from home a bit, or at least in the office only. Nothing dangerous or stressful. And Corry . . . she's concerned that your own experiences, with your mother and the attack last year – well, she thinks it's impacting on you more than you realise.'

'You said Corry. Is it Corry thinks it, or is it you?'

He paused. 'I agree with her.'

'You're so spineless sometimes.' The words were out before she could stop them.

He flinched. 'All right, if you insist, I feel you're not coping well at all. You almost died before Christmas, you almost lost your child then, but you're still refusing to scale back your duties. Now, your work has been invaluable in the past, and we need you, but we can't shoulder the responsibility of you at dangerous crime scenes. And the stress of this case . . .'

She didn't say that the most stressful thing was his presence. 'Look. I have to keep working.'

'But Paula – you won't be able to. At least for a while. You must see that. You can't imagine what it's like with a baby – no sleep, no time at all to yourself. You'll be exhausted. Naturally the force is very supportive of working mothers, but—'

'Oh, for fuck's sake, Guy. Don't talk at me like an HR manual. Like you're not even involved.'

'You won't let me be involved!' he snapped. 'I can't come to appointments, I can't ask how you are, and I can't even ask if I'm the father or not – and yes, I know you don't know, before you say it, and I know it was an accident, but try to think how other people feel for a change. Am I supposed to care for this child, look after it like a father, or am I supposed to step away?' He paused. 'I can't fail another child, but you're giving me no option.'

In the silence that followed this outburst, Paula tried not to look at the photo on Guy's desk. Two children. His troubled daughter, now sixteen, and his dead son, who'd never be older than ten. 'I'm sorry.' She was trembling, her voice thick with tears. 'I know it's hard and I wish things were different, really I do.' Fleetingly she thought of Aidan. 'But if I can't do this – if I can't find people – then what can I do?'

Guy sighed. 'You can look after yourself and get ready for the baby coming. Rest. Eat ice cream. Just take it easy.'

She frowned. 'I don't like ice cream. It hurts my teeth.'

'Well, whatever you like then. Someone should be looking after you. If you'd let me I'd—'

She stood up, with some difficulty. 'You'd be better off looking after your wife and daughter.' It was a low blow and he recoiled. 'Tell me one thing,' she said. 'Who is it? The body?'

He couldn't look at her. 'Lynch, we think. He was – his car was set alight, you know.'

'He burned to death?' One hanged, one decapitated, now one burned.

'Yes. It was – really, I don't want you there. It will be very unpleasant.'

What was wrong with her, that she'd rather go in the middle of the night to a lonely spot where a man lay charred and smoking, than be asleep, cradling her unborn child in warmth and safety? 'Please. I need to see it. Even from a distance.'

He spoke stiffly. 'If you feel up to it, I won't stop you. But at least wait till morning – the site's still on fire, for a start.'

'OK. I'll be there.'

'Should I have a word with Fiacra?'

'No. He only said what was true. I just didn't realise everyone knew.' It was an awful thought, the details of their drunken night circulating as a dirty joke, that fragile bubble of intimacy they'd made, light against the dark.

'You of all people should know that in this town, nothing's a secret for long.'

'I know. I just . . . hoped.' She wiped her sleeve over her face.

'Please . . . this is all for your own good. Will you stay off your mother's case?'

'Do I have a choice?'

'Not if you want to keep working.'

She nodded. 'Then I don't have a choice.'

It was horrible walking out, turning her back to the curious looks and ringing phones and buzz of a case to solve, and getting back in her car, but she did. Because deep down, she knew that everyone was right, and she was wrong.

Kira

The garage was quite a good one. It had spaces for six cars and there was pop music playing. It smelled of petrol, a smell Kira liked. Rose had sometimes smelled like that when she'd been out, on the back of a motorbike with one of her boyfriends.

A man was looking at her. He had on overalls and his face was oily. 'Help you, love?'

She knew she was a weird sight, in her school uniform. 'I'm looking Jamesie.'

'James-eee!' The man went back in, and he made some comment about starting young and the other men laughed. Kira tried not to understand. When Jamesie came out he was wiping his hands and not smiling. 'Kira.'

She stood there in her uniform. Now she was there she didn't know what she was going to say. 'Let's go in the tearoom,' he said. What this meant was a really small hut like a mobile classroom at school. Jamesie sat behind a desk that was cluttered with papers and magazines about cars. A calendar on the wall was still at February and had a girl on it in a bikini, licking her lips. 'Are you all right?' he asked her after a while.

Kira just looked at him. 'It's the memorial. In May. Five years.'

'I know.'

'Will you go?'

'I—' he did an awkward thing with his shoulders. 'If I can. Sometimes I can't – think about her.'

'Do you miss her?' He just shook his head, like it was annoying.

Kira was pleased. She hated being asked that too. It was like asking someone would they miss their arm or their leg or something. 'You know the group,' she said, and saw his face change.

'I can't be involved in that. I just can't.'

'Now the trial didn't work, we're thinking of doing something.'

'What can be done?'

She didn't answer. This was the tricky part, explaining. Without it sounding too awful. 'They're evil. They shouldn't be allowed to get away with it. We – some of us anyway, we think it's time they were punished for it.'

'Well, we just have to hope God punishes them.'

Kira sighed to herself. That was the problem. How could you rely on God to sort things, when he'd allowed Rose to be killed, and the bad people not to be in prison? She could see Jamesie wouldn't help. He was one of the ones who'd given into it, let it fill them up and sink them, like when you drown. Not like the ones still fighting, and struggling, and shouting. Like Dominic. Like Ann. Like her.

She stood up. It was a good thing having a reputation as being 'a wee bit turned' – you didn't have to bother with all that *how are you grand thanks is the family well drop us a wee line sometime*, like grown-ups did. 'Never mind.'

'Kira,' he said. 'Sometimes would you – would you come for a bite with me or something?'

She was astonished. 'Why?'

'I'd like to just talk about her. Like she was. Not all this court case and that.'

She nodded. 'What's your number?'

He told her and she put it in her phone. She put it under 'Jackie' just in case Mammy snooped. She remembered when she'd first met Jamesie, Rose taking her to the hotel that time – *Don't tell Mammy you saw him now. It's our secret.*

Who is he? She'd never met or heard of Jamesie until that day, but she could tell he hadn't just met Rose.

He's an old friend. From way back. Mammy never did like him. You know how she is – so, not a word.

Jamesie was OK-looking, a bit chunky, his chin raw with shaving and reeking of Lynx. He was really nervous for some reason. Rose had started a weird chat about school and after about twenty minutes they'd gone. Kira didn't even get a chance to drink her Coke.

They'd had a lot of secrets, her and Rose. This was just one of them. When someone died and you had a secret with them, you still couldn't tell anyone, and you couldn't talk to them about it any more either. It was like having a secret with yourself. It was the loneliest feeling Kira knew.

'I'll text you,' said Jamesie, now.

'Don't use your name,' said Kira. 'People read stuff.' She realised she knew more than him, more than most adults, about what was really happening. And somehow that was a very lonely feeling too.

Chapter Sixteen

How incongruous it was when you found a body on a beautiful morning. April was continuing mild and fair, and the hedgerows were beginning to fill with fuchsia and montbretia, a riot of pink and orange. Paula drove the Volvo out of town, snaked in early-morning school-run traffic. She was heading for the Drumantee Hills, a barren mountainous region that ringed Ballyterrin. Though there were no longer any checkpoints or Army patrols or any border at all, she had crossed it all the same – this body had been found in the South. And that brought a whole different set of problems. Her mind raced as she tapped the steering wheel, impatient for the car to move on. A third body. That meant someone was probably holding the other two, who could still be alive.

In contrast to the peaceful woods where Mickey Doyle had fetched up dead, hanging, the latest site was bare and flat, no tree for miles around to break the scrub of heather and gorse. She passed several TV vans, reporters doing live broadcasts in the morning breeze, and reached a cordon on the country road, manned by a Garda she didn't recognise, and hoked her ID out of her bag. 'I'm the forensic psychologist.' Always nervous saying it; many officers were suspicious of civilians at crime scenes. She was waved through and parked up, realising once again how difficult it was to get about when you were heavily pregnant. She didn't recognise anyone – even the techs were unfamiliar here. Finally she spotted Guy, but the brief burst of relief gave way to anxiety – if he saw she was struggling, he might send her home. She lumbered over to him. 'Can I see the vehicle?' She held up her hands. 'I know, I know, but it's an easy site, and there's clearly something ritualistic going on here. I need to see it.'

Guy hesitated. 'Paula, it's a really bad one.'

'You always say that.'

'They only got the fire out a few hours ago, so he's still in there. It's been soaked in petrol and set alight. He didn't try to get out, which suggests he was drugged, like the others.'

'He wasn't dead first?'

'No. Pathologist says there are scorch marks in his throat.'

'Oh. Well, I need to see anyway. How long's it been here?'

'There were reports of a fire in the early hours of the morning – it's an isolated spot but anyone driving on the lower road would have seen it.' They were walking now. Paula could see the van, a burnt-out wreck, which seemed to have once been white. There was a fire engine drawn up in the car park, and fire fighters mingled with the usual swarm of people at a murder scene. As they rounded the small hill she covered her mouth reflexively – the air stank of charred flesh and petrol. They said that was how Crossanure had smelled for weeks after the bombing.

'Not nice,' said Guy, seeing her face. 'Anyway, they're still cutting him out, so you can see if you need to.' There was a high squeal as someone wearing a mask wielded a sparking torch on the van. They halted some distance back. The sun was warm, a soft breeze twitching Paula's hair. She pulled strands from her eyes. 'Is there a note with this one too?'

'We think so. They're trying to get the door open and extract it.'

'I take it there's no sign of the others?'

'No. We may have to take helicopters up to the hills with infrared cameras. It can't be that easy to hide two people in a small town.'

Two more bodies to come. Paula struggled with the enormity of it. 'We need to find them.'

'I agree. We can't have everyone with a grudge doing this.' He waved a hand to take in the devastation, the blackened shrubs, the smell of roasted flesh in the air.

'The van's white.'

'Yes.'

'Martin's van,' she began. 'That was odd timing.'

'It was.' Guy's mouth was twisted. 'I don't know, Paula, this case . . .' A shout went up from the brow of the hill, and the noise of sawing ceased. 'They must have found something,' Guy said. 'Come on, you can meet the Detective Garda.'

This turned out to be a florid fiftyish man with white hair, who clapped Paula's hand with a firmness that made her wince. 'Garda Joe Hanlon,' said Guy. 'This is Dr Maguire, our forensic psychology consult. What can you tell us?'

'You asked us to look in his mouth? They just took something out with tweezers.' Hanlon held up a see-through bag. 'You can just about read it there, have a wee look.'

The paper was charred and brown, but the writing on it

was the same looping script as on the notes found in Mickey Doyle's mouth and Ronan Lynch's severed throat – this one said FRIENDLY FIRE.

'It's not random, if you ask me,' said the Garda. 'I've seen my fair share of Provo knock-offs – more than my share, if I'm honest. They used to like dumping the bodies over the border here, make a headache for the RUC to clean up. But nothing like this. Quick deaths. This fella – he was roasted to death, and he was alive to feel it.'

Paula was squinting at the van. 'Were you able to recover the number plate, Garda Hanlon?' The one spotted near the crime scenes had had its plate covered up.

'Yes. Do you want it?' He wrote some numbers on his notebook and passed the sheet to Paula, flapping in the wind. She turned to Guy but he'd already made the leap and was tapping on his BlackBerry.

'Is it?'

He just nodded. 'Garda, I think you'll find this vehicle is registered in the North, to a Dominic Martin.'

The man looked surprised. 'I take it you were expecting it to turn up.'

'We were. Just not so . . . audaciously.'

Paula just shook her head. As they walked back to her car, she asked, 'You didn't send Fiacra to liaise with the Gardaí.'

'No. Between you and me, he's not been coping all that well since his sister was attacked. I'm trying to keep him on lighter duties. I've sent him to Dundalk to do some paperwork.'

'That seems wise.' She was careful not to allude to the reason Fiacra had blown up at her. 'I think I'll do the same, back at the unit.'

'Good idea. I'll see you there.' How courteous they were being. As if the previous night's shouting and crying had never happened. But always there was the pressing bump of her child, reminding them that some mistakes just couldn't be ignored.

Extract from *The Blood Price: The Mayday Bombing and its Aftermath*, by Maeve Cooley (Tairise Press, 2011)

It was never fully resolved which of the Mayday bombers had played which role. The police put forward a version of events, which was rejected by the courts. But was it far from the truth, or different only in a few small brushstrokes?

Ni Chonnaill was likely chosen to act as a courier. The year before the bomb she had been convicted of ferrying explosives in the pram of her first child, who is now seven. She is believed to have sourced and shipped parts for the bomb from her father's network of supporters in Donegal and south of the border – detonators and wire from the bomb were traced back to well-known suppliers.

Lynch was the explosives expert – the two were a couple at the time, and had worked together to make and plant several devices, such as the one found beneath the car of PSNI reservist Sam Roper in 2003 (Lynch was arrested for this but once again had to be let go due to a lack of witness cooperation). It seems likely Lynch built the bomb which devastated Crossanure.

Doyle and Brady were logistics men, low down the pecking order. Brady had his IQ tested while in prison in the eighties and was borderline learning-disabled. He and Doyle probably took the bomb into Crossanure that day. Doyle's job as a refuse operative gave him access to the bin which would later that day be on the route of the planned Orange march. The two were caught on CCTV driving Doyle's work van into Crossanure several hours before the bomb went off.

Flaherty was the ringleader. That was never in any doubt. He had been high up the ranks of the IRA South Armagh battalion, but split from them in anger at what he saw as capitulation to the peace process. The mobile phone which was intended to detonate the bomb had once been registered to Flaherty, then reported missing the previous year.

And why did the Five escape justice, in the face of such compelling evidence? The pressure on security forces north and south of the border was immense after the bomb – arrests had to happen quickly. This meant corners were cut, PACE infringed in several cases, confessions extracted with perhaps too much force. Evidence was not correctly stored. There was human error. A margin of uncertainty. The need of our justice system to play by rules the terrorists ignore. Witnesses too afraid to speak out. Sheer bad luck. No one knows exactly why, but by naming them here I hope to counteract this gross miscarriage of justice and allow the families some fraction of the restitution they so desperately need.

Chapter Seventeen

Paula had been back at the unit for some time when she heard the voices. She was at her desk puzzling over the three deaths – the hanging, the beheading, the burning. What was the connection? One swinging from a tree, his purple face throttled, his bowels slack. The note in his mouth, COLLATERAL DAMAGE. The same phrase used about the bomb. The second, his head lopped off, eyes open in surprise. His note saying UNFORESEEN ESCALATION. The third, the burning man. Dying in Dominic Martin's van and the note preserved inside his mouth, the lips pulled back into a horrible grin by the shrinking of burned skin. FRIENDLY FIRE. A sick joke. Paula could never forget the smell, of scorched petrol and cooking flesh, a sweet, almost barbecue-like reek. They'd got to him before he was completely unrecognisable, his sandy hair burned off and his skin blackened, but in spots under his clothes still milky pale. He'd been wearing a plastic leather jacket, which had burned and stuck to his flesh in clumps.

She sighed and set down the gruesome pictures, wondering if they'd made any progress arresting Dominic Martin. Corry seemed determined to sit on it, whatever evidence they found. She had at least agreed to an expert taking handwriting samples from the families, now they had three notes to go on. Lorcan Finney's lab would be working on that task too. Meanwhile, the MPRU had failed utterly to find any sign of the missing, only their mutilated bodies.

'I'm sorry, you can't come—'

'I want to see Avril.' Paula looked up from her desk to see what the sudden commotion was. They didn't have a reception desk at the unit – couldn't stretch to it, and people weren't meant to walk in anyway, so they took turns to answer the glass door when it buzzed. Now a short man in slacks and a short-sleeved shirt was squaring up to six-foot-four Gerard. 'Are you him?'

'Excuse me, sir—'

'Monaghan, is that your name?'

Avril was standing up. 'Alan! What's gotten into you? Why are you here?'

Her fiancé. Paula recognised him now from the picture on Avril's desk. Unprepossessing, with a bad haircut, he was shaking like a dog in the rain. 'I know what you did. You and him.' He pointed to Gerard. 'Do your bosses know? I said you shouldn't be working in this place, it's a den of sin.'

'What's going on?' Gerard was looking baffled.

Avril's voice shook. 'I'm sorry, everyone. I don't know what he— Alan, what is this about?'

'Do they all know?' demanded Alan. 'Look at you, parading around here like a tart. Well, I want you to quit.'

Paula wondered what stretch of the imagination could accuse Avril's knee-length skirt of being 'tarty'. She stood up but stayed at her desk, cradling her bump.

Avril was pleading with him. 'Don't be silly, Alan. Can you just go home and we'll talk about this later, sensibly?'

'I can't wait. You tell me if it's true or not.' He turned his pointing finger on her.

'Is what true? I don't know what you're on about.'

'You and this Monaghan fella. Have you betrayed me, Avril?'

'No,' she said, but there was the smallest pause, and everyone heard it. 'I haven't done anything,' she said. 'Gerard is a colleague.'

'You kissed him. I know you did. At Christmas.'

The scene Paula had witnessed. She'd seen no actual kiss, but what had looked like the aftermath of one all right.

Gerard had been rendered uncharacteristically silent but now he tried to speak. 'Look. Alan—'

'Don't you dare say my name! You're no better than her. Both of you, fornicators.' He glared at Avril. 'And with a Fenian, of all people. That's the best you can do?'

Paula and Avril were in the Ladies, safe in the knowledge that they wouldn't be disturbed, given that no other women worked in the unit. Avril was sitting on an upturned toilet seat, pressing her eyes with the wads of paper towels Paula was passing to her. Her breathing was uneven. 'Nothing happened.'

'It's OK. You don't have to tell me.' She busied herself taking out more towels, the weight of her belly pushing into the sink. Behind her in the mirror she could see Avril, red-faced and weeping and apparently determined to share.

'Me and Gerard – you know how things get a bit crazy here. All work, and people are dying and you can maybe save them if you just work hard enough, except you can never work hard enough?'

'Yes.'

'I just did traffic analysis before. I never knew it would be this way.'

Paula said nothing. The last thing she wanted was to get involved in someone else's love life.

'You're close to DI Brooking.'

'Hmm-mm. Well, we're colleagues.'

'More than that. Your baby . . .'

Paula didn't know how do to this locker-room girly intimacy. 'Look, Avril. I'm not sure who this baby's father is. That's . . . inconvenient, but I still have to get on with my job. And so do you.'

Avril gave a blubbery breath. 'I can't believe he came here. Someone's been talking to him.' She caught Paula's eyes in the mirror. 'You saw – at Christmas.'

'I saw nothing,' said Paula hurriedly. 'Just you talking. Anyway, I'm not the type to tell tales.'

'I know who it was anyway,' said Avril, shredding the tissues. 'At least I think I do.'

'But nothing happened?'

'Well – no.'

'So, it'll be fine. I'm sure Alan will come round. That's if you want him to. You want the big white wedding and all that?'

'Well, what else is there?'

And to that Paula had no answer but her own swollen belly and fatherless child. 'We should go out,' she said, turning off the tap. 'It'll be OK. I've cried in work at least ten times since I started.'

'Men never do,' said Avril gloomily, dabbing her face. 'It's really unfair.'

'They do other daft things, though. Come on.'

As they went out, Fiacra was coming in the front door, his leather satchel across his chest. 'What's going on?' he said, unnaturally innocent. 'Someone's smashed a pane in the door here, look.'

'Alan came,' said Avril, very shaky.

'Your fiancé? What did he want?'

Avril went up to him. 'I know why you did it. I understand, OK? And you should have just talked to me. This is . . . beneath you.'

'No idea what you're on about.'

'I know it was you. Because I didn't tell anyone else. Because you're meant to be my friend!'

'Friend.' His face changed. 'Maybe I didn't want to be your fecking friend. How come I get that, and Monaghan gets all the good bits?'

'You are a . . . bastard.' Paula had never heard Avril swear before.

Fiacra gestured to Paula. 'Don't know why you're so chummy with her. She's just got your uncle suspended.'

'What?' said Paula and Avril together. Avril stared at her. 'Paula, is that true?'

'I . . . I don't know. I had some queries about an old case he worked on, but . . .'

'An old case.' Fiacra sneered. 'Your ma's case, is what you mean. Because you think you can do whatever you want, isn't that right, Maguire?' He glared back at Avril. 'You and her are just the same. You think the rules are for other people.'

Avril balled her fists as if she'd like to hit Fiacra, then shot back into the Ladies, sobbing.

Paula regarded Fiacra. 'What happened to you? You used to be so nice.'

'Nice,' he said bitterly. 'When did that ever help a person?' He barged into the main office.

It was a silly question she'd asked him. Paula knew exactly what had happened to him. Someone had tried to kill his pregnant sister – the same person who'd attacked Paula herself – and the girl had nearly died, and she'd lost her baby. But still. They all had issues.

'What's going on now?' Guy was coming in the door too, looking exhausted.

'Oh, just tempers fraying.' Paula would keep Avril's secrets. Call it female solidarity, or the community of liars, or whatever.

'We've got work to do. Three murders and we've achieved absolutely nothing towards finding the others. We can't afford to fall apart.'

'I think it's too late for that,' said Paula wearily. 'Did you hear what Fiacra said, about DS Hamilton? Is it true, he's been suspended?'

'I—'

'Because that wasn't what I meant! I didn't want to get him in trouble, I just wanted answers! I just need to know what happened.'

Guy turned away, rubbing his chin, which was already sprouting stubble after the early start. 'I can't talk to you about that, Paula.'

'But—'

'No. I'm sorry, but you ought to know by now – the things you do have consequences. Now, please get everyone into the meeting room.'

'Right,' said Guy. 'I hope everyone's clear on why we're here.'

'This is stupid.' Fiacra was slumped low in his seat like a sulky schoolboy, as was Gerard, as far away as possible from each other given that the room was barely three metres wide. It wasn't the best timing for a team meeting, Paula agreed. She could barely sit for ten minutes without having to pee, and Avril had so much make-up round her eyes she looked like a sunburnt panda.

'We have to work as a team. We are under huge amounts of scrutiny, as you know, and so far we have no results to show. Three of the Mayday Five are dead and we're no closer to finding the other two. Basically, we have nothing. Now, Jarlath Kenny will be officiating at the memorial service for the bombing at the weekend, in his capacity as mayor. This will bring up all manner of security issues. Kenny won't want any trouble from the dissident lot, so it's possible he will kill the remaining two members of the Five, if indeed he's involved in their kidnap.'

No one said anything.

'We work as a team,' Guy repeated. 'We're supposed to be above petty tensions – a cross border team, working in harmony. We have to set an example.'

Paula wanted to say that this wasn't really about sectarianism, just good old-fashioned jealousy, but she also sat in silence. Trying not to look at Bob's empty seat.

'So no more in-fighting,' said Guy, ploughing on. 'Leave your private lives at home, please.'

Fiacra shook his head, almost but not quite muttering something. Paula kept her eyes fixed on the desk, hands linked over her bump. The living proof that Guy and she hadn't managed to follow his own advice.

The moment stretched out, Fiacra, Gerard, and Avril all sitting in silence, either tearful or mutinous, until Paula spoke up. 'Will Corry's team be involved in policing the memorial service?'

'Not directly. The risk is so high they'll probably have the TSG there. But I feel we should attend, pay our respects. Most of the families will be there, except for a few who baulk at sharing the stage with a convicted terrorist.' A very old-fashioned attitude nowadays. You were just supposed to put it behind you.

'What will happen at it?' she asked.

He seemed grateful someone was talking. 'There'll be an unveiling service, and a journalist will read a poem – she wrote a book about it. Maeve Cooley – isn't she your friend, in fact?'

Yes, she was – or at least she had been before Paula had revealed Aidan might or might not be the father of the child currently doing flip-flops inside her. Now she clearly wasn't enough of a friend to even tell Paula she was coming to town.

Fiacra spoke up suddenly, his arms still folded. 'What about Bob? Will he be there?'

Guy shuffled his papers and stacked them neatly. 'Sergeant Hamilton is taking some time off while we look into an older case he worked on. Some allegations have been made and we need to investigate them.'

'But he's not done anything wrong, sir, so—'

Guy looked straight at Paula. 'I'd rather not discuss that at the moment. With any of you. Thanks.'

Kira

Kira didn't want to go to the memorial service. She refused to get dressed. 'You're a bad girl,' Mammy said. She was in the living room, already dressed in her suit with the pink roses, but drinking out of a glass that Kira knew had vodka in. She'd spilled some so it looked like the roses had dew on.

'Yes, Mammy.'

'The wrong one died. It should have been you. Not my Rose.'

'OK, Mammy.'

'Nobody even wanted you. A mistake is what you were.'

She was still in the T-shirt she wore to bed. It was one of Rose's and it said Rage Against the Machine on it. That was a band. It made Mammy angry – Kira had taken it from under Rose's pillow after that day and kept it.

'That dirty old thing,' said Mammy. 'Take it off or I'll tan your hide for you.'

'No, Mammy,' she said. She hid it when she was at school in case Mammy chucked it out.

Mammy threw the glass. It missed but some sprayed on the T-shirt. Kira felt it spatter onto her skin, warm from sitting out, and it was so nearly like that day she had to breathe in hard so she didn't scream. Behind Mammy, she could see Rose looking sad. Now, since it all started, she sometimes couldn't see her at all. It was getting harder and harder to hear her voice.

'I don't want to go,' she said. To Rose, not to Mammy, though Mammy answered.

'You'll do as you're told.'

Go, Rose said. *It will be OK. I'll look after you.*

I'm scared, she said, just inside her head.

You should go, Kiki. I'll be there.

'OK. I'll go.' She said that out loud but Mammy had

switched herself off again. Kira went to get some towels and wiped up the drink. The carpet was ruined anyway from drink and fags. She rinsed out the towel and got washed, then put on her nicest dress, a black one with a yellow belt, and on her feet trainers. She didn't want sore feet, and anyway, why couldn't you wear those kinds of shoes with a dress? Clothes were clothes, weren't they?

The trouble with the anniversary was you couldn't stop thinking about that day. Oh, this was when Rose and me watched Ant and Dec on TV and ate Coco Pops. This was when we drove in the car, and Rose turned the radio up high, and we sang along to that Rihanna song. Then less than an hour later Rose was dying all over the pavement and Kira had her blood running into her mouth.

She looked at herself in the mirror. She looked weird. She was weird. There was no getting around it. You dance to your own tune, pet, Rose used to say. Their pictures were out in the corridor, Rose in her party dress and Daddy in his suit. She couldn't even really remember him; he'd died when she was wee. He always looked cross in the pictures, never smiling. She'd asked Rose once what he was like. They'd been in Rose's room. She'd liked to play the CD deck and poke about in the jewellery and hairslides. One time, she'd opened Rose's bottom drawer and found a bottle of vodka there under the pants. The family had been 'dry' before Rose died, which meant you didn't drink. Daddy had been a 'strict ould bugger', Rose said one time. Then she looked sad. *God forgive me. At least he never kicked me out onto the street. She'd have done that in two shakes of a lamb's tail.*

Why would she do that? Kira had asked. Why would Mammy want to kick Rose out?

Never mind, she'd said. *Let's have a drink of Coke and some Skipps.*

'Bye,' she whispered to Daddy. Rose she knew was coming with them. She could see it in her smile in the picture.

'Show some respect,' Mammy muttered, pulling at her suit jacket. 'We have to honour Rose's memory.'

As if she didn't. As if she ever stopped.

Chapter Eighteen

Paula had a bad feeling about the service. It was the idea of crowds, after all she'd been reading about crushing and trampling, the panic on the day of the bomb.

She couldn't get used to the contours of her body being so changed and stretched. Like trying to put a glass on a table when you were drunk and missing, smashing it. She got dressed in her childhood bedroom, bumping into the shabby old furniture. She could of course have moved into her parents' room – PJ had gone and it wasn't too likely Margaret was coming back to sleep in it – but she couldn't bring herself to do it, so she stayed, ridiculously pregnant, in her single bed. Dressed in a shapeless black shift she'd bought in Dunnes, she shoved her feet into wide flats, broken down at the back, and bundled her hair up. She went into her parents' room to check her reflection in the house's only long mirror. All was still. Her mother's perfume bottles – Anaïs Anaïs, Chanel – sat on the dresser, a thin coating of dust over all. The venetian blinds let in the light in slats, dust floating in mid-air. The bed was stripped and neat. Paula held her breath and shut the door behind her.

Parking restrictions were in force for the service, so once she neared Crossanure she had to leave the car along the road. Already people were moving towards the main street in groups, families, couples, children. She was the only one alone, lumbering along, her own counterweight. Soon she was tired and needing to pee. She thought quite seriously about turning back. Standing in the heat for hours with a full bladder wasn't all that appealing. But she remembered Amber Martin, and Rose Woods, and Patrick Ward both Junior and Senior, and all who'd come into that town on a normal bank holiday, just like her, but never made it home again. She kept walking.

Despite growing up nearby, Paula had never actually been to Crossanure before, and so she saw in her mind the present day, five years on, superimposed with ghostly images of how it had looked after the bomb. The petrol station was still boarded up. It had never sold – haunted perhaps by the people who'd died there: Tom Kennedy and Lisa McShane in a car parked by the air station, Rose Woods on the forecourt as she was passing, the worker from Nigeria who was manning the pumps. The other people burned and maimed. High Street itself had been rebuilt, but it was too easy to picture the rubble, hear the screams on the bit of shaking camera footage someone had taken that day. The people they were searching for had most likely planted that bomb, hefted the bag into the bin, primed it and walked away to safety, while mothers and children were being herded to their deaths. They must have looked them in the face, knowing some of them would die. You couldn't put a bomb on a street full of children and call it *collateral damage*. And yet Paula was trying to find them, bring them home. Because that was all she knew how to do – find the lost. Whatever they'd done.

The streets of the small town were full of people. She didn't want to go further. Her body was resisting, pulling her back, but she forced her legs on to the heart of town, the square where the bomb had gone off in a litter bin. The crowd was several hundred strong, spilling all the way out of the square and down the street. She saw Guy and other police officers on a raised platform with folding seats. The families were on the other side. She recognised several faces: Ann Ward and John Lenehan, seated with his stick in front of him. He nodded to her, his differences with the group clearly put aside for this occasion. Despite the hot day, his skin was as pale as paper. The police and journalists were to the right. Corry had picked a black suit with a pencil skirt, neat and sober. The men wore black ties. Paula wondered did you own one as a matter of course, when you had to go to dozens of funerals. The crowd was ringed by officers in high-vis jackets, though there was no need. A more sombre and well-behaved gathering would have been hard to find. Somewhere in the low murmur a baby cried, but otherwise the crowd was quiet, almost weary. Paula thought she understood. More than a decade after the Good Friday Agreement, you wouldn't think you'd still need to attend peace rallies.

Guy helped her up onto the low platform, avoiding her eyes. 'How are you?'

'Fine. I needed to be here.'

Helen Corry looked tense – Paula knew she'd been closer to the bomb than most, as officer in charge of the control room that day. Her manicured hands were folded tightly in her lap.

At the lectern, Jarlath Kenny. Mayor of the town, who'd likely shot a few Protestants and police officers in his time. Was he the one behind this case; did he know where the remaining terrorists were being kept? The memorial itself was shrouded in a black curtain, casting a shadow over the crowd in the sunlit square. Already people were sweating and loosening ties. Paula wondered how long it would last, as she took her seat. She was scanning the opposite side for Kira. No sign. Then she saw two figures being hustled through the crowd by officers – Kira and the mother. She'd studied that file until she felt she knew them all, each sorrowful face, each line of loss that was etched onto them. The Woods family took their seats. None of the others looked at them.

The ceremony began at 10.30 a.m. There would be a minute's silence at 11.17 a.m., when the bomb had gone off. First there was a priest and a minister. Paula had never heard of either of them and assumed they'd been chosen to give the correct religious balance. There was also a black man in a colourful outfit who delivered a blessing in a language no one seemed to understand. This would be for the Nigerian. She assumed the African woman in the headdress was his sister, over from London. She hoped everyone had someone there for them. Even Niall McShane had come, sitting on the very back row with his folding chair pushed back, as if he might bolt. There was a young girl with him, around twelve or so, whose face was already swollen with crying. He held her hand tight. The sound of monotonous weeping had started up as soon as the blessings began. Paula realised it was Mrs Woods who'd begun it, her mouth open and slack. Perhaps she was drunk again. Her remaining child ignored her, looking stoically ahead.

The blessings had finished. She shifted in the hard chair. She was by now dying to pee and a trickle of sweat was working its way down the back of her thigh. She hoped to God she didn't go into labour right now. That would be inconvenient, but the baby had no idea she'd been brought to this ceremony of death, swimming around in the cushioned warmth inside. Guy was trying to catch her eye. She ignored him, licking the sweat from her top lip. She was very aware of Corry nearby, Avril and Gerard in the row behind. Bob, presumably, was not allowed to be there in an official capacity. Fiacra hadn't turned up. That would be a very black mark. She heard feet on the metal staircase to her left – someone was coming up it. Maeve. Her fair hair was loose, shiny, and she wore a black trouser suit with red Converse underneath, a flash of colour among the sombre mourning outfits. She didn't look at Paula.

Jarlath Kenny was saying, 'I'd now like to ask Miss Maeve Cooley to read the dedication. Miss Cooley has worked extensively with the families, and they've asked her to represent them here.' Maeve smiled at him blankly as he gave her the microphone. The smile didn't reach her eyes. Paula remembered the allegations in Maeve's book, that there was pretty much nothing to choose between Kenny and the man who'd orchestrated this bomb. So why was one on the podium and the other disappeared?

Maeve arranged some pieces of paper on the lectern, cool and in control. Her voice with its soft Dublin accent was steady. She was reading a poem. It began, 'Do not stand at my grave and weep. I am not there, I do not sleep.' A sob came from the side of the families. Paula looked and saw most of them were crying. Several of the men stared ahead, white-faced. Dominic Martin held Lily Sloane's hand as she wept. Looking over he met Paula's eyes and she felt a stab of pain. She stared at the ground while Maeve read, squinting her eyes to try not to let any tears fall out.

This wasn't her loss to cry over. In the crowd there was a low noise of sniffing. People held each other's hands and leaned together. She felt movement beside her – Guy was reaching for her hand. She let him take it, though she was lathered in sweat. His pulse was racing.

'Do not stand at my grave and cry. I am not there – I did not die.'

Maeve had finished. She looked across the square to the memorial. Later, Paula would see it on TV, Maeve with her chin raised, her eyes blinking and one strand of hair falling over her face. Two uniformed men pulled the ropes on the black curtain and the shroud fell back from the memorial. It was twelve feet high, a column of glass etched with the names of the dead, so light shone through and they floated, casting shadows over the crowd in the sun. The names seemed to radiate out. It was too far away to read them. The crowd threw up a murmur, then a faint smattering of applause rippled and died, awkward. Jarlath Kenny took the microphone again. He hadn't changed his expression at all during Maeve's recital, and Paula wondered how it made him feel, knowing he'd caused equal loss to other families. If he even felt at all.

He cleared his throat. 'We will now have the laying of wreaths by the families.' In front of the stage were piles of red roses. A walkway had been made through the crowd, fenced off with metal barriers. John Lenehan was just rising to his feet when there was a shout and sudden movement in the crowd. Something flew through the air – Guy was on his feet before anyone else, she remembered after. It sparkled, it seemed like a jewel in the bright sun, then you realised it was on fire – your body started to move before your mind caught up. More movement at the front of the crowd, confusion, people out of their seats, a child wailing somewhere. Guy was in front of Paula; he'd shielded her, she realised, he'd thrown himself in front of her. Then a metallic glint in the sun and a harsh fizzing sound and someone screaming, because everyone in Northern Ireland knew a bomb when they saw one.

Then officers were jumping on someone in the crowd, pinning them down, and there was a loud, rocking bang that reverberated in your chest and the lectern was on fire and everyone scattering, and Paula turned back to the podium, too weak to run away, reaching out for Guy. Jarlath Kenny had been at the front, mouth open in shock, and had hit the deck seconds before the grenade landed. Behind him Maeve had been standing, rooted to the spot, and the force of it had hit her. She was lying on the ground, red blooming through her white shirt, her face pale. Someone was screaming, high and pure, and Paula couldn't tear her eyes away from Maeve, as her blood ran out and pooled under her, the same scarlet shade as her trainers.

Aidan and Maeve had been friends a long time, since their first year studying journalism at UCD in Dublin. Paula herself had been stuck in Ballyterrin, finishing her A-levels, and despite the promises they'd made, tearful and Boots-17-lip-gloss smudged, she was gradually noticing Aidan's texts get fewer and fewer, and that it was a while since she'd had one of the spiralling emails he used to send her detailing the basement computer room with the smell of warm laundry from next door. Saying how much he missed her. That time of year was always hard for her anyway, the chilly nights of October leading up to the day she'd come home and her mother wasn't there. The feeling that the year was about to run out from under your feet like the end of an alley. Another year over and they hadn't found her mother. Maybe they never would.

Then Aidan's emails had stopped altogether, and he didn't answer his phone though she let it ring for forty goes, and finally there was the email with the black typeface and the sick feeling in her stomach: she knew what was coming.

She'd asked him, in one of the long, angry phone calls he'd allowed her, if it was Maeve. Was it the funny, cool journalism student he'd been mentioning a lot, was that who he'd slept with?

No, he'd said. Weary. It was just some girl. It hadn't meant anything. And she wasn't sure if that was better or worse, because he'd thrown her away for someone whose surname he didn't even know. Paula had staggered through the rest of the year, and then her results had come, a blaze of good A-levels as expected, enough to take her out of Ballyterrin to London, away from the house where she'd been waiting for five years for her mother to come back. That was when she'd realised none of it mattered, nothing was important, and she'd swallowed the contents of PJ's medicine cabinet, all his painkillers and sleeping tablets, and been rushed to Ballyterrin hospital. Aidan still didn't know about that. Glandular fever, they'd told everyone. A secret between her and PJ, never to be mentioned.

Now it was thirteen years later and Maeve was the one in the hospital bed, hooked up to tubes and drips. Her face was grey and still. Aidan was at her bedside, holding her limp hand.

'How is she?'

Aidan didn't look up. 'Holding on. That's what they said. Her ma's on the way from Dublin.'

'Is there anything I can do?'

He shook his head. 'Just have to wait.'

'Aidan.' He raised his face and she saw he'd gone. Her stomach fell away. She knew this look – the one he got when it was all too much and all he could think about was being seven years old and hiding under the table at the newspaper offices as masked IRA gunmen shot his father in the head. The one that meant he was already in his mind turning to the bottle, the dark bar, the oblivion at the bottom of the glass.

'She'll be OK,' Paula said. 'They got her in time—'

'And you know that, being medically qualified? That's not the kind of doctor you are.' He stared at Maeve's face, the slow mechanical rise of her chest. Her hair was still shining and blow-dried for the occasion, spread out around her. Lying there, she looked tiny.

'Saoirse said she'd come. She'll be able to tell you more.'

She wanted to say 'us', but this loss was not hers to claim. Maeve was only her friend through Aidan. She had little stake in the chest of that lively, talented beauty continuing to rise and fall.

'This keeps happening,' Aidan said quietly. 'It's me, I think.'

'What?'

'Me. I must be cursed or something. Dad – and you, at Christmas when she stabbed you, that woman – I thought that was it and I'd fucked it all up, you'd be gone and I'd never have— Now Maeve. I've no one.'

'I'm here. I'm fine, Aidan.'

'The baby'll come, and who knows what'll happen?'

'She'll be fine too. Everything's OK.'

'Don't even know if she's mine, but I couldn't bear it. If she wasn't OK.'

'She will be. Aidan!'

But he wasn't listening. She was about to go over, put her hand on the pale back of his neck, maybe, press his face into her vast bump, but then there was a clatter of feet and an older woman burst in. She wore a navy gilet and had fair hair in a feather cut, and she was sobbing. 'Oh God. Oh – sweetheart.'

Aidan got up and put his arms round the woman, pinning her. 'It's better than it looks, Sheila. They said she'll likely be OK.'

This must be Maeve's mother. Paula knew the father had died when Maeve was ten – it was something that linked her to Aidan.

'Oh look at her, my poor wee girl.' Sheila was sobbing. 'Let me see her.'

'OK, but they said we have to be careful, the tubes and that are a wee bit fragile.' He stood back to let her get to her daughter.

She stroked Maeve's hair, touched her forehead. 'It's Mum, love,' she said, voice shaking. 'Can you hear me? I know you can. You'll be OK, sweetheart. You did so well today. And your hair looks lovely, did you get it done like I said? You'll be OK.'

Paula was backing off to the door, letting them be. She caught Aidan's eye and he followed her out. Those hospital sounds, rattles and squeaking feet and hearts breaking. She hated it.

'Will you let me know how she is? Please?'

'If I get time.' He was still watching through the glass of the door.

'Aidan – if you go home tonight, maybe you'd – I'd like to see you. I don't want you being alone.' She put both hands on her stomach. 'I don't want to be alone.'

'Thought you loved it.'

'Please. This, being pregnant – it leaves you totally vulnerable. I'd like you to come round.'

He looked back in to Maeve. 'I don't know if I can.'

'Well. Think about it.' Her phone beeped. 'Shit, it's Corry. I have to see what she wants. I'll go now. Take care.' She drew him into a clumsy hug, her all curves and softness, him angular, unyielding. She felt his hand on the small of her back for a moment and realised he was moving her away.

'Go on, Maguire,' he said, distracted. 'You're no use to anyone here.'

Extract from *The Blood Price: The Mayday Bombing and its Aftermath*, by Maeve Cooley (Tairise Press, 2011)

The date 19th October 2010 was perhaps the most significant one since the bombing for the Mayday families. After more than four years of disappointment and waiting, they would finally hear the verdict on the terror suspects accused of murdering their loved ones. Throughout the trial, the five accused had reacted in different ways. They were held in separate docks, but the size of Belfast Crown Court meant that by necessity they were seated very close together while on trial. Lynch and Ni Chonnaill, who'd broken up the month before, traded insults several times and were held in contempt of court. Several times he was heard to call her a 'slut' and a 'dirty cheating whore'. Ni Chonnaill was five months pregnant at the start of the three-month trial, growing visibly bigger throughout, and her lawyer Grainne Devine used every advantage this offered when seeking a recess or deflecting difficult lines of questioning. Doyle wept several times, mentioning his wife and children. Brady appeared confused, addressing the judge at times as 'Sir', and once 'Your Majesty', which caused a rare burst of laughter amid such grim testimonies. Flaherty alone had refused to recognise the court or engage a solicitor, and simply ignored every question put to him.

Not all the families attended throughout. Some had nothing to do with the case. Some had planned to attend, then found work getting in the way, or couldn't sit through hours of brutal testimony on how their loved ones had died. John Lenehan was present on every day of the trial, taking the bus forty miles from his home in Ballyterrin, which may have contributed to the stroke he suffered on the day of the verdict.

As the jury came back, most of the families had gathered. Dominic Martin had also been there almost every day, despite needing to sustain his freelance energy business. Ann Ward, the group's secretary, also came, making copious notes where she could. Also present were the Woods, the Sloanes, whose daughter Lily was badly maimed in the bomb, Tom Kennedy's widow, the Connolly family, and the

Garstons. The grandfather of Daniel Jones had attended much of it, although he was in his eighties. The sight of Mr Jones and John Lenehan, leaning on canes to listen to the verdict, brought tears to many of the jurors' eyes.

Throughout the trial much interest had centred on the figure of Catherine Ni Chonnaill. A strikingly beautiful woman with long blonde hair, at five-eight taller than many of the men in court, she drew the eyes in the succession of colourful dresses she chose to wear in the dock. Scarlet and pink, vivid patterns, heavy necklaces and every day a slick of red lipstick she reapplied after eating her courtroom lunch in the cells. The lipstick was commented on widely at the time. Red as the blood on her hands, said one commentator, who shall remain nameless, violating somewhat the principle of sub judice. *She kept drawing attention to the bump of her baby, stroking it and sometimes shifting or wincing as if in discomfort. A member of the jury afterwards told me in confidence they'd found it extremely difficult to sit in judgement on Ni Chonnaill.* We were listening to the most awful stuff, wee babies blown up and that, and she was sitting there obviously expecting herself, looking so happy and calm. It was hard to imagine sending her to prison like that.

On 19th October 2010, the jury was due to give their verdict on the Mayday Five.

Chapter Nineteen

The door of Corry's office opened with a snap. She was still dressed in what she'd worn to the memorial, the sober black suit. Her fair hair was loose, still neat despite everything that had happened that day. Paula sighed at her own sweaty, unravelling self.

'Dr Maguire, come in.'

She gathered her papers and blundered in to the pin-neat office. Even the office plants were alive and blooming on the windowsill, which gave an uninspiring view over the reinforced car park with its bombproof walls.

Corry had settled herself behind the desk. 'I thought we should talk, after today. I hear there was some trouble down at the station yesterday. A complaint about intra-office relationships.'

That could have been either herself and Guy, or Gerard and Avril. Paula answered very carefully. 'There was some mention about it. I don't know, I've been so busy with the case.'

'There are rules, of course, on that sort of thing.'

'Yes.'

'Though I've often felt they were more like guidelines. People are only human.'

'Yes.'

'Just as long as it doesn't interfere with work.' The message was clear – *sort it out or get off my case.*

'It won't.'

Corry had settled behind her desk. 'How is your friend?'

'Not great. They say she should pull through, but . . . it's difficult. The grenade exploded right in front of her, and they think the blast damaged her heart. She has burns too.'

'We're getting reports that it was thrown by a fair-haired man, later seen running in two different directions out of the square – so God knows what that means. There was a lot of confusion.'

'Were they aiming at Maeve? Because of her book?'

'It's hard to say. Could have been Kenny, especially if he had something to do with these murders. But you're still convinced there's a link with the families?'

'It's clear someone is doing this for punishment. Even the staggered release of the bodies – this wasn't done to get rid of the Mayday Five. They'd have been quietly disappeared if Kenny wanted a clear election run. No, I think it's vindictive, rage-filled – but at the same time very ordered. I want us to keep looking at the relatives. After all, they had the most reason to hate the bombers. And there was Martin's van, of course. Did we take the writing samples?'

'Yes, we got samples from all the adults in the group, but none matches the writing on the notes. The type of notebook Ann Ward uses matched the one found in the caves, true enough – but you can get those anywhere. So, a dead end again.'

'You were working that day,' said Paula. 'The day of the bomb.'

Corry nodded slowly. 'I went straight to Crossanure

when it happened. We had to help dig out the bodies. There was a wee boy, he was about nine or ten. My Connor was the same age then. Daniel Jones, I think it was. I helped get him out from under a wooden door. Not a mark on him but he was dead, white as a ghost with plaster.' She stopped. 'It's hard to forget things like that.'

There was a knock at the door. 'Come in,' Corry called, switching back to a brisk tone of voice. 'This is why I asked you here. I want you to hear Dr Finney's take on it.'

He was standing in the door, dressed in a heather-coloured jumper and jeans. He carried three polystyrene cups, which was easy because his hands were huge. Paula noticed what looked like a fresh burn on the side of one. 'I thought some tea would help.' He placed them on the desk. 'Hello, Dr Maguire.'

'Hello.' She had an odd feeling seeing him, some kind of aversion mixed with something like excitement. She tried to focus on what Corry was saying.

'The samples don't match then, Dr Finney. From Dominic Martin's van.'

'I'm afraid not. Of course, there was extensive charring, but I was able to take samples from what was left. There's no trace of this particular mineral in his vehicle. Whoever did the killings would almost certainly have picked up some of it from the sea caves while transporting the bodies.'

Corry was frowning. 'But there's clearly a second site – two of the bombers are still missing, so they must have been moved elsewhere. Isn't it possible he wasn't at the caves?'

'Did you test his shoes?' Paula asked. She saw Finney look annoyed for a moment; perhaps he thought she was questioning his judgement. 'That can be useful, both for forensics and analysing footprints. The pattern of wear, and so on.'

'We can send casts off to a lab in London that does podiatry stuff,' said Corry. 'I'll see if we can get a warrant for Martin's shoes too. It's sensitive. We can't push the families too far – the press are all over me as it is.'

Finney sipped his drink. He seemed to fill the small room, giving off a warm citrus smell. 'Is there any need to involve the families at all? It must be devastating for them. I think this has all the hallmarks of IRA punishment, to be honest. And I found no traces, as I said. The van had been reported stolen anyway, hadn't it?'

It wasn't his job to say what he thought and Corry knew it. She said, rather stiffly, 'We aren't ruling anything out yet. I'd like your team to carry on searching the bogland, look for any disturbed ground. There are two other potential bodies, let's not forget. If we can find them alive, that would be something.'

Intuition was a funny thing. As a clinically trained psychologist, Paula told herself it existed in some way science hadn't yet mastered – a leap between neurons, a message in the air between people. She'd had an ancestor, her mother had once told her, with the second sight. Officially Paula did not believe in second sight, but she believed there were powerful currents between people, ways to know things without words. She knew there was something about Finney that made her uncomfortable – a way of standing too close, holding your gaze for too long with his pale eyes. He was attractive. She knew this in her bones, so she was rude to him just to be safe.

But it wasn't until she saw Corry and Finney together that she made that wordless leap. Corry had been entirely professional throughout her work with him, addressing him as Dr Finney, deferring to his expertise while drawing her own conclusions. It was because he'd brought tea that Corry made the mistake. She picked hers up and sipped it, exclaiming, 'Ah Lorcan, you know I don't take milk.' A short silence fell and in it Paula saw a momentary flicker on Corry's usually impassive face, and knew – *she is sleeping with him*. Her skin grew hot. She was actually a little shocked, while chiding herself with the reminder that she herself had slept with her boss the first week on the job, and possibly was having his baby. But Corry had fought her way up through institutionalised sexism by being both tough as nails and rigidly by the book. If it got out she'd slept with one of the forensic experts, the whole case could be compromised.

'Sorry,' he said, betraying nothing. 'I've a rubbish memory.'

'It's fine,' said Corry, too quickly. 'Won't do me any harm the once.'

Paula reached for her own and made a slight noise on finding the cup was scalding to the touch. When she looked up, Lorcan Finney was watching her.

'Thank you, Dr Finney,' said Corry, very formally. 'We won't need you for now.'

'Well, you know where I am if I can help.' His smile was a dangerous thing. Paula was glad when he'd gone, but only for a moment, because Corry immediately launched another blindsider at her, as if to cover up what had just passed.

'I know about your complaint against DS Hamilton. And I wanted to say . . . I understand, but you need to tread carefully. Are you even supposed to have that file?'

Paula looked at her hands. Even she was surprised by
what she said next. 'I want to talk to Sean Conlon. Send
me. He might know something about this case – he was in
the IRA right up till he got arrested in 'ninety-nine. It's a
good lead.'

Corry stared at her. 'You must be joking me. This being
the same Sean Conlon who said last year he might know
something about your mother's case? Sean Conlon the IRA
terrorist who wants early release in return for maybe telling
us where they buried their victims? You want me to send
you to *him*?'

'Yes.'

'And violate every ethical code and possibly get myself a
Professional Standards Enquiry?'

'Yes.'

'Pau-*la*.'

'He-*len*.' She wasn't supposed to call DCI Corry that at
work, but they'd become friends of a sort over the past
while. 'I've looked into every lead there was. I've asked
everyone who used to know my mother. I went through all
the case files. There's nothing new. And now this, from my
neighbour – I think DS Hamilton knows something that
isn't in the file.'

'She's been declared dead, Paula.'

'Yes. My dad wanted to remarry. And I can't blame
him. It's been seventeen years; he deserves some happiness.
But – I'm pregnant.'

Corry squinted in frustration. 'Which is relevant
how?'

Paula thought how to say it. 'I sort of feel . . . I need to
know what happened to my mother, before I can become
one myself.' That was so cheesy she could hardly get the

words out, but all the same fairly close to the truth of what was driving her.

Corry sighed. 'And what exactly is your plan, if I get you in to talk to Sean Conlon? What's the connection? He's been in jail for years.'

'He said he knew something. It was in the file – when the Commission for the Disappeared went to interview him last year, he said he knew her name. It's the only small link I have. Mum—' Paula's mouth still dried on the word. She swallowed. 'My mother worked in a solicitor's office where they defended Republican prisoners. Several years before she vanished, a British soldier died in her arms at a checkpoint. Sniper. She – I'm trying to piece it together, but I think it all just disgusted her. There was talk she'd leaked documents to Special Branch. And my father, as you know, was a Catholic RUC officer. They had every reason to take her.'

'So you want to dander in there and ask Sean Conlon if he kidnapped your mother?'

'I just want to see him,' Paula said. 'I want to look him in the eyes. And if I interview him, it's non-binding. He can talk to me in confidence. Clinically. I can ask him about the Mayday case too.'

Corry shook her head. 'Most of these men are dead inside, Paula. They're so sure of their cause they literally don't care about who gets killed on the way. What makes you think he would help you?'

'I have to try. I have to push at every stone.'

'All right. I'll try to help you. On two conditions. One is that you do nothing unprofessional. You don't tell him who you are. You may speak to him generally and assess him – we'll say it's a function of the MPRU. A chance for him to confess in confidence and help any families of the missing. You do not tell him you're her daughter.'

'OK,' Paula nodded. 'And the other?'

'You give me an answer on the job once and for all. I want to know if you're ever going to come and work for me.'

'But I . . .' She indicated her stomach. 'It's not the best time, surely, even if I were going to move? I'll be on leave at least for a while.'

Corry hesitated. 'I'm not supposed to tell you this, but – the MPRU. I don't know for sure, but there's a good chance it won't get funded next year.'

'Really? Does Guy know? DI Brooking, I mean.'

It was the wrong thing to say. 'Of course he knows. Why do you think he's been away at all these meetings?'

He knew their jobs were all at risk, and he hadn't told her. Paula thought about this for a moment. 'He never said anything.'

Corry gave her a hard stare. 'He doesn't tell you everything, you know.'

'No. I suppose not.' And she didn't tell him everything either, of course.

Corry looked impatient. 'I didn't officially tell you that. It's only a possibility for now. But be smart, Paula. You need to think of that wean now too. There's a job for you here, if you want it. And it would be good for you – you're far too emotionally involved in missing persons. You could do a much better job on other cases. Think about it.'

'OK. I will. Thank you.' She was speaking mechanically, trying to process it. 'But you'll help me, anyway?'

'And what if Conlon does know something? If he says he had a hand in killing your mother in 1993, and you have to sit there and write it all down, knowing you can't pin a single charge on him?'

'That might be the case.'

'You could handle that, could you, knowing the man will likely be free in a few months and you might bump into him in Dunnes?'

'I usually do my shopping in Sainsbury's,' said Paula vaguely.

Corry gave an exasperated sigh. 'I wonder why it is, Dr Maguire, that you seem to continually get away with poking at the rules.'

'You know how it is,' said Paula riskily. 'Some rules are more like guidelines anyway.'

There was a long, dangerous pause. Could have gone either way. But she was getting to know Helen Corry better, and suspected there was nothing that warmed the DCI's heart more than an equally bolshie woman on her team. 'Dr Maguire,' she said levelly. 'Go home. You've been overdoing it and I haven't the budget for washing afterbirth out of the carpet.'

She got up, slow and ponderous as a ship turning in harbour. She'd pushed her luck too far. 'Thank you for helping me. With Conlon, I mean. I know it's caused some problems.'

'Hmph. I meant what I said. I don't want to see you hanging round here trying to pretend you aren't massively pregnant. Get some rest, for God's sake.'

'I'll try,' Paula said, knowing that she couldn't. She had the sense that time was running out, that perhaps she'd had the first chance in seventeen years to find out what happened to her mother, and it was about to slip through her puffy pregnant fingers.

She flexed them as she got up, seeing only dark branches and the gleam of moon on bone, feeling the grit of soil in her nails. *I have to find her. I have to keep digging.*

As Paula lumbered out of the room, about to follow Corry's advice and go home, she was intercepted by a sweaty Gerard, jogging down the long carpeted corridor towards the interview rooms. 'Hey Maguire. I was looking for you. We've found the fella who threw the grenade.'

'Already?'

'It wasn't hard. They handed themselves in.'

Paula frowned at him in puzzlement. 'They?'

'Come on. I'll explain on the way.'

'So they're twins. I guess that explains how the same man was seen in two places at once.'

'Yep. Joseph and Danny Walsh. Danny has a scar over one eye, see. Otherwise they're dead-on identical.'

In two adjacent interview rooms, the same man was sitting. He was dressed in two variants of a T-shirt and tracksuit bottoms, and the tattoos on both arms were different, but the cropped sandy hair and eyebrows and narrow, suspicious faces – those were exactly the same. Twins.

'And they're confessing to the attack on Maeve?'

'They were aiming for Kenny, apparently.'

'But – I thought all the Provos loved him round here?'

'Something shifted. I did say it was coming.'

'Yeah yeah, you're amazing.'

'I know.'

She elbowed him in the side.

'Ow! Don't be jealous of my awesomeness.'

Corry and Guy appeared, walking briskly down the

corridor, deep in conversation. 'Right,' said Corry. 'These two clowns want to confess to everything back to the kidnap of Shergar, it seems. Let's try to get the truth about why they targeted Kenny. Monaghan, you're with me. DI Brooking will have one of my team. Dr Maguire . . . I thought I sent you home?'

'I got waylaid. Can I observe?'

'If you must. You can listen for any inconsistencies between the two.'

Paula tried to switch between both rooms, putting the earpieces in and out and sometimes getting muddled. Joseph Walsh's first comment was, 'I want to go into that there protective custody. Someone's trying to kill me.'

Danny's was: 'Where's my brother?'

'We have to interview you both separately, Danny.' Guy took a seat beside one of Corry's constables, a DC Ryan from deepest South Armagh. Paula wondered was that deliberate – it was the last stronghold of diehard Republicanism.

In the next room, Corry said, 'So Joseph. Tell us what happened. You threw a grenade at the mayor, hitting Ms Cooley instead?'

'Well, our Danny threw it. But aye.'

'So why are you here?'

'We never meant to catch the wee blonde girl. Just that bastard Kenny. He's trying to kill us, so he is.'

Paula tuned in to Danny's account of it. '. . . We was heading back from the pub earlier when this van comes flying back, tries to flatten us. I says to Joseph, hit the deck! And we both lepped over a wall and ran. Next thing someone's shooting at us.'

'Which pub was this?' asked Corry. Paula tried not to

think about the fact they'd almost killed Maeve, then merrily gone for a drink.

'Wolfe Tone's.' The very pub where Gerard met his informants. She wondered if he'd spoken to these two.

She went back to Joseph's interview. He seemed a bit more with it.

'And why did you try to attack Mr Kenny?' Corry was asking. 'We understood you two were associates of his. "Fixers" was the word used.'

Joseph became evasive. 'I want assurances. We'll give him to yis but I'm not going down with him.'

Corry didn't bat an eyelid. 'Mr Walsh, you came to us for protection. I will have no qualms in booting you out on the street if you don't answer my questions. Whether you incriminate yourself or not is a side issue – we've already got you on attempted murder.'

'All right,' he said sulkily. 'We done a wee job for him recently.'

'How wee?'

'Em . . . he wanted some people picked up and dropped off.'

'I assume you're not talking about a taxi service,' said Corry severely. 'Who are we on about here?'

'That Ireland First lot. The ones that got done over – but it wasn't us, I swear. We just dropped them off. At them caves down by the beach.'

Paula could see Corry trying not to react. 'You're saying you abducted Callum Brady, Mickey Doyle and Ronan Lynch, who have since turned up dead?'

'Aye. Kenny asked us to. Said he'd pay us and all.'

'Did he say why?'

Joseph shrugged. 'Naw. I never asked no questions.'

She tuned in to Danny, who was telling the same story.
'. . . Kenny said we'd to meet these two other fellas who'd
have a van, and they'd be under the Old Mill Bridge.'

'What kind of van?' Guy asked.

'I dunno. White.'

'And who were the two men?'

'I couldn't say, boss. They had on masks, like, and so
did we. One was driving and the other fella – when we got
them in the van he gave them a shot of something and they
was out like a light.'

'Danny. These are very serious allegations. You're
saying Jarlath Kenny paid you to meet two other men and
abduct the Mayday bombers?'

'Aye. 'Cept he never paid us yet.'

'And that's why you hurled a bomb at him?'

'Well, sorta – he was after us, swear to God. Earlier on,
that wasn't the first time. Me and Joseph been followed
since it happened. Same ould white van with the plates
covered up.'

'You can't tell me anything about the two men?'

'Naw. The one who drove, he wasn't a pro. He was all
over the road – nervous like. But the one with the injections
– he knew what he was about. His hands never even shook.'

'Right.' Guy took a deep breath. 'For the tape, talk us
right through it. Who exactly was in the van that day?'

He counted it off laboriously on his fingers. 'Me, our
Joseph, them two guys, the four we lifted . . . that's it.'

Guy paused with his pen over his pad. 'Four? You don't
mean five?'

'Naw. Them fellas that are dead and the woman. I'd tell
you where she was if I knew. Don't hold with killing
women.'

'That's . . . noble. You didn't pick up Martin Flaherty?'

'No way.' He shook his head. 'I'd not go near him. Man like that, you'd need a SWAT team to get him in the van.'

'And you left the other four at the caves?'

'Aye. They was all out of it, me and Joseph dragged them in. The two fellas tied them up, then off we went. It was a long ould walk back through them woods.'

'These men . . . were they local?'

'Aye. Local accents. Tallish fellas. I couldn't tell you anything else, they never said much. 'Cept one was really nervous.'

She buzzed into Corry's earpiece. 'Ask him how many people were in the van.'

Corry blinked, but picked it up seamlessly. 'How many people did you abduct that day, Joseph?'

'There was four,' he said immediately. 'Three fellas and the girl. We was a bit squashed up in the van like.'

'So four, plus you two, and the two men who drove. Nobody else?'

'Naw.'

'Right. Is there anything you can tell us? If you help us find the men, it would be advantageous for you. Try to remember.'

Joseph creased his face, identical to his brother's. 'One thing . . . in the van, there was this weird thing, like a big massive bit of dark glass.'

'Dark glass?'

'It looked like one of them, whatcha call it. Solar panels.'

Kira

Kira had always been a bit afraid of John. He'd been their obvious leader since the group started, when Kira was too young to go. He was the one who could stop Dominic from shouting and punching the wall, or Tom Kennedy's wife from turning up drunk and crying, and even make the Presbyterian Sheerans sit in the same room as the Connollys, who'd been a Sinn Fein family for years, everyone knew. When he looked at her, under his bushy white eyebrows, she felt all the words she had pile up in her mouth and clump there.

After the last meeting – the one where people had said yes or no, and taken their pick, and made their promise not to say anything about it ever again, whatever they decided, and John had looked at them all in silence, and then said he was stepping down, he'd been the last one left in the hall. The others had gone to Dominic's for a drink – people seemed almost excited at first, crying and then laughing too, like they'd had too much alcohol already. Kira was too young to go, of course. She hung back, helping John pack up his papers. He wasn't good since the stroke, but that day he seemed to be going as slow as possible, touching every page as he put it away. John had been Chair for nearly five years. There was a lot of paper.

She held the door as he stumped out on his stick. He looked her right in the eye. 'You're too young to be involved in this.'

'They killed Rose!' She didn't like the way he looked at her, cross but sad too.

'It won't bring her back, your sister.'

'I know.' Stupid. 'But it's what they deserve. They're bad people.'

'Who are we to sit in judgement?'

She'd turned her head, annoyed. 'We're exactly the ones. The judge and jury people, they don't really know, they get to go home to their own families and forget. We can't do that. I'm never going to see Rose again and it isn't fair!' She felt her voice go funny, which was annoying, because after five years you'd think she would be done crying about it.

John put his hand on her shoulder, almost like he was so unsteady he had to lean on her. 'You're only young, pet. None of this was your fault. They took so much. Don't let them take your heart too.'

She'd pulled away. She made herself be less angry by thinking of his son, big, good-looking Danny, and his poor wife who'd done the worst possible sin and taken her own life. John stumped off to the bus stop and Kira watched him go, every step like a heart breaking.

Chapter Twenty

'Where's the switch on this yoke?' Gerard was fumbling for the button on the overhead projector. It was the next day and they'd gathered in the conference room to hear about some breakthrough he'd made. The Walshes were in protective custody awaiting charges. With Bob still off, Guy and Paula were presiding with difficulty over the tensions between the three younger staff. As Aidan wasn't replying to any of her texts, Paula had called the hospital that morning. Maeve was no worse, at any rate.

'Look on the side.' It was the first thing they'd heard Avril say to Gerard for days.

He found it. 'Right, the Walshes brought this in with them, some kinda bargaining chip or something – take a wee look.'

They were looking at a picture of two men. From the exposure and the clothes, it seemed to have been taken in the seventies. It showed the two arm in arm, holding large rifles and smiling. They wore balaclavas, but pushed up round their heads so you could clearly see their faces. Like so many IRA volunteers, they were heartbreakingly young, no more than eighteen. Gerard pointed with one squat finger. 'That's Kenny there on the right. And look who's on his left.'

'Is that Martin Flaherty?' Guy was peering. Even Fiacra

sat up in his seat, where he'd been sulkily slumped.

'It is, boss. Best of friends, they were, back then, like we thought. South Armagh Brigade. Then Kenny threw his lot in with Sinn Fein and the peace process, and Flaherty went out on a limb – thought they were dirty rotten traitors, the lot of them, as he said.'

Paula stayed silent. Any of those men could have ordered the abduction of her mother. Not Sean Conlon – he'd been too far down the ranks, a foot soldier. Someone else had given the orders for every shot that was fired.

Guy looked annoyed. 'So Kenny lied to us.'

'Hardly surprising, the same fella.'

'I found something too,' said Avril, addressing Guy and ignoring Gerard. 'The phrase "friendly fire", the one that was in Lynch's mouth – the most significant use of that is in a speech Jarlath Kenny made a few years back, after the funeral of Christy Magee. He condemned the killing of Republicans by other Republicans, or "friendly fire", as he called it.'

'Who's Christy Magee?' Guy was looking puzzled.

'Informer who was leaking stuff to Special Branch back in the eighties,' Fiacra supplied. He also didn't look at Avril. 'Got shot in 2007.'

Guy glanced at him in some surprise; he hadn't contributed much in meetings since the outburst with Alan. Avril made a small noise of contempt in her throat.

Guy was putting it together in his head. 'Right, so friendly fire could refer to an intra-Republican feud, also suggesting Kenny is behind all this.'

'It makes sense,' Gerard was saying. 'Kenny's gone straight, wants to do a Westminster bid – Flaherty could easily cause problems for him. Could be he can prove

Kenny was linked to some of the murders he's always denied.'

'What about the notes?' asked Paula. She wished Gerard would take down the photo. They looked so happy, like boys waving toy guns. 'The notes explicitly link the deaths to the bomb, suggesting a revenge motive. Then there's the pictures in the caves, and the mode of death – hanging, fire, beheading – it's all very similar to how people died in the bomb.' She'd been thinking a lot about this. 'In fact, it's exactly the same, isn't it – several people burned to death when the petrol station exploded, and some were beheaded by debris. Plus there was Walsh's comment about the solar glass in the van. I mean, we all know who works with solar panels. Why aren't we arresting him?'

'And the hanging?' Guy was frowning. 'How does that fit with this theory?'

Paula thought for a second. 'Mary Lenehan hanged herself after her son was killed – I bet she wasn't the only one. The Mayday Five are being killed in the same ways people died because of the bomb.'

Gerard wasn't giving up. 'But it's also how the Provos got rid of people.'

'Not really,' she argued. 'A shot to the base of the skull was the most common one. Beheading is definitely not in their bag of tricks.'

Gerard shrugged. 'Maybe they got a tip or two off their Taliban colleagues.'

She didn't laugh. 'It doesn't feel like internecine murder to me. I think it's personal, intimate – beheading suggests total contempt for the victim, a desire to rob them of all humanity. Not even the dignity of a quick shot to the brain stem.'

'OK,' said Guy. 'So what do we do? It's going to be tricky arresting the mayor, if we're just going on hearsay from a pair of miscreants like the Walshes.'

'Why aren't we arresting Dominic Martin?' asked Paula again, bewildered. 'How much more evidence do we need?'

'Corry is considering it.' Guy's face was creased with worry. 'She's going to discuss it with the Chief Constable. Do you have a plan, Gerard?'

'I think we need to go in further.' Gerard punched his hand forward. 'I want to lean on some of my guys to testify, offer inducements, maybe.'

Guy was looking even less happy. 'You'd need to run that past Corry, you realise. I think we should swoop now and arrest Kenny before he has time to skip town.'

'You've used informants before, sir, have you? Sorry, covert human sources?'

'Yes. It was a part of our anti-gang strategy in London. But it was very dangerous. Several of our contacts were killed when their cover was blown. One of them turned up on the station doorstep. Or rather, bits of him did.'

'This isn't the same. I'm only talking a wee kickback. Info for a helping hand – and maybe we can get some definite info on Kenny, once and for all.'

Incredibly, Guy was nodding. 'If Corry says no now, we'll do that. I agree it's the best plan we have.'

'*What?*' Paula and Avril both exploded, for very different reasons, talking over each other.

'We can't pay off terrorists!' said Avril, appalled.

'I really feel we should be looking at the revenge motive,' Paula insisted. 'There was evidence of abuse on the bodies, sustained torture. This wasn't done to get rid of inconvenient witnesses.'

'The IRA never tortured anyone?' said Gerard scornfully.

'I know they did, of course, but I still don't feel it's them—'

'Nonetheless, Gerard's plan is the best option we have,' said Guy. 'I'll speak to Corry and see if we can get Kenny now, but I doubt it.'

As he went to make the phone call, Paula was left alone with the three angles of the office's little love triangle. Gerard was ostentatiously packing away the overhead projector, while Fiacra gazed sullenly at the ceiling. Avril was typing something on her laptop. Paula noticed the analyst's eyes were red and swollen and – shit – she wasn't wearing her engagement ring any more. Avril saw her glance and put her hand quickly under the table, but not before Fiacra had noticed.

He cleared his throat. 'So what's your strategy then, Monaghan?'

Gerard straightened his tie. 'Usual. Go and talk to some of my boys on their home turf.'

'So hang about in a pub,' said Fiacra neutrally. 'That's good evidence there, that is.'

'You've a better plan, do you?'

'We should arrest the damn mayor, like the boss wants. Kenny's guilty as sin. What is it about you lot up here in the North, that you let these people walk about free?'

'You don't understand, son,' said Gerard.

'Oh, I don't, do I? Listen, *son*, my da was a Guard for near-on thirty years. Dropped dead with a heart attack from the stress. Don't you tell me I'm not affected.'

'I . . .'

They stopped as Avril stood up, pushing back her chair with a scrape. 'I think we should all get on with our work,' she said pointedly to the air. 'Paula, are you going to be at Kenny's arrest, if it happens?'

'If I'm asked to.'

'Yeah, well, you always are when the boss decides, aren't you?' Fiacra delivered this with a glare at her, then stormed out.

Paula met Avril's eyes; saw she was barely holding back tears, and got up to leave. She couldn't cope with any more drama on top of what was already unfolding.

Guy put his head back in. 'Right. Gerard, Paula, get yourselves ready. We're going to Kenny's.'

'Corry said yes to arresting him?' Paula was surprised.

'Too late for that. Kenny's wife just reported him missing. Let's go.'

Paula was thinking it all through as they drove to Kenny's five-bed house in the centre of town. In any other situation, he would have been the first arrest made. Guy had seen it from the start. The rest of them, including her, had too easily fallen into the trap that this island laid for you – understanding the context. Knowing why people were the way they were. Assuming a sort of immunity because of the past. And by understanding, forgiving. Guy's approach was bracing in its simplicity – context be damned. This country was part of the UK, and subject to its law. They didn't have to make the law, they only had to enforce it. It was a buoy to cling to in the shifting sands of Irish history.

She parked up and showed her ID to the officer at the gate. Outside the house was in good repair, recently painted, lawn trimmed, windows washed, as befitted a man of Kenny's standing. Inside told a different story.

'Jesus.' Paula stared at the devastation, the furniture

turned over, the air dusty with feathers from the cushions that had been slashed. Underfoot, broken glass gritted.

Guy was wearing gloves and passed her some. 'Be careful not to get cut. Look.'

Every picture on the mantelpiece had been shattered. Behind the fractures, children smiled, and Kenny walked his wife down the aisle on their wedding day.

'Where are his kids?'

'With their mother. They've been living apart, secretly – Mrs Kenny just comes out for campaigning pictures and so on. She called round and found the place like this.'

'This was done on purpose,' said Paula. 'The pictures haven't even fallen over.'

'I agree. And there's signs of a struggle out back – soil churned up, the back door broken down.'

'He was kidnapped too?'

'I'd say it was the same people, wouldn't you?'

On the cabinet was a framed picture of Kenny as a young man, happy and smiling, holding a rifle. 'Look at this.' The picture had been removed from its frame and left on the side. A corner was folded back, and Guy now straightened it out with gloved hands.

'Flaherty,' said Paula. There he was, their missing bomber, arm in arm with Kenny. A copy of the picture they'd already seen.

'All very cosy,' said Guy, bagging it up. 'Why on earth would he have a thing like that in his house?'

'Because he thinks he's above the law. He thinks he's untouchable.'

'Up to now, I can see why,' said Guy drily. 'What's your opinion?'

She turned slowly, taking in the remnants of the smart

living room. Even the massive TV had a shattered screen, and all the crystal animals had been tossed to the floor. Pat had the same ones; Paula had loved them as a child. 'Not a burglary,' she said. 'This is deliberate, and targeted. Someone wanted Kenny's house ruined, and smashing the pictures of the kids – that's just callous. I'd say there was more than one person. He's a big guy, and he'd have put up quite a fight. Did you find any weapons?'

'A revolver in the kitchen cabinet. The door was open, and some of the china broken, as if he'd been trying to get into it.'

'So he was overpowered, dragged out. They'd have had some kind of van – maybe there are tracks.'

'Yes, we're photographing them now.'

'I suppose none of the neighbours saw anything?'

'They never do in this country,' sighed Guy. His phone buzzed and he looked at it; sighed again. 'Another meeting. The mayor going missing is getting a lot more attention than some washed-up dissidents.'

She looked at him, the hint of grey in his fair hair, the curve of his chin above the sharp tie and suit. She thought back to what Corry had said about the unit – *he doesn't tell you everything, you know.* Wondered how much that was true.

'So, any thoughts?' he said, removing his gloves.

She moved her foot away from a broken crystal duck, which was casting fractured rainbows on the wall. 'Someone will know who did this. That's what's frustrating – it's so close. You can almost feel them. They're not even trying to hide.' She looked around again. 'There's bound to be forensics here – this is too messy to be professional. Hairs, fibres – even blood, maybe, with all this smashing. But it might be too late for Kenny, even if we find him.'

'Why do you say that?'

She gestured to the mess of his family photos. 'Well, look. Someone *really* hates him.'

Extract from *The Blood Price: The Mayday Bombing and its Aftermath*, by Maeve Cooley (Tairise Press, 2011)

It's a common belief in the rest of the UK that 'the Troubles' in Ireland are long over. It's true to an extent that people now feel safe to walk the streets. We have a regional government who spend at least some time on issues like healthcare and schooling. There have been only – only – three police officers killed since 'peace'.

The Mayday bombing was, we are led to believe, an accident – intending to hit commercial targets, and perhaps kill a few Orangemen as they marched in the town. Due to the early detonation and bungled warning, which led police to group evacuees right near the blast centre, there were unfortunately civilian casualties. This is the view taken by Ireland First.

The most shocking aspect of the bomb is that it wasn't the end. These groups are still operating. They still have weapons, and funding, and support. In 2010 over three hundred devices were found and defused in Northern Ireland, many of which had the capacity to cause serious explosions. Though the majority of people in Ireland simply want an end to funerals, to blood running in the streets, to dead children and ruptured lives, there are some, like those behind Ireland First, who will never give up. Not even the 'accidental' murder of sixteen people stopped them. Not even a criminal trial. Not even killing babies and blinding children and burning people alive. It beggars the question of what, short of their deaths, would actually convince these people to cease their murderous campaign.

Chapter Twenty-One

'Right, everyone. Now Kenny has gone, I can't stress enough how much pressure we're under to solve this. I'm afraid we're looking at overtime for the foreseeable future. Let's review what we know.'

Fiacra was squinting as Guy spoke, trying to piece together the clues. Paula's own head hurt. Guy was scribbling things on the whiteboard – he'd learned this in some management class and insisted on it, even though the rest took the piss behind his back.

'So we have Dominic Martin's van, the clues leading to the families . . . the notebook and so on, and the fact there was obviously some important occurrence at the end of March, when John Lenehan stepped down. From what the Walshes say, it's possible Kenny and the families were working together – however far-fetched that seems.'

'And Flaherty knew he was going somewhere,' Paula said. 'He may not have known where, or when . . . but he said goodbye to his daughter.'

Guy nodded. 'Right. Corry wants us to go back to Flaherty's house to see if we can find any clues about why he wasn't in the van with the Walshes. He was definitely in the caves, we found his DNA. So why did they not pick him up with the others? And how did he know to change his will before he disappeared?'

'But none of the others knew they were going,' Gerard said. 'Except for that text of Ni Chonnaill's – but it mightn't of been her, of course.'

'I think someone knew she had children and wanted to make sure they were all right, even though they were kidnapping their mother.' Paula tried to work it out. 'I wish we knew who fathered her third child. If you remember the court testimony, Lynch called her a whore a few times – maybe she cheated on him while they were together. If we knew it might give us a lead.'

'How'd we know who to test, though?' said Fiacra grouchily. 'Do you not, like, need the fella's DNA to prove it?'

This conversation was the last one she wanted to be having right now. 'Yes. But perhaps we could screen any men she knew, work colleagues and so on, her former boyfriends. Someone will have an idea.'

'That'll be more work for me, I suppose,' Gerard grumbled. 'Seeing as you can hardly drag yourself round the office, let alone out on interviews.'

Guy shot him a look. 'I'll see about getting you some back-up, DC Monaghan.' His eyes lingered on Fiacra, then he seemed to think better of it. There was Bob, of course, but he was suspended and could hardly be sent to interview Republican families. That was the hard part of Guy's job, skipping over the tripwires of religion, politics, and the grim, looming past. An outsider, he did it with aplomb – one of the many things she admired about him. 'Anything else?' He held his pen poised near the whiteboard. The surface had become a tangle of clues and connections, nothing making any sense. 'We need some new angles, and fast. I'm having to justify our work on this to the Chief Constable, and so far I've got nothing to say.'

Paula heard herself say, 'The best thing to do would be to keep on looking. Bring in aerial search teams if we have to. The others have to be somewhere, if they're still alive.' Searching was expensive, and often fruitless, but it was either that or go back to interrogating people who'd had their hearts torn right out of them, and she just didn't think she could do that any more.

Luckily, at that point, Avril stuck her head into the room. 'Everyone, you're wanted up the hill. DCI Corry has Dominic Martin under arrest. They've matched samples from his shoes to the mineral from the caves, and they've lifted Lily Sloane for questioning too.'

Even in the unflattering lighting of Ballyterrin police station, Lily Sloane was beautiful, her skin luminous, her hair shining under the fluorescents. She was wearing jeans and Uggs and chewing on a fingernail. She looked up when Gerard and Paula went in – Corry had decided it was best to continue the rapport they'd supposedly built up, even though last time this had resulted in Lily crying.

'Hi, Lily. Are you OK?' asked Paula.

'Well, not really. What am I doing here?'

'We've arrested Dominic, I'm afraid. We just need to ask you a few questions about him.'

'What sort of questions?'

Gerard sat down, clearly trying to curb his usual hard-man approach. 'I'm sorry. We need to check where everyone was on the day the Mayday Five disappeared. It's called eliminating from enquiries. He's already told us he doesn't have an alibi. But if Dominic messaged you that day, say, or if you spoke to him, it might help us let him go. Do you see? Would he have texted you?'

'Not while driving,' she said, stern.

Gerard almost smiled. 'Of course not. But during stops? Do you keep his messages?'

She looked blank. 'Messages?'

'Your texts,' said Paula, getting a little tired of Lily's ingénue act. The girl was twenty-three, after all, not fifteen.

'I get loads,' she said vaguely. 'My phone doesn't keep them after a week or so. They like get erased.'

'The phone company should have them.'

'I don't know.' Lily went back to chewing on her nails.

'Do you remember where Dominic was on the first of April?' Gerard was still pushing on.

'When was that?' Lily was vague, distracted.

'When the Mayday bombers went missing.'

'Duh. I mean, like how long ago?'

'It was a month ago, Lily,' said Paula, shifting forward. The baby rolled with her. 'You need to tell us if you know anything. It could be very serious if you don't and we find out later you lied. Dominic says he was out on the road that day. Were you with him?'

'I don't go with him,' she said, sulkily. 'I've got my college course. Probably I was there.'

'Do they take attendance?'

'Yeah. Usually.'

'So we can check if you were there.'

'You could if you could be bothered.'

Paula and Gerard exchanged a glance. Paula began to speak quietly. 'Lily. I know you want to protect Dominic. I know you've all been through hell. But three people have been murdered, and another three are missing, and we have to follow that up, no matter who they were. We have a lot of evidence linking Dominic to the crimes. He might go to prison for a long time. You can help him.'

Lily was staring at the table, her long hair pooling on it. 'How?' she said in a small voice.

'Tell us everything you know.'

With trembling hands, Lily was reaching under the table into the rear pocket of her jeans. She unlocked her phone with a click and passed it to Paula. 'Look. I want you to.'

Paula scrolled up the message list, trying not to read them but getting a general impression of smileys and kisses from Lily, a more restrained tone from Dominic. Contrary to what Lily had said, they went all the way back to 1st April. There were several from that day, but all from Lily asking where he was and was he missing her, the kisses gradually dropping off as the day went on, culminating in CALL ME PLEASE.

Paula looked up. Lily's head was drooping, so her caramel hair pooled on her lap. 'Did he ever call?'

'Later. He got busy, he said. He doesn't like to answer when he's driving. He's . . . he's very good.'

'Lily.'

A small sob came in answer. 'What will happen to him?'

'Well, we can check his phone data. He might have made business calls that day. And we can talk to his customers – he keeps records?'

'He writes it down in a little book. But some days he just goes up into the hills to see where they can put a windmill or something.'

'A wind turbine?'

Lily was anxious now, wanting to help. 'Yeah. One of those things. Can you check that?'

'I'm sure we can. Now one last time, Lily – if you know anything about these disappearances, you really have to tell me now. You might have seen that the mayor is also missing now, and we think it's connected. It's very serious.'

'I – I don't know anything.'

Gerard jumped on it. 'Ms Sloane, please tell us. Have you ever heard Dominic or anyone else talk about revenge, anything like that?'

'It'll help Dominic if I tell you?'

'Of course.'

'Well – I don't know if this has anything to do with it. I don't go to all the meetings. I have college and stuff. But one time I went – it was after the court case all fell through, you know. There was talk in the meeting about what to do next. John was in charge. You know old John. He always talks to me like I'm five. Anyway, Dominic stood up and he started shouting. He said we had to do something. Did John not understand these people had killed his child, and was he supposed to sit back and take it? John said they'd killed his child too – you know, Danny, that was his son, he was at my school – but there wasn't anything left to do. All the money was spent and they just had to leave it in God's hands. Dominic said where was God when his wee girl was dying under him.'

'And what did John say?'

Lily's face was streaked with tears on one side. She'd put on heavy make-up to see them, thick mascara on her one good eye. It was a terrible thing to see, someone with one missing eye trying to cry out of it. Paula knew it was unprofessional, but she moved to the other side of the table and awkwardly put her arm round the girl.

'He said . . . he said he didn't know where God was,

and if he thought about it too much he'd lose his faith, and he couldn't because that was all he had left now. That's all I know. Honest.'

Paula looked at Gerard over the girl's shaking shoulders. He nodded reluctantly. 'Come on, Lily,' she said. 'Let's get you a cup of tea or something.'

'Can I go home?' she sniffed.

'You can go home for now, yes.'

As she led Lily into the reception area, the girl bolted and ran into the arms of a woman wearing an expensive jumper and jeans, who from the resemblance had to be her mother, Katrine. Only forty-five herself, she had shorter, highlighted blonde hair, and the same turquoise eyes as Lily – except hers were intact.

'Mum!'

'What's going on here?' Katrine Sloane fixed them with a cold glare over her daughter's shoulder. Lily was several inches taller. 'How dare you arrest her without me or her father?'

'She's twenty-three, ma'am,' said Gerard, following behind. 'It's perfectly legal. Anyway, she wasn't under arrest, we were just questioning her.'

'I'm not saying it's illegal,' she snapped. 'I'm talking about basic human decency. Have you people no idea what my daughter's been through?'

'Just take me home,' Lily wept, her voice muffled in her mother's shoulder. 'Please, Mum. Get me out of here.'

Gerard looked at Paula again, sighed. 'Corry wants you to observe the interview with Martin.'

'Mr Martin,' said Corry briskly. 'I'm sorry we've had to take you in today. We're sympathetic to your loss, please believe that.' She was sitting across the table from him, Gerard at her side. Paula was watching from outside the room.

He sat relaxed in his chair, watching Corry from his green eyes. He wore jeans and a blue T-shirt with paint on it. 'But I'm here in the interview room.'

'It's unavoidable. You were caught on camera making death threats to people who later turn up murdered. You own a van of the same description as one seen at the crime scenes, which we are reliably informed was used to pick up the victims – and one of them actually died in it. You must see we had to bring you in.'

'It was stolen,' said Martin calmly. 'Terrible time, when you can't leave a vehicle without it being stolen.'

Gerard leaned in. 'Bit of a coincidence, isn't it? With your link to the bombers.'

He met their gazes steadily. 'Could be I was targeted. An easy suspect.'

Corry made an impatient gesture. 'There's reported stolen and there's stolen, Mr Martin. I think we both know the difference, so let's not waste each other's time. You had the means to carry out the kidnap and we found mineral traces from one of the crime scenes on your shoes, the sea caves down at the coast.'

He eased back in his chair. 'Well, I go there a lot. I used to take my daughter. Amber. She's dead now, so I go alone.'

Corry looked at him closely. 'I was working that day,' she said, changing her tone. 'I was in the control room when the warning came in. We missed it.'

He said nothing, but his jaw tightened almost imperceptibly.

'I just wanted you to know,' she went on. 'The dispatcher

who missed the warning lost her job. Of course, we get hundreds of threats all the time. There was no code word and the warning was vague. But it was in my power to stop it, Mr Martin. It was in my power to save Amber, and I didn't. I'm so sorry.'

He looked away – score one for Corry. 'It was no one's fault but the people who primed and set the bomb,' he said. 'I've never blamed anyone else.'

'But still. We felt responsible. My supervisor put a gun in his mouth.'

Dominic almost smiled. It was one of the most chilling things Paula had ever seen. 'Collateral damage,' he said.

Corry stiffened. 'I'm sorry?'

'That was the phrase they used, wasn't it? The Ireland First lot. They hadn't meant for children or women to die – that was just unfortunate. There'd been – what was the phrase they used?' He paused as if trying to recall. 'I can't remember.'

Corry watched him. 'I'm not sure what you mean, Mr Martin.'

'Oh, I'm sure you do. It was reported quite widely in the press. They got their voices heard, that lot. My daughter meanwhile had barely learned to talk. She could say three words. Do you know what they were? One was "doggy". One was "no".'

'Mr Martin—'

'The other was "dada". A daddy's girl even then – well. Do you have children?'

Corry ignored him. 'Where were you on the first of April, Mr Martin?'

'Out on the road, like I said. I was siting a new wind turbine. Planning laws, you know – it's a nightmare.'

'You were in your van?'

'Yes, of course. Can't get my equipment in the Lotus.'

'You were in your white transit van.'

'Yes.'

'Alone.'

'I work alone, yes, and the reception up there is dire.' He smiled. 'Not that more masts are the answer.'

Corry put a picture on the table. 'For the tape, I'm showing Mr Martin image forty-two, a white transit van proceeding down Bluebell Road, home of the deceased Callum Brady. Is that your van, Mr Martin?'

'It's hard to say.'

'Why is it?'

'You can't see the registration. It's been covered up.'

'I'm aware of that. What I'm asking is if you were driving on that road on April the first – the day when Callum Brady and the other four suspects went missing.'

'I can't say. Who can remember where they go?'

'Mr Martin, we have witnesses. The two brothers who went with you that day – Joseph and Danny Walsh. The men Jarlath Kenny sent to help you. They'll testify they were in your van. But if you cooperate it might go easier on you. Tell us where they are – Kenny, and Flaherty, and Catherine Ni Chonnaill. She has three children, you know. They don't deserve to be orphaned, whatever their mother may have done.'

'Who are the Walshes?' he said, frowning. 'Never heard of them.'

'You're denying all this?'

'My van was searched after it got torched. There was nothing to link me to the case, no forensics, nothing, isn't that right?'

'Not that we could find. There's the shoes.'

'That's circumstantial and you know it. You've inter-viewed me already, DCI Corry. I've cooperated. We all have – we've let you into our homes, even though we know you're trying to find the people who murdered our loved ones. Are you going to charge me? Because if you are, I'd like you to get on with it. Use these witnesses that you say you have.'

'You made threats after the trial. To kill the Mayday Five.'

'I was upset. They murdered my wee girl and they walked free. You'd feel the same.'

She watched him for a long time. 'I might feel the same, Mr Martin, and I might even say it, but I wouldn't ever do it.'

'Why not?' he asked, with what looked like genuine interest. 'If you'd nothing to lose. If a prison sentence didn't frighten you.'

'I don't have it in me,' said Corry. 'I'm a rule-follower. Always have been.'

'That's a shame. For you.'

'And for you,' said Corry. 'I'm sympathetic, but I don't do allowances, Mr Martin. There's been far too much of that in this country. I do the law and nothing but.'

He smiled. 'I'm glad to hear it. No doubt you wouldn't have made mistakes and blunders, like the police and Gardai who let the case collapse against my daughter's killers.'

She watched him, seeming to come to some decision. 'OK, Mr Martin,' she said. 'We aren't going to charge you. Not yet anyway. You're free to go.'

'Thank you. Could I have my jacket please?' He clicked

his fingers as he stood up. 'Oh, I remember what the phrase was. "Unforeseen escalation." Isn't that what they said, in the Ireland First statement? There was an unforeseen escalation.'

Corry didn't turn a hair. 'If you say so, Mr Martin. I don't have a memory for such things myself. I'll send an officer to show you out.'

'Thank you.' And he smiled right at the camera, as if he knew they were all watching there, looking out for a slip-up and finding absolutely none.

Thump, thump, thump. Paula heard the noise before she saw it. She'd just arrived back at the station to get some files, bone-weary from dragging the baby around all day.

Avril was standing in the yard outside the unit building, shivering in a light blouse and grey skirt. She had the lid open on the large blue bin and was systematically throwing things into it from a cardboard box at her feet. Paula recognised in her gestures a certain desperate theatricality. 'What are you doing?'

Thud. Another item went in. 'Getting rid of these.'

Bridal magazines, Paula could now see. The smiling women, perfect-teethed, shiny-eyed, elaborately coiffed, clutching flowers and generally looking as if they couldn't take one more bit of happiness or they might explode in a puff of taffeta and lace. 'The wedding stuff? Why?'

'It's not happening.' Thump, thump. The smiling women disappeared under the mounds of old teabags and sandwich wrappings in the bin.

'What? Are you joking me?'

'Of course I'm not joking! Alan wouldn't believe me about Gerard, and he said some awful things about, about religion and that. Unforgivable things. I never knew I was engaged to a bigot, I said.'

Paula glanced at Avril's hand, which was indeed still bare of the sparkler that had adorned it, save for a reddened band of skin. 'Are you OK?'

'Yes! It's for the best. I can't marry him if he's a bigot, can I?'

'And your family?'

'It doesn't matter about my family!' She stopped her throwing and ran an angry hand across her face. 'I thought you might understand, at least. I mean you didn't . . . and you had . . .'

'I do understand. Hey, if it's not right you should definitely break if off. As long as you're sure.'

Avril sounded miserable. 'I'm not sure. How can you be?'

'I've no idea. If I can make a suggestion, Avril, the best thing to do at a time like this is . . .'

'What? Don't say pray. I get enough of that at home.'

'No. I was going to say – have a drink. Then have another one. Then another, until you feel better.'

'You mean go into a pub? On my *own*?'

'Well, or get a bottle of wine in the shop.'

'Mammy wouldn't let me. She'd call in the minister to get me exorcised or something. They don't really drink at all.'

If she wasn't so heavily pregnant, Paula would have taken her to the pub and fed some drink into her. Though the idea of boozing with Bob Hamilton's niece, who was from a hardcore temperance family, did make her mind boggle a bit. 'Trust me. It will help. There are worse ways. But I'm sure you're doing the right thing.'

THE SILENT DEAD

'Thanks.' Avril's lip was trembling. 'I'm sorry to be so . . . when your friend isn't well. I know it's not important, not really.'

'It's OK.' Paula still hadn't been back to visit Maeve. She knew she should, but she hadn't, and despite her own excuses about how busy the case was, she knew this was not the real reason. 'I'm sorry about your uncle too. I didn't . . . I never meant for that to happen.'

'It's – let's not talk about it. I know you had your reasons.'

'Yeah.'

Avril had come to the end of her pile of magazines and was shivering in her thin cotton top. 'Did they let him go? Dominic Martin?'

'They had to. We can't link him to anything, not solidly, anyway.'

'So . . . what do we do now?'

Paula wasn't sure if she meant the case, or something wider. Either way the answer was the same. 'I have absolutely no idea.'

Kira

Sometimes she couldn't believe it was really happening. So long spent so angry – why did they get away with it? Why did they kill Rose and walk around laughing, filling up their cars, going to their children's schools? She'd once ripped out an article about them from the paper and kept it under her mattress. Every day she looked at it, the Five, their faces, running her eyes over and over the pictures in case she ever saw them in town. Waking up, fumbling to look at it one more time, panicking she couldn't remember. Doyle, lighting a cigarette. Lynch waiting at a bus stop. Brady on an undercover camera, making bets in a bookies' shop. Flaherty at the BP garage. And the woman, worst of all – she had two wee kids with her, one in her arms and one by the hand. Their faces had been blanked out but you could see it was a boy and a girl.

One day Kira came home from school and her bed was stripped and the article was gone, and Mammy never mentioned it and neither did she. It was too late anyway. She could see their faces when she closed her eyes. She was ready for it to happen.

Other things went by. They announced the trial, and some of the families were happy and some said only hanging was good enough, but no one expected it would all fall through because of something Kira didn't understand about warrants and phones and tampering, and she didn't understand, honestly could not take it in, how the defence lawyers could find this out and why it mattered. She'd wanted to go in and shout at the judge – *Come on! It's not fair! One stupid hour out on the warrant thing!*

She hadn't been allowed to go into the court, so on the day of the verdict she'd sat in the old-fashioned café in the courthouse and sprinkled too much chocolate on her cappuccino to make it less bitter, and watched people coming and going. When it all ended there'd been a big shout and people had started coming out, filling the space. Kira's heart had started to hammer. She went out, pushing through the people, trying to hear what had happened.

Tears on faces. She couldn't see Mammy. There was lots of shouting and she was afraid, so afraid. Then she saw Dominic, behind a big crowd of reporters and cameras, and he was crying and shouting. 'It's a travesty. My daughter. They killed my daughter. They should be killed too. They're like animals. They should be strung up.'

Kira had pushed her way over to him, through all the scrum. He was trying to move to the door, some woman in a suit running after him. 'Leave me! You're as bad as the lawyers. Bloody vultures, feasting off our loss. Get away.' He was walking away, almost running out of court. He just kept walking. Soon the reporters tailed off, muttering. But Kira could run. She had her trainers on. She followed him down to the waterfront and over the bridge. He was clutching the rails and his face was frozen. He saw her. 'Kira— you shouldn't be here.'

She was panting. 'I heard you. I think it too. They should be punished. Eye for an eye. We should punish them. We can. They got off. I agree with you. They say about God and forgiveness – well, I don't want a God who forgives them. We should punish them, Dominic. We should show them what they did to us.'

She could see he wasn't listening. She realised she was crying. 'I want to punish them, but I can't! I'm too small, I'm not strong, I'm afraid – but I want to punish them. You have to help me.'

Dominic put his hands over his face, scrunching them into his eyes. When he took them away, his face had a different expression.

Chapter Twenty-Two

'He'd made a bit of money for himself then,' said Guy.

'Must have done. Left his Beemer behind and all.'

Flaherty's silver BMW sat outside his house, collecting leaves and dust. The house was large, with white pillars at the front and a sweep of garden containing a wishing well and a pond with gnomes around it. Paula thought it pretty tacky, but it was clear that the man had done well for himself. It was less clear how – the other members of the Mayday Five were all struggling, working in dead-end jobs or not at all. After the bombing, the local Republican movement had made sure they were frozen out, unwelcome in their own town. But then every report on Flaherty had mentioned his charisma, the strength of his presence.

Guy was snapping on gloves and handed her a pair. 'Let's go in. I want your first impressions on anything of note. We need to get inside his head.'

She almost shuddered. A man who'd mastermind the murder of children, refuse to apologise for it, then fill his garden with plaster gnomes? She wasn't sure she wanted to be anywhere near his head.

Inside the air lay heavy, undisturbed for several weeks. It had been left clean, every item of furniture aligned, but dust was settling on the window blinds and hall table. In the kitchen, which was marble and steel, no dishes sat out.

The fridge was empty, several letters pinned to it. Paula stood looking about her while the search team fanned out into the rest of the house, overturning cushions and pulling pictures away from the wall. There wasn't anything much. An old map of Ireland, framed. There were no pictures of his wife or of Flaherty himself. The television was neat, all the leads tucked away in brackets, and one of the chairs still had its plastic covers on.

'Any thoughts?' Guy was standing in the bathroom door, a set of scales in his gloved hands.

She shook her head and moved forward to open some of the cupboards, feeling her bump press against the counter. Not much in them – cereal, tubs containing teabags and instant coffee, sugar. Again everything was neatly arranged. She wondered if that was what made Flaherty so good at what he did. He was organised. He knew where to find things. He left no loose ends. And he'd killed; he'd killed so many people you would expect blood to drip from his feet as he walked.

She turned to the notices on the fridge, pinned up with magnets, one in the shape of Ireland, made out of Connemara Marble. The kind of thing a grandchild might give, which made her wonder again about how much Flaherty had really seen his daughter over the years. One was a flyer about recycling collections. A library schedule – her mind failed slightly at the idea of Flaherty checking out large-print paperbacks – and the last thing had a logo on it that she recognised, having spent rather more time than she wanted looking at it recently. She ran her gloved fingers over the typeface.

'Sir?' she called. Best to call him by his title around the other officers, strange as it felt. He reappeared. 'There's a letter from the hospital here. An appointment for next week.'

'Interesting. Could be proof he didn't plan to disappear at all.'

'I don't know.' She examined it. 'Dr Andrew Fuller. It says oncology department.'

'Flaherty had cancer?'

She scanned the letter. 'Stage four, Guy. He was dying.'

Guy was digging out his phone. 'This could change things.'

Her mind was racing. She knew they'd find no more from this sterile house – someone had left the place clean, swept, locked up. But this, leaving a letter out, with something so red-hot on it . . .

'I think we were meant to find this,' she said.

Guy nodded. 'I think you're right. But why?'

'Someone's trying to send a message. Add this to what the Walshes had to say about there being four bombers in the van . . . Maybe that Flaherty wasn't kidnapped at all? Maybe he's out there, on the run?'

'So why was his DNA in the caves then?'

She shook her head, frustrated. 'I don't know. But I think this is deliberate.'

'So do I. And if so, I wonder how much of the rest we were meant to find as well.'

Paula's father was in the kitchen when she got home that evening, brushing the floor up into a dustpan. 'You shouldn't be doing that, with your leg.' He looked well, she thought, his face fuller than it had been when she'd moved back eight months ago to find him living alone in the gloomy terraced house, existing on toast and biscuits.

Though it wasn't very flattering that he seemed to think she couldn't so much as wash up a cup by herself – even if it was close to the truth.

'Well, pet.' He emptied the dustpan into the bin. 'What were you about?'

'Just work.' She busied herself putting away some dishes from the rack – she knew he'd have dried them up and put them away immediately. 'Long day.'

'You're still looking for those Ireland First scumbags then?'

'Yeah. Well, the ones that haven't turned up dead yet. How's Pat?'

'Ah, she's grand. Young Aidan was down for his tea the other night. Seems the paper's doing well again.'

'Mmm.'

'You've seen him yourself?'

'The odd time.' She kept her voice light. PJ didn't seem to know what to say. She wondered if Pat had sent him on a fishing expedition. 'What brings you over?'

'Oh! I thought I'd measure up for the builders.' She saw there was a tape measure on the side.

'Are they actually going to do it then?'

'Who knows with those fellas? They're all working in Dublin these days.'

The long-term plan was to get the cupboards replaced, rip up the old lino and put in wooden floors. All the things a young family would expect if buying it, and hopefully they'd not remember what had happened there in 1993. After that Paula didn't know what she'd do – move somewhere else in Ballyterrin, or go back to London with her baby. She couldn't seem to think beyond her due date.

She took her jacket off and put it on the chair; then

thought better of it and picked it up again before her father could make a comment about hanging it on the proper peg. 'Is . . . do you know if Maeve is OK? I mean, I thought Pat might have been down to see her.'

'She's much the same, I think. No worse, anyway.'

'That's good. I need to go, but . . . work . . .'

Her father seemed to understand. 'She'll be grand, I'm sure.'

'How's life at Pat's?'

'It's grand. Haven't seen you for a while. You never call down.'

'Busy with work.' The truth was that the more time she spent in their house, the more Pat would then start acting like the coming baby's grandmother, and Aidan would be hanging around, and then the blissful denial she'd been keeping up about the paternity test matter would crumble apart. 'Did you come up just to clean the place?'

Looking around, it did need a good scrub, but she had neither the time nor the energy. She thought about what had happened that week – she'd got one of her colleagues suspended while they looked into the possibility he'd deliberately kept back evidence in the case of Margaret Maguire, aged thirty-seven, who'd gone missing on 28th October 1993. If only she could keep it behind those words, safe, screened off. She couldn't begin to tell her father. He didn't officially even know she had the file, except he probably did, in that space somewhere between people who know each other too well.

'Not really. I needed to talk to you. You better sit down, pet.'

Nothing good was ever prefaced with those words, *you better sit down*. It was as bad as 'we need to talk'. Paula folded her arms. 'It takes me five minutes to get up again. I'll stand. What's wrong?'

'I had a call from the PSNI this afternoon. About the case you're working on.'

'Oh yeah? You're lucky, they keep trying to send me home.'

PJ leaned the brush against the wall. 'They found a body,' he said.

'Another one? Flaherty?' She was getting annoyed. 'I can't believe they didn't tell me after last time. I was only at his place today as well.'

'A woman.'

'Oh no. It's Catherine? Is . . . is she dead?'

'It's not her. Paula, it's an older body. They phoned me.'

It took a long time for the understanding to travel up her spine and into her brain. They thought it was her mother. A body the right age. 'Where?' she asked, when she could speak.

'On the beach at Mallin sands. The search team were looking there for your other two bombers.'

A well-known IRA burial place. A car park development ten years before had yielded up two decomposed bodies, bound and gagged, shot in the skull execution-style. Families pleased to have answers at last. It was a fucked-up world when you were glad to find the mutilated body of your loved one. It was a fucked-up Northern Irish world. Paula realised she hadn't said anything for a while. PJ was brushing non-existent dust off the counters.

'I want to see,' she heard herself say. 'I want to identify her.'

'Ah, pet. You're about ready to pop. You don't want to be standing around the morgue in your condition.' But she could tell his heart wasn't in dissuading her. He knew it wouldn't work.

'I mean it. I'll be fine. I need to know.'

PJ just nodded. 'We'll both go then. First thing tomorrow.'

Paula had been to the morgue a few times before, supporting families, watching their reactions when they were suspects, and on training. She was well used to the smell of bleach and blood and told herself she was just going to find it all interesting instead of upsetting. Posters on the wall. Grime on the windows of the waiting room, a cross on the wall. A prayer room provided, in case you were of different faith. They were very modern in the Northern Ireland Forensic Pathology Service.

PJ sat two seats down from her, arms folded, eyes on the grey-tiled ceiling. One tile was missing in the corner, like a knocked-out tooth. Paula's fingers roamed over her stomach, trying to cling to the solidity of it. She was grimly aware that Maeve was upstairs in the hospital, still in the ICU, and Aidan probably hanging over her bedside. On the table in the waiting room was a folded newspaper. The front cover carried the faces of the Mayday Five – three of them dead now. Paula turned her head back to the ceiling.

'Mr Maguire. Miss Maguire.' The attendant wore scrubs, and spoke in the hushed tones of a top-end spa employee. She thought about saying, *It's Doctor,* just to be a bitch. How dare she, with her kind brown eyes behind glasses and her little ponytail. How dare she be nice.

PJ was up. Shit, she had to get up too. She found the corridor endless and at the same time nowhere near long enough.

The chief pathologist, a white-haired man, knew PJ, it seemed. He was shaking hands and murmuring. 'Paula,' he said, turning to her. 'I remember you when you were wee.'

What to say to that? They were outside a room with a long window like they had at the station. Inside something lay on a gurney under a blue sheet. A white-masked attendant stood by.

'Are you ready?' asked the pathologist.

What a question. As if you could ever be ready to see a dead body that was possibly your mother. It was all happening so fast. She'd expected a fair amount of bureaucratic faffing around. But it was happening. Right now.

The sheet was going back. PJ gripped the windowsill. Paula tried to take it in from the head down.

The hair was red, but with a ginger tint. Hard to tell if it could have turned that way after death.

The face was gone. A brown, gaping skeleton, scraps of leathery flesh still attached.

One ear remained, in it a hoop earring.

The body was emaciated, some skin remaining, pale as maggots.

Paula had braced herself for the moment when something she saw made the realisation come. *It's her, it's her.* It didn't come. She stared at the body, frustrated. PJ caught her eye and she shrugged. He twisted his mouth. 'I'm afraid we can't say for sure, Simon.'

'We can let you see her clothes, if that would help.'

Do I have to, Paula wanted to say. *I've already looked, I already faced the prospect it could be her.* But they were uncovering another gurney and again she was looking. As soon as she saw the clothes, a wave of relief swamped her. She didn't know these things. Any of them. A denim skirt, torn bomber jacket. The items cheap, sad and soil-stained. Paula shook her head. 'I don't think she'd wear anything like this.' Have worn. Hard to know what tense to use.

'She had her ears pierced,' said the assistant, reading from the clipboard. 'And she'd broken her left arm some years before.'

Paula looked at her father, who shook his head. 'She never broke her arm that I knew of.'

'So . . .' Paula was reluctant to let herself say it. 'No, then?'

'From what you're saying, it's unlikely this is the body of Margaret Maguire,' said the assistant. And why would she say it any differently? The name meant nothing to her.

'Who is it then?'

'We don't know.'

Paula was so used to it the other way around – someone went missing and you didn't know where they were – that this baffled her. 'You don't know?'

'It happens a lot. Some we never identify at all.'

'But aren't people looking for her?'

'You'd be surprised. People wash off boats, for example, or they drift about the continent. If they have families, sometimes they'll have no idea the person was even in Ireland. You can't look for someone when you haven't the foggiest what country they're in.'

PJ was buttoning his jacket. 'Let's go, pet.'

'OK, but—' She looked back at the forlorn array of clothes. 'What will happen to her?'

'We'll carry on looking. Sometimes we can source the clothes to another country and look in their files. She'll stay in the morgue for now, and at some point maybe we'll bury her.'

'It doesn't seem right.'

'I know. I can't think of anything worse than being lost and no one even looking for you.' The assistant pushed back her glasses. 'I'm sorry you didn't find what you needed, Miss Maguire. But there's always hope.'

'I'm not sure about that,' Paula muttered.

She thought it was rubbish, in fact, but the assistant smiled slightly. 'Until you're in here, anyway, there's always hope.'

Paula couldn't face talking about it any further. It was there between her and her father, the dead woman on the table, her face eaten away, the nearness of it – today could have been the day they knew for sure, Margaret was dead. Today could have been the day they took her bones and buried them and sold the house, finally, and Paula got on with her life, had her baby, stopped digging up the past with its worms and dirt and secrets. But it hadn't been.

She couldn't bear the idea of going back home, her mother's ghost still hovering, so she was glad when she spotted a familiar face in the waiting room on their way out. 'Dad, would you mind getting a taxi back to Pat's? I need to do something here. There's a rank out the front of the hospital – do you mind? Sorry.'

PJ passed her the car keys. 'Aye, OK, but pet, would you not be better off taking a break after that?'

'No.' A break would mean having to think about what she'd just seen. And not seen. 'There's someone I want to talk to.'

Lorcan Finney rose from the plastic seats as she went back into the waiting room. 'Dr Maguire. I thought I should be here when you came, to explain what happened. We were able to locate the body using geothermal equipment, which shows up disturbed ground. We were thinking obviously it would be one of the bombers, but then a different suggestion was made. I'm sorry it wasn't the right one. But we'll keep on trying to find out who this is.'

She was nodding but she wasn't listening.

Finney was watching her intently with his violet-blue eyes. 'Look, if you don't mind me saying, you seem like you should sit down. You're as pale as a sheet.'

She let him lead her into a small private room and return with tea in Styrofoam cups, tasting of nothing but plastic. She felt the bland heat fill her mouth, providing some comfort, until she could speak again. Wordlessly, he reached out and took her wrist, feeling her pulse. She felt the warmth of his rough hand on her skin, smelled the citrus tingle of his aftershave. She wondered again about him and Corry. Was she right? Corry would never tell her even if she was. Gently, she disengaged her hand from his.

'Sorry. You're just so pale, and with the baby . . .'

'I didn't think you were a medical doctor,' she said weakly.

'I have some basic training. I was out in Afghanistan before I came here, helping to look for mass graves.'

That got her attention. 'Really? So you do know all about disturbed ground.'

'More than I'd like to. That's why I've got some medical training – you need it somewhere like that.'

'How long have you been back?'

He drained his tea. 'Not long. Six months or so. There was a job going so I thought it was time to come home.'

Not long at all. She wondered how he was coping.

'Dr Maguire – your mother – has the case been reopened?'

'Not officially. There's no new evidence, not really. I just . . . can't leave it.'

'The IRA disappeared my father,' said Lorcan baldly. 'In the seventies. I was six.'

'I'm sorry. Did they ever find him?'

'He was dug up in the eighties by accident, on a building site. It would have been like this, I suppose. I – they didn't let me go to the funeral. My sister and I were split up when he died, put in care. She was adopted. They felt it was best.'

Paula fell silent. How lucky she'd been to have PJ, doing his ham-fisted best with school lunches and ironing her uniform. 'I'm sorry. That's awful.'

He just nodded. 'It's how it goes, isn't it? There's always collateral damage.'

She looked at him sideways, wondering if he'd used the phrase on purpose. 'I suppose.'

He raised his empty cup to her ironically. 'That's us, isn't it? Collateral damage in their bloody pointless war. And there's Kenny and his like in their suits, collecting their thirty pieces of silver, and we're just supposed to forget everything that happened back then.'

She stirred. 'Dr Finney . . .'

'Please, call me Lorcan.'

'OK. You can submit evidence to the forensics lab for testing, can you?'

'I can.'

'If I gave you a sample of handwriting, would you be able to have it analysed against the notes in the mouths?'

He looked at her, his eyes framed by sandy lashes. 'Did you get it through proper channels?'

'What do you think? I just want to check something. It's not official. We wouldn't be able to use it anyway.'

'All right.' He fished out an evidence bag from the pocket of his waterproof jacket, and she opened her notebook and tore out the strip that had Kira Woods' number written on it, in her loopy schoolgirl script.

Paula finished her plastic-tasting tea, and with difficulty, stood up. 'Thanks for this. And for listening. I have to be somewhere now.'

He watched her with his strange eyes. 'All right. Just look after yourself, Paula.'

Extract from *The Blood Price: The Mayday
Bombing and its Aftermath*, by Maeve Cooley
(Tairise Press, 2011)

In the course of writing this book, I have tried to interview each of the alleged bombers, in order to see how they can justify carrying on a struggle that has killed so indiscriminately. Last year I attended a fundraising meeting for Ireland First, which was held in a pub in County Monaghan. I there encountered Brady and Lynch, both trying to drum up cash and support. The former was intoxicated and shouted at me to 'Eff off, you Mexican bitch' (Mexican is what some residents north of the border call Southern Irelanders). Lynch was more persuasive, taking time to explain that they were defending Ireland from 'London rule by stealth' and honouring the legacy of the Republican dead. He is superficially plausible, and it's easy to see why many have fallen for his tall, fair good looks. I also spotted Doyle, who was chain-smoking outside the door, and refused to answer any of my questions or speak to me.

I asked them about the Mayday bombing, and Lynch simply said they had no comment on that. They'd been acquitted in court, and legally they had nothing further to say. I asked again how they could carry on fundraising after so many people had died. At this he became angry, pointing out there had been no 'evidentiary proof' of their involvement and that 'justice had prevailed'. I asked about the statement, where they used the words 'collateral damage', and he tried to remove me from the premises. I stood my ground, asking my questions again. We were then approached by a tall, grey-haired man, who I recognised as Martin Flaherty. 'Is there a problem?' Flaherty asked. Lynch said that I was a journalist who had come to 'spy' on them and 'write lies'.

Flaherty looked at me. He is very softly spoken, powerfully built for his fifty-five years. He could have been handsome in other circumstances. 'Ms Cooley, isn't it?' he said. 'It would be wise if you would leave now, please. This is a legal political meeting and your presence would not be welcome. Don't make us remove you.' I have interviewed many killers in my time, but I would be hard pressed to think of one more chilling than Flaherty, with his quiet voice and neatly pressed polo shirt. I left.

Chapter Twenty-Three

It was easy enough to find Bob Hamilton's address on the database. Security had eased since the days of regular car bombs, and the unit was considered something of a backwater. Bob lived in a white-washed bungalow in the Protestant end of town – the kerbstones painted red, white and blue and the Red Hand of Ulster flag flying over the nearby housing estates. She told herself not to be silly as she went to the door, down a neat garden path, garden gnomes fishing in a little pond. Just like at Flaherty's.

There was a ramp leading up to the frosted glass door, and Paula suddenly realised she had no idea who else Bob lived with. She remembered there was at least one child, but in truth she'd never really thought of Bob as a person with a life. She was vaguely ashamed of this fact as he opened the door, in a short-sleeved shirt and slacks. She'd never seen him before out of the suit he wore like uniform. 'Miss Maguire?' He looked baffled. 'What are you doing here?'

'Sergeant, I'm so sorry to land in on you. I need a quick word.'

She waited in the living room while he went to get her some water. It was very clean, a glass carriage clock on the mantelpiece ticking away, a piano in the corner left sitting with music on it. She wondered who played. She sat awkwardly on a velvet sofa, her feet digging into the thick cream carpet. It was a warm day and she could feel sweat patches seeping out from under the arms of her shirt.

She smiled uncomfortably as he came in, placing a glass of water on a coaster on a small table. He had nothing himself. 'You're feeling well?'

'Ah, I'm not too bad. Hot. You're all right?'

He looked blank. 'You know how it is. Lots to do round here.'

'I'm sure. The garden. It looks like it keeps you busy.'

'That's mostly Linda. The wife.'

Paula had a vague memory of Linda Hamilton coming when Paula's mother had disappeared, bringing buns or a casserole or something. Pretending her husband, PJ's former partner, wasn't the one investigating him. 'I'm sorry for what happened.'

He looked away. Said nothing.

Paula had drained the glass of water already. 'Bob – can I call you that? I really am sorry. It wasn't my intention. I just had to try everything, and you know – the baby coming, it makes it more urgent—' She stopped, a little ashamed of herself for playing the pregnancy card. Even if it was true. 'When Mrs Flynn told me what she'd seen, and that she'd made a statement – I just had to know if everything was done. Please believe me. I didn't mean it personally. At you, I mean.' Guilt was making her inarticulate.

Bob still wouldn't meet her eyes. 'Can I get you anything else, Miss Maguire?'

'Please, it's Paula. Will you call me that?'

He nodded stiffly and she knew he'd call her nothing at all now. 'I remember you back then. Your daddy and me – we spent a lot of time together and you'd be with him the odd time, in the car, you know, or if I had to call round to the house. You were just the same as you are now.'

She wasn't sure what this meant – angry? Difficult? 'You knew my mother, then? I mean before . . . all that.'

'A wee bit. To say hello to.'

'Did you – what did you think, when she went?'

Pause. 'I don't remember. We did our best for her. You have to remember, miss, the nineties, back then, it was very bad again for a while.'

'I do remember. I was thirteen.' It was the year before the IRA ceasefire. A last hurrah of shootings and bombings. She remembered only too well the sense of things falling apart, the backsliding, the helplessness.

'A lot of people go missing. You know that. Usually, they have their reasons. We had to do what seemed right at the time.'

'But why would she go?' Paula burst out. 'She was just a wife, a normal person. She was my mum.'

He examined the carpet closely. 'Sometimes, miss, the families aren't the people who can see the reasons. But the reasons are there all the same.'

She opened her mouth to say: what is it you're not telling me? He met her eyes and she saw it very plainly: *please don't ask me*. She swallowed. 'Look, the reason I came here – it's not right, that this happened. So I thought I could tell them. I'll tell Corry and Brooking, say I made a mistake, there was no statement from Mrs Flynn. I just – I just needed to know. I'm sorry.'

'We did what we thought was right at the time. That's all I can say.'

'Let me talk to them. Please.'

'There's no point. I'm getting on. I been working for the

police forty years now. Seen a lot of good people die. Seen two police forces. Maybe it's time I called it a day.'

'You mean . . . you'd resign? But we need you at the unit.'

'The unit. Miss – I don't want to speak out of turn, but you know as well as I do the unit's on borrowed time. Even now, this is our job, and have we found any of the Mayday lot? We have not. They're turning up dead. And why are we even looking for them? You weren't there that day, were you?'

'Mayday? No – I was in London.'

'Then I'm glad for you.'

'Was it as bad as they say?'

Bob didn't speak for a moment. 'No. It was worse.'

'Oh.'

'I wouldn't wish it on anyone, the things I saw that day. Linda . . .' He stopped. 'It took weeks to even wash all the blood off the floor, I'd walked in that much of it. So. You see. Sometimes you just have to say enough.' He got up. 'I hope you don't mind but I need to get on. Linda would like to say hello, though, before you go.'

She lumbered after him, mind swirling, noticing in distracted passing the Orange sash framed on the wall. Linda Hamilton was in the kitchen, which was filled with light. She was sitting down with a man in a wheelchair, feeding his lunch to him off a spoon. His head drooped onto his chest, hands curled in his lap.

Linda jumped up, setting down the bowl and spoon, which Paula saw now were plastic and decorated with cartoon characters. For a child, but this was a man. 'Hello, Paula!' She shook Paula's hand with her cool one. 'Look at you, all grown up.'

'How are you, Mrs Hamilton?'

'Oh, keeping well. And your daddy?'

'He's all right. Grand.' She didn't want to say he'd remarried, as that in itself raised a number of difficult questions.

'He must be glad to have you home from England.'

'Oh yes, it's lovely.' No mention was made of her bump – Bob had likely briefed her on the lack of father situation. Linda indicated the man in the chair. 'I don't know if you'd remember our Ian? I think you'd have met him once, there was a party at the station way back.'

She didn't. 'Hello, Ian.' Could he understand? There was no reaction. A thin stream of drool trailed from his mouth.

Linda beamed. 'You two are the same age and all.'

She remembered it vaguely now – the suggestion that Bob's son wasn't 'well' – something genetic, wasn't it, meaning there were no other kids, just Ian in his wheelchair?

'Well . . . I best be off now. Bye.'

After that Paula went. A heavy feeling dogged her steps to the car, and she remembered its taste in her mouth – shame. She was ashamed. Bob walked her out, courteously, shading his eyes in the sun. 'Take care driving now. I'll see you soon.'

She got into the car, leaving the door open. 'Was there a statement?' she asked, looking out at the road. 'Just tell me yes or no. I won't ask again. I promise. I can see that I . . . well, there's a lot I don't know, obviously. But I want to. I'm trying.'

'Sometimes it's better not to know.' His voice was neutral.

'Please,' she said again. 'I just need to know the statement existed, that it's not just . . . a lonely old lady getting confused. I need something concrete.'

Nothing. She looked up at him; he nodded shortly, almost looking away. Paula's hands contracted on the wheel. 'Thank you.' Her voice shook.

He stepped away. 'Safe home now, Miss Maguire.'

Paula jumped as the prison gates buzzed open, trying to stand up straight, her heart thudding as the locked-up bleach smell of the place surrounded her. She'd visited prisons many times before, of course. She'd even spent a year doing doctoral research in a high-security hospital. Men who'd grab you if you dropped your guard for so much as a second, men whose eyes crawled over your chest, who'd speculate in front of your boss about what your breasts looked like. This prison – a medium-security one for prisoners reaching the end of their sentence – should have been easy. But she'd never gone to one when heavily pregnant. And she'd never come face to face with the man who'd possibly been responsible for the disappearance of her mother.

The security guards of the prison, all cut from the same cloth of small-hard-Ballyterrin-man-with-moustache, did not know what to do with Paula at all. Trailing cardigans and scarves, red hair escaping from a plait, and her bump held out in front of her, she didn't quite fit in. They took a look at her and retreated for a lengthy discussion, which seemed to be about whether or not she could safely pass through the metal detector.

'Wait there a wee second, love,' one told her, sweating under the arms of his epauletted workshirt. Eventually a grim-faced woman was procured, who patted Paula down as if she might be smuggling Semtex in her belly.

'When are you due?' It seemed more of a test than a kindly enquiry.

'Er . . . in June.'

The woman's hands probed her stomach, stretched so tight now that a foot or hand could often be detected emerging from the thin drum of skin. It was very unnerving.

'On you go,' said the guard, stepping back. 'Good luck.'

Paula wasn't sure if she meant for the baby or for what she was about to do. She was given a temporary ID badge, and arranged her clothing as the first set of doors buzzed open. Her Virgil through the inferno was a white-haired prison officer, his belt jingling with keys. 'Never worry, he'll be on his best behaviour. He wants out, our Sean. You're here to give him the say-so?'

'I'm asking him what he knows about some missing persons' cases. I work with the MPRU in Ballyterrin.'

Her guide paused by the last door. 'He'll tell you whatever you want, miss. But I'd believe him as far as I could throw him, the same fella. He's not got a truthful bone in his body.' They were now at a small interview room, the pane of glass webbed in protective wire, the walls and floor bare, echoing concrete. 'Maguire,' mused her guide as he swiped a key card. 'Catholic Maguire, is that?'

'Yes,' she bridled.

'Ah, you'll be OK then. Just don't trust him.'

'Thanks.'

He opened the door and she stepped into the comfortless room. There was a wall of reflective glass, and a bare fluorescent light. There was a chipboard table and two plastic chairs. On one of them sat a middle-aged man in a sweatshirt. He was paunchy and pale, his dark hair thinning, and with manacled hands he was scratching at his nose. Paula felt the horror go through her – here was the man, the actual man she'd seen on TV and in mug shots, who'd most likely shot Aidan's father in front of him back in 1986, and maybe her own mother too.

Sean Conlon was now fifty, Paula knew. He had three children with two different women and he'd not seen any of them in twelve years. He'd joined the IRA at fifteen. Allegedly he'd helped shoot John O'Hara when he was twenty-five. Planted the bomb he was doing time for at thirty-eight. But he looked like any man you'd see on the poorer streets in town, a little chubby, a little pasty. Tattoos up and down his arms. Wary. When she came in he gave her a weary nod. He'd done this a hundred times before.

'Hello. I'm Dr Ma—' She stopped. Swallowed. 'I'm a forensic psychologist.'

He nodded. 'You'd be with the missing persons crowd?'

'Yes. Our remit is to open old cases, look for new evidence, as well as coordinating new ones. We don't have a specific political focus but we do work closely with the Commission for the Disappeared.'

Sean moved, the metal of his handcuffs making a tinkling sound that was oddly cheerful. He knew the drill. 'My assurances?'

She was ready for this. 'We're an independent commission, so not part of the CPS. However, I am authorised to report back to the parole board if you've been helpful or not. I understand you may not have any knowledge of these specific cases.'

Again he just nodded and held out his cuffed hands. 'Let me see.'

She rooted in her bag for a few moments, willing the surge of blood to her face to subside. She had a bundle of printouts, each one with the name and picture of a missing person, carefully screened for all staples, clips or rogue pens. She knew a psychologist who'd lost an eye that way in one prison.

Sean Conlon leafed through them with one hand. The fingers were squat, hairy, a tattoo on the back of a Celtic cross. Around his neck a crucifix. He read in silence, Paula watching. She was as jittery as the man was calm. His eyes flicked to her when she adjusted her jumper over her bump. 'When are you due?'

She flushed. 'June.' She wanted to hide it with her arms.

He turned a page. 'Not a nice place to come when you're expecting.'

She said nothing. He cleared his throat. 'You could save your time, doc, if there's any of these you think I might be linked with. We didn't always know their names, see. It'd be dark and we'd have masks on too.' He pushed some away. 'No weans. Never got involved with no weans.'

'Women?'

He didn't flinch. 'The odd time.'

Paula reached for the pile of papers. Her hands were shaking so badly it took her several goes to find the right one. Averting her eyes from the familiar photo – she'd taken it, for God's sake, playing with the camera as a kid – she placed it before Sean Conlon. He studied it, then put out one stubby finger and framed the face, squinting as if trying to see something. His lips pursed. Paula realised she was holding her breath.

'Hm,' he said. 'I know this one. She was from Ballyterrin.'

'Y-yes. She was.'

261

'The nineties.' He said it oddly, almost nostalgically. ''Ninety-nine it was they got me.' It explained why he was still in prison while so many equally notorious terrorists were free and walking the streets. The Good Friday Agreement of 1998 had been seen as a watershed, and everything before it was supposed to be washed away, forgiven. But people could still be convicted for anything that happened after. 'Can I hold on to these?'

'I suppose so.' It was just paper, after all. Names and dates and faces of the lost.

'I'm not saying I know anything, now. I'll think. It might just be from posters or that. If I remember, how do I get you?'

'Tell the governor,' said Paula. She didn't want this man knowing her number, or anything about her. And yet he might be the only person who could help.

'OK.' He was done. 'I'll have a wee think. No immediate bells.'

'All right. Thank you.' *Thanks for telling us who you might have murdered, Sean!* What a mad post-conflict world it was. She took a breath. 'You may also have heard that the mayor's gone missing.'

'Kenny? Aye, I heard someone lifted him. Not surprising, really.'

'No?'

'Aye, he was talking about taking his seat in Westminster. Swearing the oath to the Queen and all. That'd annoy a lot of people.'

'Is there anything you could tell us about that?'

'Ah, no. I know the background. But you've come to the wrong place if you think I know anything more. Sure I've been stuck in here over a decade.'

She watched him; quailed before his stare. 'I'll . . . if you think of anything, perhaps you'd let us know.'

Paula rapped on the door to show they were finished, and Sean placed both wrists on the table. '*An bhfuil Gaeilge agat?*' He asked it quietly, not looking at her. Anyone listening might have missed it over the buzzing of the door.

Paula froze with her back to him. She nodded very slightly. Yes, she spoke some Irish.

'*Tá sí do mháthair?*' Is she your mother?

Maguire. Of course. For fuck's sake. It was written on the badge round her neck. She had the same name, same face, same hair.

She turned to look at him, mute. His face was very strange. Interested. Compassionate, maybe. He nodded, as if seeing something that satisfied him. Then the guard was coming in and leading him out. 'Good luck with the baby, miss,' called the man who'd murdered five people. That they knew of, at least.

Kira

The office was much nicer than she'd thought. There was a machine with water and plastic cups, and a thick blue carpet. His assistant asked them all did they want tea or coffee, and Kira said coffee to look grown up, and when it came it was black and horrible but she drank it anyway.

'Welcome,' he said, briskly, shaking her hand, then Dominic's, then Ann's. 'It's an honour to have you here. And please accept my condolences for your loss. We're all united in condemnation of such a brutal act.'

Kira was a bit confused about it, but she knew this man had been in the IRA too – everyone knew that, though they weren't allowed to say so on the news, they had to call him Mayor Jarlath Kenny, and talk about how he was going to run to be their local MP. But maybe he'd killed some people too. Not everyone in the group knew they were here, because of that, but Dominic just said something about strange bedfellows.

'I wanted to meet you as representatives of the group and say that if I'm elected I will of course pursue all avenues of compensation available to you.'

'What about legal avenues?' said Ann in her dry, cross way.

'The five suspects were acquitted,' Kenny said.

'We know that, we were there. But they are clearly guilty.' Dominic sounded annoyed, underneath his 'talking to official people' voice.

'There's little we can do if the justice system has played out,' said Kenny, and he really sounded sad. 'I think the key now is to focus on the memorial, and ensuring this doesn't happen again by supporting the peace process.'

'So you're saying we have to accept the verdict?'

'What else can we do, Mr Martin?' Kira didn't like the way he was saying *we*, like it was something to do with him. 'The civil trial option is so expensive and gruelling, are you sure you'd want to put yourselves through that . . .'

Dominic caught her eye. It was up to her now. Kira leaned forward. Outside in the office there were people typing, phones ringing, chatter and the odd laugh. 'We have another idea,' she said quietly. 'Mr Kenny, we want you to help us with something.'

Chapter Twenty-Four

Paula lumbered back to the unit, in a thoroughly foul mood as a soaking May rain fell over the town, the mugginess of the day finally broken. The working day was nearly over, but the team had been on near-constant duty. They were short on manpower with Bob's suspension – her fault, though hardly the outcome she'd expected – and she was needed there. There were still two bombers to find as well as Kenny. That was what mattered. Find the lost things, put them back where they belonged, and everything would fall into place, and it wouldn't matter about Aidan being up at the hospital at Maeve's bedside, or about the fact she'd had to look at a dead woman that no one cared enough to find, or the impending birth of her child, which could not be gotten around without going through, or that she'd just come face to face with the man who maybe knew what had happened to her mother. None of that would matter at all, if she just kept looking.

Back at the unit the mood was equally sombre. The band of journalists who'd been door-stepping the unit had scattered in the rain, sheltering in the coffee shop opposite. Inside Avril and Fiacra sat at their desks in rigid silence, where once they would have played music or made each other cups of tea or gossiped in a familiar undertone that could make you feel like a total outsider. Every few minutes the phone buzzed with an irritating three-note cheep. No one picked it up. Paula glanced at it, wondering why. 'What's the latest?'

'Oh, the usual.' Avril didn't look up from her clacking keys. 'I checked with the hospital and you were right, Flaherty's dying of stage four lung cancer. He'd been offered palliative care but refused any treatment or pain medication.'

She put her bag down on the chair, frowning. What did it mean? He was dying, and his house had been left so neat and tidy, and he hadn't gone in the van with the other bombers – so where was he?

'Boss wants to see you,' said Fiacra, also not looking up.

Paula sighed. 'In his office?'

'Yeah, and the DCI is there too.'

Avril looked up. 'Are you in trouble, Paula?'

'I guess I'll find out, won't I?' She trudged to the office, rubbing her aching back, knocked on the door and went in. 'What's the problem?'

Corry and Guy were very still, he at his desk, she standing by the window.

Paula saw a look pass between them and some feeling went pop inside her. 'Is something wrong?'

'Sit down, Dr Maguire. Shut the door.' Corry.

That phrase again. 'I'd rather stand, if you're going to. Is someone going to tell me what's going on?'

Another look. Guy placed his hands on the desk. 'We think there's a leak in the investigation.'

'The notes,' said Corry. 'No one is supposed to know about them. So how come Dominic Martin was able to quote them back to me?'

'It could just be coincidence. Those phrases were in the public domain, after all. Or maybe, like I've always said, he wrote them and we just haven't been able to prove it.'

Another look. Corry placed something on the desk. 'There's also this.'

It was a page from the *Ballyterrin Gazette*. She'd largely stopped reading it because it only made her cross with Aidan. He was always sticking the boot into the police somehow, and the unit was often the focus of his scorn. Aidan didn't believe in offering immunity to terrorists, even if it helped find the bodies of the lost, and was furious they were working with the Commission for the Disappeared. The story was about the Mayday Five – he'd plastered it with their pictures, and Maeve's book was also detailed, accompanied by a stern but beautiful picture of her leaning against a wall with her arms folded. The Mayday Five were all named as the perpetrators of the bomb.

'That's libel,' she said absently.

'You can't libel the dead,' said Corry tersely. 'Three of them are in the morgue, in case you forgot. Look at page six – he knows about the notes.'

She peered at it. 'Oh. That's not good.'

'We were keeping that back on purpose, so we could eliminate suspects. Now that's blown. Now the *Gazette* has it it'll be all over the media.'

She looked up at them, Corry glaring with folded arms, Guy frowning down at his desk. 'I see. You think I did this?'

Corry stared her down. 'Dr Maguire. We're aware of your – relationship with the editor of the paper. I'm afraid we have to ask you formally if you have allowed him access to any of the case notes. It wouldn't be the first time, would it?'

She opened her mouth. Guy jumped in. 'He could have got them himself. Perhaps it wasn't even your fault.'

'Aidan wouldn't do that! He's an old-fashioned journalist. He gets people to talk, he doesn't go through their things.'

Corry sighed. 'Paula. This is very serious; I don't need to tell you that. May I remind you that the unit has had this case for over a month and so far you haven't found any of the missing alive? All we have is dead bodies, and now the mayor, the actual mayor of the town, is also missing. I'd say that for a missing persons unit, that constitutes a pretty big failure. And I'm not doing much better – we've got eyewitness testimony against Kenny and what sounds like some of the Mayday families, but we haven't been able to pin a thing on them. Why is this happening? I should have realised sooner there might be a leak. The damn phone's been ringing off the hook all morning since this came out.'

'It isn't me,' Paula said stonily. 'I'm doing my best to find them. You were the one who said I was working too hard on the case!'

'Does he have access to your phone?' Guy asked the question uncomfortably.

She quelled him with a glare. 'I haven't seen Mr O'Hara for a number of weeks – except in hospital, where we were a bit more concerned about our friend who's seriously injured. Aside from our family connection, which is hardly rare in a town this size – half the PSNI are related to someone – we are not in contact, and he certainly could not get access to my work email. Your leak is somewhere else.' She leafed through the paper. 'Can I take this?'

Corry was pursing her lips, looking at Guy to say something. Paula didn't wait for an answer – she took the paper and stalked out, allowing the door to close that bit harder than usual behind her.

* * *

'Why do you do it?'

In the past Aidan would have greeted her with a sarky comment, a lippy remark, and that would have been them away, trading insults. What passed for flirting, with them. But now he gave her a look that was fast becoming familiar, his eyes moving straight to her bump, avoiding her gaze. 'Can I help you?'

Paula had found him in her least favourite place, Ballyterrin General Hospital, and she'd made herself go up to where Maeve lay in the ICU. There was an officer on the door but she'd argued her way in, all five foot ten of her and two extra stone of baby. Aidan was sitting outside the glass-walled private room, his head in his hands. She said, 'The notes. How did you know?'

He looked at the paper she was slapping against the seat. 'The notes in the mouths?'

'Yes of course the bloody notes in the mouths. That was deliberately withheld, and now you've plastered it all over the paper. Who told you?'

'I hope that's not a serious attempt to get me to reveal my sources. You should know I don't do that.'

'Aidan. They think I told you. They even think you might have gone through my phone. I might get suspended.'

'Why would they think that?'

'Because hardly anyone knows, and you and me, we're – you know.'

He scratched his neck – he needed a shave, and a haircut. His dark hair flopped over the collar of his Springsteen T-shirt. 'Look, Maguire, I don't reveal sources, not for anyone. But in this case it was an anonymous tip-off. I'm no wiser than you. Look.' He took out his phone and called up an email, passed it to her, the address just a string of numbers – 010506. The name on the email said A Source.

Paula thumbed through it, frowning. 'Someone trying to be clever?'

'I didn't ask. There's scans of the notes, the lot.'

'Why would someone do this?'

'You're the psychologist, Maguire.'

'They must be working with us. Only a police insider would know this – or else the killer. Look, I'm going to have to take this to Corry and Brooking. They need to know.' She thought suddenly of Fiacra, his angry truculence, the sneakiness of what he'd done to Avril. But he wouldn't damage the investigation – would he? She fell silent, following Aidan's gaze to the room where Maeve lay, the machines still breathing for her. A woman with a short dark bob bent over her, talking, even though Maeve clearly could not hear. 'Is she . . .'

'She's all right,' Aidan said. 'Not that you asked. She hasn't woken up yet but . . . they're hopeful.'

'I'm sorry. I did phone to check on her. I just . . . couldn't be here.'

'I noticed.'

'Why did you use it?' she burst out. 'This isn't the first time you've bollixed up a case for us by printing stuff. Don't you ever realise it might mean justice isn't done?'

Aidan turned back to the room. He seemed too distant these days to even fight with her, as if vital circuits were shorted out on their old connection. 'Was it justice when those Five walked free from court, tell me? I've my own brand of justice – telling people the truth, and letting them decide.'

'People. The mob, you mean.'

'Maybe. And you've your own brand, too, and as I recall it isn't always the exact definition of the law.'

'Oh for God's . . .' She stopped.

'What?' He followed her gaze.

She stared at the screen of the phone in her hand. 'The numbers – it's the date of the bomb. First of May, 2006. It's the bomb.'

Aidan's forehead creased. 'Why would someone send us this?'

'Publicity. The notes were done for a reason. My guess is someone doesn't want this dismissed as an IRA feud. They want the punishment to be seen. To get their voices heard.'

'Like a public hanging.'

'Exactly like that.' She thought of Dominic Martin's angry words after the trial. *They should be strung up . . . My daughter didn't have much of a voice.*

Aidan rubbed a hand over his face. 'What do you think's going on here, Maguire? Your instincts are usually right, even if you do run off on some awful half-cocked missions sometimes.'

'You're one to talk. Honestly – and this is hard to admit, knowing what I know – I think the families did it. Dominic Martin definitely knows something, and there's this teenage girl, Kira Woods, she's only thirteen but she knows something. I'm sure of it.'

'Who else?' Aidan was hunting through his jeans pockets, pulling out a pen and receipt to scribble on. Paula heard the words pour out of her, as if the pressure of not talking to him about the case was piling up in her and had to burst. He had all the evidence now, so why not tell him everything, see if he could help as he had before?

'Ann Ward, she's the secretary, she had the same notebooks as we found at the caves, same ones the notes were written on. She handed them over to us bold as brass. Lily Sloane, the girl who lost an eye – she's tied up in it, I'd say, even if she doesn't know the whole story. I'm pretty sure John Lenehan knows what's going on. Dominic Martin even has a white van, just like we found on CCTV. It was just parked outside his house in plain view. But we've not been able to prove any of it. They're getting away with it somehow.'

'Like the bombers did.'

'Exactly. A crime in plain sight, but somehow you walk free.'

'Maybe that's the idea.'

Paula thought about this for a moment. 'If that's so, then . . . shit.' Her own phone was ringing in her bag. Guy, checking up on her?

The ring was very loud; the woman with the dark bob was coming to the door to complain. 'Those aren't allowed in here.' She didn't introduce herself.

'Sorry, sorry,' Paula said. She moved to the corridor and answered it. 'Dr Maguire.'

'Maguire?' It was Gerard. 'Where are you?'

'Checking up on a few things.'

'Well, you can't moan no one tells you about bodies if you're not around when it happens.'

'There's another body?' She saw Aidan's face change; he'd overheard.

'Aye. A woman. Can you get here now? I'll text you the details.'

'I'm on my way.' She hung up.

Kira

The courthouse was suffocating her. People everywhere, cameras going off, reporters with microphones and notebooks, families crying. She recognised Ann Ward, shaking, one of her sons holding her up. Lily Sloane shouting, *No, no, it's not fair*, as her parents led her away. She couldn't see Mammy. Dominic had told her to go away, go home, but she didn't know how to get home, and anyway, it wasn't home without Rose, it never would be again. Kira sank down on the hard wooden bench in the middle of the big hall, echoing with shouts and feet and flashes of light from cameras. Everything was spinning. Everything had fallen apart.

Not Guilty. They'd said Not Guilty.

'It's not FAIR,' she said out loud, her voice swallowed up in the noise.

'I know it's not.' She looked up. A man was standing over her. She didn't know him, didn't recognise him as one of the relatives. He was very tall, with hair the colour of sand. He was wearing a blue jumper and jeans.

'You're Kira,' he said.

She nodded. People often knew her from TV and that.

'What if I told you this didn't have to be the end?'

She didn't know what to say. 'We already said we wouldn't take it further. We don't have any money.'

'I'm not talking about something that costs money.'

The man sat down beside her in the crowded courtroom, and what he said to her then meant nothing was ever going to be the same again.

Chapter Twenty-Five

In late spring the hills around Ballyterrin bloomed with butter-yellow gorse, ringing the town like a protective fortress. She could see the crime scene from far away, the hills touched with dying light like the beginning of a forest fire. The earlier rain had let off, leaving a pale haze in the air as the sun went down. At this time of year the weather changed in a heartbeat.

Aidan had tried to talk her out of going. 'Fuck's sake, Maguire, you're mental to be doing this. It's too close to your due date.'

'Who are you, Doctor Bloody Spock?'

'Star Trek?' His forehead creased.

'Never mind. It's just annoying you seem to think you're some kind of childbirth expert. I'm not due for a month. I'm going. I have to see if it's her, Ni Chonnaill – Christ, she has three kids, Aidan. The youngest isn't even one.'

'Paula. Mum told me about the other day, at the morgue. You're sure you don't think this is someone else?'

'Fuck off. It's a recent body.'

'Paaaaula.' He sighed. 'This is happening, you know. You're going to have to slow down. What will you do, bring the baby to the crime scenes in her pushchair?'

'Maybe her father can mind her,' she snapped, riled. Shit. She realised from the look that cracked across his face she'd gone too far. 'Sorry. Sorry, I'm just scared. I didn't mean anything.' He said nothing. 'Aidan. I don't know, OK? I was just – lashing out.' She swallowed her pride. 'Please – will you come with me?'

He stood up. He didn't put on a jacket or jumper or look her in the eyes.

'Well – will you?'

He had his car keys in his hand. 'Course I bloody will. You know you don't have to ask.'

They said nothing driving out of town, that witchy orange glow in the sky, as if bonfire season had come too soon. She'd had to put her seat back as far as it would go to fit in, and her belt would barely go around her bump. Luckily, Aidan's car was far too ancient to have dangerous airbags. She felt dizzy, as if the ground beneath her feet were slipping and sliding. 'Can you go any faster?'

'You want to be pulled over by your mates in green?'

She sighed. 'No.'

They couldn't get all the way in the end – police vehicles made a fence around the muddy field where the body had been found, trying to keep back journalists and rubber-neckers. Someone's farm, out near the border. Paula put on her wellies, stooping with difficulty. Aidan just watched her struggle, still in his jeans and vintage Adidas. 'Maguire,' he said softly. 'Would you ever catch a grip?'

She ignored him. She knew what he was thinking. Of Mickey Doyle hanging, his face livid. A punishment for the families he'd left to live with what he'd done, and those who'd killed themselves, unable to. Of Ronan Lynch, his skin hanging off him in blackened strips, left sitting in his car. That was for those who'd been burned alive near the petrol station, clawing at the doors and windows and dying in desperation. Of Callum Brady, his head cut off and sitting several yards away, wide-eyed. For all the people blown apart, studded in shrapnel and glass, brick forced inside their bodies. What could this be? What could those unseen hands have done to Catherine Ni Chonnaill? Paula thought of her three children, the two oldest sullen, swollen-eyed, the little one with the unknown father – just bewildered, crying for his mother. He didn't know she had helped murder young babies like him. He'd no idea what she'd done – just that she was his mother, and he needed her.

She got out of the car. 'You'll have to help me walk.'

He gave her his arm stiffly, refusing to speak, cursing softly as his trainers were quickly clabbered in mud. At the cordon she disengaged, rearranging her cardigan. 'You can't come in. No press.'

The old Aidan would have wheedled and bribed, seeking the story at any cost. This one just stepped back. 'Be careful. Please.'

She ignored him, though the 'please' was like a knife in her chest. It wasn't his place to tell her what to do. For all they knew it wasn't even his baby.

Guy was there, the orange sunset shining on his fair hair, suit trousers tucked into green wellies and over them those plastic covers. He frowned at her approach, waddling through the crowd. She wondered if they believed her that she wasn't behind the leak.

'I know, I know,' she said wearily. 'But I'm here. Show me.'

'It's bad.'

Duh. 'Is it her?'

'We think so.' He led her close by, to where a white tent had been erected, lights shining out and shadows moving behind its thin walls. Catherine Ni Chonnaill's last resting place was a field in the fertile agricultural land around South Armagh.

'Buried deep this time?' The other bodies had not been well-hidden, clearly meant to be found in as startling a way as possible. 'That's different. She could have been here for a while.'

Guy hesitated. 'Yes, but – well. You'll see. Are you OK for this?'

'Just because I'm pregnant, sir, it doesn't mean I forgot how to do my job.'

Without comment, he passed her some gloves and foot covers and they pushed back the tent flap. Paula blinked. Surrounded by rapidly working CSIs was a shallow trench in the earth. A grave. The earth was rich and heavy, the smell of soil stronger than any decay. She hadn't been there long.

Catherine Ni Chonnaill had been a striking woman in life, tall, fair-haired, beautiful. The Republican Mata Hari, she'd once been called during one of her trials. Now that lovely hair was spread about her, brown with earth like a bad dye-job, and her face, once beautiful, was a mask of horror. Soil caked her mouth and nose, as if she'd choked on it, and her arms were stiffening up, the hands clawed and covered in dirt. Nestled in the earth, she looked like a tree root burrowing desperately to the light.

'What do you think?' asked Guy quietly. 'She was found exactly like this, only covered in around two foot of soil and with a heavy stone dragged on top.'

Paula stared down, transfixed. 'Was it—'

'Yes.' He dropped the flap. 'We're pretty sure she was put down there alive.'

Exactly like those who'd died under the rubble in Crossanure that day. Buried alive, suffocating, their nails splintered in their desperation to live, dying in a heap near the door of the collapsed bank. 'Is there a note?' she asked. Her own voice seemed to be coming from far away.

Guy said nothing, just passed her a plastic bag. This note was soil-stained, barely legible. In the lights of the crime scene she read the words: 'LEGITIMATE TARGET'.

Paula had the strangest feeling she was sinking into the ground. She looked at the woman's blue-grey face for a long time. She'd died in terror, you could see that. Clawing through the cold ground, feeling it fill up her lungs, fighting until the end with the dawning terror it was going to be too late. Paula had been there too, when someone had tried to kill her at Christmas – watching the blade move towards her belly, thinking *no no this can't be it no* and then realising it was, the knife was in her, it was happening. It had been the same for Catherine Ni Chonnaill. She was sure of it. Her last thought would have been of her children, at home in their beds, wondering where their mother was.

'Paula?' Guy was gripping her arm. 'For God's sake, I told you not to come. You've gone grey.'

'I'm fine! I – oh.' Paula gasped. A fist had punched her from the inside.

'What is it? The baby?'

She was going to say no, it was fine, it was too early, but then she felt a cramp move through her, crushing her, and she felt herself give up. She'd fought for months – fought with herself about even having the baby, and then fought to keep it alive, fought with Aidan's hostility and

Guy's pained politeness, and fought with everyone who wanted her to stop working, and now she'd lost. Her own body had won, as snakes began to coil and writhe in her, and a terrible fear took hold of her, a sense of slipping, of cogs and gears whirring into life. She could almost feel the child strain within her. How could Paula birth her into this, a grave, a crime scene?

'Help me,' she gasped, groping for Guy's arm like a drowning woman. 'Get me away, please.'

'Can you walk?'

She opened her mouth, shook her head. Gave up. 'No.'

Guy picked her up with a small grunt, heaving up her legs and getting mud on his suit from her wellies. 'Come on.'

She put her arms round his neck, and as the pain took hold she made a mewling noise in her throat, like a stepped-on cat. *Oh, fuck.*

'Coming through!' Guy whisked her past the cordon, panting with the effort. He probably would have struggled even if she hadn't been pregnant; she was nearly as tall as him. He kept up a soothing monologue. 'My car's just there. I'll drive you to hospital, and it will be fine. It takes ages, especially a first baby. You've got hours yet. Don't worry.'

'My things,' she gasped. 'I can't go. I don't have any things.'

'We can call for them. I'll phone your dad. Will he know?'

She nodded helplessly. What did it matter if she had the wrong pyjamas? Guy was so good at this. He was good at it because he'd already had two children. With his wife. His wife he was still married to. She began to shake. 'Put me down.'

'What? Paula, you're going into labour. We have to get you out of here.'

She was crying. 'Not you. You're still with her. I can't – not like this.'

Then Aidan was at their side. 'Maguire? What's wrong with her?'

'She's in labour,' said Guy curtly. 'I'm taking her to hospital.'

'Why the feck should you be the one do it?'

Paula had clambered down from Guy's arms, bent double with a cramp as they argued.

'O'Hara, there isn't time for this. She needs help.'

Aidan scowled. 'Do you want him to take you, Maguire?'

She tried to shake her head, grunting with the pain. 'Nnnn – no.'

'See? You're married, Brooking. You should be with your wife.'

'I'm responsible for her.'

'You are in your hole. You barely know her.'

Paula found her voice. She gripped Guy's arm and heaved herself up. 'You two. You will SHUT. The fuck. UP.' She tugged at Guy. 'Drive me home. Aidan – phone Dad. Tell him to meet us at the house. I need to pack the rest of my things.'

'Why is he driving you? I brought you here.'

She closed her eyes, grinding her teeth against the pain. When she could speak she said, 'Because his car is cleaner. Now fecking do what I said, or so help me God I will never forgive you.'

* * *

The following twelve hours were something Paula never quite got right in her head. Time was out of joint – she'd look at the clock on the delivery room wall, and an age would pass and she'd look again and it would be the same time. The contractions seemed to take an eternity. She counted through them – one two three four five six. Clawing at her was the anxiety of Guy and Aidan – when they went to the house her dad and Pat were there, throwing clothes in bags, and they'd never met Guy before, so she was aware of certain awkward introductions, while she sat on the sofa, gritting her teeth and counting through the pain. She overhead comments from Pat and Guy, who seemed to have appointed themselves childbirth experts: '. . . really close together already . . . not due for another month . . .' Then Pat must have rung the hospital. 'They said bring her if they're this close . . .' Then she was in the car, retreating somewhere into herself, bracing her hands against the dashboard and making a grunting noise like an animal, trying not to throw up in the footwell. It was Guy's car, so clean she couldn't see a speck on the carpet as she breathed in the smell of his air freshener. She'd have liked to stay there. Aidan was in the back, shouting directions, and Guy irritated, saying he'd lived there for a year, he could find the bloody hospital. Then they were there and Saoirse came, her face excited and scared but her voice calm. She took Paula's hand in her cold, clean one. 'It's too early,' Paula tried to say. 'Why's she coming so early?'

'We don't know yet. But we'll look after you.' Then there were charts and murmurs and people's hands on her, in her even, and mutters about being three centimetres and why wasn't she progressing, and she knew you had to get to ten but it was too soon for this surely? Guy and Aidan were there, and her last view was of them standing side by side as she plunged through double doors. There was the wheels of the bed squeaking and a siren noise that must be for her. A pen was in her hand and Saoirse's voice. 'You have to sign your consent, Paula. They need to give you a caesarean.'

'But I didn't want one.' She wasn't sure if this came out or not.

'I know, but it's too late. You have to sign.'

She clutched Saoirse's hand, which was cool and strong. There was one thing she was clinging to, stopping her from being sucked under. 'Will you tell him . . . Guy . . . will you ask him to find her for me? Ask him to find out more.'

Saoirse's face a blank oval over her. 'Find who, Paula?'

'Find Mum. Ask him to help me find her.'

Then the blinding overhead lights of the theatre, four lights blacking out on the edges and a sharp pain in her hand and faces overhead, masked faces dissolving, and finally, gladly, Paula gave up and disappeared.

Extract from *The Blood Price: The Mayday Bombing and its Aftermath*, by Maeve Cooley (Tairise Press, 2011)

After my encounter with the Ireland First fundraiser, I tried to seek out Catherine Ni Chonnaill for a statement. I visited her house, where she lives with her three children, since her split from Lynch just before the trial. When I arrived she was getting out of her car with bags of shopping and lifting the youngest, a very young baby, from his car seat. She was very beautiful, even dressed in a tracksuit with her fair hair pulled back.

'Ms Ni Chonnaill?' *I asked.*

She jumped – as someone might who had a small child and death threats from the IRA. 'What do you want?'

I explained I was writing a book about the Mayday bombing and wanted to get her point of view. She was immediately cagey. 'I had nothing to do with that, as I've said. It was a tragedy but not caused by Ireland First.'

I asked her why she'd gone on trial then, and she said something about persecution by a Diplock court – totally inaccurate as her trial had a jury and she was acquitted anyway. She said I should speak to Flaherty. 'Martin's the one in charge. He'll tell you we weren't involved.'

I said I had spoken to him already. She became agitated at that. 'Did he tell you about me? Did he say where I lived?'

He hadn't, but I didn't answer this. 'Have you anything to say to me, Ms Ni Chonnaill? Anything to say to the victims and families of those killed?'

She paused on her doorstep. She was covering the baby's head with her scarf, as if she didn't want me to see him, or him to see me. 'I have nothing to say.'

'Nothing?'

'Just . . . it was never meant to happen. It wasn't meant to be . . . the way it was. Not all those people.'

'Then why did you do it?'

'Please. Please leave me alone.'

I stopped then, because I did not feel right

accosting a woman with a baby. Which was not, of course, a qualm she had herself when her actions led to the deaths of sixteen people, including two infants and three children.

Chapter Twenty-Six

It was a baby. Of course it was, what else could it have been?

Paula had never been maternal. Even as a child playing with Saoirse, she'd been the one to give her dolls Mohicans and draw on their faces with green fluorescent marker, or remove their jointed limbs in a sad amputation storyline (it was no wonder she'd ended up working with murderers all day). But this baby was different. It was hers.

She regarded her – Maggie – through the glass of the cot. It didn't seem right that she'd been allowed to name another human being. She'd told her father when he came in, waiting for the reaction: 'I want to call her Margaret.' Would it feel like a judgement, since he'd just married another woman? He'd been quiet for a while, rocking the baby in his big arms. Paula was an only child, so she'd never seen him hold a baby before. He'd said, 'Aye, that's nice, but maybe a short name . . . something her own.'

'Maggie, I thought.' Maggie. She'd been thinking of the child as this for so long, a secret name. Now she was out, and other people could know her too. Paula had known her a long time.

'Wee Maggie.' He tasted the name. 'That suits her.'

'She was never Maggie, was she – Mum?'

It felt wrong to say her name, but it was OK.

'No. Just Margaret. Wee Maggie. Welcome, pet.' The baby stretched her starfish fingers and blinked, making those little cat noises Paula had become accustomed to. She was so small, her skin red like a blister, born too soon. Now the baby was out, she still felt tied to her by every inch of skin. The pull was almost physically sore if someone took her away to be weighed or changed.

'Can Pat come in?' asked PJ suddenly.

Paula was startled. 'Of course! You mean she's outside?'

'She thought . . . you know, with things the way they are.' Pat was Aidan's mother. That meant none of them knew if she was this baby's grandma, or its step-grandma, or both. Paula closed her eyes, feeling the slow seep of pain from various parts of her body. 'I'm sorry, Dad. I can't deal with this now.'

She'd been so focused on getting the baby out, surviving the horror stories of childbirth. And now Maggie was here, pink as a seashell, and Paula still had no idea who her father was. She'd researched it half-heartedly while pregnant, her belly pushing against the laptop. It was quite simple, apparently. You could buy tests in Boots. A little cotton bud in the cheek, it wouldn't even hurt Maggie. But Paula, arms already itching to take her back, press her against her face, knew she couldn't bear the idea. 'She's only hours old. I don't want – things done to her. She's herself. It doesn't matter who – you see?' *She's mine*, was what Paula meant. *I made her and I gave birth to her*, and right then it didn't seem very important which stupid encounter had resulted in this chubby little body squirming in her arms.

PJ was embarrassed. 'Aye, aye, plenty of time for that. Pat just wants to see her is all.'

'Will Pat mind? I mean . . . she's still her granny. Either way.'

It was the second risky thing she'd said, but he seemed pleased. 'Would you tell her that, love? Would you say she's her grandma? It would mean the world to Pat, it really would.'

'Of course.' It wasn't as if Maggie had any others at the moment. Paula wondered fleetingly what Guy's mother was like. Was she even alive? She pictured a stern, cold Englishwoman, maybe with pearls and a Labrador. Which was unfair, given that Paula had no idea what background Guy was from. His mother could just as easily be a Cockney pensioner with a blue rinse. All a world away from plump Irish Pat, bustling in the door, arms bursting with teddies and flowers and chocolates. The latter made Paula wince a little – she would now have to lose the several spare tyres, more than enough to meet Road Safety guidelines, which had settled around her midriff.

Pat was well meaning, but tiring. Paula forced herself to say, as casually as she could, 'And here's Granny, Maggie,' then ignore the misting in Pat's eyes as she held the child.

'Maggie,' she repeated. 'It's a lovely name.' Awkwardness was glossed over with good will. As much as they could, anyway. No one mentioned Aidan, but she could feel them searching the child's face, looking for a telltale dark eye there, a curve of the chin here. A Brooking or O'Hara. Neither – she was to be Maggie Maguire. Maggie deserved a little while to get used to the world before people began to label her. Paula herself could see nothing but a baby, dark blue eyes and a fuzz of red hair, as if she'd made Maggie entirely of herself.

'Well, we'll let you rest,' said PJ, when the nurses came.

No one mentioned Aidan but surely he'd be there, somewhere? Surely they were both still there? Aidan would be in with Maeve, if nothing else. The thought threatened to pull her down into some complicated darkness, so she pushed it away.

When they'd gone, she turned to the child almost as a conspirator. 'Just us, pet.' She realised she was looking forward to getting home just the two of them, shutting the door. As Maggie had come so early, she had to be kept in for a few days.

Later, Saoirse had come. Which was nice, but also tiring, because Paula hadn't tried for five years, right at the start of the queue for IVF before she was even thirty. She hadn't tried at all. But why should she feel guilty? She realised she was holding herself tense when her friend arrived, laden down with flowers and toys. Overkill, maybe to mask her own guilt at feeling jealous. 'Hiya.'

'Hi.' She struggled up. 'Sorry – I'm a mess of stitches.'

Saoirse's eyes were riveted on the baby. 'Oh Paula. She's gorgeous. She's just gorgeous.'

She was, of course, but did all mothers think that? Her little nose, her dark lashes, the wise look already in her eyes. 'Do you want to hold her?'

Saoirse hesitated. 'I might hurt her.'

'Ah no. She's pretty sturdy, though she was so early.' She passed the baby over, the light weight of her – so light it hardly seemed credible – with a pang. She'd sworn she wouldn't be one of those 'once you've had one, you'll understand' women. 'I've no idea what I'll do,' she confided. 'I've to take her home in a few days. Imagine! I never even had a goldfish before.'

Saoirse said, almost to herself: 'I want one.'

'I know you do, love.' What did you say? It'll happen? Paula knew enough to be sure that false hope was often worse than no hope at all, and so she said nothing.

Within a day or two, the ceiling above Paula's head had become her main point of interest. It was cream, with a pipe running down it and a large, rusting stain. It wasn't very interesting at all, in fact, and so she had to rely on her brain for the hours when her father or Pat or Saoirse weren't visiting her. She'd asked her dad to buy a notebook, and he kept forgetting on purpose. He didn't think she should be working, so in the end she'd begged the nurse to give her a bit of clipboard paper and a chewed biro. All the while her body was pumped in and out, the catheter slowly draining her and the drip filling her up, like a machine. She wished her mind was a machine that could compute the facts of this case and spit out a neat answer, someone to arrest, a knot tied in its long tail.

What she knew was this – four of the Mayday Five were dead. Brady, Lynch, Doyle, and Ni Chonnaill, with her soil-stained hair and three orphaned children. Each had been kidnapped on the same day five weeks before, and killed deliberately in ways that echoed the brutal deaths of the bomb victims. The notes slipped into their mouths proved that. Now Jarlath Kenny was gone too, and if the Walshes could be believed, he and the families might have been in on it together – but how would that ever have happened?

She found she was going over the families in her mind, as if feeling a joint for a weak spot. How to break them, prove that those ordinary people were the ones who had abducted and killed the Mayday Five, left them in scraped-out graves, marked their own pain and loss onto human skin. Maeve was likely to know more than had appeared in her book, but she was still too ill to talk. Later, perhaps the arrival of Maggie might soften the coolness that had appeared between them. Maggie. At the thought of her daughter, Paula's breasts began to ache. She pulled herself up to a sitting position, cursing her weak body. She didn't want to be stuck in this room, staring at the rust-coloured ceiling. She wanted to scoop up Maggie and run, go back to the office with the baby strapped to her and work until this tangle of evidence was somehow combed out.

The door opened, and she lay back down sharply. The nurses were always berating her for not taking convalescence seriously enough. It was PJ.

'Well, pet. I've brought you some grapes.'

Bloody grapes. She'd be able to stock her own fruit and veg stall with that lot.

'What's wrong? Are you sore?'

'I'm bored out of my mind. Will they let me back to work soon?'

'You had a big operation, Paula. You're meant to take at least three months off.'

'I know! And now I'm fine. I can't take three months off. I need to find out what happened.'

'Why?'

It was an obvious question, but she suddenly couldn't think of the answer. 'Well – Flaherty's still missing. We could find him. And Kenny.'

PJ seated himself, rustling plastic bags. 'I doubt if their own mothers would mourn them. They're scum. Why upset yourself over that bunch?'

'You should understand, of all people. It shouldn't be

like this any more – people can't just dispense justice however they see fit. We have laws. We shouldn't have border justice – judge, jury, and executioner in one.'

PJ looked surprised at her vehemence. 'Well, no, but it's happened now. It's most likely green on green killings – sure the Loyalists were all bumping each other off in the early nineties and no one shed too many tears.'

'It isn't right.' She struggled to explain. 'I don't want to bring Maggie up somewhere like this. They should have been convicted properly.'

'They tried. Everyone tried. Sometimes justice just isn't done.'

'I know. It's just . . . it doesn't seem right.' She spotted a national paper sticking out of one of his carrier bags – Catherine Ni Chonnaill's face was clearly visible on the fold, her eyes staring boldly out. Closed forever now, her children left alone. And that was four bodies now and still no answers from the unit that was supposed to find them alive. She changed the subject. 'No Pat?'

'She – hmm.' PJ cleared his throat. 'She stopped off on the way for a minute. Went to see the wee journalist girl who was hurt.'

Paula understood. She'd gone to see Aidan. Aidan was in the hospital right now, and not coming to see her. 'How is she? Maeve?'

'Better, they said. She's awake now, so they're going to move her to Dublin. She'll not be herself for a while yet, though.'

'If you see her . . .' Paula stopped. She couldn't think of a word to send to Maeve, or to Aidan. She wondered if their little family would be able to sort themselves out one day.

'You'll have to let him come sometime,' said PJ, reading her mind.

'Will I?' she bridled. 'I didn't notice him asking.'

'No. But somebody's that wean's father.' They both looked at Maggie, her face already so utterly her own it was impossible to tell who her parents were.

'All right,' she said. 'He can see her if he wants. But I'm not doing any tests. I'm not even thinking about tests for a while yet. She's only just got here. Right?'

'Right, right. Whatever you say. Listen, your boss is here to see you. The English fella.'

Paula lay back on the pillows, wondering how long traumatic early labour and thirty-five stitches meant she was allowed to get her own way. Ages, hopefully.

Kira

'Look at the picture,' Liam was saying. 'Go on, look at her.'

The man – Brady – was crying. So was one of the other ones – Lynch. Doyle was looking down at his chest. He might not have been awake. Earlier on, there had been some hitting. Kira was standing near the back of the caves. She didn't know how she'd got there but the stone was cold on her back through her sweatshirt. There were other people there, in the dark – Ann, and Dominic, of course, Lily. It was better not to look too closely – this was something all of them had to do by themselves.

It would be her turn soon. She didn't want it to be. She didn't know what she was going to say. She had Rose's picture in the pocket of her hoody, the corners curling up in the heat, and she could almost feel her smile burning through the material.

Liam was still shouting. 'Look at her, look at my wee sister. You killed her. You murdering scum.'

The big man wasn't reacting at all. He just looked right ahead all the time, even if someone lost it and spat on him, or hurt him. The woman didn't cry either. She looked at them like she was furious, like if she could get her hands out of the ropes she would kill them all. Kira was most afraid of her, she thought.

Dominic was going over to Liam now, leading him away, the boy shaking and angry and almost crying himself. *Bastards, the bastards.*

Ann was sitting at the table, writing everything down, her face just the same as it always was. The place smelled of damp, and blood, and a terrible stink from the bucket they went to the toilet in.

'Who wants to be next?' Dominic asked, once Liam had slumped off to the side, the noise of his crying filling the place like a whimpering dog.

Kira pressed herself harder against the wall of the caves. In her pocket, she stroked Rose's picture, and tried to hear her voice, but there was nothing at all.

Chapter Twenty-Seven

The hospital was a good place to talk secrets. Something about the hush of machines, the slow ebb and flow of life. 'I haven't got long,' she said. 'I have to feed Maggie.' Already her breasts were aching, ready for the next feed. As if she'd become nothing but a sophisticated milk delivery system.

'How is she?' Guy's awkwardness made her look down at the sheets, their ragged threads, washed over and over to softness.

'She's fine. I can't – talk about that yet, OK? Can you just give me time?'

'All right.' He drank his coffee from a cardboard cup. She was sure he'd bought it for something to do. She just had a glass of tepid water. God, she missed using caffeine as a crutch.

'So?'

'Do you remember what you asked, before you went under? What you said to Saoirse?'

She nodded. It had come back to her in vague shreds. She recognised the voice he was using. It was his 'giving bad news to relatives' one. She had a version of it herself. She clutched the glass, feeling beads of moisture inch down the outside.

'Well, I did some digging like you asked. Strictly off the

record.' He traced a pattern on the side of his coffee, scraping the cardboard sleeve. 'You know I used to be in the Army.'

'Um – I guessed.' They'd never really spoken about this but it was obvious in everything he did, even the way he held himself.

'It was only for a few years. But I have contacts, people who would have worked over here during the Troubles. Army intelligence. So I asked about your mother. If they knew whether anyone ran her as an informer.'

Paula flinched at the word. 'She wasn't an informer!' A tout. Worst thing you could call a Catholic. That, coupled with her father's RUC job, would definitely have made her family what they called a legitimate target. It was the phrase they'd found in Catherine Ni Chonnaill's mouth. She shivered.

'OK, informing is a very loaded word. But, Paula, this was five years before the peace process. There wasn't some mythical freedom struggle. The IRA had been bleeding Ireland to death for years at that point. You know what I mean. I asked around, to see if anyone knew of her.'

'And?'

'Paula, are you sure you want to hear all this?'

She didn't look up. 'Tell me. Everything.'

'My contact – he said there'd been rumours your mother was involved with someone at Special Branch in the town.'

'Involved?'

She could tell from his voice he was blushing. '"Carrying on with" was the phrase he used.'

'Oh.'

'So, because of that, and her job at the solicitors, it was

believed that Margaret was passing information to Special Branch about terror suspects.'

That was better. Call her Margaret. Keep her distant, just a name in a file.

'Did they take her?' she asked, under the gentle hush of the hospital. She wasn't the first person to hear bad news inside these walls. They could absorb it. 'Did they know if the IRA took her?'

Guy hesitated. 'He wasn't sure. But it was known that there were plans to kidnap her and her – contact at Special Branch. For interrogation. He didn't know any more after that – he was moved to Kosovo.'

Contact. Her lover, that meant. According to Guy's friend, her mother had been having an affair, passing on secrets from her work to him. Paula tried to fit this in with what she knew of her mother, homely and quiet, and failed utterly.

'I'm sorry,' Guy said.

'It's not your fault. At least it's something.' And it was, a bit of solid ground she could rest her feet on.

'If it's true. It was so long ago, and most of the files are classified.'

'It fits, though. Her boss at the solicitors, Colin McCready, he'd heard some rumours too. And—'

And there was the man. The day before her mother's disappearance – October, dark and cold already – Paula had come home to find her mother in her dressing gown. That was strange enough. Even stranger, she'd been talking to someone at the back door. No one ever came there. Her mother had closed the door rapidly as Paula went in, asking her normal questions and telling her not to make toast as dinner was nearly ready, saying she'd come home sick from work. Going past the kitchen window Paula had seen a man, an old-fashioned hat hiding his face. He'd gone down the narrow side passage and left. She couldn't bring herself to tell Guy this, give him this private little memory like a thorn in her flesh. 'It fits,' she said again.

'Well – that's all I could find out. I hope it helps, in some way.'

Paula took a drink of her water, now muggy and warm, and nodded, not trusting herself to speak. Was she wrong to pry open this box, long buried? Sometimes she thought it was better not to know. But she couldn't let it rest, not now she'd opened it a crack. 'Thank you.'

'It's OK. I want to help.' The strained look returned to his face. 'Can I see her, since I'm here? Please? I'd just really like to see her.'

Paula said nothing.

'I know you're not ready to find out.' He spoke in a rush. 'I do understand, it's best for her, and to be honest, I think Tess – well, it would be very hard on her right now. At the moment she's managing to pretend it isn't happening. But I haven't even seen Maggie. I'd like to. Is that OK?'

'All right,' she said. 'I need to feed her anyway. Stay.' It wasn't as if he'd given her much choice.

'Thank you.' He looked intensely relieved. 'I wanted to tell you what's been going on with the case, anyway. If you're interested.'

'Are you kidding? I want to know everything.'

'Well, there's not much to tell. No sign of Kenny or Flaherty, though we've thrown all our resources at the search. You can imagine the media interest since the notes were released. We've also not been able to trace the source of the leak, so all information is being restricted. Corry's been interviewing to see if it's an internal leak but we haven't found any evidence yet.'

She was pleased he was telling her; that meant she was no longer under suspicion. 'OK. Listen, you know how Fiacra's been lately . . . Did you ever think, you know?'

He said nothing for a moment. 'I know what you mean. But like I say, we've found nothing. One other thing is that Catherine Ni Chonnaill's mother has given consent for a DNA test on the child. The youngest one.'

Peadar. She pictured him, snotty and bewildered, and remembered that despite her best efforts, his mother was never coming home to him. 'Is she allowed to do that?'

'The mother's dead, and we don't know who else has parental responsibility, do we?'

It was close to the bone. 'OK. And what did it reveal? It definitely wasn't Lynch?'

'No. And here's the interesting thing – he wasn't the father of the girl, either. The older boy, yes, but not the girl.'

'And who was? Do we know?'

'Same as Peadar. Turns out we already had his DNA.'

She was growing impatient. 'Tell me, Guy.'

'The father of Catherine Ni Chonnaill's two youngest children was Martin Flaherty. We'll need to ask his older daughter for a comparison to make sure, but the lab is pretty confident it was him.'

Paula had to assimilate this. 'They had a relationship? Ni Chonnaill and Flaherty?' He was fifteen years older than her.

'Looks that way. And at the same time as she was with Lynch.'

'I suppose that's why he called her a whore in court.' The topic seemed to become too heavy, and she fell silent, fiddling with the drip. 'Well, thanks for telling me.'

The silence was broken by the nurse bustling in with Maggie in her cot. 'Here we are! Here's Mummy.'

Paula froze for a second, then breathed in. It had to happen sometime, after all. She accepted the baby into her arms, and tried to cut short the nurse's curious glances. 'Thanks. Could I just feed her by myself today? I'll call if we have trouble.' She knew there was fierce speculation on the ward as to who might be the father of the wean – was it the cop who'd brought Paula in that day, or the angry-looking man in the band T-shirt? She'd have told them the truth if they'd asked – she had no idea.

Guy stood by the door, where he'd moved to let the nurse in. 'That's her then.'

'No, it's another random baby.' But there was no sting in her voice.

'I'll leave you.' He got up, buttoning his suit jacket.

'You don't have to. It's a bit dull. Talk to me.'

She tucked the sheets up to hide her breasts – ridiculous, he'd already seen that and more besides – and gasped as Maggie latched on. 'Good girl. She's getting the hang of it. They struggle sometimes, when they're premature.'

Guy watched her from the door.

'You don't mind?' she asked, for form's sake. She didn't care if he minded.

'Of course not. I always thought – it's beautiful, isn't it? I envy women that. The bonding. It can be hard for men. You just know they're yours, don't you?'

'Well, that and she came ripping out of me, yes.'

The silence shrouded them, soft and warm. Paula let

herself breathe. Knowing he was watching her. She said, 'Would you like to hold her? When I'm done?'

He said nothing for a while. 'I – another time, maybe. I should go in a minute.'

She nodded. She felt Maggie's mouth sag and transferred her, the scrabble and pop as she latched on, the relief of it.

'It's amazing.' Guy was watching, not averting his eyes politely from her breast. It would be worse somehow if he looked in the middle distance, as other people did. 'How do you know how to do it?'

'It's not that easy at first. After all, I never saw my own mother feed. I'm an only child.' That she knew of. She quailed suddenly. Thinking of what the murderous psychic had told her months before, when Maggie was just a whisper inside her – *your mother's alive. Alive over the water. There's another family. She's forgotten about you.*

It wasn't true. How could she know? But on the long winter nights, as Maggie turned over inside her, Paula had found herself worrying over the details of other things the woman had known, or seemed to know – that she was having a baby, that it was a girl, that Guy might be the father. Now she found herself looking from the curve of Maggie's face to the broad sweep of his forehead, the high cheekbones. 'Do you have brothers and sisters?' she asked. How could she not know this about him, when they'd worked together so closely they could almost hear each other's thoughts?

'A sister,' he said. 'We're not that close.'

'OK.'

'Was I right to tell you all that? I wasn't sure if I should.'

'Guy. Will you please stop trying to protect me? I'm a

grown-up, I've been without my mother now for longer than I ever had her.'

'I can't stop,' he said simply. 'It doesn't work that way. Even if you don't want to be protected, I have to try. Was it really worth it? To find out – that?'

'Yes.' She answered right away. 'I decided a long time ago I had to know. Whatever the truth was, it doesn't kill like lies do. Like you said – there's a law for a reason.'

'You do listen, then.'

'On occasion.'

He shifted. 'I must go. Please let me know if there's anything I can do, at all.'

'Bring me work. Anything. I'm mad with boredom.' But she knew that wasn't at all what he'd meant.

'I'll leave you two in peace. I'll do my best to look into that for you, I promise.'

You two. She wondered if there would ever be three.

'Guy?'

'Yes?' He stopped in the door.

'When I'm out of here, do I need to look for a new job?'

'What?'

'The unit – if it's going to be axed, you need to tell me. I'm on my own now with Maggie.'

'It's not going to be axed.'

'But they're discussing it.'

'I won't let that happen. I didn't want to worry you with it. It will be OK.'

'Just please – tell me, if there's anything I need to know.'

'I promise. And since you mention it, when you're out, when things are a bit settled, maybe . . .'

'Yeah?' She waited. The silence between them stretched. Guy was staring at his feet. 'Things are different now.

You have the baby. And you and I . . . well, I think we need to decide what we're going to do.'

Paula spoke carefully, looking at the baby and not at him. 'What do you mean?'

'Let's talk when you're out.' He crossed the room swiftly and planted a quick kiss on her forehead before she could react. 'Look after yourself.'

When he went, she felt strangely bereft, his kiss still burning on her skin. She couldn't even begin to process what he'd almost said, or not said. And it reminded her once again that Maggie was now three days old and Aidan, who at the very least was her step-uncle, still hadn't even come to see her.

Extract from *The Blood Price: The Mayday Bombing and its Aftermath*, by Maeve Cooley (Tairise Press, 2011)

On the day of the verdict Ni Chonnaill was all in black, her lipstick like a scar across her face. Her lawyer asked if she could stay seated for it as her legs were painful, and this was agreed to. The men stood, as if preparing to take a penalty shoot-out. The jury was, by its very nature, made up of ordinary people. Eight women and four men. Almost all white, given the area. The youngest was nineteen, the oldest seventy. The foreman was a middle-aged woman in a suit, by day a civil servant.

She said they had reached a conclusion. The judge asked what it was. She hesitated. The judge asked again, a little tetchy. The families were all on their feet, except those too old to stand. She said, Not guilty. For Brady. For Doyle. For Lynch. For Ni Chonnaill. And for Flaherty. She said not guilty five times in all. The evidence had not been enough. The flimsy case of the police and CPS, error-ridden and bungled even before the bomb stopped smoking, had not been strong enough. As she sat down, the forewoman looked up to the gallery, as if to say she was sorry.

I don't think any of the families ever blamed the jury. They knew the case didn't hold. After all, they'd sat through every word.

There was the sound of shouting as the prisoners were taken down to be let out. Murdering scum! They should be strung up! It isn't right. It isn't right.

The person shouting those words was Dominic Martin. He was restrained by bailiffs, and the dock was opened and the prisoners stepped out, blinking as if they couldn't quite believe it themselves. None of them looked at each other.

Doing my interviews for this book, I spoke to the solicitor for Ni Chonnaill, Grainne Devine. She was defensive, giving me a string of legal arguments about due process and right to trial. In the end I stopped asking why she defended people like the Mayday bombers, and simply asked how it made her feel. Standing up there with the eyes of the families boring into her. She thought about this for a moment. She is a young woman, stylish, assured. She said, I feel like I'm doing my job. I feel like I'm lucky to live in a country where we have the right to be presumed innocent, no matter what the evidence looks like, and you can't really understand what that means until you've defended someone who looks guilty as sin. *She said,* If I were ever to be on trial, on the other side of the dock, I'd want to know someone was defending me.

When she put it like that, I couldn't argue.

Chapter Twenty-Eight

'You've a visitor, so you have,' said the nurse. It was the young one, who wore a pink uniform and thick glasses and was very rough with her pillow-plumping technique.

'Who?' After five days in hospital, Paula was getting fed up with visitors being sprung on her. She much preferred it the other way, arriving at people's doors to question them.

The nurse tittered. 'A fella. Dead handsome.'

Aidan, she assumed. Girls always went silly around his air of tortured abstraction. Finally, the bastard. She was already planning out how to be – aloof, making it clear his behaviour was as usual not acceptable, and yet there was a quickening in her pulse at the idea of seeing him. But as she pulled herself up to sitting, she saw someone totally unexpected approach across the ward. Dominic Martin. He wore jeans and a short-sleeved navy shirt buttoned tight. He had a few days' stubble growing. 'Eh – hi.' She'd last seen him on the other side of the interview room glass.

'Hello, Dr Maguire.' He was carrying a Pampers box. 'I'm sorry to land in on you. I rang the office and they said you'd had your baby – a little girl. This is her?'

'Er – yeah.' It was clearly Maggie beside Paula's bed in her cot. She'd insisted on white Babygros only, though Pat, knowing unfortunately that a girl was expected, had

305

already bought up the entire stock of frilly pink clothes in the Ballyterrin area.

'What's her name?' Dominic was looking at the baby.

'Maggie.' She wanted to say – *I named her for my mother. She's gone. She's probably dead.* She wanted somehow to make a connection in their loss, but couldn't. He stood alone, and she was here with her brand-new child.

He seemed to realise he needed to explain his presence. 'I hope you don't mind, but I had a lot of toys in the house for a baby girl. Some of them never got opened – they were birthday presents.' Of course, Amber had died just days shy of her second birthday. 'I wondered if you'd – I mean they'll just go to waste otherwise.'

Paula understood. In this box he had packed up his dead daughter's toys to give to Maggie.

'Maybe you'd think – but she never got these ones, there wasn't time, and I'd like them to get played with. You know.'

She had to say something. 'That's really kind of you. How nice.'

He placed the box on the bed and she looked into it. Pink plastic, a rag doll, colourful picture books. 'She'd be too wee for them now,' he said. 'But later . . .'

Paula took a deep breath. 'Would you sit down, Dominic? I'm going spare here. I'd be glad of the company.'

He sat on the edge of the plastic chair. 'They've kept you in a while then.'

'Just a few days, they said. She was a bit early, and I had a caesarean.' She felt embarrassed talking about this with him. A suspect, however much she tried to avoid it. It was hard to believe he wasn't one of the men the Walshes had described. The nervous one, driving the white van. Paula looked at him. He was a good-looking man, and this bringing the toys was a heart-rending act of small kindness. Could she really see him arranging the murder of five people? They had no idea how extensive the leak was – did that explain why they'd not been able to pin any evidence on him?

'It's boring, isn't it?' he said. 'I was in myself after . . . everything. Amazing how boring it all was. Waiting for your tea to come, hoping they'd put something decent on the telly.'

'I didn't know you were injured too.'

'Just my back.' He touched it. 'Burns and cuts. I lay on top of her when it happened. When the roof of the bank came down. But the shock waves, they said – well, she was too wee to stand it.'

Of course, she remembered now. He'd covered Amber with his body, trying to shield her, but they'd both been buried in the rubble when the bank collapsed. Paula realised she should say something but couldn't find the words. Her mind was as exhausted as her body.

He changed the subject. 'I had another visit from your boss. The English fella. Asking me all about the mayor and did I know where he is. He is your boss, is he?'

'Yes. DI Brooking.'

'We're happy to help, as long as he's sensitive to people's loss. I know it might not seem like much, if you're over from England, but to us it was – devastating.'

'His son died.' She said it before realising she probably shouldn't have. But she hated the way some locals looked at Guy, the fair-haired Englishman with the military bearing, coming over there telling them to sort out their differences. They didn't know what he'd been through.

Dominic's face was still. 'I didn't know. How old?'

'Ten. He got killed. In London.' Jamie Brooking had been shot because of his father's job in anti-gang work, but she shouldn't say that.

Dominic nodded slowly. 'I'm sorry for his loss. Can't be easy to work on cases like this, then. Trying to find murderers who killed wee kids.'

She could have said, *It's a job to him. He doesn't know how to break the rules even if he wanted to.* She could have said, *He really believes in it, a fair trial and acquittal and innocent until proven guilty. He really believes we have a duty to look for everyone who's lost, no matter what they did.* Instead she said, 'Thank you for the toys. It was very thoughtful.'

'I hope you get some use out of them. Amber didn't.'

There was a silence that was painfully full of unsaid things and suspicion and apologies and he stood to go, putting his hands in the pockets of his jeans. His forearms were tanned and strong from working outside. Why had he come – to make a point, to get them to back off? To show he was a decent man, whatever she suspected him of? She wanted to ask how Lily was, but baulked at it.

'His son,' said Dominic, turning back. 'When did he die?'

'Early last year. Before he came here.' And precipitating his family into crisis, his daughter lost and his wife deranged, and Paula making it all worse by having this child.

'If he'd ever like a chat – you could tell him I'd be happy to. I mean, I learned a few things about it. Coping. I've had longer.'

'That's—' Words escaped her. 'That's very kind. Thank

you.' She looked at him for a moment, so handsome, so sad. *Could you really have done this? Are you the killer I'm hunting?*

'I'll be off then. Hope you feel better.'

He went, drawing glances from the women in the ward. Paula looked at the bright plastic toys, one with a scrap of wrapping paper still on it, and then at her own sleeping daughter, new-minted. She knew there was nothing she wanted to do less than give Maggie a dead child's toys to play with – but also that when Maggie was old enough, that was exactly what she would do.

Paula was eventually allowed out of hospital five days later, minus a lot of weight, plus one baby and thirty-five stitches. Her father picked her up, and she did her best to smile and act normally and not think about what she'd learned from Guy. Was it really possible her mother had been unfaithful? And had her father known, had he any idea?

'Er, what's this?' As they drew up to the doorway of the house, she could see pink balloons on the gate. 'Dad?'

PJ was opening his car door. 'It's Pat – she wanted to do a wee thing to welcome the baby.'

'Dad!'

'I'm sorry, love. There's a few people round.'

For God's sake. The last thing she wanted to do was smile and chat to people, when she was still struggling to walk.

Pat was delighted to see her. 'There you are, both of you! Welcome home, pet!' She cooed at Maggie in her sling.

Paula was holding the baby in front of her like a human shield. 'You didn't have to do all this, Pat.'

'Oh, it's no trouble. Just a few friends and family.'

This translated to around twenty people – Paula's aunt Philomena being one, the image of Paula's mother but with the ferreting-out skills of a bloodhound, and her cousin Cassie, now a lawyer and correctly engaged to a man she wasn't yet living with like you were supposed to, and Saoirse and Dave, loaded up with presents that Paula felt uncomfortably were meant to replace the joy her friend couldn't feel for her, Avril in a pretty pink dress, finger still bare, plus assorted mates of Pat's, who all wanted to devour baby Maggie. She was passed from arm to arm, luckily staying asleep, her face a crumpled rose petal. Thankfully, Mrs Flynn from next door was not there. Paula couldn't have coped with that. There was pink everywhere – pink bunting, pink cupcakes (or 'wee buns', as Paula's father insisted on calling them), pink wrapping paper, pink rosé wine, pink flowers. It was like an explosion in a patriarchal factory. Aside from the baby, all the talk, hushed in corners, was about the case and the four dead people turning up one by one. The case they still hadn't solved.

While Maggie was being cuddled by Cassie and Auntie Phil – 'Who's a lovely girl? Ah look, she has the family red hair and all' – Paula followed Pat out to the kitchen, where she was putting flowers (pink) in a vase.

'You'll be glad to be home, love.'

She'd have been gladder if said home were not filled with people, but said nothing about that. 'Yeah. Listen, Pat – I need to ask you something. About Mum.'

Pat's face changed. 'I'll close the door over there.' She did, the noise of the party receding.

'The thing I always think about you is, you've always

310

helped me when I needed it.' Paula spoke looking out of the window; it was easier that way. 'I'm going to ask you something, and I promise it will never get back to Dad, or to Aidan. I know things have been awkward because of Maggie—' She could hear Pat start to make some protest, something no doubt about Maggie being the best and sweetest baby in the world, and she steam-rollered on. 'Sorry. I need to get through this. I've heard a few things now about Mum, and I think you'd have known best what she was up to that autumn she disappeared. And I'd like to ask, was there a man? Was she seeing someone?'

Pat spoke carefully, arranging the flowers. 'What do you mean, seeing?'

'At first I thought it was something to do with her work, maybe she was informing, like they said, passing on confidential files. But now I wonder – was she seeing him as well? Like an affair?' It almost killed her to say these words to Pat, the noise of the party next door, people gurgling at the baby, who mercifully stayed quiet.

'I don't know anything for sure.' Pat's voice was very small. 'But one day when I called round, there was a man there, yes. I don't mean – not like that. She was in the kitchen with him. I went to the back door, like I normally did – she wanted to borrow a cookbook I had, to make a cake for your birthday.'

That placed it as September then, around a month before the disappearance. Paula remembered the cake well, two records on a turntable, shaped in liquorice laces. She'd thought it was pretty cool, and it was a good thing she did because it was the last birthday cake she'd ever had. The following year PJ had mentioned something about it, and she'd said she was too old at fourteen, even though she didn't think this at all, just to save him having to think of one more thing.

'Anyway, your man was there clearing up his papers. He'd a briefcase with him. She was all flustered, I remember, but he was the calmest thing you've ever seen. She never told me who he was, and that wasn't like her, she was always polite, you know. He shook my hand. "Hello," I said. "I'm Pat O'Hara. I'd better be off, Mrs Maguire," he said to her. "Lovely to meet you, Mrs O'Hara." I didn't realise until after he'd never said who he was, and she just started talking about your party and how you wanted a sleepover and what did I think about that.'

Paula's head was bowed. How little she'd known, consumed by teenage worries, such as would she be allowed to stay up to watch *The X-files* that week and would a boy ever talk to her. Even Aidan had totally ignored her back then, for all their mothers were best friends. Actually, he was still ignoring her now – no sign of him at the party, of course.

Pat was biting her lip. 'The thing is, pet – I didn't mean to snoop, honest I didn't, but I saw his papers when he put them away, and there was an Army crest on them. And the way he walked, and shook my hand all firm like – I think he was one of them. I worried about it after. That I'd shaken his hand. Whether someone might find out. It was daft, but that's how things were then.'

'He was English.'

'Aye, I think so.'

'Did he have a hat? A sort of old-fashioned one?'

She could see Pat frown in the reflection of the window. 'I think he did, now you mention it.'

The same man she'd seen at the door the day before it happened. When, crucially, Paula had come home to find her mother in her dressing gown at four p.m.

'OK,' she said heavily. 'I won't ask you any more. Thanks.'

Pat was twisting her wedding ring – the one she'd so recently had from PJ. She'd moved the one from John, Aidan's father, to her right hand. 'I keep thinking I'd know,' she said distractedly. From the next room came the noise of the party, chatting, laughing, cooing over Maggie. Paula was like a tuning fork waiting for the smallest cry.

'Know what?'

'If I did the right thing. Marrying again. It took me a long, long time. But PJ needs someone to mind him, with that ould leg, and it just – I was selfish, I suppose.'

Paula leaned away from the counter. 'You're allowed to be happy, the two of you.'

'But I see how you are, running round trying to find her, and you and my fella don't even talk any more, and I think what if it was meant to be you two wed? What if we took your happiness, us old ones? Just being selfish, looking for a second go.'

Paula sighed. 'It's nothing to do with that. Honest it isn't. Aidan and I always had our differences. This is nothing to do with you and Dad. I'm happy for you. I just needed to try and find out. I can't explain it. I need to know I did everything I could to find her. Her bones, even. Pat – they were after her, weren't they? They knew there was a man she was . . .' She groped for the right word, a minefield of meaning – 'talking to. They came for her, didn't they? The IRA.'

Pat was turned away, filling the kettle at the sink. Paula

saw her eyes reflected in her glasses. 'That's – that's what I always thought. But who knows for sure?'

'So she's probably – gone.'

'I don't know, pet. I never did. But . . .'

'But you married Dad. And that's why. You think she's dead.' Suddenly it was all so clear. There was no way Pat would have done that, married PJ, if she thought there was any chance at all his wife was still alive. Pat, the good Catholic, who'd deny herself any happiness if she thought it was the right thing to do. Standing in the kitchen, looking at the pink cake, smelling the sugar-pink roses, it hit Paula like the world was slowing down and stopped. Pat and her father thought her mother was dead, long dead. They'd thought so for a long time. There was no one but Paula who still had the hope to look.

She pulled herself together. 'Listen, I need to go out for an hour or so. Would you look after Maggie for me? I'll feed her first, so she shouldn't be any trouble.'

'Of course, pet.'

'And don't tell Dad where I've gone,' said Paula. 'If you don't mind, I mean. Tell him I just went to get nappies or something. He doesn't need to know any of this.' Pat thought about it for a minute, and then nodded. Paula thought she looked relieved.

She rescued Maggie from grasping arms and took her upstairs, relaxing as she breathed in the smell of the baby's head. In the bedroom were Dave and Saoirse. Saoirse was sitting on the bed with Dave bending over her.

Paula blundered in the doorway. 'Oh God, sorry.'

'Sorry, Pat said we could come up. It'll only be a minute.'

As Paula watched, unable to look away, Dave lifted

Saoirse's wool jumper and rubbed at the soft white skin of her stomach with cotton wool. Then with surprising force he stabbed her in it with the needle. Paula flinched. Saoirse didn't move. The syringe of drugs flowed into her with several breaths and it was done.

'You do that every day?'

'Every day, sometimes twice.'

'God.'

'No choice,' said Saoirse grimly, then forced on a smile. 'Not if we want one of our own. There's wee Maggie. How are you, sweetheart?'

Paula's hands tightened on Maggie's little body, so much more skin than mass, almost missing her even though she was in her arms. She thought that her body would never forget having the child within it. But she had to leave her now, because there was something that needed to be done.

Kira

Kira was trying to spell the words out. They'd asked her to write the notes, she thought probably so she wouldn't see what was going on down the back of the cave.

U-N-F-O-R . . .

She focused on the page in front of her, the sheets of the exercise book a bit damp from the cave and the sweat off her hands. She tried to keep writing and not look.

She could hear it, though. A noise like in a butcher's shop, a sort of horrible crunching, and a smell coming on the damp cold air of the cave. At least it was dark, and with the torches you could pretend you hadn't seen anything in the shadows. They'd said he wouldn't feel a thing. They'd given him an injection. The others were out too, slumped in their chairs with the ropes pulled tight. Except for the first, who was already gone. This one would be gone soon too when they'd finished. And then, she supposed, the others.

She hadn't really imagined it getting to this point. She hadn't known what they would do once they had them. But she should have. Oh, she should have and it was all her fault.

She just had to concentrate on the writing. E-S-C-A-L. She realised that her hands were shaking so much she could hardly move them over the page.

Afterwards, no one was sure how the woman got away. It seemed like Dominic hadn't tied her up as tight as the others, maybe he felt sorry for her or something. Anyway they were all busy trying to deal with the man over in the corner, and the noises he was making. She was busy pressing her pen into the paper, writing the note for him, then suddenly there was a movement and the woman was out of her seat. She lurched forward, then fell over on her knees on the dusty cave floor, making a little noise like she was hurt. Then before anyone could stop her she was out the front and into the woods.

That was the worst night. The idea that she might get away, tell people what had happened – no one could look each other in the eyes, as if they were only just realising how it seemed – the people tied up, the man in the corner who had stopped shouting, and she didn't want to look over into the darkness and see why. They spread out into the woods to find her. Calling her name. Kira realised when she was deep in the dark trees she wasn't even afraid. That the woman was probably afraid of her. Things had changed that much.

In the end it was easy to find her, she made so much

noise in the bushes, and the crying, wheezing sound of her voice. She was caught onto some trees by her hair and couldn't get free. They took her back. They tied her up again. The main man had woken up by then, sitting tied onto his chair, and the woman was shouting *Martin Martin help me don't let them do it*, and also *My baby, oh my baby*. Nobody listened. Kira caught the man's eye for a second, and she had to look away or she thought she might fall down herself.

Chapter Twenty-Nine

Conlon was in his cell, a space about three metres across, with small dirty windows. He was sitting on his single bed, writing in a notebook. Paula couldn't speak for a moment – she didn't want to call his name, not Sean, like a friend might say, not Conlon like calling a dog. 'Hello,' she said. He looked up, freezing slowly with the pencil in his hand. She could see the reactions were still there, the stillness of a warrior. She was glad of the door between them. It had been easy enough to get in, with her PSNI credentials and Corry's previous introduction. Of course, she wasn't supposed to be here at all. No matter. She didn't care any more.

'Dr Maguire,' he said cordially. 'Back again.'

'Yes.' Her voice wavered.

'Did you have your baby?' His eyes were moving over her, framed in the hatch of the doorway. 'Looks like you did. Boy or girl?'

She was trembling. Her hands holding the latch were slippery with sweat. 'I don't want anything from you. I'm just going to ask you one thing. Then I'll go. If you do know anything about those other missing people, maybe you'd see your way to telling someone. Even if you think it's too late to make a difference – well, take it from me, it would. To have them back. Bury the bones. That's all people want.'

'Easy to say,' he said idly. 'People always want more. Dr Maguire, have you ever heard that thing people say, the past is another country?'

'Yeah.'

'I believe that. Soon as you start poking too far into who did what back then, it'll all come crawling out. People always want more. My sorry wouldn't be enough for them.'

'We don't want sorry,' she burst out. 'We just want to know what happened to our goddamned families.'

'Dr Maguire, if I knew where your mammy was, I'd tell you.' He spread his arms. 'I've not much to lose and lots to gain. I don't know if she's even dead. And that's the truth.'

'But there was an order given. To take her for interrogation.'

His face was impassive. 'There may have been.'

'I know some people went to the house. They were there that day. I know it. Two men. Maybe you were one – it doesn't really matter now, as you said. But I know they went.'

'Well well, you've been playing detective.'

'Was she there? Did they take her?'

He said nothing.

'Look. Just say yes or no. You don't know what it would mean to me. Did they take her?' Paula remembered the haste of the last morning she'd seen her mother, the snatched plate, the last hug. The sense of a clock ticking, though she hadn't realised it at the time.

Sean Conlon said, 'I don't know. All I can say is I don't know if anything was done to your mother.'

'And would you have known, if it was?'

'Aye, probably. Can't say for sure. Now that's all I know, miss.'

'I—' She wanted to say thank you, but couldn't. 'That's what I needed to know.'

'I don't know anything else. There were orders, and you went and did things, and that was all. It's hard to remember sometimes.'

Paula stepped back from the door, holding the flap. 'Well, you'll have a lot more time to remember now, Mr Conlon. I'm afraid that in light of your inaccurate information I won't be recommending you for early release.' She dropped it back and walked off, her steps echoing, but she could feel his eyes on her back all the way through the concrete and stone that kept him in.

'You can do this. How hard can it be?'

Paula looked down at the baby wriggling on the changing mat. She had no idea what time it was, three a.m. possibly. She thought she had slept for a while but couldn't be sure – the hours seemed to blend into each other. She'd changed Maggie's nappy again, maybe for the tenth time since coming back from the prison. She'd fed her. But the baby was still crying, a desperate, choking wail as if her tiny heart was breaking.

She scooped her up, feeling the little pulse fluttering like a trapped bird. 'It's OK, sweetheart. What's the matter?' She walked her to the window, where the sky was lightening over the shrouded rooftops of Ballyterrin. 'Look, it's night-time still. We should be asleep. Sleeping!'

Maggie continued her ragged cries. Paula walked her between the kitchen and the living room, keeping up a monologue as she went. 'Look, there's a picture of Grand-dad. That's Granny with him. Other Granny. She isn't here any more. We don't know where she is. And that's your toy that Granny Pat gave you.' Which just reminded her there was still no word or visit from Aidan, and resentment boiled up in her stomach like acid. 'Well, this is it, Maggie.' She showed the baby the living room, the seventies-style velvet couch, the cabinet of glass and silver knick-knacks, the silent TV coated in a layer of dust. She'd switched it off after the news channels rolled with endless updates on the Mayday case and the missing mayor. 'I'm sorry it isn't much. Maybe you'd rather go to London, what do you think? They have big red buses there. And nightclubs and bars and stuff. But you're maybe a wee bit young for that.' She sat down on the sofa, allowing herself to think briefly of her London life – transient men, long drinks in dark bars, running at night along the river, the city's slowly pumping heart. That was all gone now. Now she had this instead – her parents' sad old house, a town where everyone knew her name and her story, and this little baby, tangling angry fists in Paula's hair and jumper. 'What is it, love? Do you want more food?' She tried latching the baby on, but Maggie turned crossly away. She wasn't hungry. She wasn't wet. Maybe she was just really, really annoyed. Paula would sort of understand that.

'I'm sorry!' Paula started walking her again. The kitchen, the living room, the hall. The kitchen, the living room, the hall. Still the crying didn't stop. Her jumper was soon soaked in baby snot and tears, and she caught a glimpse of herself in the hall mirror – whey-faced, grubby, her hair in knots. 'Is that why you're sad, Mags? Because Mummy looks so awful?'

Mummy. That was her now. It was hard to believe. She was still pacing semi-dementedly when the doorbell rang. It was five a.m., who could that be? She rushed into the hall, hoping for deliverance of some kind. On the doorstep was Helen Corry, turned out despite the early hour in a swanky trench coat and trouser suit.

Corry winced at the wailing. 'What are you doing to her?'

Paula wiped the sweaty hair out of her eyes. 'I really don't know. She's been crying for hours, I think I've gone deaf in one ear.'

'Give her here.' Corry stepped into the hall, taking the baby and cradling her over one arm in a rocking movement. Maggie's cries swelled like a passing siren and then subsided into sad hiccups.

'How did you do that?'

'Years of being up with crying weans, then called out to crime scenes at six a.m.'

Paula collapsed back on the sofa. 'I'm not sure I can do this on my own.'

'Course you can. I'd a husband and he was next to useless. Never heard them crying, apparently, even when I took them into the bed and held them beside his ear.'

'How did you know to come?'

'I'd a feeling you might be up.' Corry looked at her kindly. 'It's tough the first few months.'

'*Months?*'

'Yes. But you'll get through it. Anyway – I'm here with something that'll cheer you up.'

'What's that, a full-time nanny?' Either that or Aidan's head on a plate.

'Gerard's got some anonymous tip-off about what happened to Kenny. You realise I mean cheer you up in that ghoulish sort of way you like.'

'Oh really?'

'Word is there's been some kind of power shift in the local IRA leadership and someone wants to talk.'

Paula's mind was racing, trying to put the pieces together, but then she sighed. 'I'm not supposed to be working. What's the point in telling me?'

'I know you're not, but how would you like a few hours in the office? If I know you, it's doing your head in that you didn't get to clear your desk.' She nursed the now-sleeping baby. 'I'll mind this wee one while you nip out.'

'Are you sure it's OK?'

'Call it one of those Keeping in Touch days or something. We have to stick together, us working mothers,' said Corry, with a heavy tang of irony. Paula could have hugged her.

Gerard was in the car park as she pulled up. He was zipped up against the morning chill in a waterproof jacket. 'You're here, Maguire?'

'Just pretend I'm not. What's going on?'

'Dunno. Apparently someone knows what happened to Kenny and they're prepared to talk.'

'Where are you off to now? You're not going to see them on your own?'

'Er, no, I'm not daft. I want to talk to my boys some more. I've an idea about something I want to check.'

'What's that?'

'I don't want to say as I might be wrong. But it would explain a lot about why we've not been able to get any solid evidence.'

Paula looked at him suspiciously. 'Where are you going?'

'There's a pub on the Knockvarragh estate where I sometimes meet them,' he said, naming the dodgiest Republican enclave in the town.

'You better not take the jeep then,' said Paula.

'Yeah, yeah.' He paused. 'How's your, eh, baby and all that?'

'Baby and all that is fine. Good luck with your terrorists.'

'Republican soldiers, they prefer.' Gerard went, beeping open the Skoda; no doubt he imagined he was in some Ballyterrin-set version of *The Wire*. 'Catch you later.'

In the office, all was quiet. It was too early for Avril or Fiacra to be in, and Bob was still on suspension anyway.

Paula sat at her desk but didn't turn her computer on. Her mind was full to bursting. First there was the four dead terrorists and the other missing two. Was it possible the leak was somewhere in their small team, so close-knit until recently? Then there was everything she'd found out about her mother. Sean Conlon said he didn't know if they'd taken her mother or not, but they'd certainly planned to. Did that mean she was dead after all? Mrs Flynn had known something. She'd put it in her statement, and Bob had suppressed it, not to cover himself as she'd imagined, but to spare her and her father. What was the piece of knowledge it contained, that lost slip of paper? Paula sat on, and found she was thinking of the man. The man in the hat. The one her mother had been talking to at the back door that day. Something told her that to find out about him would be the trailing thread that unravelled the whole rotten fabric of the past.

Sighing, she looked around her at the empty office, dust hanging in a shaft of morning light. So many files, new cases, old cases, the long-lost and the recently gone. The unit had been set up to try to find these people, bring home the ones who'd been missing for years, either alive or dead, and look for the ones who'd just disappeared before they too became lost for good. But had they done it? Four of the Mayday Five were dead and the unit hadn't managed to find anything. For the first time Paula found herself wondering what was the point of it all. Why hadn't she stayed in London, with her safe, controlled life there, where every case wasn't as close to her as her own pumping blood?

She sighed again. Reaching for her desk phone, she dialled a number and waited for the sound of his voice, rich and full. She said, 'Hello. This is Paula Maguire here.'

'Dr Maguire, back to work so soon?' Lorcan Finney sounded guarded.

'Not really. Just sorting out a few things. Sorry, have I caught you at a bad time? I know it's early.' She could hear the sounds of traffic behind him.

'It's fine. Just out for my morning run.'

'Right. I was wondering, did you run that writing sample?'

'Oh yes, the one you officially didn't give me. I did, but there was no match with the notes.'

'Really?'

'No.'

She'd been so sure. 'Well, OK, thank you anyway.'

'How's your wee one?'

'Oh, she's grand, yes.' She wasn't comfortable talking about this with him. 'So there's no more news from forensics?'

'Nothing. The note from Ni Chonnaill's mouth said LEGITIMATE TARGET, as you know. That's a pretty standard phrase, so I don't think we'll get much from it.'

'Same paper and everything again? Same writing?'

'Same.'

She sighed. 'Well. I'm not supposed to be working anyway. Thanks for looking at it.'

'Take care, Dr Maguire.'

She was pottering about collecting case files, enjoying the silence of the office with the morning sun slanting in, when the main phone began to ring. She picked it up. 'MPRU?'

'Paula! Is anyone there with you?' Fiacra was on the line, shouting. Fear in his voice.

'No, it's just me. What's wrong?'

'Call the hospital. Now. Tell them we're coming. Then get outside, I'm coming to pick you up.'

'Why? What's wrong?' She was reaching for her mobile.

'Gerard's been shot. His meeting, it was a set-up. We need to go and get him. I'm almost there.'

'Oh . . . OK.' Paula rang the hospital, giving the details as quickly as she could. Her hands shook as she put her coat on, went outside. She found herself locking up the door. *For God's sake, Maguire, leave it.* Fiacra's Fiesta was already screeching into the car park, engine chugging.

Fiacra wound the window down. 'Get in!'

Paula had barely shut the door when Fiacra sped off, throwing her against the dashboard. She leant awkwardly on the tape deck. 'Christ! Where are we going?'

'To the estate. He was on his way to the pub. Someone took a shot at him.' Fiacra was cutting up the morning traffic.

'How do you know?'

'I was on the phone with him. Heard it all happen. He knew it was bad.' The estate was only minutes away and Fiacra rounded into it, turning the wheel wildly. 'He said he was running down the alley by the pub . . . shit.'

There, slumped on the tarmac in a weed-grown alley between two council homes, was a familiar body. Gerard's eyes were shut and he wasn't moving, except for the blood seeping out from under him. As they drew up there was a screech of tyres, and a white van accelerated out of a side road, from which every resident seemed to have vanished.

'Get down!' Fiacra was grabbing for her head, pushing her down. 'Shit. I think that was them. That was the shooter.'

'Did you see anything?' She'd had a momentary glimpse of a dirty white van, no number plate, the windows tinted out.

Fiacra was scrabbling at the door. 'No. Shit. Come on, we have to grab him and get out of here. It's not safe.'

Kira

'Did you ever love anyone?' she asked.

From the corner, Lily called out – 'Don't talk to him, Kira.' She was always on her phone when it was their turn to mind the man, her hair falling over her face in a big shiny curtain. Kira ignored her. They didn't tell Lily everything because she didn't understand. They didn't even tell her on the day it all happened, because she couldn't be trusted. The man was in his cage in the corner, head slumped onto his chest. He never said much.

Kira asked again. 'You must have. You have kids? I saw pictures.'

'My daughter,' he said, his voice rusty. 'She doesn't see me much.'

'But you must have loved someone – a woman? Your wife? I mean, loved someone so much that when you lost them you thought you might die without them?'

He said nothing for a long time, so she didn't think he was going to answer. Sometimes he just didn't, not for hours. She sat back against the wall, looking around the little hut. Lily was in her usual spot in the old green armchair Dominic had brought up there, her long legs propped on the windowsill. Kira thought she did this so men would see, even though the only man there was *the* man. She just couldn't help it.

After a while he coughed – he coughed a lot, usually horrible ones full of phlegm that made her want to cover her ears. 'Her,' he said.

'What?'

'I loved her. Catherine.'

The woman? Kira stared at him but his head was still bowed, hands laced together over his knees. He looked broken. Kira was remembering things she'd told herself she wasn't going to think about ever – the moonlight catching the woman's blonde hair, the sound of her crashing about in the trees and the way she was crying. What she'd said when they'd caught her and it was time for the end – *please, my baby. My baby.*

And how she'd called out to the man – *Martin, please don't let them—*

He hadn't even looked at her. He hadn't done a thing to save her; instead he'd given her up to them. Kira couldn't understand it. 'You loved her?'

'Aye. We met because our . . . what we believed in. She was with another man, and she'd a child already, but she wanted me. She was younger, too young, but she was beautiful, so beautiful, and I . . . I was weak. I loved her. Now she's dead because of it.'

He was talking to her like an adult, or more likely, as if he'd forgotten she was there. Rambling. His eyes didn't seem to be looking at anything. 'We didn't mean it,' he said, staring past her. 'It was never meant to go like that . . . All those people, dead. Blood in the street. Those wee kids. It wasn't meant to be like that.'

Kira leaned in towards his bars, so she could smell the stink of his bucket in the corner. 'Why did you do it?' she whispered. 'How could you?'

Lily turned her head, annoyed, but was distracted by her phone. Probably texting Dominic or looking at one of her stupid fashion blogs. He said nothing, and Kira was almost glad, because she didn't really know what it was she was asking.

Chapter Thirty

'Where are you hurt?' Blood was bubbling up from under Gerard's white T-shirt. Her hands were already covered in it from where they'd dragged him into the car. *Shit*. She took off her scarf with the clock pattern, her favourite, and pressed it firmly against his stomach. His heart was racing so fast it was almost a blur, but at least that meant he was still alive. 'What happened? Why did they shoot him?'

'Total fuck-up,' said Fiacra succinctly, running a red light on Market Street. 'He went to meet the tipster on his own. I'd guess it's the local Ra, and they didn't take too kindly to him snooping around. He was being set up with this meet.'

'For fuck's sake. I told him not to! He went on his own to meet an anonymous source?'

'Aye, he's an eejit. Help him, will you? He's losing fuckloads of blood.'

In the back, Gerard was filling most of the car seat. A smell of hot blood. His face was clammy and his breath came in pants.

'S'OK,' muttered Gerard. 'S'not too bad.'

Fiacra said, 'You've been shot, you fecking eejit.'

'You're OK. You'll be OK.' Knowing this was a stupid thing to say, Paula tried not to look out the front, pressing down as hard as she could on Gerard. With the size of him and her own remaining baby weight they were pressed up so close she could smell the frightened sweat under his Lynx. 'You'll be OK.' She felt his fingers on her wrist. 'What is it?'

'Mum,' he breathed. 'Call my ma. Tell her.'

'I will, of course, but you're fine, you'll be fine. Listen, Gerard, do you know why this happened? Did you find out something? What was your hunch?'

His eyes were fluttering. 'Knew he wasn't right . . .'

'Who? Gerard, tell us!'

It was too late. He was slumped over, unconscious from blood loss. Most of it seemed to be over Paula's clothes and hands. She could hear the panic in her voice. 'For God's sake, drive!'

'We're there.'

Though she'd always hated Ballyterrin General Hospital, Paula had never been happier to see the blue door of A & E come into view. Fiacra slammed on the brakes, halfway up the pavement, and Paula was thrown forward again. A fresh spurt of Gerard's blood pumped through the scarf and over her wrist. Then doctors were running up with a stretcher, and Saoirse was one of them, and they were taking Gerard off her and removing the scarf, bringing clean bandages.

'We've got him from here.' Attaching an IV, Saoirse threw Paula a brisk backwards look. 'You should sit down. You look like you're in shock.'

'Come on.' Fiacra was taking her by the shoulders and moving her into the waiting room. 'We have to leave him now. They know what they're doing.'

'My hands.' She held them up, like Lady Macbeth. The cuffs of her grey jumper were sodden, and blood stuck in her nails and skin. On the front of her top, it made what looked like an abstract painting. 'It'll not come off,' said Fiacra grimly. 'Hope it wasn't your favourite.'

She sank down on a plastic chair, the legs crumpling under her. Fiacra remained standing. He rubbed his face and Paula saw the front of his shirt was also bathed in blood. 'How did you know he was there?'

'He rang me. The van was following him – he was in some alley on the estate and he knew he wouldn't get away. He said he'd try to protect his head and run to the main road and I was to get him and go straight to hospital. He knew no one on the estate would call him an ambulance.'

'So you just went?'

'Course I did. I'm not – well, I know what you think of me. But you don't know everything that went on, OK? You don't know what I've been going through with my family and all that business with – Avril. You know – nothing.' His voice went high and cracked.

Paula let him finish. Then she stood up and put her arms awkwardly round him, smearing blood over his blue work shirt. She was ashamed she'd ever wondered about him – he was just a boy, really, hurting and confused. 'It's OK,' she said. 'He'll be all right. You saved his life.'

Fiacra rubbed his eyes with screwed up fists. He pulled away. 'Thanks. Sorry.'

'It's all right.'

It was a long ten minutes for Fiacra and Paula, waiting in the stark room with the posters on sexual health. Having just come to the end of a surprise (stupidity-induced) pregnancy, that was the last thing Paula wanted to see. She'd rung the house several times but there was no answer

– Corry must have taken Maggie somewhere else. Fiacra was pacing up and down, occasionally pushing his fists against the walls or chairs, and she longed to tell him to stop fidgeting, but didn't. He might start crying again. Eventually Corry came in, grim-faced.

'Is he—' Fiacra stopped in his tracks.

'He's all right,' said Corry. 'Bloody eejit. This is a publicity nightmare.' She saw their faces. 'Yes, yes, I know, but Monaghan will be fine, though he might have a bit of damage to the six-pack he's so fond of flaunting in the station changing room.'

'Where's Maggie?' asked Paula, feeling her heartbeat slow a little. 'Is she all right?'

'I left her at your father's. She's grand. I'm more worried about you two. Honestly, Dr Maguire, can you not stay out of trouble for even one day?'

'What have we got to do with it?' Paula was bewildered.

'You were seen picking him up, weren't you? DC Monaghan was sent an anonymous email claiming to have information about the case – same person who emailed the *Ballyterrin Gazette* with the leaked notes, it turns out.'

'Was the email a string of numbers, the date of the bomb?'

Corry glared at Paula and nodded. 'Yes, and rather than bring it to me as further evidence of the leak, he went alone to meet them. Someone clearly wanted him out of the way – maybe he was getting too close to the truth with those informers of his. And I've no doubt they saw you and know exactly who you are. DC Monaghan will be moved to a secure unit where they used to put injured soldiers. You two better lie low. Why didn't you ring an ambulance?'

'He called me,' said Fiacra stubbornly. 'He said the ambulance might not go down there. He was in big trouble, he said. The blood. He knew it was bad.'

'Yes, I can see.' Corry wrinkled her nose. 'You two look like extras from a horror film. I'd send you home to clean up but I can't spare the officers to guard you right now.'

'It can't be that serious,' said Paula, shocked.

Another glare. 'Do you really want to risk finding out, Dr Maguire? You with a new baby at home?'

'No,' she muttered.

'Right. So you'll stay here until I can have you escorted home.'

Fiacra and Paula spent the next hour as virtual prisoners in the waiting room, Corry and a uniformed officer stationed outside. Paula had read the same poster about gonorrhoea about a hundred times when she heard loud steps outside, running down the corridor.

'Where is he?'

'Ms Wright, you can't—'

'I need to see him!'

Paula tried hard not to look at Fiacra as the sound of Avril's panicked voice reached them in the room. She got up, slowly, and looked out the glass panel of the door to see Corry remonstrating with Avril, whose face was shiny with tears. 'You can't see him, he's in theatre.'

'Oh no, oh no . . .'

'His spleen is lacerated but he can live without that, so let's not panic, all right?'

More noisy sobs. Corry rolled her eyes at Paula through the glass, then opened the door and propelled Avril in with a gesture halfway between a pat and a shove. 'There now, Dr Maguire will have a wee chat with you, sure isn't that what she's good at?'

Paula shot Corry an irritated glare and led Avril in. 'What's the matter?'

'He – they said he got shot – oh!'

'Come on, sit down. Calm yourself.' The analyst, normally so neatly turned out, was dressed in jeans and a hoody, on the back of which was printed QUEEN'S UNIVERSITY GIRLS HOCKEY 2005. Her shoulders were heaving. Paula reflected that comforting weeping women was becoming a large part of her job – though she could hardly talk after she'd made a holy show of herself the night Lynch's body had been found. 'He'll be fine Avril, honest.'

'What happened? How did he get shot – oh!' she caught sight of Paula's stained jumper. 'Is that *blood*?'

Paula hastily folded her arms. 'It's not as bad as it it looks. They said he'd be OK.'

Avril shook her head, giving out more noisy mewling. Fiacra lurched over from his seat in the corner, looking as pale and miserable as she did. 'They did say he'd be grand, honest.'

'You were with him.' It could almost have been an accusation.

'Naw, he rang me, like. The van was chasing him, and they must have known he had intel, so he said he'd run to the main road and I was to pick him up there. It was too late. But we got him here as fast as I could, honest.'

Avril wiped a shaky hand over her eyes. 'I wish I could see him. Last time I – oh, I said some awful things. Said it was all his fault. Told him he was an arrogant you-know-what – getting involved with the IRA, and also . . . you know, what happened with Alan.'

Fiacra took her hand clumsily. 'Well, so did I. I nearly took a swing at him and all. But when he got in diffs, he rang me. He may be an arrogant fecker but he doesn't hold grudges.'

She continued to cry, her face screwed up, and Fiacra looked stricken. He slid to his knees in front of her. 'Ah, here. I'm sorry, OK? I never should have said a word to Alan. What I did was awful, but sure I never thought – I was just in a mess over Aisling and her wean, but it's no excuse. I'm sorry, Avril. You were a good friend to me and I blew it, just because I wanted more.'

With an inarticulate noise she grabbed him to her in a hug. Paula saw his eyes close and thought he still wanted more, whatever he might say. She went back to the door and tapped on the glass. Corry turned her head. *Please let me out,* she mouthed.

Corry just smiled and shook her head. It made a change, Paula thought, grumpily sitting down again, when she and Guy were not the most emotionally messed-up members of the team.

Kira

Kira couldn't look at them. 'Do I have to do it?'

'Yes. She knows too much, and she won't suspect you. You're only a kid.'

'But . . .'

'You agreed, Kira. This is for Rose, and all the others.'

'But she didn't do anything!'

'No, but she'd put us in prison if she could. She's close

to finding out. We need to stop her. It was her picked up the other officer, the one who was nearly on to us.'

'And . . . you'll just talk to her, you promise? You won't hurt her.'

'We won't need to. She hasn't done anything wrong, like you said.'

'But . . .'

'We can just persuade her. She'll understand. They've hurt her too, the bad people.'

'She has a little baby.'

'We just want to talk to her. It has to be you, Kira. Or else this whole thing, it will be for nothing, and we'll go to prison, while those people got away with it.'

But they didn't get away with it. They were dead, all of them except the last. She couldn't think what to do. Rose's voice had been fading since they killed the first man. Since everything started to go wrong. She'd wanted them dead, yeah, but when it really happened she'd thought they would just talk to them. She'd thought they would show photos, make them see what they'd done, and maybe they'd confess and go to prison. She didn't know this was the plan, the hurting, and then taking them away and killing them somewhere. And hurting the policeman, when he hadn't done anything wrong, he was trying to *help* them . . .

'I . . .'

He was looking at her. His eyes were flat and cold. 'Kira. You're in this now. It was all your idea. You don't have a choice.'

Still looking at her feet, so they wouldn't see she was nearly crying, she nodded. The weird thing was the only person she could think to ask what to do was the man, and he was in his cage again in the corner, and anyway, what would she ask? She knew the answers already, and inside her head, so did Rose. But it was too late.

Chapter Thirty-One

Paula spent an awkward night with officers on her doorstep, Maggie sleeping fitfully and waking up to feed, then cry, then sleep, then repeat again. She had the baby nestled beside her in her single bed, thinking over what Corry had said. It was an exaggeration, surely. She wouldn't be targeted. Whoever was in the van couldn't have seen her in that split-second. But she thought of Maeve, and of Gerard, both lying injured in hospital, and clasped Maggie so tight the baby squawked. 'Sorry, pet. Let's try to get some sleep. Let's put you in your cot.'

She was woken out of a hazy doze several hours later, by voices outside. She sat bolt upright, checking Maggie in her nearby cot. The baby slept, small fists clutched under her chin. Paula looked out the window and saw someone remonstrating with the officer at the front door. A man.

Wrapping a shabby red dressing gown round her, she crept downstairs, listening.

'Sir, you can't go in.'

'Ah for God's sake. She knows me!'

She opened the door on its chain, feeling the cold morning air on her legs. 'It's OK, Constable. He can come in.'

'If you're sure, ma'am.'

'Yeah. Er . . . are you OK out here, by the way?' The man looked frozen in his reflective jacket and helmet.

'Fine, ma'am.'

She opened the door properly, and moved back to let Aidan in. He stood there in the hallway, wearing just a T-shirt, his arms stippled with gooseflesh. She crossed her arms, hugging the dressing gown round her, neither of them speaking for a full minute.

'Are you all right?' he said finally. 'I heard what happened with Monaghan.'

'He'll be OK. They've moved him to an army hospital. This is just a precaution.'

'Quite the precaution, armed peelers on your doorstep.'

'What do you want, Aidan?'

'To see if you're OK.'

'You're running a bit late for that.'

'I . . .' Whatever he was going to say was lost as a thin wail started up from upstairs. Aidan froze. 'Is that . . . ?'

'That's Maggie, yes. That's her name. My baby. Not that you've been around to ask, or see, or . . .' She had to stop as tears suddenly filled her mouth. 'She needs feeding. Give me a minute, will you? Go in the kitchen.'

Paula went upstairs and quickly pulled on jeans and the first jumper she could find that wasn't too encrusted with milk or sick or snot. She scraped her hair into a loose ponytail and then scooped up Maggie from her cot. The baby was hot and smelled of milk and talcum powder. Paula held her close, murmuring into her head. 'He's here. He came.' She couldn't put a name to what she felt, anger and excitement and something even stronger, a need that was like a kick in the gut. God, she'd missed him. It was hard to admit in the cold light of dawn, her child in her arms. She had missed him. She needed him. Trouble was, he'd never had anything to give.

She took the baby downstairs wrapped in a blanket, not looking Aidan in the eye. He was in the kitchen, leaning awkwardly against the counter. 'Sit down if you want. I need to feed her.'

'Oh, should I . . . ?'

'Just stay.' She was too weary to explain. She pushed up her jumper. The pull of Maggie's mouth brought a gasp of relief, the little starfish hands grasping. This she could do. This was helping someone.

Aidan was staring at the baby, half-hidden by the blanket Paula had wrapped around them. Usually she didn't care if her breastfeeding bothered people, but this situation just felt too fraught to add anything else to. 'Red hair.' He nodded to the fuzz on Maggie's head, already gingery in the dull light of dawn.

'Yep. Hardly surprising.'

'What colour are her eyes?'

'Well, blue. But most babies have blue eyes at first.'

'Oh.'

The weight of the unasked questions was suffocating. Maggie had finished, her mouth going slack as she fell back to sleep. Paula rearranged herself. 'Do you want to hold her?'

'Me?'

'Well, yeah, that's what most people do when they come to see a newborn.'

He seemed paralysed. She stood up and walked the few paces to him, placing the baby in his arms. Close enough to smell his skin. Maggie was asleep, lolling like a doll. Aidan stared at her. 'She's so light.'

'Yeah, not when you carry her round howling for hours.'

He still stared. The only sound in the kitchen was the hum of the fridge, and traffic starting up in the road below, Maggie's soft breathing. Paula stood watching the two of them. Aidan spoke slowly. 'She's . . . she looks just like you.'

'Poor kid.'

'No. She's beautiful, Maguire. She's . . .' he tailed off, staring at the baby. Paula leaned against the counter, registering in some part of her brain that this was the exact place she'd last seen her mother, washing the dishes that morning. She hardly dared breathe in case she shattered the moment.

'It's hard to take in,' she said. 'I've got a baby now. Me. I mean . . . it's daft.'

'Everything's changed, hasn't it?'

'Yeah.'

Aidan kept looking at the baby rather than Paula. 'So do we need to talk about that?'

'What do you mean?'

'Ah Maguire. Are you not sick of this? Falling out, making up, having all these stupid misunderstandings . . . I mean, we've known each other all our lives. Why is it still so hard?'

'I don't know. I never mean it to be.'

'Me either. But it is, isn't it? And now she's here . . . what's that going to mean?'

She might have said something then – something, anything, forgiven him, scolded him, answered his question – but the peace was ended by her phone suddenly trilling on the counter. Aidan jumped slightly, holding the baby tighter to himself; her blue eyes flew open but she didn't cry.

'Sorry. I'll just . . .' Paula answered her phone, listened to the unfamiliar voice on the other end for a minute, and hung up. She took a deep breath. 'I have to go out. Will you watch her for me for an hour?'

'You're leaving her?'

'I have to.'

'You're her *mother*, Maguire . . .'

'Look, John Lenehan's had another stroke. He's asked for me, apparently. He hasn't got long left. He's dying, Aidan.'

'Why you?'

'Why not?' She was taking her coat down from the peg in the hallway. 'Thanks to Flaherty and his lot, he has no one else. They're all dead. And he may well tell me what's been going on.'

Aidan was shaking his head. 'Pumping a dying man for information. Nice, Maguire.'

She stared at him coldly. 'He asked for me. And this is my job.'

Aidan nodded to Maggie in his arms. 'That's your job now. Not running off trying to find murderers. You have to stop, Paula. Stop running. You're out of road. Stop looking for your mother, stop with this case – think of Maggie.'

'You sanctimonious bastard,' she said quietly. 'You're a bloody dinosaur. This isn't the dark ages! I can have a child and not be tied to the house forever. How am I supposed to manage? I'm a single mother, or have you not noticed?'

'Only through choice, Maguire. You've gotten exactly what you wanted, just like always.'

There was so much she could have said, angry, bitter words that once flung out could never be taken back. Only the latest in a string of their rows. Paula picked up her bag, flipping her hair out from under her coat. 'Will you mind her? I won't be long. She's just been fed so she should sleep again.'

He said nothing.

'Will you help me? Look, I'm so close. Gerard was probably shot because he was on to something. Kenny's gone. The families are involved, I'm sure of it. And I think maybe Flaherty knew . . . if you'd help me, then maybe I could . . .'

He still wouldn't look at her. 'No, you do whatever you want. You always do.'

'Aidan! Grow up. Will you look after Maggie for me?'

'Of course I bloody will. You don't have to ask, if you need it. But you shouldn't need it, not for this.'

She was pulling open the door, preparing to argue with the constable. 'I don't have time for this. There's expressed milk in the fridge if I get really held up. Call your mum if you have any problems. And if you let one hair on her head get hurt, I will kill you.'

The man in the bed was the colour of overwashed socks, a grey tinged with green. A mask over his face was helping him breathe.

'We could only find your number,' said the nurse, hushed. 'Is there any family?'

'No,' said Paula. 'Not any more.'

The noises coming from John were alarming, even with the mask. She turned back to the nurse. 'Can you not do anything for him?'

'We've done our best. It'll kick in soon. We hope.'

'Is there . . .'

The nurse shook her head firmly. 'We're making him comfortable. Those are his wishes.'

She pulled up her chair beside him and saw his eyes flicker open. He knew she was there. 'Hello, John,' she said quietly. 'How are you?'

He made a wheezing coughing noise that could almost have been a laugh.

'I can see.' She wanted to take his hand, gnarled and shaking on the hospital blanket, but he was a dignified man and he might not like it. She'd do him the courtesy of not showing pity. His hand reached up, scrabbling at the mask. Though she knew the nurse would shout at her, she helped him. His skin was cold and clammy. He slurred, 'You had your wean?'

'Yes. A little girl. Maggie.'

'She's . . . well?'

'Yes, thank you. I think so.'

'You're . . . working?'

She knew what he was asking, heard the fuller speech behind his hoarded handfuls of words.

'Yes, I – I just have to see it through, John. I know it's hard. But I have to do the same for them as for anyone else.'

A storm of coughing shook him. Paula looked round anxiously; no nurse to be seen. 'Tried to forgive them,' said John hoarsely. 'Tried to follow the Bible. But . . . Danny. And Mary.'

'I know. You lost them all.' And here he was dying alone, after a life lived to the letter of the law, the wife and son and grandchildren that should have been his all taken from him. His hand clutched hers suddenly. 'Wanted to go to Heaven . . . but – I couldn't. Forgive them. Too much to ask. I despaired. Despaired of God. And Mary – a sin.'

She remembered, the church's teaching that suicide was a mortal sin. It wasn't long since people who'd died that way had been buried outside the walls of the graveyard. 'I don't believe that,' Paula said. 'I don't think a just God would punish someone further.'

Tears were leaking from his old eyes. 'But that lot – these evil, evil people – they walked free. No punishment.'

'They've been punished now,' said Paula quietly. 'Four of them are dead, John, even the woman. She won't be coming home to her children – the youngest is only a baby.'

He closed his eyes. His hand was cold in hers. 'John,' she said, 'if you know something, please tell me now. Before it's too late. If we can find Flaherty, even – if we can just know what happened . . .'

'Already too late.' His voice was exhausted, used up. 'Was too late . . . long ago.'

'I've got this problem,' she said, almost whispering. 'I'm no good at giving up. I can't give up trying to find my mother, whoever I hurt in the process, and I can't give up on this case. I need to know. I know it won't do any good, and maybe they deserved it – but John, there was a reason you left the group. You couldn't go along with their idea, could you? You knew justice was only God's to deal out.'

He muttered something. 'C'mere.' She leaned in close, so her ear almost touched his mouth. His breath was weak. He smelled of hospitals and old damp clothes. 'The wee girl,' he gasped.

'Kira? Kira Woods?'

'Aye. The wee one.'

'What about her?' One of John's machines began to beep, and outside she could hear a commotion of feet. 'John! Is she in danger? Tell me!'

He pushed his head up, with great effort, like an old tortoise. 'It was her idea,' he said, right into Paula's ear. Then she was thrust aside.

'Let us work please, miss!' John was swamped by nurses, and a terribly young girl in scrubs who was apparently the doctor. The machine kept beeping.

'Are you family, miss?' asked a different nurse.

'No, there is no family.'

'You'll have to go then. Please.' The curtains were swished around, and Paula got her last glimpse of his face, white as if he were already dead.

'Is he dying?'

Paula turned at the sound of the small, stricken voice. A thin, pale girl in school uniform was at her side – Kira Woods herself. 'You shouldn't be here, Kira.'

'I heard he was sick – he's not got anyone to be here with him. He wouldn't let Dominic . . .' She was shuddering. 'You shouldn't be on your own when you die.'

'He's all right, Kira. They'll look after him.'

Kira just looked at her. 'He's dying, miss. I know he is. Please don't lie to me.'

'Well, OK, but there's nothing we can do. He's old. He's . . . he'll be with his son and wife again, maybe.'

'Do you really believe that, miss?'

'I don't know, Kira. There's no way to know.'

The girl was shaking. Paula looked at her watch. 'Come on, I'll wait with you.'

It wasn't long. They'd been in the waiting room for ten minutes when the young doctor came, reading from her clipboard. 'I'm sorry, but he was very weak, and he did sign the DNR order . . . he wasn't in any pain.'

Kira was pale and composed. 'Did he die?'

'Yes. I'm sorry. Are you his granddaughter?'

Kira tutted. 'He didn't have any. His son died in the bomb.'

'The bomb?' The doctor looked tired, confused.

Kira sighed. 'Never mind.' She looked at Paula, and her eyes were hollow. 'Thanks for waiting with me, miss. It's all right. I think he's happier now, it's just . . . I feel sad for me.'

Paula had the car keys in her hand. She knew Maggie was waiting for her, needing a feed. She'd be starting her small snuffling noises, pulling at the top of whoever was holding her. Aidan, maybe still. She looked at the girl, who was slumped in her chair, head down. 'Can I drop you somewhere, Kira? Do you not have school today?'

'Yes, but I can't . . . I don't want to go home yet. Mammy . . .' She shuddered. 'She's cross with me.'

'Well, a friend's, maybe? I can't leave you here on your own. I'd stay but I really have to get back to my baby.' She could all too easily picture herself. In her maroon school uniform, the same age, thirteen or so, answering all their endless questions in the police station, sitting in this same hospital waiting for PJ to identify a body they'd found that might have been her mother. *Did your mammy say anything to you? Did you see anyone near the house?* At least she hadn't had to watch her mother die in front of her, covered in her blood, as this girl had watched her sister Rose. She thought of what John had said – what did it mean, it was all her idea?

'Come on,' she said. 'Get your coat on. I'll drop you wherever you want.' And maybe on the journey she could find out what Kira knew.

Kira seemed to relax as they moved out of town in the early morning traffic. The streets were full of kids in uniform, the navy of Kira's Protestant school, the black of the Catholic boys, the maroon of Paula's own convent school and the pale blue sweatshirts of the integrated high school. The girl sat quietly beside her, school bag on her knee. 'Where is it you want to go?'

'Can we go out of town, miss? Like in the country, in the hills.'

'You have a friend there?'

'Yeah. A few friends.'

'OK. And you'll call your mother and tell her you're there?'

'I already did. Earlier, I mean.'

'OK. Good.' She found herself taking looks at the girl, with her scars and slightly unnerving silences – she wasn't pretty, as Rose had been, but there was a steel core in there, a tough little nugget that hadn't shattered when her family did.

'Kira – John said something to me, there now . . .'

'How's your little baby?' Kira asked suddenly. She was still looking straight ahead.

'Oh – she's OK, thanks. Very little still. I'm not sure she even knows who I am.' She glanced at the dashboard clock; she really had to get back. The traffic was awful.

Kira was saying, 'I bet she does. People always know who their mum is. I did.'

Paula frowned. 'Your mother? But . . .'

'Not *her*. I knew she wasn't really. She didn't love me.'

'What do you mean, Kira?'

Kira looked at her in the car mirror. 'Rose was my real mum. Did you not know? Mammy isn't my mum at all.'

Paula stalled for time. 'Er – what makes you think that?'

'I just knew. Mammy used to say things, when she'd

drunk too much. So I asked Jamesie – that was Rose's boyfriend. I knew she used to go out with him way back. He said he was my dad. Rose was having me, only she was too young, she was fifteen, so they pretended I was Mammy's and Rose didn't see Jamesie again for years.'

'Oh. That must have been very difficult.' Paula's mind was racing. It was a common practice in Irish families, the youngest member actually being the first grandchild. She looked at the road ahead, now empty as the bog stretched out on either side, heather and gorse blooming. They hadn't seen another car in some time.

'Not really.' Kira's chin was raised; she looked different. 'I knew it, you see. I could tell Rose loved me. She talks to me sometimes, still. She said she'd have gladly died like that, instead of me, if that was the choice she had to make. You'd do the same, wouldn't you, miss? For your little girl? You'd die for her. That's what it means when you really love someone.'

'I—'

'Maggie.' Kira flashed her a look. 'You named her for your own mammy, Dominic said. I bet she didn't want to leave you, miss. Like Rose didn't want to leave me. I bet she didn't go by herself.'

'Kira—this isn't . . .'

'Can you slow down, miss?'

She was so flustered she did hit the brakes, and the car slowed right down.

'I'm sorry,' said Kira, and then she was wrenching open the door, tumbling out onto the road, hitting it knees first. Paula slammed on the brakes and the car stopped, but Kira was up, rubbing her cut legs, and sprinting with surprising speed over the bog.

Kira

It was something that, when she knew for sure and no messing, she realised she had always known. Like there being no Santa Claus. For years you didn't want to know the truth, trying to hold yourself away from it, and then it hit and it was OK. It was something solid to stand on.

There were little things. Rose's story about Daddy almost kicking her out for something she'd done. The comments Mammy used to make about being sinful and no better than she should be. There were no pictures of herself and Mammy in hospital, but there was a picture of Rose holding her that she'd seen in Rose's sock drawer. Rose looked fat and shiny and Kira had thought at the time this was why it was hidden.

Then the time a neighbour calling in said he'd got his car fixed by 'that fella Jamesie you used to go with, Rose' and that he'd done a good job. And everyone had gone quiet and Kira had remembered the strange meeting in the hotel. But she didn't really know it until the night of Rose's birthday, just before the last bomb anniversary. Rose had only turned twenty-three when the bomb happened. She'd have been twenty-eight now, nearly thirty. On her last birthday they'd gone out to a pizza restaurant in town, and Mammy had sighed that there was no boiled spuds, but Rose and Kira had put on party hats and made each other laugh, and like always, it didn't matter how Mammy was.

Mammy got drunk this year on Rose's birthday. Whiskey this time, mixed with Fanta. Kira could smell it on her breath. 'I'd have thrown her a party, she'd have had weans, her own proper weans. She'd have been wed. Making something of herself.'

Kira had been trying to help. 'She did make something of herself. She had a boyfriend. I think she liked him.'

Mammy stared at her, her eyes bloodshot.

'Jamesie. You know, he fixes cars. I think she might have married him.' This was after she'd seen Jamesie at the garage, after all the plans were in place, when it was too late to turn back or change what she'd done.

The finger pointed. 'Where did you hear that name?'

'I met him.'

The whiskey was dripping out of Mammy's glass. 'That dirty wee slut. She promised me you'd never meet him.'

'She's not a slut! You take that back!'

'And what would you know about it? Having a baby at fifteen years of age, so I could hardly hold my head up in church?' Mammy started to cry. 'I'm sorry, Rosie. I was hard on you. But you sinned.'

Kira was counting in her head, and feeling odd, like sinking down into the bottom of the sea. 'Mammy?' She gasped. 'Mammy?'

Mammy just stared at her. 'What's the point of you calling me that? I'm no more your mother than I am the dog's. Get out of my sight.'

Chapter Thirty-Two

Shit. Shit! Paula looked at the clock. 8.36 a.m. Maggie flashed into her mind, the small, compact body, the lullaby of her cot mobile. That was where she was supposed to be. Maggie might be still asleep, but she'd wake at some point, howling for the mother who wasn't there.

'Shit,' she said again, parking the car up beside the road. She took off her seat belt and set off after Kira. It wasn't easy. The birth had left her out of shape, and she could feel every step as she herpelled through the sticky bog. Bog cotton waved in the breeze and the ground squelched underfoot – step in the wrong place and she'd break her ankle, get stuck out here. Her breasts ached with milk. Maggie, Maggie . . .

'Kira!' she shouted. The girl had vanished into trees up ahead. 'Please come back! I can't go after you – I need to go to my baby. Kira. *Kira!*'

Nothing. She somehow made it to the trees, where the ground was harder, paved in pine needles. The morning sun slanted through the trunks like pillars in some enormous cathedral. She was glad she'd at least worn ankle boots with flat heels. 'Kira! For God's sake, please come back.' She followed the girl's progress onto the pine track, trying to listen for breathing or running teenage feet. There was nothing but her own panicky wheeze, and distant birds way up high.

'Help!' she shouted, she wasn't sure who to. But someone stepped onto the path ahead of her.

'Paula!'

'Dr Finney?' She ran to him. 'What are you doing here?' He was dressed in jeans and a light red rain jacket.

'I'm out with the search team – are you all right?' He took her arm. 'You look pale.'

'Just too soon to be running, after the baby. I was driving Kira Woods home and she ran off on me. I can't just leave her out here.'

He nodded. 'Look, I think there's something going on – there's a sort of hut up here. Let's look.'

She was panting. 'Is it safe?'

'You'll be safe with me. I think Kira went there.' Still breathing hard, she let him lead her to the end of a path, where a wooden hut sat in the trees. It was small – no more than ten metres long.

'What is this place?' Paula stopped.

'I think it's an old forestry hut. Come on, she went in here.'

'What did you say you were doing here?'

There was a moment when she could have run, maybe even got away, had it not been twelve days since she'd given birth, and she wasn't thinking straight. Most of her brain focused on her baby needing to be fed across town. Then it was too late anyway. His hand closed on her arm, hard this time, and he pushed her in.

Inside the hut was dark, and for a moment she couldn't see who was there. Then faces emerged – Dominic Martin was standing over someone in a chair. Kira was there, and

Lily Sloane. Tied to the chair, apparently unconscious, was Jarlath Kenny. And in the corner, in a sort of makeshift cage created by bars set into the wall, was a very much alive man she recognised from pictures as Martin Flaherty.

'I'm sorry, Dr Maguire. It's nothing personal.' Lorcan had turned. For a long moment, maybe for five seconds, she genuinely didn't understand what had happened. There was a gun in his hand, pointed at her.

Then it all fell into place, beautifully, horribly. The way they'd been led straight to the sea caves, but no one was there. The fact that Dominic Martin's van had, against all common sense, shown no traces linking it to the murders, yet his shoes – sent to London – had. The fact that Finney also drove a white van, which he'd been standing beside when she'd first met him. He had been tampering with the evidence. He was the leak. She remembered, vividly, handing him that scrap of paper with Kira's writing on.

'But – why you?'

He shifted the gun. 'One of the dead women. Lisa. Do you know her maiden name?'

Paula mentally leafed through the file she'd committed to memory. All the dead, their faces, their lives. Their names. Lisa McShane, dead in the car park, her hands clasping forever onto the man she couldn't bear to let go.

'She was your sister? Lisa McShane was your sister? But how . . .'

'No one knew. I've been away in England for years. Like you. We were separated when the terrorists disappeared our father. They tore my family apart, and then they killed Lisa too. Even now they're destroying her. The things they say about her! So ugly. It isn't fair. I came home for the trial, hoping I'd see some justice – well, you know how that ended. So what choice did we have?'

Paula looked round at them. The man in the cage, sitting on the ground with his head bowed, unmoving. The teenage girl, blank-faced, and Dominic, and Lily, weeping. Ordinary people, brought to this crazy place. 'So you lifted them – you went in the van with the Walshes, and you?' She looked at Dominic, who lowered his head. She looked at the gun in Finney's hand. 'You shot at the Walshes too, I take it? Not Kenny. He was already gone by then. Did you . . . was it you who hurt Gerard?'

Lorcan shifted on his feet. 'He'd worked out it was me. He was looking for proof. We couldn't let him get any closer.'

'You put him in the hospital. You almost killed him. And now you've kidnapped me too.'

Dominic spoke. 'We haven't . . . There was no other way, Dr Maguire. We know you saw John before he passed, and it was you picked up DC Monaghan too. We knew you were getting close to us when you gave Kira's writing sample to Lorcan.'

'So what happens now? You kill me?' She gestured to Flaherty. 'I guess this was some kind of vengeance. You can't kill me. I've done nothing wrong, and I have a child at home.' She turned to Dominic. 'You came to see me in hospital, when I was holding my baby – why did you do that?'

He lowered his head. 'I . . . I wanted to show you we aren't bad people. We're the victims here.'

'And what's your plan now you have me?'

'You can let it go,' Lorcan said. 'No one has to know. I've got Corry exactly where I want her – especially when she finds out the leak's been coming from her all along.'

'What?' said Paula.

'Let's just say she isn't as careful of her BlackBerry as she should be when I'm distracting her. So look. We can pin it on Kenny. It's all set up.'

'You kidnapped him too? Why?' She looked at the unconscious mayor. A bubble of blood sat near his mouth.

'He was getting spooked. He was happy enough when we went to him and asked if he could help us out when we lifted this lot and got them out of his way too. That was Kira – she persuaded him. No one could know I was involved. Then when you started figuring it out he'd have shopped us. Didn't want to get his hands dirty, now he could be an MP.'

'But he had nothing to do with the Mayday bomb!'

Lorcan made an impatient gesture. 'He's just as bad. He's killed people, and not only is he free, we've elected him mayor of our town! It's a joke, it really is. He thought he could do whatever he liked and walk away. He's a liar and a hypocrite.'

'You're no better than he is,' said Paula steadily. 'You're a murderer too. Don't make things any worse than they are. Let me call someone and we can sort all this out.'

'Shut up. What would you know about it?'

'Plenty. My mother's been gone for seventeen years. Most likely killed by the IRA, though I don't think I'll ever know.'

'And if you had them here –' he pointed with the gun to where Flaherty sat behind bars, his head bowed – 'if you had the person who killed her, and no one would find out, are you telling me you wouldn't take your revenge?'

'No. Because we're not like them. They killed without

remorse or regret, but there has to be some end to it, Lorcan. To the killing. Or else there'll be no one left alive.'

The gun was pointing at her again. She clenched her fists. Thought of Maggie. 'You won't hurt me.' She tried not to look in his violet eyes. 'You were nice to me. I know you understand how it's been for me . . . if anyone can understand me, you can.'

'A word, Lorcan.' Dominic dragged him by the arm to the corner, along with Lily. Kira sat in the window, very still, watching them all. Lily stood awkwardly, her feet wide apart, looking back at Paula. She looked beautiful, and very young. Paula heard whispered words – *knows too much, she'll go right to them* – she tried to keep steady. She'd been in worse situations. These were good people, if hopelessly damaged. She did her best not to look at the caged terrorist. Kenny was, mercifully, totally out of it. Blood ran down from his nose.

Lorcan was back, still holding the gun.

'Let me ask you this, Dr Maguire.' He pointed the gun at Kenny. 'What if I told you he knew something about your mother? What if, by doing the right thing to him, and in the right way, you could get all the answers you're looking for?'

'No.'

'You don't want to know what happened to her?' His face mocked.

'I want that more than anything. But he would tell me anything I wanted to hear, and I wouldn't know the difference. The only confession you can trust is one that comes for the right reason. Not fear. Remorse.'

'Men like him don't feel remorse,' said Lorcan. 'He's a monster. He's no better than the Mayday lot, for all his fancy suits. So you'd have no use for him? Is that what you're saying? If I said, here he is, do what you want with him?'

'I wouldn't torture him like you did. For God's sake, you're just as bad as they are.'

'So no then?'

'No, I wouldn't have—'

'OK,' said Lorcan, and lifted the gun, and shot Kenny in the head.

Paula flinched. She looked down at the red matter sprayed on her jumper and the wall. Kenny's eyes had flown open in death, surprised. Blood leaked from his mouth.

'Jesus Christ, Lorcan,' said Dominic faintly. 'We can't hurt her. She's done nothing wrong.'

'She's in our way! I want to finish this!' He was snarling. 'The plan was to pin it on Kenny.'

'And how do we do that now you've blown his damn head off?'

Lorcan waved the gun at Flaherty, who hadn't stirred at the noise of the shot. 'Make it look like him. A shoot-out. They're old mates. Get rid of them both – who's going to look into it?'

'Give me that, for Christ's sake.' Dominic moved towards him. 'We'll finish it. We stick to the plan. Dr Maguire knows what we went through. She'll do the right thing.' He turned to her. 'We just wanted to get their voices heard, the people who died . . . my daughter, Lorcan's sister, and Rose . . . they couldn't speak, and the people who killed them get to walk around free, saying what they like – it isn't right.' He turned again. 'Come on, Lorcan. This is too much.'

'I don't trust her.' The gun was still pointing right at Paula. 'No, she has to go.'

Dominic held Paula's eye, steady. She'd never see so much contained sorrow. *I'm sorry*, he seemed to be saying, and she felt the first dart of panic under her ribcage. *He wasn't going to help her.*

There was a creaking noise; everyone looked round. The door of Flaherty's cage was swinging open and he was coming out. It was open from the inside.

It seemed to take a moment for Lorcan to process events. He sprang back, a slow dawn spreading over his face as he looked round them all, coming to rest on Dominic. 'You. You . . . traitor!'

'Lorcan, we can explain—'

Flaherty was coming out. He looked tired and unkempt, his grey hair dirty, his face unshaven. But he drew the eye. This commander of men, this general in a war everyone else had long stopped fighting. 'Put the gun down,' he said to Lorcan. His voice was hoarse, as if he hadn't spoken in weeks.

Lorcan hesitated, and Dominic stepped in and took the gun from him, easily, lightly, like a pass in Gaelic football. Lorcan was struggling. 'Someone better explain this to me. Now. Why the hell isn't he locked up?'

'He wanted to come!' Kira burst out. 'He . . . he helped us. He told us where the others would be that day.'

'What are you telling me? Is that why we didn't pick him up with the others – you lied to me all along?'

'The wee girl,' said Flaherty, in a hoarse voice. 'She came to see me. She said it was a way to do . . . something.'

'We were going to take him,' Kira babbled. 'But he said he'd come, he said he wanted to end things. He said he was dying and he couldn't meet his maker that way. He said he'd help us get the others. That's how we – that's why it was easy. He told us where they'd be.' She turned to Paula, tearful, frantic. 'Miss, we never thought Lorcan would hurt them so much – it was just meant to be some justice, so we could come to them and show them what they'd done. We thought maybe they'd turn themselves in, go to prison. So Mr Kenny said he'd help and he'd send some men and Lorcan and Dominic went and lifted them and we did it. But – Lorcan just lost it, and Liam, Siofra's brother, he kept punching one of them, he wouldn't stop, and the guy's face like exploded and there was all blood everywhere – oh God.' She swallowed thickly. 'I didn't think it'd be like this. I just wanted them punished. It was Lorcan. He said we should kill them like our people died, so Kenny helped us lift them all, and we were in the caves, and Lorcan and Dominic took Doyle into the woods and hung him up, and with Brady, he wouldn't stop cutting him – they were going to cut his head off in the caves and the noise – it was like in a butcher's shop, and then he really lost it, he put Lynch in the van and they burned him – he was still alive . . . then the woman, she ran away, and she'd hardly any clothes on – that was Lorcan too, he said we had to make them suffer, take everything they had – and . . . she just kept crying and saying she had to go back to her baby, her children – and Lorcan just shouted she'd killed children, so why should she get to be with her own. Then we had to move them, we had to keep taking them to new places to hide them . . . It was awful, miss.' Kira caught her breath in her throat. 'And it was me. I started it. Lorcan was there at the court and he spoke to me, he said it didn't have to be this way. We could punish them. We were planning it for ages – then that journalist, her book came out and they said there might be another trial and Lorcan said we have to do it now before it's too late . . . And I . . .'

Flaherty spoke again, wearily. 'Leave it now, girl. It's too late.'

Lorcan seized Flaherty's wrists and pulled the cuffs. They fell away easily, clattering to the floor. 'All this time?' Lorcan was in disbelief. 'Why didn't you fight back?'

'I gave my word.' The contempt sounded in Flaherty's voice. 'As did you. Not to take anyone who didn't deserve it. And you've brought this woman here all the same.'

'You can say that? You?'

'Aye. Because I know what it's like to have your soul burned out. You wanted to kill – well, this is how it is, son. Every time you kill you put the knife in yourself too. Think on that. Now finish it.' He looked at Dominic, who was holding the gun. 'Finish me. I've had enough of this. I'm dying anyway, and I've done my piece, so let me go.'

Kira was moving towards him. 'Mr – I . . .'

Flaherty looked at her, his eyes almost kind. 'You started it, wee girl. This is how it ends.'

'But I didn't know – I never thought this would happen . . .'

'Unforeseen escalation,' said Flaherty. Kira was crying. He shut his eyes. 'Finish it, man, for God's sake. You promised.'

Dominic had the gun trained on him, but his arm shook and Paula saw it in his eyes – *he can't do it*. 'Look, maybe we should just . . .'

Then Lorcan was behind Paula, squeezing her neck with his arm. 'This doesn't end here. Not like this.'

Paula tried to buckle, kick back with her booted feet,

but he was strong, much stronger than she'd imagined, and she was so weak from her stitches, and he didn't even flinch. His breath was in her ear, his smell of panicky sweat reeking from under the aftershave, and she couldn't believe she'd ever thought him attractive.

'Lorcan,' said Dominic quietly. 'What are you doing?'

'I won't go to prison. Not when those animals got away with it. She said we can sort it out. You know what that means. She's going to shop us.'

The pressure on Paula's windpipe increased. She gasped. She thought of Maggie, Maggie in her cot, clutching her fists, eyes jewel-bright. She thought of Guy watching her feed and Aidan holding the baby in his arms. A thousand futures began to spin away. This wasn't how it ended.

Dominic was trying to keep his voice calm. 'I trust Dr Maguire. She's known loss. She'll help us. We can stick to the plan, stage a shoot-out like you said.'

'I don't believe you.' He tightened his grip. Paula felt a tattoo of panic release into her blood – *he isn't stopping. Oh God, he means this.*

'Lorcan!' Lily screamed. 'You're hurting her! For God's sake, Dominic, do something!'

With her fading vision, Paula looked to the man with the gun for help, and saw he was just as helpless as her.

She wasn't sure what happened next. There was a loud noise, and she felt Lorcan sag and release her, and she fell to her knees, panting. When she looked up Flaherty was somehow holding the gun. Lily was screaming on and on. Flaherty held the gun to his own chin. 'No –' Kira said, swallowing it down into a cry. She was standing in front of the terrorist. 'Stop, I take it back.'

'You can't take things back, girl,' said Flaherty. 'That's

what I kept trying to tell you. Do you feel you've got justice now for your Rose?'

'No . . . I didn't mean . . . this wasn't . . .'

'God bless you, child. None of this was your fault.' And he fired.

The whole thing took seconds, the space in between heartbeats. She blinked and Lorcan was on the floor slumped against her legs, clearly dead. Blood seeped from the perfect black hole in his forehead – Flaherty, the expert marksman, had not missed his target. Her throat was raw and bruised. Flaherty had fallen to the ground, and Kira was scrabbling at his bloody throat. 'I killed him.' Her voice was empty with shock. 'I killed him. It was me. It was all my idea.'

Lily's screaming had become a background drone. Dominic was frozen. After what seemed like hours he gave a shuddering sigh and took a phone from his pocket. He wiped blood from it – Flaherty's had sodden him – and handed it to Paula. 'It's up to you. I don't know any more. I don't what we're doing. Lorcan – he had you – all I could see was your baby.' His hands were bloody, and when he raked them over his face he looked as he had on the day of the bomb five years before, staggering up to find his child's dead body beneath him. 'He had you and I did nothing – I couldn't shoot.'

It was a cheap phone, disposable. Paula looked at the number he'd keyed in. 'Dominic – I—'

'I know. Do what you have to.' He bent to Kira, who was also as covered in blood as she'd been after the bomb. She was cradling the dead terrorist in the same way she'd held her sister – her mother – on the day of the bombing, howling and wailing. Lily was the only one not blood-soaked, and she was keening, rocking herself in a corner. Dominic lifted Kira to her feet, half carrying her, and put out his hand to the other girl. 'It's over. Come on, Lily, love. It's over.'

She crept to him, dazed as a child. 'What will happen now?' She averted her eyes from all three dead bodies.

'Dr Maguire is going to ring someone to get us.'

'OK.' Lily was shaking. 'Can we go home? I want to see my mum.'

'Yes, pet. It's over.' He met Paula's eyes over Lily's smooth head, and nodded. She looked down at the phone. Plastic, cheap, the same as the one meant to trigger the bombs, setting off so many shockwaves that they were still detonating. It seemed crazy that such a little button, pressed in the space of a heartbeat, could bring down a mountain, topple onto you, rebound back and keep on rolling until nothing stayed standing. She thought about what Guy had said – how you could lose your ability to judge, to say who was right and who was wrong, and that was why we had the law, so we didn't have to make those choices ourselves, in all our human weakness and pain. She looked at Flaherty. The terrorist's face seemed strangely at peace. From the way the gun had torn his mouth, he could almost have been smiling.

'I'm sorry,' she said – she wasn't sure who to – and she pressed the button.

Epilogue

'What will happen to her?'

'I don't know,' said Guy. They were watching Kira Woods through the window of the hospital room where she was currently in bed, looking tiny amid the medical equipment. An officer was posted just inside the door. 'I've sent for a juvenile liaison officer. She really planned the whole thing?'

'It seems so. She was the one convinced Kenny to help them, and Flaherty to bring the others in, make amends. Or at least what he thought amounted to that. I don't think she had any idea Finney was planning to kill them all. I don't think the other families knew what was going on – or at least not enough. Maybe they let it happen, turned a blind eye.'

'You were very lucky.'

She knew he was looking at her, but she couldn't bear his gaze. 'I'm fine.'

'You need to get yourself checked out. Finney choked you, you said.'

'A bit. What will happen to Corry?'

As soon as Paula had broken the news, Corry had confessed to her relationship with Finney, who had been able to derail the investigation from within and leak information to the press. Guy winced. 'I don't know. There'll be a standards hearing to see just how far her misconduct went.'

'It's not fair. She couldn't have known. No one knew who he was.'

'Still, it could have been a lot worse. Are you sure you're OK?'

'Yes.'

'Why don't you tell me before you run off and do these things? There's Maggie to think of now.'

Paula bit her tongue. She remembered Corry's words about the unit possibly closing – what was Guy not telling her? 'All right,' she said. 'I'll get myself checked out. Since you're so concerned.'

As she turned she saw a young man had approached. He was dressed in oil-stained overalls and his face was with raw with shaving over acne. 'I . . . is Kira . . . is she OK?'

'She's fine, physically at least.' Guy frowned at him. 'Could I take your name, sir? We're waiting for Mrs Woods to arrive and no one can see her until then.'

'I'm . . .' He was twisting a baseball cap in his nervous hands. 'I'm Jamesie . . . James Carter.'

'Are you some relation to Kira?'

'Well, yeah. I'm her dad.'

Aidan sighed. 'Bit sick of this, Maguire. Seeing you in a hospital bed, I mean.'

'I'm just sitting on it this time.' She pointed to it. 'It's only a bruised neck, I'm fine.'

After Maggie had been fed, PJ and Pat had taken her to the canteen, perhaps tactfully giving Aidan and Paula a bit of space.

'A man tried to strangle you. You asked me for help and I wouldn't give it.' He shuddered. 'It's only a miracle you didn't take the wee one with you. Christ. Doesn't bear thinking about.'

'Well, I did tell you to fuck off.'

'Not for the first time. But I deserved it.'

'Maybe.'

'What about wee Maggie?'

'Oh for God's sake . . . I don't have to listen to you pontificate. It wasn't my fault – the girl tricked me, OK?' She wondered what they'd do with a thirteen-year-old girl who'd somehow masterminded the kidnap and murder of five hardened terrorists. Dominic was doing his best to take the blame, but with Lorcan dead and clearly the leak they'd been looking for, she thought he'd probably get away with Accessory to Murder. Either way, Lily wouldn't be seeing him for a while. She might get away with it herself, though she'd obviously been involved. Paula wondered if it had made things any better, taking their retribution.

'Woah now.' Aidan held up both palms. 'I'm not a, whatever you said, misogynistic dinosaur from the dark ages. Incidentally, they didn't have dinosaurs in the dark ages. I'm not going to say you can't work because you've a child and you're a woman. But Maguire, you're all that wee girl has. She has no da. And you of all people know what it's like when you've only the one parent to depend on.'

'So you're saying I need to get the DNA test, is that it? And a father will magically appear for her? Cos it's that simple.'

'Jesus, Maguire. You're a terrible woman for jumping ahead in rows. I'm on my best behaviour here. George

Mitchell and his peacekeeping team have nothing on me. Did I say anything about a test?'

'Fine, fine,' she said grouchily. 'Just make your point. As you say, Maggie has no one else, so I have to get back to her.' The several hours she'd been gone from her that morning had seemed like forever.

'What if she did have someone else?'

'Who?' She said it casually, but her heart began to beat.

'This fella Brooking – he's not such a bad being, I'll admit. He does his best. He was frantic when they realised you hadn't made it home from the hospital. But he has a wife, yes?'

'I don't know what's happening with them. They were splitting up, I thought.'

'For now, though, there's a wife, and a kid, am I right?'

'She's sixteen.'

'Maguire . . .'

'Yes, yes, Guy is married, OK? I didn't exactly plan all this.'

'Never mind. He can't be there for you, that's my point. But there's me, Maguire. I'm unwed.'

She looked away. 'You're seeing Maeve, though, aren't you?'

'Maeve? Maeve Cooley?'

'Yes, Maeve who was lying upstairs there in the ICU, whose bedside you've hardly left in weeks. You were in her bedroom in your pants, that time in Dublin. Don't pretend you don't remember. I'm not stupid.'

'Ah Maguire.' Aidan began to laugh heartily, leaning on his knees. 'Me and Maeve?'

'Is it so unlikely? I saw you, Aidan. I saw how upset you were when she got hurt.'

'And here's me thinking you were observant, Maguire. I love Maeve, right enough, but like a sister. That woman who was there at the ICU, giving out to you about your phone?'

'Yeah?' He meant the one with the dark bob. Some friend, she'd assumed.

'Maeve's girlfriend. Sinead. Nice girl, you'd like her.'

'Oh.' Paula thought about this, things fell into place. *Oh.*

'So I'm not with Maeve, or anyone, and you're not with Brooking, nor are you likely to be any time soon.'

'What exactly is your point?' She folded her arms huffily.

'You. Me. How about it? Get the old band back together.'

'You want me to go out with you? Again? After everything?' She was gaping. 'Jesus, Aidan, you're mad.'

'Am I? Anyway, that's not what I mean. We're not eighteen this time. I don't want you to "go steady" with me.'

'So?'

'Thought we could do better this time. I want you to marry me.'

She just stared at him. 'Fucking hell. You've lost it. I better call a psych consult.'

He took her hand, which was lying limp on the bed, and she let him, still in disbelief. His was rough and warm, inkstains on the knuckles. 'I mean it. Don't do a paternity test. Forget about all that bollocks. Just marry me. I'll be Maggie's da – honest. I don't care whose she is. We're family anyway, you and me. We should be there for each other. Especially if you keep doing mad things. I want to be there for you, and for her. What do you say, Maguire? Will you marry me?'

A jingle of the curtains announced three new arrivals into the cubicle – PJ, Pat, and baby Maggie, held in Aidan's mother's arms.

'Are we interrupting?' said Pat, looking between the two of them.

Kira

She was surprised by how little Rose's grave had changed over time. Someone else had been looking after it – Mammy, probably, though they hadn't talked about it. Someone had put daffodils in the jar, fresh and yellow, the colour of hope, and cut the grass. Otherwise it was all the same, the black granite stone, the wind through the trees, the quiet of the place. Kira walked a few steps and then dropped onto her knees. She'd get grass stains on her jeans but she didn't care.

'Hi,' she said out loud. 'I'm sorry I haven't been for a long time. I've been . . . away.'

She didn't tell the truth, but she felt Rose would know anyway. Maybe she'd even been watching over Kira in the young offender place, with all the angry girls, scars up their arms, bruises under their eyes. It had been a year now and Kira was out. Ready to get on with her life, whatever that meant. Lily was still in the women's prison, though she'd get out in another year. Dominic had been sent to jail for a long time, but Kira thought in some weird way he was glad. There was no one outside he really wanted to see now his little girl was dead. Ann had managed to get off without prison, since she hadn't been there at the end, and Liam had been inside for six months. No one else had really known what they'd planned, or if they had, they were dead.

So many other graves to visit after this – John, and the new memorial in town, and even Lorcan deserved a visit from someone, she thought, though no one else wanted to mention his name.

She heard the breeze through the leaves, like a soft whisper, like a hand across her forehead. 'I'm all right,' she told Rose. 'Mammy's better, and there's Jamesie . . . I've been spending time with him. I think that's what you wanted, isn't it? He says I should call him Dad.'

No answer. She had stopped expecting one, and maybe that was right. She stood up, resting her hand on the cool stone of the grave. *Rose Sarah Woods. 1983–2006. Beloved sister and daughter.* Beloved mother, it should read, but it didn't matter. Everyone important knew the truth. She knew. Jamesie knew. And Rose, wherever she was, Rose knew too. 'Goodbye,' said Kira softly. 'I hope that you're all right. And maybe . . . maybe I'll see you again.'

A bird sounded again in the tree, sweet, out of sight. Kira smiled, and turned to go back to the car where Jamesie was waiting for her. She shut the gate to the graveyard with a squeak, and she didn't look back.

Author's Note

This book is not intended to represent any specific events during the Troubles, but sadly there are parallels with real-life atrocities, most notably the Enniskillen and Omagh bombs. I was sixteen when the Omagh bomb exploded, killing 29 people and unborn twins. At the time, in the stunned devastation that followed, it seemed impossible to believe the country could ever move towards a lasting peace. However, for the most part, it has, something which I and most people from Northern Ireland are grateful for every single day.

I hope this book will serve as some reminder of the losses which are still being endured every day, the unbelievable strength of the victims and bereaved, and the incredible progress that has been made even in my lifetime. The worst days are behind us now. May we never go back.

I am indebted to the book *Aftermath* by Ruth Dudley Edwards, which sets out the stark consequences of terrorism with much more insight and detail than I ever could. I urge you to read it.

'Norn Irish' Glossary

I've been living in England for 14 years now and I'm still surprised when I use words that make people look at me blankly. So, here's a short glossary to explain what on earth the characters are talking about.

A yoke – a thing
A galoot – a useless person, an idiot
Provos – the Provisional IRA, ie the main IRA
Footering – fiddling with
Black as your boot – insulting way to say someone is very Unionist/Protestant
The Orange Order – kind of a long story. Involves sashes and marching.
An Garda Siochana – the southern Irish police force
PSNI – Police Service of Northern Ireland. Replaced the RUC.
Wean – a child
Peelers- the police
Hoke – to root about for or to extract ('hoke it out')
Baldy – a clue, ie I haven't a clue
Herpelling – to walk awkwardly, to limp
Flitters – tatters
Hot press– airing cupboard (not sure this is in the book but I do get a lot of blank stares when I say this one)